*L*achlan dropped Flora on the bed.

"You can't mean for me to sleep here?"

Flora's horrified tone only fueled his anger. "Is there someplace you would rather sleep?" He moved closer, looming over her until only a few inches separated them. "My bed, perhaps?"

Her eyes widened. "Never."

He didn't move. Tension crackled between them thick and heavy. God, he could smell her. He could almost taste the warmth of her lips beneath his. His body ached with pent-up desire. He should take her right now. It would be over, and she would be his. And God knows he wanted her. Many men in his position would. . . .

But not him.

Lachlan jerked away, furious, his body drumming with anger and lust. He'd never used force to get what he wanted, and he wouldn't start now. Now matter how tempted. He'd have her. And soon. Even if she didn't know it yet.

Also by Monica McCarty

Highlander Untamed
Highlander Unmasked

HIGHLANDER
A Novel
UNCHAINED

MONICA McCARTY

BALLANTINE BOOKS • NEW YORK

A Ballantine Books Mass Market Original

Copyright © 2007 by Monica McCarty

Published in the United States by Ballantine Books, an imprint of The Random House Publishing Group, a division of Random House, Inc., New York.

BALLANTINE and colophon are registered trademarks of Random House, Inc.

ISBN 978-0-345-49438-2

Cover illustration: Craig White

Printed in the United States of America

www.ballantinebooks.com

OPM 9 8 7 6 5 4 3 2 1

To Penny and Tracy, for one *long* afternoon of plotting. And as always to Nyree and Jami, for your encouragement, enthusiasm, and unerring brilliance.

Acknowledgments

Publishing a trilogy in back-to-back months is an enormous undertaking and requires a special effort on the part of everyone involved in editorial and production. My heartfelt thanks to all, especially my fabulous editor Charlotte Herscher, Signe Pike, and the copyeditor who worked on all three books.

A special thanks to Barbara Freethy, Candice Hern, and Carol Culver who thought the story of Lady's Rock would make a great prologue. And also to my Golden Heart finalist buddy Kalen Hughes for her invaluable costuming resources.

None of this would have been possible without my wonderful agents Kelly Harms and Andrea Cirillo, my husband Dave, and my understanding (most of the time) kids Reid and Maxine. Thank you!

Prologue

"I dreamt of my lady, I dreamt of her grief,
 I dreamt that her lord was a barbarous chief:
 On a rock of the ocean fair Ellen did seem;
 Glenara! Glenara! now read me my dream!"
—From "Glenara," by Thomas Campbell, 1777–1844

The Firth of Lorn, a Rock Between Lismore and Mull

*On a cold winter's day nearly a hundred years gone
past, a curse was born. . . .*

Lady Elizabeth Campbell Maclean wouldn't beg. Not
for his love, and not for her life. But she was scared.
More scared than she'd ever been in her preciously short
life. Six and twenty was far too young to die.

With each minute that passed, Elizabeth had to fight
to hold to her vow. But her pleas she knew if uttered
would go unheeded. And that more than anything prevented her from dropping to her knees and begging for
mercy.

He had none.

He wouldn't even look at her. Lachlan Cattanach
Maclean, Chief of Maclean. Her husband. The man
she'd been fool enough to love. Her eyes fastened on the
familiar handsome features. The rough, battle-scarred
face, the piercing blue eyes, the wide mouth and hard
implacable jaw. Her chest squeezed. Even now, in the
face of this ultimate betrayal, she could not deny his appeal.

Lachlan Cattanach was a fortress of masculine strength.
A powerful Highland chief. And an unwavering one.
The very qualities she'd once admired—his decisiveness,

his steely determination, his single-minded purpose—
had now conspired against her. He'd made his decision.

She was as good as dead.

One of her husband's *luchd-taighe* guardsmen took
her hand and helped her from the *birlinn* with a courtesy
that belied his murderous task. She would have laughed
at the absurdity if she didn't fear that laughter would
send her spiraling into a descent of hysteria from which
she might never return.

An involuntary shudder coursed through her as her
foot touched the hard, unyielding rock. The impulse to
retreat back to the safety of the boat was strong, but she
knew they would only drag her back. Resolve forced
one foot after the other. Her heart might be in tatters,
but she would not give him the satisfaction of doing the
same to her pride.

Taking a deep breath, she allowed the guardsman to
bind her wrists. With an uneasy glance that hinted of an
apology, the clansman tied the other end of the rope to
the buoy intended to alert passing boats to the danger
posed by the rock. Mooring her to the rock was an unnecessary precaution. She couldn't swim. There was
nowhere for her to go . . . but under.

Fear slid down her spine. Her senses seemed unnaturally heightened, and she felt everything with a painful
raw intensity, from the tiniest droplet of icy sea spray to
each prickly fiber of rope that bit into the tender skin at
her wrists. But most of all, she felt the agony of her
breaking heart.

Dear God, how could he do this to her? How could he
leave her to die like this? To be buried alive by the merciless rising tide? Her heart clamored in her chest as she
struggled with the horrible truth.

Her husband didn't want her anymore. He'd already
found another to take her place. But he would not risk

angering the powerful Campbell clan—including her brother, the Earl of Argyll—by putting her aside. So he'd devised his barbarous plan.

She wished he would take a blade across her neck. But he wanted it to look like an accident. A drowned wife was much easier to explain than one whose throat had been cut.

A sharp gust of wind blew across the sea, freezing everything in its powerful wake. She had to fight to keep her footing on the slippery rock. Her teeth chattered; with only a thin cloak for added warmth, she was cold—painfully so. But it would only get worse. Much worse.

They were almost done. The men climbed back into the boat and started to pull off. Tears ran down her cheeks as she stared at the retreating faces of the men who'd once called her their lady, and then at the man she'd loved.

The man who'd forsaken her. Though she'd raised his two sons as her own, her doom had been in providing none of her own.

They were almost out of view. The thought of being left all alone finally broke her. She couldn't bear it any longer. "Please, don't—"

At the sound of her cry, his eyes shifted toward hers. He met her plea with stony indifference.

—*leave me,* she finished silently.

In the flat of his eyes, all hope was extinguished. He had no mercy. It was over.

But she wouldn't let him go so easily. *By all that was holy, he would pay for the cursed deed done this day*.

Anger and terror forged a powerful weapon. Her voice shook as she called down her promise of vengeance. "A curse upon you, Lachlan Cattanach, and all who shall come after you. As you have murdered me for barrenness, so your lands shall suffer in kind. As you have tied me to this rock, so too will the fortunes of your clan be tied to a Campbell. No Maclean chief will prosper without a Campbell by his side. This will be your legacy until the wrong you've done is atoned and a Maclean life is given in love for a Campbell."

His eyes flickered. She felt a rush of satisfaction, seeing the spark of alarm.

The power of her curse reverberated with an unmistakable ring of prophecy, conjured not from sorcery, but from injustice. A power that not even her husband could deny.

The misty wind pelted Elizabeth like icy nails as the water covered her feet . . . her ankles . . . and then her knees. She clutched the rope that was now her lifeline as the surge of each wave tried to knock her off the quickly sinking rock.

It was pitch black, but she could feel the water moving closer. Rising. Inch by torturous inch.

How long would it take? She prayed it would be quick. Every nerve ending in her body poised for what would happen next. She couldn't breathe. It was as if she were drowning already.

Her gaze lifted to the moonless sky. *Oh God, please help me!*

In cruel heavenly response, the next wave knocked her down, pulling her under. Drenched, she wiped the sodden tangle of hair from her eyes as she struggled to keep her hold on the rock. She tried to stand, but another wave came and pushed her down again.

She slumped forward, losing the strength to fight. *Please, just let it be done.*

She started to close her eyes, intending to allow the water to take her. Her eyes flickered and then snapped open again.

What was that? A light, she realized. The soft glow of a torch appeared out of the darkness. She held her breath and listened, hearing the unmistakable lap of water off an oar.

Her heart soared.

It's him. He's come back. He still loves me. I knew he couldn't do it.

Using the rope for leverage, Elizabeth found the strength to pull herself to her knees and finally to her feet.

"Here!" she yelled. "Husband, help me, I'm here!"

The sounds of the oars quickened as the boat headed toward her. The excited exchange of voices grew louder and louder until the small fishing boat—

Realization struck, followed hard by crushing disappointment. *It wasn't him.* Her husband had not returned.

As her eyes scanned the shocked occupants of the boat, she realized her life had been spared by fishermen.

"My lady?" one man asked with surprise.

Not just any fishermen, she realized. *Her* fishermen. Campbells.

She laughed then, giving in to the hysteria that had threatened in the darkness. With tears streaming down her face, she laughed until she thought her sides would tear apart. The irony was bittersweet. A life had indeed been taken tonight, but it would not be hers.

Elizabeth Campbell—for she would never call herself a Maclean again—did not drown that day. She lived long enough to be returned to her brother's house and to see the surprise on her husband's face when he arrived at Inveraray Castle to break the news of her "unfortunate death" to her family. But there was precious little satisfaction in defying death on Lady's Rock—as the place of her attempted murder became known. For it found her not long after. She died not from the rising tide, but of a broken heart. With the amulet that had been ripped from her husband's neck as her brother took his life clutched in her hand.

But Lady Elizabeth Campbell's legacy lived on, passed down with the amulet from generation to generation.

Chapter 1

❖

"Second thoughts?"

Flora MacLeod turned her gaze from the window to peer into the darkness at the man seated opposite her. She never had second thoughts, which—given that it was too late to change her mind—she supposed was a good thing. No, once she made a decision, she stuck with it. A small army couldn't turn her from her course. In the matter of her marriage, there was no exception.

"Don't be silly," she replied. "I couldn't be happier."

It was clear, however, that her soon-to-be husband, William, Lord Murray, son of the newly created Earl of Tullibardine, didn't believe her. "Happy? I haven't seen you so subdued in months." He paused. "It's not too late to turn back, you know."

But it was. She'd made her decision the moment she'd snuck out of Holyrood House and scrambled into the waiting carriage.

"I don't want to turn back." But the vehemence she'd intended was lost when her voice vibrated with the clattering carriage. A carriage that was fighting to stay upright on the uneven road. She grabbed the seat as best she could when they hit another bump and tried not to crash sidelong into the glossy, wood-paneled walls. A battle she was sure to lose before this day was done. The road leading from Edinburgh would only get worse as they neared the parish of Falkirk.

"Maybe we would have been better off riding after all?" she ventured. It was at Lord Murray's insistence that they'd taken the carriage—luxurious, but impractical on the road to the Highland divide.

"No need to worry on that account. We're perfectly safe. My coachman is an excellent driver." William tried to hand her back her purse, which had slid off the bench beside her, but it slipped through her fingers, landing on the floor again. He laughed. "I never thought I'd see the day that Flora MacLeod was nervous."

Her mouth twitched, caught. "Perhaps I *am* a bit anxious. I've never done this before, you know."

He gave her hand a friendly pat. "I should hope not. But no need to worry, everything is all arranged. It shouldn't be much longer now."

She sat back against the seat and tried to relax. If all went according to plan, in a few hours she would be Lady Murray. Lord Murray—*William*, she reminded herself—had found a minister willing to preside over the clandestine marriage ceremony without proclaiming the banns. Every man had his price, and for the minister of the St. Mary's Kirk it happened to be a cask of fine claret and five hundred merks. More than enough to soften the blow of any fine that might be levied against him for performing the irregular marriage ceremony.

An irregular marriage was Flora's only option. She would not take a chance that one of her brothers, or her powerful cousin, would hear of her plans beforehand and try to stop her.

If she had to marry, she thought grimly, it would be a man of *her* choosing.

She cursed the fates for putting her in this position. She had no desire to marry at all. But it was her great misfortune to be half-sister to not one, but *two* powerful Highland chiefs. And if that weren't enough, her cousin was the most influential Highlander in Scotland. But this "marriage prize," as she was infuriatingly referred to, would rather avoid the state altogether. Marriage brought nothing but unhappiness.

Her mother's misery was all too fresh in Flora's mind.

But about the only thing worse than being married was being forced to marry. So rather than risk the alternative, she'd decided to take the matter of her husband in her own hands. In this case by riding at breakneck speed through the countryside to find a minister of questionable repute in an out-of-the-way parish where she would not be recognized.

She gazed sidelong at the man seated opposite her. Even in the darkness of the carriage she could see the silvery sheen of blond hair cascading across a face that could only be described as sublime. But though he was undeniably pleasing to the eye, it was not his looks that had made her decide to accept his proposal. Nor was it his wit and intelligence, of which he also had a superfluity. It was because William had wealth, power, and position of his own—he did not need hers. She had no need to question his motives beyond what he'd stated: Their union was of friends who would seek their mutual advantage by their union.

As an added boon, he didn't seem particularly concerned with Highland politics. And of *that* subject, she'd heard her fill. The lessons of the mother had indeed been well learned by the daughter. She would sooner marry a toad than a Highlander.

And Lord Murray was infinitely more appealing than a toad.

"And what of you, William. Any second thoughts?"

"None whatsoever."

"Don't you worry what will happen when they discover—"

"Is that what this is about?" He took her hand and gave it a reassuring squeeze. "You wrote the letters, did you not?"

She nodded. One good thing about having so many relatives was that there were many places she could claim to be with none the wiser. Fortunately, the one person who might question her whereabouts—her cousin Elizabeth Campbell—was on Skye attending to the birth of Flora's latest nephew. The second son in as many years of her half-brother Alex and his wife, Meg—a wife Flora had never met. Her mother had been too ill to travel the year they'd come to court.

"Then there is no reason to assume they will find out," William said confidently. "And thanks to your disguise, no one will have noticed you leaving the palace."

Noting the direction of his gaze, she touched the white linen cap she wore on her head. She grinned, amused by the image she must present. Flora was well-known for her propensity to find mischief at Holyrood House. But sneaking out of the palace at midnight to elope with one of the most powerful young men at court, dressed as a maidservant, was sure to top all that had come before. She'd outdone herself. And coming from the girl who'd once donned breeches and climbed halfway down the parapet beneath her balcony at Castle Campbell before her cousin Jamie caught her, that was saying something.

Uncomfortably aware of the scratchy woolen dress she was wearing that poked right through the fine linen of her shift, she asked, "You were able to pick up my gown?"

"As charmingly rustic as you look, my dear, I hardly think the future Countess of Tullibardine should be married dressed as a servant. Your gown is in the trunk, though procuring it from your dressmaker did take some explaining."

Flora chuckled, thinking of the dour Frenchwoman.

The court's preference for French fashion was the one lasting legacy from the reign of Mary Queen of Scots—other than her son, King James, of course. "It seemed the easiest thing to do. I could hardly sneak it out with me. Madame de Ville already thinks me horribly indecorous. I doubt anything you could say would change her opinion." Indecorous was probably an understatement. Flora had a reputation at court for being more than a touch unruly.

Fortunately, William had never seemed to be bothered by her reputation. If anything, her penchant for finding trouble seemed to amuse him. After news of tonight's events spread, he was going to need that sense of humor. Their elopement was sure to cause a scandal far greater than anything she'd ever managed before.

She bit her lip. He was taking a risk. Not much older than her four and twenty years, he'd already made a name for himself in King James's northern court. He wielded considerable influence among the privy councillors—the men left in charge while the king wooed his recalcitrant English subjects at Whitehall. Eloping with the Earl of Argyll's cousin, and the half-sister of Rory MacLeod and Hector Maclean, was a potentially dangerous move for a young man of ambition.

One that might be excused by strength of affection, but Flora did not delude herself in that regard. Although attentive, her soon-to-be husband could hardly be described as besotted. As her feelings were similarly disengaged, it was actually another element in his favor. There would be no pretense on either side. They were friends, nothing more. It was far more than could be said of most marriages.

Most important, she knew him well enough to know that he would not try to control her. She would live her life, and he would live his. It was all she wanted.

But what of him? What did he want?

Flora had known William for years, ever since she'd first made her appearance at court six years ago. But unlike most of the young men of her acquaintance, he'd never pursued her. His sudden courtship—in earnest—upon her recent return to Edinburgh was thus unexpected but admittedly well timed.

For scarcely a few days after he'd made his intentions known, a letter from her half-brother Rory, Chief of MacLeod, arrived requesting her presence at Dunvegan Castle to "discuss her future." Ironically, the request from Rory was followed not long after by one from her half-brother Hector, Chief of Maclean, requesting her presence on the Isle of Mull. Flora was hardly fooled by the near simultaneous requests. A discussion about her future could mean only one thing for a young woman of four and twenty left alone by the sudden death of her mother: marriage. Or, more specifically, the right to control her marriage.

With her mother gone and her father buried long before, the right belonged to Rory. A brother she hardly knew. From what she did remember of him, he didn't seem as if he would force her to marry a man not of her choosing. But she could not take the chance. Even if Rory could be persuaded, Hector and her cousin Argyll wouldn't let the matter be decided without interference.

All three would be furious to discover what she'd done.

Her brothers should have known better than to try to force her hand. Though she hadn't seen them in some time, in some ways she hadn't changed. But perhaps they'd forgotten the little girl who hated to be backed into a corner?

Flora gazed at William again, peering through the darkness to study him a little longer, wondering not for the first time why he'd agreed to her plan to elope. But she quickly pushed aside the sudden twinge of uncertainty.

He was the perfect choice. Her brothers might even approve, she thought wryly. Not that she would give them a chance to have a say in the matter.

"You have nothing to fear," Lord Murray reassured her, seeming to know where her mind was going. "Even if they hear of it, it won't be in time. We're nearly there."

Flora arched a brow. "You don't know my brothers."

In the soft glow of moonlight, an odd look crossed his face. "Not well," he admitted. "Mostly by reputation."

Flora repressed an indelicate snort. "Then you will know that there is much to fear. My infamously fierce brothers are not men to anger." She paused. "Though admittedly, I don't know them very well anymore."

"When did you last see them?"

She thought for a minute. "Quite some time ago. My mother preferred to stay at court or Castle Campbell." The Lowland stronghold of the Earl of Argyll. Thereby avoiding the "barbarians," as Highlanders were considered at court, who'd caused her so much misery. "My brothers do their best not to leave the Highlands," she explained. "I see far more of my cousin Argyll than I do of Rory and Hector." Or any of the other half-siblings, for that matter.

Other than a few brief times at court, Flora had not spent significant time with anyone in her family since she was a child. Though she had eight half-brothers and -sisters—five MacLeods (sharing the same father) and three Macleans (sharing the same mother)—she might as well have been an only child.

Not that she'd minded. She'd always had her mother.

But her mother was gone.

Flora swallowed the ball that had suddenly formed in her throat. She missed her desperately.

She could only hope that in death, her mother had

found the happiness that eluded her in life. Married four times to men not of her choosing, her mother had endeavored to ensure that her daughter not suffer the same fate, and her dying wish was that Flora not marry without love. A wish was that she'd secured with a deathbed promise.

Promise me, Flora. Whatever it takes, never marry someone you do not love.

Flora shook off the memories—and the guilt. She didn't love William. But how could she keep her promise to her mother? Without her mother's protection, Flora was left to the mercy of the men who would seek to control her. A woman could not choose her own destiny. Like it or not, Flora *was* a marriage prize. Her duty was to marry where her brother wanted her to.

But was it her duty to have a life of unhappiness?

No. She refused to be bartered like a prized heifer. She'd made her decision.

"Did it belong to your mother?"

Startled, she turned back toward William. "What?"

"The necklace. You always hold it when you mention her."

Flora smiled softly, not realizing she'd been clasping the amulet. The amulet that her mother had never been without but that had belonged to Flora for the last six months. Since the day her mother's unhappiness was finally put to rest. "Yes."

"It's unusual. Where did it come from?"

She paused, for some reason unwilling to share the story of the necklace. It seemed so personal somehow. Ridiculous, she knew, given that this man would soon be her husband. The legend and the curse associated with the amulet were hardly a secret. Still, she hesitated. "It was passed to my mother's mother by her aunt, who . . ." She paused. "Died without children. And then to my mother as the youngest daughter, and then to me. But originally, it belonged to the Macleans."

"Your brother's clan?"

She nodded.

They hit another bump. Flora held her breath as the carriage perched sideways for a long moment, then settled back down on all four wheels. When it came to a sudden halt, she thought they must have damaged something.

"I'll have the coachman's head for this—"

But Lord Murray's threat was lost in the deafening thunder of horses and the sudden burst of loud voices coming from outside.

Her pulse shot up in an explosion of comprehension: They were being attacked.

From the quizzical expression on his face, it was clear that William had not yet realized what was happening. He was a Lowlander to the core—a courtier, not a fighter. For a moment, Flora felt a stab of frustration; then she chastised herself for being unfair. She wouldn't want it otherwise. But clearly, in this situation, he was going to be of little help.

She could hear the sporadic clash of steel against steel moving closer. They didn't have much time. Grabbing his arm, she forced his gaze to hers. "We're under attack." A shot rang out, punctuating her words. "Do you have anything? A weapon of any sort?"

He shook his head. "I have no use for weaponry, my men are well armed."

Flora cursed, not bothering to curb her tongue.

His frown returned. "Really, my dear. You mustn't say such things. Not when we are married."

Another shot rang out.

She bit back the sarcastic retort that sprang to her lips. Married? They might not be alive in an hour. Did he not understand the desperation of their situation? Scotland was rife with brigands who roamed the countryside. Outlaws. Broken men without clans who weren't known for their mercy. Flora had thought there would be some protection in staying close to Edinburgh. She was wrong.

Lord Murray was exhibiting the arrogant obtuseness characteristic of many courtiers—the confidence that rank and wealth would protect him. But a few muskets would not stop a Highland sword or bow for long. They needed something to defend themselves with.

"A sword," she said urgently, trying to mask her impatience. "Surely you have a sword?"

"Of course. Every man at court carries one. But I did not want to be bothered with it at my side during the journey, so the driver strapped it to the box with your gown. I do still have my dagger." He slid the blade from the scabbard at his waist and held it out to her. From the heavily jewel-encrusted hilt, Flora could tell that it was intended for adornment and not battle. But the six-inch blade would suffice well enough.

From the awkward way he held the blade, as if it were distasteful, it was obvious he didn't know how to use it. "I'm afraid I don't have much experience—"

She did. "I'll take it." Flora slid the dagger into the fold of her cloak right before the door swung open with a crash.

And everything happened at once.

Before she could scream or make a move to defend herself, she was plucked roughly from the safety of the carriage into the viselike hold of a man. A very large man. Who from the feel of him was as strong as an ox.

She gasped from the force of being brought up hard against the granite wall of his chest. Laid out against him, the full length of her body was plastered against hard, unyielding stone.

Dear God, no one had ever dared to hold her like this. She'd never been this aware of . . . anything. Her cheeks burned with indignation and from the sudden blast of heat that seemed to radiate from him. He'd wrapped his arm around her waist and pressed it up snuggly under the heavy weight of her bosom, making her deeply conscious of the rise and fall of her breasts against his arm. Although she was not a small woman, her head tucked easily under his chin. But the worst part was that with her back to his chest, her bottom was pressed directly against his groin.

Instinctively, she rebelled at the closeness. At the intimacy of being molded against the hard-muscled body of a filthy villain.

Except that he didn't smell filthy at all. He smelled of myrtle and heather, with the faintest hint of the sea.

Furious at the direction of her thoughts, she turned her outrage on her captor. "Get your hands off me!" She struggled to wrench free, but it was useless. His arm was as rigid as steel. Though he was restraining her with only one arm, she'd barely moved an inch.

"I'm afraid not, my sweet."

She froze at the lilting sound of the burr in his voice. A Highlander. His voice made the hair on her arms stand straight on end. It was almost hypnotic. Deep and dark, with an indisputable edge of danger.

Her blood ran cold. The direness of their predicament had just grown markedly worse. Highlanders had the morals of the devil. Unless she could think of something, they were as good as dead.

Repressing the impulse to struggle further, Flora stilled, feigning submission, giving herself a moment to appraise the situation. The night was dark, but the full moon softly lit the wide expanse of moorland, enabling her to see just enough—or perhaps too much. Because what she saw wasn't good. They were surrounded by about a score of powerful-looking men dressed in *breacan feiles*, the belted plaids of the Highlands, all brandishing enormous two-handed claymores. To a one, their faces were hard and uncompromising. These were fighting men, warriors.

But they did not bear the hungry, feral look of hunted men. Glancing down, she noticed the finely spun linen shirt of the man holding her. His plaid was also of fine quality—soft and smooth to the touch.

If they weren't outlaws, just who were they, and what did they want?

She didn't intend to stay and find out. Every nerve in her body clamored to break free, to escape from danger. But her options were few.

The handful of men whom Lord Murray had brought as an escort were greatly outnumbered and, from the looks of things, had given up without much of a fight. She saw a few muskets and hagbuts scattered at their feet, although most still held their swords.

But surrender was not in Flora's nature. *Especially* to barbarians. And she had no doubt that these men were Highlanders. If their speech hadn't given them away, the manner of their dress left no doubt.

"What do you want?" Flora recognized the haughty voice of her betrothed. "And get your filthy hands off her."

Lord Murray had been pulled from the carriage behind her and was being restrained by a fearsome-looking Highlander. His size, piercing blue eyes, and shock of white blond hair left little doubt of his Viking ancestry.

The brigand gave her a moment's pause, leaving her to wonder whether the brute holding her was equally as formidable. Perhaps she was glad she could not see him; she was frightened enough as it was. Her heart was beating so hard, she was sure he must feel it.

"Take whatever it is you want and leave us," Lord

Murray added. "We are on important business this night."

The man behind her stiffened, and Flora realized why. She'd never noticed the tinge of condescension that threaded through William's speech until now.

"You are hardly in any position to be issuing orders, *my lord*," her captor said with unveiled contempt. His arm tightened possessively around her middle. "But you are free to go. Take your men with you. I have everything I want."

Her blood drained to her feet as his meaning became clear. *Me. He means me.*

William would die before he allowed a barbarian to take her, and Flora couldn't be the cause of his death. Nor would she contemplate what the villain might do to her. Her gaze darted around frantically as she tried to come up with a plan.

"You can't be serious. Do you know who we are?" William paused. "Is that what this is about? Do you intend to ransom her?" He laughed scornfully, causing the man behind her to stiffen further. Flora wished William would be quiet, before he got them all killed. "You'll wish for a simple hanging if you take her. You will be hunted like a dog."

"They'd have to catch me," the brigand said flatly.

From his tone, it was obvious he thought it impossible. This was no typical brigand, Flora realized. She could tell from his voice and his facility with Scots, the tongue of the Lowlands, that he had at least some education.

A glint of silver coming from the rear of the carriage flashed in the moonlight like a shimmering beacon. There it was. Her chance. She only hoped that William's men would be ready.

William had started issuing more threats. It was now

or never. She hoped the man holding her didn't notice the sudden spike in her heartbeat.

She prayed she remembered what to do. It had been a long time since her brothers Alex and Rory and her cousin Jamie Campbell had taught her how to defend herself.

She took a deep breath and stomped down as hard as she could with the wooden heel of her patten on the brigand's instep, causing him to loosen his hold just enough. In one swift movement, she slid the dagger from her cloak, spun, and thrust the blade deep into his stomach. But he'd turned slightly, and the blade sank into his side instead.

He let out a pained curse and fell to his knees, grabbing the handle of the dirk that was still in his side.

Horror crept up her throat. She'd never stabbed a man before. She hoped . . .

Nonsense. The brute intended to kidnap her . . . and worse.

She turned around long enough to see the surprise on his face. A face that was not what she'd expected. A face that made her hesitate. Their eyes locked, and she felt a strange jolt. *God's breath, he was the most ruggedly handsome man she'd ever seen.*

But he was a villain.

Turning from the wounded man, she leapt toward the carriage.

"Fight!" she yelled to Lord Murray's gaping men.

Lunging for the flash of silver she'd glimpsed, she prayed, letting out a sigh of relief when her hand found steel and she pulled Lord Murray's sword from the box.

Her daring had spurred the men back into action. The fighting began again in earnest.

Escape. She couldn't let them take her. Perhaps if she could cross the moors a few hundred yards to the edge of the forest. She turned to look for William, relieved to see that the man holding him had made a move toward his injured leader—for she had no doubt that the man she'd stabbed was the leader—and then found himself engaged in a sword fight with one of William's men. After tossing the sword to William, she pulled him behind the carriage. "We have to run," she whispered.

He stood frozen, looking at her with the strangest expression on his face, as if he couldn't quite tell whether to be awed or repulsed.

She tamped down her rising irritation. He should be thanking her, not gaping at her as if she were a Gorgon. "Look, we don't have much time." Not giving him an opportunity to reply, she pulled him toward the moors and started to run toward the line of trees that loomed in the distance like an oasis.

But freedom was swift. She hadn't taken more than a few steps onto the heather before she was brought down from behind, landing hard against the ground with the full weight of a man on top of her. Her breath slammed against her chest.

She couldn't move. Or breathe. Heather, dirt, and twigs pressed into her cheek, and her mouth tasted dirt.

She didn't have to look; she knew who it was just by the feel of him.

He wasn't dead.

He stayed like that for a minute, letting her feel his weight, letting her feel her helplessness, before rolling her over onto her back. Since she had lost her cap in the fracas, her hair streamed across her face and tangled in her lashes. He pinned her shoulders to the ground with his arms and pressed the long length of his body against her to keep her down.

He didn't say a word. But he didn't need to. Anger radiated from him as bright and hot as wildfire.

A movement out of the corner of her eye caught her attention. "William! Help me." He had the sword, and sprawled out on top of her, the brigand was vulnerable. William stood stone still, as if he hadn't heard her. "William!" Their eyes met. She saw fear—for himself— and guilt. The blood drained out of her. *He's going to leave me.* And before she could react, he turned and ran.

Stunned, Flora watched as he disappeared into the darkness. She couldn't believe it. Her betrothed had left her to the mercy—assuming they had any—of the brigands.

The man on top of her murmured an uncomplimentary expletive, echoing her thoughts exactly. She'd erred badly. To think she might have married him.

But her mind was quickly driven from Lord Murray's betrayal.

The brigand was touching her. Covering her body with his enormous hands. Sliding over her breasts, hips, around her bottom, and down the length of her legs. She froze, shock slipping into panic.

"What are you doing? Stop!" She tried to break free, but he had her trapped. With his weight on her, she couldn't budge. She'd never felt so helpless. Tears burned her eyes. "Please. Don't do this."

Ignoring her frightened pleas, his hands, so large and unfamiliar on her body, continued their methodical plunder. He didn't miss an inch. There was something hard and calculated about his movements, almost detached. But when his hand slid between her legs, she lashed out as if scalded. With the quick burst of strength, she managed to free a hand long enough to rake her nails across his cheek.

He swore and caught hold of her wrists, pinning them together above her head. Lowering his face to hers, he said menacingly, "Enough. You test my patience, my wee banshee." Stretched out beneath him, she stared up into his eyes—breathing hard from her struggles, her bosom heaving conspicuously. He stilled, and something changed. The detachment was gone. His eyes fell on her breasts, lingering. Heat spread across her chest. But his gaze hardened and snapped back to her face. "Your fears on that score are unfounded. I simply do not relish another dirk in my back."

Side. But she thought it best not to argue the point. "I'm unarmed."

"I don't think I'll take your word for it."

When he'd satisfied himself that she was telling the truth, he sprang to his feet, and she found herself unceremoniously pulled up after him. She'd calmed, but her heart still pounded.

Without the heat of his body, she immediately noticed that her gown felt wet. She placed a hand on her stomach, then jerked it away. The sharp metallic smell sent a wave of nausea crashing over her. It was blood. His blood. She glanced at his chest and blanched, noticing the dark crimson stain that penetrated the thick wool of his plaid. It must hurt him something fierce, but he gave no evidence of any injury.

But any guilt she might have experienced was swiftly eradicated. He dragged her back toward the carriage, her arm clenched in a viselike grip, a physical reminder of her circumstances.

"You're hurting me."

He spun her around and pinned her with his gaze. His eyes glowed in the moonlight. Blue. A penetrating blue that bored right into her. His gaze was like the rest of him, hard and uncompromising—with an unmistakable tinge of danger. Her stomach fluttered. With fear? It should be.

His face was strong and lean, all hard angles and raw masculinity—there was nothing soft about him. His nose had been broken more than once, but that and the scattering of scars across his face only added to his rugged appeal. Four fresh scratches scored down his cheek. Flora wouldn't feel sorry for it, but they didn't look deep enough to scar.

His squared jaw was firmly clenched, and tiny white lines were etched around his mouth. For a Highlander, his hair was unusually short and well groomed, just long enough to fall in gentle waves past his ears. It was either dark brown or black, she couldn't tell.

Standing before him, face-to-face, she realized for the first time just how big he was. Tall, broad-shouldered, and heavily muscled. But she wouldn't allow his size to intimidate her. She was used to large men—her brothers were all similarly built. Still, she'd felt his strength first-hand, and it was hard not to be unsettled.

"It's either my hand or I can tie you up." He gave her a long look, one that made her think he would like nothing more. "You decide."

Mortified heat burned her cheeks. She lifted her chin a little to glare at him. "Hand."

"Good decision. But if you try to run again, I will not be so generous."

"Generous." She made a sharp sound of derision. "You are kidnapping me. Am I supposed to thank you?"

"You're welcome."

"I was not . . ." But her reprimand dropped off as they rounded the carriage. She tensed, sure that she would see many of Lord Murray's men lying dead on the ground. Her gaze darted around, then widened, shocked to find them all accounted for. They had surrendered, and this time the brigands had made sure to divest them of their weapons, but otherwise Lord Murray's men appeared largely unharmed. The worst injury appeared to belong to a Highlander who'd been shot in the arm.

It didn't make any sense. It was almost as if their attackers had gone out of their way not to hurt anyone. Not what she expected from barbarians. She turned to look at him appraisingly. "What do you want with me?"

His face was like stone, giving no hint of his thoughts. "Where are you taking me?"

"To my keep."

"And where is that?"

He paused for a moment, obviously debating whether to tell her. "Drimnin. In Morvern."

Her mother had lands in Morvern, which wasn't unusual since her mother had held lands all over the Highlands, so Flora knew that the keep belonged to Lachlan Maclean, the Maclean of Coll. The embittered enemy of her half-brother Hector Maclean of Duart. Her eyes narrowed. "Does your laird know what you have done?"

"You might say that." His mouth curved, the first sign of lightness in his stony expression. The transformation was stunning, turning his fierce visage into something far more dangerous. Her gaze fixed on the charming twinkle in his eyes and the sensual curve of his wide mouth. Her stomach fluttered.

It was only because she was watching him so closely that she saw him flinch. He was in more pain than he was letting on, but he quickly masked it.

A few of the brigands were staring at her with strange expressions.

The Viking ventured the question that was apparently on everyone's minds. "Are you sure you've got the right lass? This one doesn't look like the bonniest heiress in Scotland. Or anywhere else, for that matter."

Flora bristled. She didn't care much for her nickname, but no woman liked to be told she was not pleasing to the eye. Vanity stung, she opened her mouth to offer a torrid rebuke when she suddenly realized how she must look. Blond hair a tangled nest, dirt streaked across her face, blood on her gown . . . Ah yes, she'd forgotten about her shapeless gray wool maidservant's gown.

"It's her," her captor replied flatly.

He couldn't know who I am. What could he possibly want with me?

Her heart crashed to the floor. *Why did women of fortune usually get abducted? Good God, this barbarian couldn't intend to marry her?*

There had to be some mistake.

Chapter 2

❖

The stubborn lass hadn't said a word all night, not since he'd ignored her protests and set her atop his horse. She would ride with him. Where he could keep his eye on her.

Lachlan Maclean, Chief of Coll, had no doubt that it was Flora MacLeod. The bonniest heiress in Scotland. The Holyrood hellion. Take your pick. No matter the nickname, she was the most gossiped-about woman at court. A renowned beauty who left a path of broken hearts in her troublemaking wake.

Well, she'd definitely lived up to her reputation in temperament—he had the marks on his face and a gaping hole in his side to prove it. She was aptly named. Flora. The ancient Roman goddess of flowers and spring. She was a flower all right. A beautiful rose with the thorns to match.

Aye, she was a beauty. With a strong family resemblance to the MacLeods, thankfully, and not to the Maclean of Duart. Delicate oval face, wide blue eyes, tiny pert nose, lush red lips, and long silky golden hair. With a body . . .

Hell, with a body built for a man's pleasure.

His men might not have seen through the dirt and sackcloth, but he'd had a better perspective. A *much* better perspective. He hadn't meant to land on top of her, but he'd lunged, she'd lost her footing, and momentum had carried them both forward.

Focused on the task at hand, namely making sure she was not hiding another dirk, he hadn't realized he was frightening her until she'd raked her fingers across his face. Ravishment had been the furthest thing from his mind. Had been. Until all of a sudden he'd become very aware of every well-curved inch of her. For a moment, with that sweet red mouth merely inches away and those luscious breasts straining against him, he'd been tempted to taste the spoils. Hell, he would have had to be a bloody eunuch not to be at least tempted.

And the memory of that incredible body writhing underneath him was brought back full force every time her soft bottom nudged against his groin when the movement of the horse caused her to slide against him. It had been one of the longest nights of his life. His side hurt like hell, and he was as hard as a damn rock. You'd think he hadn't had a woman in weeks, though it had been only a few days.

That he wanted her didn't bother him. A pretty—nay, a lovely—face and lush body would not endear him to his task, although it might make it more palatable. Abducting a lass, no matter how fair, was not his way. But he had no choice; too much was depending on the wee termagant. And Lachlan would do whatever it took to protect his clan and family, even if he had to kidnap a stubborn, headstrong lass to do so.

A burst of white hot pain fired in his side. He gritted his teeth and waited for it to pass. But each time it seemed to take longer for the flare of pain to ebb. The hard ride had only made it worse. Though he'd bound the wound as best he could with a strip of linen, he was still losing blood. Too much blood. He'd be lucky if he could stand when they arrived at Drimnin.

She'd stabbed him. It was a rare lapse. But he'd never known a woman to handle a blade with such proficiency. Never hesitating. He shook his head, unable to believe that a lass had succeeded where many formidable men before her had failed. Including her damn halfbrother Hector Maclean, Chief of Duart. His fiercest enemy and the source of his current troubles.

Still, in spite of his pain, he had to admit that her spirit impressed him. She knew how to defend herself. Which was more than he could say for the cowardly popinjay she'd been with. What kind of man would leave his woman to kidnappers?

Lowlanders, he thought with disgust, glad that the wretched place was behind him.

From Falkirk they'd headed west, crossing the Lomond Hills, skirting the higher peaks, entering into the rugged, mountainous terrain of the Highlands. As dawn broke across the majestic landscape, a layer of dew sparkled across the green glens and heather-filled moors. The land rose in gentle, rounded hills as far as the eye could see.

No matter how many times he left, returning home to the Highlands never ceased to move him.

It baffled him how the lass could choose to live in the Lowlands, forsaking her kin in the Highlands. He knew little about Flora MacLeod, except that since the death of her father when just a child, she'd lived with her mother in the Lowlands—shifting between Edinburgh and Castle Campbell—and only occasionally traveling into the Highlands to Inveraray. Her half-brother Rory had spoken of her a few times—usually in tones of frustration with some sort of mischief she'd gotten herself in. Apparently, whenever he asked her to do something, she unfailingly did the opposite. Her visits to Dunvegan had been infrequent. Everything else he'd heard had to do with her reputation at court. For once, in that respect, the rumors seemed to be true.

Hellion was an understatement. He had little patience for courtiers, spoiled headstrong ones even less.

Despite her efforts to sit stiffly before him, the long
night in the saddle had eventually worn her down. From
the way her body sagged gently against him, and the
calming evenness of her breath against his chest, he
knew that she slept. Although she wore a cloak over her
dress, he'd taken the opportunity to wrap his plaid
around her, creating a cocoon of warmth against the
cold night air.

She was so soft and sweet like this. Relaxed. Almost
trusting. He felt an unexpected tug in his chest. A feeling
he hadn't had since his sisters were young. He shook off
the uncharacteristic bout of sentiment. She shouldn't
trust him. He would do what he had to do for the good
of his clan. And for his family. Even if it meant using her
to do so.

But in repose, the wee hellion looked almost . . . vulnerable. Until the pain hit again and he brutally recalled
her blade.

He'd never studied a woman so closely. But after the
long night, he felt his gaze falling to her face again and
again, until it seemed as if he'd memorized every inch of
her. He no longer needed to look to see the long lashes
fanned against the flawless ivory skin of her cheek, the
soft red lips gently parted, and the long winding strands
of pale blond hair tumbling wildly around her shoulders. Her features seemed permanently imprinted on his
mind.

More than once while she slept, he'd been unable to
resist bending down, sinking his face into her hair, and
inhaling the soft scent—like fresh flowers warmed in the
sun.

Everything about her was dainty and sweetly feminine. He found himself fascinated with the perfect arch
of her brows and the delicate tilt of her nose. Knowing
that it would wake her, he fought the powerful urge to

sweep his finger down the curve of her cheek just to see if her skin was as baby soft as it looked.

He cursed and focused on the path ahead of him. The loss of blood from his wound must have addled him to be so engrossed with the lass.

As the first rays of sunshine fell across her pale cheek, she stirred. He wondered how long it would take her to realize . . .

Sure enough, in a matter of seconds she jerked up straight, putting as much distance between them on the saddle as she could manage.

Aye, the lass was stubborn and prideful. That would change. A firm hand was what she needed.

They rode a little while longer, and at the north end of Loch Nell, he ordered his men to stop. There were still many hours of riding ahead of them before they reached Oban. From Oban, they would trade their horses for a *birlinn* and navigate the oft treacherous Sound of Mull to his keep at Drimnin. Like most men from the Isles, Lachlan felt most at home on the water.

First, however, they needed to eat, water the horses, and do something about his wound. He knew of only one way to stop the bleeding.

Clenching his jaw, he slid from his mount and helped her down after him, trying to control the light-headedness that threatened to yank his legs out from under him. He gripped his saddle, pretending to tend to his horse while he fought the pull of nausea.

It was worse than he'd feared. The lass had done some damage.

He hated any form of weakness. "Go tend to your needs," he said roughly. "But stay where I can see you."

She didn't move. "Who are you? What do you want with me? Is it ransom?"

A fiery twist in his side threatened to buckle him. Was

the damn woman deaf? "Not now, Flora," he said through clenched teeth.

"You *do* know who I am."

He paused, giving the pain a chance to pass. The ground steadied a little, and taking a deep breath, he turned around to face her. He started to order her away, but the expression on her face stopped him. For the first time, she'd realized it was not a mistake. He looked for signs of fear, but she appeared more bemused than anything else. "Did you think I did not?"

"I wondered that any man could be fool enough to kidnap the sister of Rory Mor MacLeod and Hector Maclean." She gave him a long look. "My brothers will kill you."

He caught the unmistakable gleam in her eye, and his mouth curved in a half-smile. "I wouldn't plan the *ceilidh* yet, my bloodthirsty one. Hector has tried—repeatedly—and failed. Rory I consider a friend." But she was partly correct. Rory would be furious if he ever discovered the truth. "In fact, I think he may have cause to thank me."

She scoffed. "What for? For abducting his sister? You must be mad."

His voice grew hard. If she were his sister, he'd take her across his knee for what she'd attempted to do. "For saving you from a foolish mistake."

"Lord Murray is not—" She stopped. "I don't know what you are talking about."

He cupped her chin with a firm hand and looked deep into those wide, defiant eyes. Remarkable eyes that in the morning light were as blue as the stormy sea. "I think you know exactly what I'm talking about. Do you deny that you were running off to marry your wee Lowlander?"

"How could you possibly . . ." She jerked her chin away. "It's none of your damn business."

He laughed. He couldn't help it, even though it hurt like perdition. The chit had spirit. Misplaced, perhaps, but she would learn her place. He did not tolerate disrespect, especially from a woman. But with her eyes blazing, hands on her hips, and stubborn little chin lifted toward him, he was glad she didn't have another dirk.

"Such foul language for a proper 'lady' of court."

She looked as though she'd like to rattle off a few others. Instead, she studied him with increasing scrutiny. "How did you know where I'd be?"

He shrugged.

Her eyes narrowed. "You were spying on me."

He didn't deny it.

"But I don't understand. Even if you were watching me, how could you possibly know it was me leaving the palace? Even Lord Murray didn't realize it was me until I climbed into the carriage."

He hadn't. Not right away. But then again, he'd also had the advantage in knowing what she intended. He'd waited outside the palace gates for three nights. And he'd seen the woman stepping into Lord Murray's carriage and almost dismissed her, thinking it was a maid-servant. But something niggled at him, and he'd taken a closer look. And happened to glance down.

He pointed at her feet. At the tips of the delicately embroidered silk slippers now covered in mud that peeked out from beneath her gown. "The shoes." He bent a little closer and said in a low voice, "Next time you don a disguise, try not to let vanity interfere."

Her cheeks flamed. He'd guessed correctly. Glaring daggers, she whirled around and started off. Giving him the space he needed to tend to his wound.

"Don't take too long, Flora," he called after her. "Or I will come after you." There was no mistaking the threat in his voice.

She pretended not to hear him and stomped off in the direction of a meadow.

Undone by a pair of slippers, Flora thought morosely, kicking the dirt with the tip of her ruined shoe.

He was right, curse his wretched soul. She knew it was ridiculous, but she *loved* shoes. They were her one indulgence. She just couldn't bear the thought of being married in plain leather, and with her wooden pattens on to protect her from the mud, she didn't think anyone would notice the delicate satin slippers.

But he had. He noticed everything with those penetrating eyes. Blast him.

Flora nibbled on a dry bit of oatcake, which she'd never liked even in the best of circumstances, and washed down the offending grain with a sip of ale. By the time he'd finally decided to stop, she'd been close to begging to attend to her personal needs. Not to mention starving. Hungry enough to choke down oatcakes and be glad of them. The bit of dried beef one of his men had brought her was considerably better, but she'd finished that off quickly.

She sat on a rock a little away from the others, grateful for the moment of reprieve. Sitting for so long, practically in his lap, had been maddening. Every time she tried not to think about him, it seemed she couldn't think of *anything but* him.

Awareness had been her constant unwelcome companion. After the long journey, she was as tightly wound as a coiled spring, every nerve ending on edge and fraught with tension. It was only natural, she told herself. He'd abducted her. Touched her. Taken liberties with her person that no man had ever dared. What woman wouldn't be nervous? But it was more than nervousness that had her keenly aware of his every movement, every command he'd issued to his men, even the distinctive masculine scent of him. A scent that made her yearn to curl up against his warm chest and fall asleep.

How humiliating that she'd actually done so. He was her abductor, for heaven's sake.

But exhaustion and the gentle sway of the horse had cut through her resolve to stay as far away as possible from him, as easily as a knife slid through butter. The uncharacteristic weakness annoyed her.

What did he want with her? And more important, how was she going to escape?

There was a ruthless edge to the man that gave her pause. He was not used to disobedience—that was obvious. His gruff manner, his brusque tone, his natural authority, all spoke of a man who was used to giving orders. But he was too rough around the edges—a leader, not a laird. Probably one of Coll's *luchd-taighe* guardsmen. Or a captain of one of his castles. Or, more likely, his henchman.

Yet despite what she'd done to him, he'd treated her with remarkable courtesy. But she sensed that he did not make idle threats. So unless she wanted to be tied up, next time she tried to escape she'd better make sure she wasn't caught.

She sank her chin in her hands and stared at the large standing stone at the edge of the grassy meadow. Watching as the rising sun created a shadow across the ground. These odd stones that were scattered all over Scotland had always fascinated her. Some said they belonged to the Druids, but most believed the stones were placed there by the faerie folk.

Though normally she did not give much credence to the rampant superstition that seemed part of the very fabric of the Highlands, the stones did have a magical quality to them. It wasn't hard to understand why such abundant lore surrounded them.

A large shadow fell over her, this one from a living

rock, and she glanced up to see him standing before her. With the sun shining behind his head and the enormous sword slung over his back, he looked like some Norse god of war coming to wreak havoc and destruction—on her.

"Here, eat this." He held out a bit more of the beef. "It will be the last until we reach Drimnin."

She took it with a nod.

"You found the faerie circle?"

"You mean the standing stone," she corrected.

"No." He pointed to the circle of rocks around her. "The circle of stones you are sitting on."

She jumped up, not realizing the stone she was sitting on was one of about thirty low boulders set about in a circle.

He smiled. "Afraid you will have bad luck?"

"I'd say it's rather too late for that."

He ignored her barb. "Are you superstitious?"

She shook her head. "No. Not exactly. Respectful, perhaps." She looked around and thought for a moment. "There is something magical about the place."

"It's the Highlands, lass. There is magic everywhere you look."

He was right. It was impossible not to be struck by the beauty of the landscape around her. The hills, the lochs, the brilliant shades of green for as far as the eye could see. But she knew it was as deceptive as the men who lived here. She knew how quickly this place could change, turning cold, brutal, and remote. Barbarous. An unforgiving place of ancient feuds and endless killing. A place where men raised in war took what they wanted with no thought to the lives they were destroying.

It had happened to her mother, and it had happened to her. Abducted like Persephone on her own descent into Hades.

A hell that looked like the Garden of Eden.

It had been different when she was a child. The few times she'd seen one of her brothers or sisters, they'd recounted stories of how she used to run wild around the hills of Dunvegan. But she didn't remember. Her father had died when she was only five, and she'd left Dunvegan and never returned. Rory had tried repeatedly to bring her back, but her mother always made some excuse to prevent her from going. Soon, she'd stopped wanting to.

But once in a while, something would jog her memory—like a whisper of something that was just out of reach.

She shook off the memory. No matter what she'd once felt for the Highlands, it had all changed when she'd learned the truth of what had happened to her mother. Of why she rarely smiled. Of why she hated the Highlands and the brutal men who lived there.

Janet Maclean Maclean (twice) MacIan MacLeod née Campbell had been sold from husband to husband, a pawn in the political machinations of men. Manipulated by those who should have protected her. Used. She was a commodity, and they never let her forget it. She was married the first time at fifteen to a man nearly four times her age. The second to a husband who was murdered. The third she never spoke of. And the last, Flora's father, was another much older man. Finally, on his death, Janet was too old to have children, and for the first time in her life she was free. But it was already too late.

The damage had been done.

Flora straightened her back and turned away from the beautiful vistas. "I prefer the city to the wilds." Like the others of his ilk, this Highland warrior had abducted her for his own ends. With no care to the plans he'd upset. "And the company of gentlemen to barbarians."

His face hardened, and he took a dangerous step

toward her. "Like the *gentleman* who left you without a backward glance?"

She flinched. Flora was more hurt by Lord Murray's abandonment than she wanted to admit. "I'm sure he only thought to get help."

"He only thought to save his foul hide."

"I'm sure you're wrong." She didn't know why she was defending Lord Murray. Her pride stung. Both that she'd been wrong about him and at how quickly he'd left her. The Highlander might have opened her eyes, but she wouldn't thank him for doing so. What woman wanted to be publicly humiliated by the man who was supposed to be her husband? Who was supposed to care for her, but had so little regard for her that he would leave her to the company of brigands?

But they weren't brigands. They were Macleans. She hoped there was a difference.

He reached down and took her chin in his hand. Holding firm when she tried to jerk away. His eyes were truly remarkable. A crisp and vivid blue.

"Don't count on a rescue, my sweet. Not from him. He's not likely to run back to Edinburgh shouting to the rooftops of a failed elopement—or of his own lack of honor." He dropped her chin. "If you are done with the flagon, I have need of it." She handed it to him. "We will be leaving soon. Be ready when I call." He turned and walked away, leaving her feeling strangely unsettled. A feeling she was becoming used to when he was around.

She watched him return to his men, continuing on toward the edge of the loch. Her pulse jumped. Though it seemed an odd time for a swim, he quickly removed his plaid, leather jerkin, and boots and waded into the water.

She couldn't look away. He was a striking man. Not just handsome, but blatantly masculine. His features seemed forged of iron, strong and hard. His damp shirt molded against an impressive array of stomach muscles. In his shirt and leather trews, she realized that he was less bulky than she'd initially thought. Muscular and broad-shouldered, but honed tight as a bow. It somehow made him seem more dangerous.

She gasped. Even from here she could see the enormous dark red stain that covered his shirt from under his arm to his waist. He winced as he used the water to loosen the cloth, pulling it away from his skin. She realized what he was doing. Cleaning the wound where she'd stabbed him.

She bit her lip. It must hurt something horrible, but he barely reacted. She turned away, refusing to feel guilty, and found another rock to sit on—this one she made sure was not part of a circle. She sat down and waited.

Her gaze slid to his men. They'd finished tending the horses and had started to build a fire. From the looks of it, a very hot fire.

She frowned, perplexed by the odd behavior.

Her abductor emerged from the loch and sat on the bank, pulling on his boots. The man who looked like a Viking—Allan, she'd heard him called—handed him the flagon. Her abductor grabbed it with a nod and took a long swig. Handing it back to the Viking, he said something that seemed to cause a minor disagreement.

Her heart pounded as if she almost guessed what it was about. He lifted his shirt.

No.

He turned to look at her, as if she'd said it out loud, as the Viking poured from the flagon onto his open wound.

Her chest squeezed as his body jerked, but his face remained impassive. The pain must be excruciating. But except for the tightness around his mouth, she wouldn't have known it.

She jumped up from the rock, at once understanding the reason for the fire. She'd seen it done once before, as a child. She took a step toward him and stopped when one of his men lifted a dagger from the fire. A dagger with a blade that glowed a fiery red.

Unconsciously, she clenched her hand, recalling the time she'd been trying to help in the kitchen and accidentally knocked over the large iron stew pot that had been simmering over the fire. Without thinking, she'd grabbed for it, burning her hand badly. She still bore the scars on her palm. She couldn't imagine how much it would hurt on an open wound.

One of the men tried to give him a stick to put between his teeth, but he refused. He lifted his shirt, and her stomach lurched. She could see the gaping wound from here.

She took a step toward him and stopped. His eyes found hers as the side of the blade hit the wound.

The sizzling sound of the blade upon his flesh made her chest twist. Yet despite the pain, he barely flinched. And through it all, he held her gaze.

She could smell . . . it was horrible. She turned, breaking the connection, unable to bear it any longer.

She'd never witnessed anything like it. It was the most impressive display of control and strength she'd ever seen.

She wouldn't apologize, but neither could she ignore the fact that she'd done that to him. Nor could she ignore the strange conflicting feelings he aroused in her. How could she admire a man who'd kidnapped her?

She had to get out of here.

It was her worst nightmare. Banished to the Highlands and forced to marry an uncouth savage. Now would be the best time to escape, while he was weakened. Slowly, she started moving back.

His head snapped around, and she froze.

"Flora." His voice was hard and steady. "Take one more step and you'll regret it."

Not weakened at all. The man was inhuman.

Another night had passed by the time they climbed up the sea-gate stairs to Drimnin Castle. Lachlan's side ached, and his head felt as if it had been split in two with Allan's battle-ax. The bleeding had stopped, but if he didn't get some rest soon, he knew fever would set in. If it hadn't already.

He led them across the yard and up the timber forestairs to the entry of the keep. As was common with most tower house castles, the only entry was from the first floor. If any attackers made it through the gate, the stairs could easily be removed or burned.

It was more of a relief than he would admit when they entered the warmth of the keep.

Flora looked around the entry, obviously unimpressed, and spun on him immediately, eyes flashing. "Where is he? I demand that you take me to your laird, now."

"Demand?" His temper flared. He was in no mood for her sharp tongue. "Have care, little one. Remember your status here."

"How could I forget? I'm a prisoner. Abducted by a band of Highland barbarians."

His hand whipped out to grip her arm, and he peered down into that beautiful mutinous face. "I do not like that word." His voice cut like steel. "Do not use it again."

He saw the spark in her eyes, delighting in the knowledge that she'd gotten to him. "The truth too painful?"

His gaze slid down the length of her body. A barbarian would know exactly how to shut her up. "Would you like it to be?"

"How dare you—"

"There's not much I wouldn't dare, and you'd do best to remember it." He nodded, and his men and the servants retreated, leaving them alone.

She didn't miss the silent command. "Just who do you think you are?"

He smiled, but it was without humor. "Who do you think? Your host."

Her eyes widened. "You couldn't be."

Her disbelief shouldn't bother him, but it did. He was the Laird of Coll, and she'd damn well better believe it.

"But . . ." Her voice dropped off.

He could tell by her expression what she was thinking. That he wasn't refined enough and had none of the courtly graces of a laird. Damn right. He was too damn busy fighting her brother. Too damn busy protecting his clan from years of floods and famine. And war. What learning he'd had was forged on the battlefield.

"Why have you brought me here?" she asked.

"You'll find out soon enough."

"I'll never marry you."

The certainty in her voice infuriated him. "I don't recall asking," he said coldly.

"A man like you wouldn't ask. He'd take."

He took a step closer to her. She didn't know when to stop. By God, she would learn. "And what kind of man am I?" he asked in a dangerous tone.

She lifted her chin and met him square in the eye, refusing to cower before his intimidation. "The kind who abducts a lady with no care for the plans he's upset and forcibly brings her to his keep."

"You would have been miserable with him."

"He was *my* choice."

He didn't understand her. She didn't deny that her marriage would have been a mistake, but she was still angry that he'd interrupted her elopement. There wasn't enough time in the day to decipher the mind of a lass.

She gave him a sidelong look from under her long lashes. "So you do not intend to force me to marry you?"

"No," he answered truthfully.

Her nose wrinkled, as if she weren't sure whether to believe him. "Then it's my brother Hector. You intend to use me to get to him."

It hadn't taken her long to figure it out. Part of it, anyway. The lass did not have just a sharp tongue and beauty, she had wits as well. He gave her a long appraising glance. He would have to be careful. If she learned what he was about, it could make his task difficult.

She had a smug expression on her face. "Well, you are in for a disappointment if you think to use me to bargain with Hector. I barely know him."

"But I do."

Too well. Lachlan and Hector had been at each other's throats for years, since the day of Lachlan's father's funeral, when Lachlan was not yet ten and Hector had used the burial as an opportunity to take over Coll. Lachlan's uncle Neil Mor had thwarted the brash invasion, cutting off the heads of the Duart Macleans and tossing them into the stream now known as *Struthan nan Ceann*, the Stream of Heads.

Hector had never forgotten—or forgiven—his defeat, and Lachlan had been fighting for what was his ever since.

Tensions had run high between the two branches of the clan for years, but the feuding resumed not long ago when Lachlan refused to bow to Hector as the superior branch of the clan. It was a bit of posturing by Hector to answer for his invasion of Lachlan's lands in Morvern. Hector claimed that his actions were justified by Lachlan's refusal to take his part in his blood feud with the MacDonalds—a duty that was owed to a chief. The kinship between the two branches of Macleans, descended long ago from brothers, was all but forgotten. As a feudal baron, Lachlan didn't owe fealty to anyone, except perhaps the king. And with King James's recent maneuverings, even that was debatable.

"Hector has something of mine. Now I have something of his."

"What does he have? Your favorite dog?"

"No," he said flatly. "My favorite castle."

Her eyes widened appreciably. "Breacachadh, on the Isle of Coll?"

"Yes." His fists clenched. With Hector's ancestral seat, Duart Castle, sequestered and seized by the king's commissioners for his treasonous dealings with Queen Elizabeth, he'd turned his sights to Lachlan's.

"But how?"

"I was away." While Lachlan was gone, Hector had led a force to Coll and, using trickery, captured the castle. But Hector would pay for his treachery.

"Why did you not appeal to the king?"

His jaw clenched. "I did." He'd tried to follow the rules, but it had only made things worse. Much worse. He would never make that mistake again.

"You've kidnapped me for nothing. My brother has been after Coll for some time, he will not exchange it for me. A sister he barely knows."

"You underestimate your worth, Flora."

He knew right away that it was the wrong thing to say.

Her face went taut, and her voice grew thick with emotion. "I know exactly my worth."

There was something significant about her words, but he didn't have the energy to figure it out. He wouldn't feel pity. She was a means to an end. He was finished with this conversation. Before she guessed what he intended, he lifted her in his arms and started to carry her up the stairs.

"What are you doing?"

"Taking you to your room."

"W-h-h-y?"

To shut her up so he could get some sleep. And it had seemed like the most effective method at first—until he was forcefully reminded of his injury.

"You shouldn't be carrying me. You'll reopen the wound."

"Since you're the one who put it there, I'm surprised you care."

"I didn't mean—" She stopped. "Well, I did, but . . . well . . . Forget it. You can bleed to death for all I care."

"Your concern is touching."

He swung open the door; it squeaked and rattled off its hinges a little. The years of famine had taken its toll. Drimnin Castle was old and in desperate need of repair. He looked around the sparse room, knowing that it was far different from what she was used to, but until he got his castle back, it would be her home.

He dropped her on the bed.

"You can't mean for me to sleep here?"

Her horrified tone only fueled his anger. "Is there someplace you would rather sleep?" He leaned over her, and she tried scooting back away from him, but there was not much room to maneuver on the small bed.

He moved closer, looming over her. Only a few inches separated them. "My bed, perhaps?"

Her eyes widened. "Never."

He didn't move. Tension crackled between them thick and heavy. God, he could smell her. Could hear the furious beat of her heart. He could almost taste the warmth of her lips beneath his. Opening. So soft and sweet. His body ached with pent-up desire.

He should take her right now. It would be over, and she would be his. And God knows he wanted her. Many men in his position would.

But not him.

He jerked away, furious, his body drumming with anger and lust. He'd never used force to get what he wanted, and he wouldn't start now. Now matter how tempted. He'd have her. And soon. Even if she didn't know it yet.

Flora MacLeod would be his bride. The ransom demand to Hector would give him the time to convince the lass to marry him. Like it or not, he needed her. And it couldn't be done with force. But pandering to the contrariness of a termagant left a bitter taste in his mouth. He cursed the need for her approval, but there was no doubt about it, she would be his.

And if she tried to stand in his way . . .

There would be no mercy.

Chapter 3

❖

Three days later, Flora was ready to leap from her tower prison.

The first time she'd tried to leave, about five minutes after he'd left her, her path had been blocked by two imposing guardsmen. *Two* men were entirely unnecessary, as it took only *one* to completely fill the doorway. If there was a man in this keep under six feet tall, she'd yet to see him.

A pleasant-looking man of about forty years escorted her—gently but firmly—back into the room. "The laird wishes for you to enjoy his hospitality in your room for now, my lady."

"So I'm to be a prisoner?" she asked, employing her most haughty voice.

"Aw, now, lass, don't think of it that way."

"How else do you suggest I think of it?"

"As a brief respite. When the laird is ready, he will send for you."

She pursed her mouth. It galled her no end to be at *his* beck and call. "And when, pray tell, will that be?"

The guardsman's face shadowed. "Soon, lass. The laird is a very busy man."

"I'm sure he is," she said sweetly. "Abducting any more helpless lassies this week?"

"Helpless?" He chuckled. "Ah, lass, you have a fine sense of humor," he chortled, closing the door behind her.

Busy. More like he enjoyed torturing her. The Laird of Coll. She still couldn't believe that the handsome kidnapper with enough raw masculinity to entice a nun was Lachlan Maclean. Why had she never seen him at court? She would have remembered him. He was a difficult man to forget.

Even days later, the memory of his presence filled the room. For a moment, with his body leaning over her and a glint in his hard blue gaze that made her feel warm and syrupy, she'd thought . . .

She'd thought he was going to kiss her.

And she'd frozen like a silly fool, caught up in the powerful magnetism that seemed to surround him. Irresistibly drawn to him like Icarus to the sun. For a moment, she'd wanted him to kiss her. To feel his mouth on hers. To melt against his heat. Her cheeks burned with the knowledge of how badly her body had betrayed her.

At least her initial fears had proved unfounded—he did not intend to force her into marriage. But discovering that he meant to use her as a bargaining chip against her brother to exchange her for his castle wasn't much better. A man who made no bones about using her for his own ends was exactly the type of man she wished to avoid.

Up to a point.

For the next two days, she waited for his summons. Patiently. Or about as patiently as anyone could be expected to wait, when there was nothing to do but stare out the window for hours on end at the churning seas and the undulating dipping and soaring of the gulls.

Her sole sources of conversation were the hourly exchanges with the guardsmen every time she tried to leave her room, the occasional appearance of a very taciturn serving woman named Morag, and the two lads who'd brought up the wooden tub for her bath.

But on the morning of her third day in captivity, her

patience was exhausted. The fir-planked walls of the room were closing in on her. She knew every inch of the small space.

Fortunately, the chamber wasn't as horrible as she'd initially thought. Though rustic and sparse, it was clean. Upon first seeing the threadbare linens and rushes on the wooden floors, she'd feared fleas and mice. But the bed linens—although a far cry from the rich silk taffeta hangings she was used to—smelled of lavender; and the old-fashioned rushes were still green and strewn with fresh herbs. Her pillow was stuffed not with feathers, but with surprisingly comfortable bog cotton.

A small fireplace and wooden bench took up one wall, the bed another, and a rickety wooden table with a pitcher for washing occupied the place beneath the sole window opposite the door. Though small, the window was paned with glass and had a wooden shutter for added protection from the wind and cold. Other than the door, which was well guarded, it was her only means of escape. But even if she could manage to squeeze through the small opening, there was nowhere to go. Situated on a level summit overlooking the Sound of Mull, Drimnin keep was a simple rectangular tower house with a single external stair turret on the east side of the southern wall. The laird had placed her in the uppermost chamber of the tower in a small garret. To escape, she'd have to climb down about forty feet of sheer stone.

Too ambitious by half, even for her. Although if she was locked in here much longer, she might be willing to take her chances.

A trunk containing an extra plaid, a brush, and a small hand mirror had been placed at the foot of the bed. Not long after she'd arrived, a tub had been sent up along with a change of clothing to replace her mud- and blood-spattered dress. In quality, it was not much better than the gown it had replaced, but at least it was clean. She'd cleaned her satin slippers as best she could with a small brush, but for more reasons than one, she wished she'd worn her new leather boots.

She finished pulling the brush through her hair and headed for the door. The drawbar had been removed, preventing her from locking *him*—or anyone else, for that matter—out. Swinging it open, she was shocked to find empty space.

"Good morning, my lady."

She turned to her jailer, who stood waiting to the side of the door. "Well, aren't you going to block the door-way, Alasdair?" she asked, referring to the little dance they engaged in every time she tried to leave.

He smiled, revealing the crooked grin that despite his advanced years still managed quite a bit of roguish charm. "Nay, not today, my lady."

She turned to the other guardsman. "Is it to be you today, then, Murdoch?"

He shook his head and wouldn't meet her eyes. Murdoch couldn't be much older than eight and ten, and despite his towering height, he seemed flustered by her presence. "Nay, my lady."

"Then I am free to go?"

Alasdair's grin deepened, a twinkle in his well-lined eyes. "Well now, lass, not *go*, exactly. The laird has requested you join him in the great hall to break your fast."

She crossed her arms, her gaze shifting back and forth between the two men. "Oh, has he now?" She tapped her foot. Her summons had apparently come. She was tempted to ignore it but was too desperate to leave the room to allow stubbornness to interfere. "It's about time." And with her shoulders pushed back as regally as any queen, she alighted through the open doorway and proceeded down the winding stairs.

As in most tower houses, the great hall was on the first floor. Perhaps she should just call it a hall. There was nothing "great" about the room at all. Austere was an understatement. Wooden floors strewn with rushes, plastered walls, wooden-beamed ceiling, a fireplace, iron sconces to hold the candles, about four arrow slits sufficed for windows, half a dozen wooden tables and benches, and that was it. No dais, no tapestries, no oil lamps, no rugs, no decoration of any kind.

And standing before a window with his back toward her was the laird himself. The Chief of Maclean of Coll. How could she have not realized who he was right away? Even his stance was commanding. But also wary. Much like the man, she suspected.

He turned as she entered the room. The sun beamed down on his head, catching the occasional strand of gold in his dark brown hair. She resisted the urge to draw in her breath. She couldn't, however, prevent the sudden spike in her pulse. It seemed from the first, this man had a strange effect on her that had not lessened in the intervening days. Her body felt blanketed with awareness. That the mere sight of him should affect her was troubling. But perhaps not surprising. He was an impressive man.

Strong and dangerously handsome. In the stark light, the hard lines of his face seemed carved from stone. Tall, broad-shouldered, and muscular, he was a force to be reckoned with. Never had she met a man whose physical strength blended so seamlessly with his appearance. Or one who was so undeniably masculine, almost primitive in his appeal. He dominated his surroundings, radiating an unmistakable aura of authority and command that had been forged by generations of the proud warriors and leaders who had come before him.

He was everything she'd been taught by her mother to revile: a Highlander, a warrior, and a chief. Yet she didn't revile him at all. It was disconcerting, appalling even, but she could not deny it. Lachlan Maclean wasn't at all what she'd expected.

In the Lowlands, Highlanders were looked on as rough, uncouth brutes. The wild savages of the North. A sentiment perpetuated by King James, who referred to his Highland subjects as "barbarians." Her mother had spoken of proud, cruel, warlike men incapable of emotion. Men who thought themselves kings over their own fiefdoms.

In some ways, the prejudice was warranted. Lachlan Maclean, like her brothers, was inalienably proud and more primitive—less refined—than Lowland courtiers. An authority unto himself. He'd abducted her, after all.

But he hadn't ravished her. Nor could she forget that he'd seemed to purposefully avoid killing any of Lord Murray's men. Hardly the bloodthirsty warmonger she'd come to expect. Indeed, even though she'd stabbed him, he'd treated her with surprising courtesy.

His strength, control, and blatant sensuality were difficult to ignore.

Paradoxically, the very things that should repel her were the very things she found appealing. On a base level, she was deeply attracted to this man who'd abducted her. The type of man she'd avoided most of her life. But acknowledging the truth only hardened her resolve to leave this wretched place. She would never let him know the effect he had on her.

He held her gaze as she approached. As she drew closer, she could see that something was different. He looked tired and slightly pale. As if he'd been ill.

The realization struck. He *had* been ill. He hadn't been ignoring her; he'd been recovering from his wound. He was human, after all.

She halted a few feet away from him, plastering her

hands to her side before she did something embarrassing like reach out and touch his arm. "You've been unwell."

His already gruff expression hardened. "No. I'm sorry you were confined to your room, but I had other matters to attend to."

He lied. He was not the type of man to explain his actions. Obviously, he was too proud to condescend to weakness of any kind.

The same sense of regret hit her as when she'd watched him with the hot blade. She hadn't meant to . . .

But she had. She'd wanted to hurt him. She knew she shouldn't feel guilt or regret, but the truth was that it bothered her to be the source of his pain.

"I'm . . ." It was on the tip of her tongue to apologize, but she couldn't quite get the words out. Her cheeks flooded with heat.

"You defended yourself well, Flora," he said, acknowledging her discomfort. "The fault was mine. I underestimated you. But only once. Never again." His voice held the unmistakable ring of a warning. "Come, sit." He indicated a seat at what must be the laird's table, because it had carved wooden chairs instead of benches.

She considered refusing, but when platters of steaming bread and beef started appearing, she thought better of it. She'd hoped for an improvement from the meals brought to her room, but the fare wasn't much better down here—bland and overcooked. At least it was hot.

They ate in silence, but she could feel his eyes on her. She tried to ignore it, but it made her self-conscious.

Finally he spoke. "You've been well treated?"

She finished chewing the bit of coarse brown bread that could use more salt and considered him over the rim of her ale. The combination of his dark, almost black hair and blue eyes was truly striking. She was glad to see that her nail marks across his cheek had nearly healed. "If you consider being locked in a small room for three days well treated. Actually, I've been bored out of my wits."

Her response seemed to annoy him. "I'm afraid we do not have time for masques and revels at Drimnin."

Clearly, he thought her just another spoiled courtier, and his barb was not without effect. The differences between their lifestyles could not be more divergent. But this time, she hadn't been criticizing him. She ventured another glance and saw his frown. "That's not what I meant. I hardly expect courtly entertainment, but I doubt even Highland women sit in their rooms for hours on end with nothing to do."

He leaned back in his chair and paused thoughtfully. "No, you're right, they don't."

The concession surprised her. Prompted by the apparent thaw in his temper, she decided to broach what had been on her mind for the past few days—leaving. "Have you written to my brother?"

He lifted a dark brow. "So anxious to go? But you've only just arrived."

She ignored his attempt to defray the question. "Have you?"

"A messenger left for Coll not long after we arrived."

"And has Hector acceded to your demands?"

"Not yet."

"Nor will he."

"We'll see."

He sounded so confident. But she wasn't so sure. A terrible thought suddenly occurred to her. "What will you do with me if he does not agree?"

He held her gaze with piercing blue eyes that seemed to see right through her. "He'll agree."

"But what if he does not? You can't keep me here forever. Eventually someone will realize I'm missing."

"Eventually. But I would wager that you've bought me quite a bit of time with your attempted elopement."

"What do you mean?"

"I rather doubt that you left Holyrood in the middle of the night without explanation."

Her face fell. She thought of the notes she'd written to both Rory and her cousin Argyll that she'd gone to see Hector. Notes that would prevent anyone from looking for her for some time.

But how had he guessed?

Hector would know soon enough, but he was on ill terms with both Argyll and Rory. Her only hope was that William would alert her cousin to what had happened. But then there would be some explaining to do. Would he risk it?

The laird was watching with an inscrutable expression on his face. "Why have you never married?" he asked suddenly. "You are certainly of age."

Her body went rigid. "I hardly think that is any of your concern."

His gaze swept over her face and down her breasts. "You are pleasing enough."

She gasped. Did that suffice for a compliment? Blandishments were obviously not his forte. But it wasn't the lack of gallantry that stung. He could have been inspecting her like a horse at market. The simple gesture summed up everything she despised about her position. She was flesh and blood, but no one would ever see her as such. All they saw was the wealth and connections she would bring them. And this man saw her only as a bargaining chip.

"You are too kind." Her voice dripped with sarcasm. "But what has marriage to offer me that I don't already have?"

There were many ways to answer that question, but having care for her innocence, Lachlan refrained from the blunt one. One glance at that beautiful face and lush body, and he need look no further for a reason why the lass should be wed: swiving. And lots of it.

It had been the foremost thing on his mind since she'd walked into the room. When he'd had to force himself not to blink to see if she was real—there was such an ethereal, almost fey quality to her beauty. The face that had haunted his dreams while he recovered from his wound was even more breathtaking in the flesh. There was no mud to obscure her features or horrible cap to hide her hair.

The old gown he'd borrowed from his sister was a shade small and clung to her breasts and hips, emphasizing the seductive curves of her body. Her long blond hair tumbled in loose waves around her shoulders, catching the sun in a golden halo of light. Freshly scrubbed cheeks revealed the translucence of her pale skin, a luminous contrast to sea blue eyes framed in thick dark lashes and to her bold red lips.

It was her mouth that was driving him mad. Filling his mind with dark, erotic images. Her lips were soft and wide with a deep, sensual curve, highlighted by a tiny naughty dimple on one cheek. He thought of how close he'd been to kissing her and regretted the forbearance that had only increased his hunger. He wasn't a patient man by nature, especially when he wanted something. And he wanted Flora MacLeod. With a force that sent a surge of heat rushing through his veins.

Tearing his gaze from her mouth, he realized she was waiting for his response. Though she'd spoken derisively, Lachlan heard the underlying challenge in her question. What *did* marriage have to offer her? Stretching his legs out in front of him, he leaned back in his chair and took a long draught of ale. "Obviously you have no need of connections or additional wealth." He wished he could say the same.

She lifted a finely arched brow, surprised that he was taking her question seriously. "Obviously."

"Hmm . . ." He paused, considering. "May I presume that love is too trite a reason?" Although in his experience, young women—his sisters included—thought of nothing else.

"It's as good as any, I suppose. Though perhaps not a practical one. One may wait a lifetime for such an occurrence—if it happens at all."

Her answer surprised him. He would have thought her pragmatic like him. Romantic love had no part in his decision to marry, simply because he would never allow emotion to influence his decisions. Love was for other people. His devotion and loyalty belonged to his clan and to his family. No one woman would ever change that. And certainly not this one. He was too old to confuse lust with love.

She would bring him much. But love wasn't part of the bargain.

But Flora was not wholly without illusions of romantic love. He filed the knowledge away for later, when it might be helpful. First he needed to understand the way she thought, before he decided how best to approach her with his offer. He hadn't told her of his intentions from the first, because he knew she would be too angry to see reason. And he'd been warned of her contrariness. But he would do whatever it took to secure her agreement to marry. When he played, he played to win. He hadn't survived the years of attack by shirking from doing what was necessary.

He held her gaze. "Then what of passion as a reason to marry?"

He thought a tinge of pink appeared upon her cheeks, but if she was embarrassed, her response gave no hint of the fact. "I do not believe one is a prerequisite for the other."

The flash of anger hit him swift and hard. Had she and that popinjay . . . ? The mere thought filled him with rage and a feeling of incomprehensible possessiveness. Why the lass's innocence was important to him, he didn't know. Simply that it was.

"What do you mean?" He held his voice even, though his knuckles turned white as he gripped his goblet.

She shrugged. "I do not believe passion is confined to the marriage bed. In fact, from what I can tell, the marriage bed rarely holds much passion at all."

He didn't like the cynicism of her answer—even if he happened to agree with it. Lack of passion in the marriage bed was one of the many reasons he'd delayed taking a wife. That and the fact that he'd been too busy defending his land from attack and his people from starvation.

"Yet the marriage bed is the only respectable place for a woman of your position to find it."

She bristled. "I do not need to be lectured on respectability by you. A man who abducts women is hardly in a position to be casting stones."

He didn't miss that she hadn't answered him. He leaned closer and looked her straight in the eye. "And are you respectable, Flora?"

Her eyes sparked with anger. "How dare you! It's none of your damn business."

God, she provoked him. This woman possessed an uncanny ability to rile his anger. He wanted to grab her arm and shake the truth out of her, but instead he took another drink of his ale and allowed his blood to cool. It *was* his business, although she didn't know it yet.

But she would.

She pushed back from her chair and started to stand up. "If you have run out of reasons—"

"Protection." He took her wrist, holding her in her seat. His fingers wrapped around bare skin. Incredibly soft, bare skin. Though tall for a woman and well curved, she had slim, delicate bones. Suggesting a fragility otherwise obscured by the outward strength of her character. "An unmarried woman, especially one with wealth and lands, is vulnerable without a husband to protect her."

"I don't need—" She stopped, realizing that her very presence in his keep was proof to the contrary. She lifted her chin. "My mother protected me."

"But your mother is gone." He stated it simply, as a fact, but she flinched as if he'd struck her.

She turned to him with such a look of despair in her eyes, it cut him to the quick. "I'm well aware of that," she said softly.

He felt a strong urge to comfort her but held it back. Feeling sorry for her would only complicate matters. He couldn't allow compassion to interfere. But he didn't miss the flash of loneliness.

"And yet for all your protesting to the contrary, you've implicitly acknowledged that there is some benefit to marriage."

"What do you mean?"

"Do you forget your betrothed already?"

Her cheeks fired. "Of course not."

But it was clear she had. "So was it protection or love, Flora?" he asked quietly. The answer was somehow important. He wouldn't consider the other possibility— passion.

She looked away. "Lord Murray was my choice."

She'd said as much before. He was beginning to understand what might have caused her to elope. "Rory would not force you to wed." Which was the very reason he was in this predicament. He needed her agreement.

A wry smile turned her lips. "You know him so well?"

"Well enough. He's spoken of you."

It surprised her. "He has?"

She tried to hide her eagerness by shifting her gaze to her plate, but not before Lachlan had glimpsed the yearning. Did she think her family had forgotten her?

"Of course. You are his sister." He saw the disappointment in her face, and before he could stop himself he added, "He cares about you."

Her eyes brightened, and he felt a sharp tug in his chest. This urge to please her was dangerous, and one that he would need to keep a tight rein on.

"Even so," she countered, "my cousin might."

The Earl of Argyll. Lachlan masked his reaction, understanding too well why she would fear her cousin's interference. Her fear was warranted. Although Rory controlled her marriage, he—like Lachlan—had entered into a bond of manrent with Argyll. That alone gave Argyll plenty of influence in the decision.

"Your cousin has a habit of interfering where he does not belong."

"And I've seen too often the misery that type of interference can bring. When I marry, *if* I marry, it will be my decision and no one else's. Not my brothers', not my cousin's, but mine."

She spoke with such passion, he knew that this was the crux of understanding her. Her elopement was not simply the actions of a spoiled, headstrong girl, as he'd first thought. There was a far deeper reason. A real fear behind her actions. It wasn't marriage itself she feared, but being forced into it.

He tested his theory. "But it isn't a woman's right to make such decisions. Like it or not, the choice of your husband doesn't belong to you."

She looked at him as if he'd struck her. The irony, of course, was that she had more power than she realized. But perhaps it was better for his purposes if she remained unsure.

"So it's a woman's lot to be bartered to the highest bidder?"

It was rather crude when put that way, but accurate nonetheless. "It is."

"Well, it's a lot I do not accept." A glint of steel appeared in her eyes. "Headstrong" was putting it mildly. He would need to tread carefully, but time was a constant weapon.

He suspected the source of her discontent. He knew something of Janet Campbell. Like her daughter, Janet had been one of the most sought-after heiresses of her day. Married to four powerful Highland chiefs. Unhappily, it was said. "Your mother was wrong to put such ideas in your head."

"You presume too much. You don't know anything about my mother." Her hand went to a large pendant she wore around her neck.

Suddenly, his entire body froze. He nearly ripped it out of her hand. "Where did you get that?" It wasn't a pendant, as he'd first thought, but a brooch hanging from a chain with a large stone set in the center.

She paled and tried to slip it down the bodice of her gown. "It belonged to my mother."

He reached out to stop her, taking the amulet in his hand. He couldn't believe it. Excitement coursed through him as he examined the faded etchings of axes and thistle in silver that surrounded a large center stone of cairngorm—the yellowish brown stone of the Highlands. Axes and thistle were the emblems of the Macleans. He turned it over to read the inscription on the back: *To my beloved husband, on the day of our marriage.*

He couldn't believe it.

The irony could have made him laugh. Marrying Flora MacLeod would be a boon in more ways than one. Their marriage would be a powerful symbol. An end to a curse. A curse that he didn't believe in, but that didn't matter, his people believed in it. They blamed the curse for the misfortune that had haunted their clan for the last eighty years.

Still holding the amulet, he looked deep into her eyes. "It's you. You're the Campbell lass."

Flora cursed herself for her stupidity. She should have kept the amulet well hidden. But how could she have guessed that he would recognize it so easily?

He was a Maclean; of course he knew the legend. The chief who had chained poor Elizabeth Campbell to the rock had been his ancestor—his grandfather's father's father, if she wasn't mistaken. But she wouldn't have expected him to give it much credence. Not in this day and age.

But how could she have forgotten that putting an end to the curse was one of the reasons her mother had been forced to marry her first husband?

"You can't believe in that old tale," she said dismissively.

"No."

Her relief was short-lived.

"Although many in these parts do," he finished.

"It's ridiculous. My mother's marriage to Hector's father should have put all those old superstitions to rest."

"Instead it strengthened them."

He was right. For a few years, with her mother's marriage to Hector's father, the Maclean of Duart, the bad luck that seemed to follow the Macleans had temporarily ended. Until his death, when the misfortune returned. The small lapse had only fueled the superstition.

What had she done? Had Coll reconsidered his intention not to marry her? She couldn't let that happen. "It doesn't matter. The amulet belongs to me, and I will never willingly bestow it." *On you,* she left unsaid. Most believed that the curse would end when the amulet was bestowed willingly on a Maclean—something her mother had never done.

Something sparked in his eyes. He'd taken her words as a challenge. He leaned closer, invading the safe buffer of space between them, engulfing her senses. He was big and strong and thoroughly overwhelming. And he smelled amazing. Warm and spicy, with just a hint of myrtle and soap. Awareness surrounded her. She became achingly conscious of his mouth only inches from hers. Of fine stubble along his jaw. His lashes were so long and feather soft, a sharp contrast to the hard angles of his face.

He reached out, and she froze, thinking he meant to touch her, to kiss her. Instead, he untangled a strand of hair that had caught in her lashes and tucked it gently behind her ear. Her stomach clenched as she breathed in the scent of him. Of myrtle, soap, and man. The sensation of his fingers on her skin made her shiver.

How did he do this to her? Turn her into a quivering mess in a matter of seconds.

He held her gaze, letting her feel the power of the tension sizzling between them. His thumb strayed for just a moment across her cheek in a soft caress. "Can you be so sure?"

"I . . . I . . . yes." She couldn't think.

And the arrogant brute knew it. He chuckled and released her. "We'll see."

Outrage fired her cheeks. "Do I need protection from you, my laird?"

He gave her a long bold look, one that was blatantly sensual. "You might."

"You promised."

He seemed unabashedly unconcerned. "So I did."

"You have no honor."

He quirked a brow, infuriatingly amused. "Obviously, or you wouldn't be here."

"A prisoner," she said forlornly.

"Whether you are prisoner or guest is up to you." His gaze narrowed. "Do not defy me and your stay here will be pleasant."

She stiffened, her deep-seated resentment of being told what to do flared. "And what am I supposed to do while I'm your *guest*?" she asked, not bothering to hide her sarcasm.

"Whatever it is that women do to keep themselves busy. Do what you like, as long as you do not try to leave the walls of the keep."

She spun around to hide the smile on her face, her mind swarming with all kinds of ideas. She would keep herself occupied all right.

Lachlan Maclean had abducted the wrong woman. And she was going to make him sorry for it. Very sorry indeed.

Chapter 4

❖

"I don't know, Flora. Are you sure he won't be angry?"

I certainly hope he will be. Flora looked back and forth between the two girls. She'd caught the laird's young sisters lurking in the shadows and watching her with unabashed curiosity a few days ago and had pretended to ignore them—which, of course, had the opposite effect of increasing their curiosity. Finally, they'd ventured out of the shadows to ask her what she was doing. When she'd told them, they'd offered to help, thereby becoming her unwitting accomplices.

Which only served him right, since the poor darlings were bored to tears. Buried in this barren wilderness with nothing to do. And no female companionship to speak of.

Mary, the elder at seven and ten, was a feminine version of her brother, possessing the same striking coloring—dark brown hair and light blue eyes. Her features were a tad too strong for true beauty, but her sweet disposition more than compensated. Gillian was two years younger and by far the more adventuresome of the two. She couldn't look more different from her elder siblings. Red-haired and green-eyed, with the palest pink skin, she would be a true beauty in a few years. Gillian was also a kindred spirit, as Flora had discovered within minutes of meeting her. Mary, on the other hand, tended to need a wee bit of encouragement. Like now.

"I'm simply keeping myself busy, just as your brother instructed," Flora answered. "What else is there to do? He's barred me from the kitchens and the aleroom."

"With good reason," Mary said gently.

Flora shrugged. "I was only trying to help."

Gilly wasn't fooled. Her eyes lit with mischief. "By salting the food and sweetening the ale?"

Flora smiled at the memory. Salting the food had been the first test. Despite her bold vow to torment him, she'd been a little worried—he was rather fierce and imposing and clearly not a man to be trifled with. So the day following their exchange, she'd visited the kitchens. Heart pounding, she'd watched nervously as he'd raised his spoon and filled his mouth with her special gruel, and then smiled when he'd nearly spat it right back out. His piercing eyes narrowed on her with understanding, and she could see him struggle to bite back the tongue-lashing he'd clearly wanted to give her. He was controlling himself. Flora didn't know why, but it didn't matter—he was.

"It didn't look to be too much going in," Flora protested. And in this case, it might even have been an improvement. "I haven't had much experience in the kitchens before." At least not since her cousin Argyll had run her out of the kitchens at Inveraray for doing the same thing.

"And don't forget you are also barred from helping with the laundry and the mending," Mary said.

Flora pressed her lips together to keep from giggling. "It's quite unfair. I thought his shirts smelled lovely."

"Oh, they did," Gilly said, amusement bubbling in her voice. "As lovely as any lass."

Fitting, since Flora had dipped them in rosewater. "I thought it matched well with the embroidery," she explained. She'd sewn large pink flowers all over his best linen shirt.

"Which might have been fine had you not sewed the arm closed," Gilly said.

"And hemmed his trews too short," Mary added.

Not to mention the nettles that she'd aired his plaid on. It had been worth every hour of drudgery removing the prickly leaves, simply to hear the bellow.

Ah yes, she'd been busy. But he was being infuriatingly calm about everything. No matter what she did, he demonstrated extreme patience. And steely control. Almost as if he were humoring her. Which only made her more determined to rattle him.

She hadn't had this much fun in years. Though admittedly she'd had lots of practice. Even as a girl, Flora had understood her place in life and rebelled—with her mother's encouragement—against the future that seemed to be predetermined. But by the time she'd arrived at court, what had started as a way to avoid her mother's sad fate, by discouraging suitors with harmless misdeeds, had escalated beyond her control. She didn't need to look for trouble, it seemed to find her easily enough. Unfortunately, her reputation for mischief didn't discourage her bevy of suitors one whit. With her fortune and connections, they'd want her even if she had horns on her head.

But Flora intended to make sure Lachlan Maclean had no such inclinations.

Mary shook her head. "My brother is quite particular about his weapons."

"Well then, won't he be pleased to see them so bright and shiny," Flora countered.

"He'll be angry," Mary warned. "And he has squires for that."

"He hasn't been angry about anything before."

Mary frowned. "Yes, he's been remarkably understanding."

"Perhaps he feels guilty," Flora offered.

Gilly laughed. "I doubt that. Lachlan knows exactly what he's doing. When he makes a decision, he never looks back." There was more than a touch of admiration in her voice.

"You can't mean you think he was right to abduct me?"

Gilly flushed, looking uncomfortable. "No. Yes . . ." She twisted her hands. "He has his reasons."

Flora decided not to press the matter. She did not want to put a wedge between the girls and their brother, even if she could. The girls idolized the laird, speaking of him in somewhat reverent tones. That he cared deeply for his two sisters was obvious, though it was equally obvious that he didn't know how to show it. As her own brothers had done with her, he seemed to be trying to fill the position of father rather than brother. Understandable when the girls were young, perhaps, but Flora could see how desperately they wanted the teasing affection of a brother. She swallowed hard, her throat suddenly tight. Just as she'd wanted.

Hector she'd never spent much time with, but Rory and Alex had fostered with their uncle, the Earl of Argyll, the present earl's father, at Inveraray Castle, and returned often when she was a young girl. Rory and Alex, both so much older than she, had tried to stand in for the father she'd never known. Looking back, Flora realized they were doing only what they thought best, but at the time she'd resented their authority when she'd wanted desperately to be one of them.

Like her, Mary and Gilly were bound to be disappointed. Wringing affection from Coll would be like trying to squeeze water from a stone. But oddly enough, in some ways Flora found his gruff male awkwardness around his sisters charming. Watching him interact with the young girls had shown her another side of him. He was attentive and understanding, if firm, listening to their excited girlish prattle with remarkable patience. He cared. He might not like to think so, but he did.

He was different from what she'd first thought.

She'd often felt his gaze on her the past few days, watching her with an intensity that was both unnerving and exhilarating. Thrusting aside the odd sentiment, Flora took a minute to gather the necessary items from the storeroom, then turned back around to the two girls. "Well, what will it be?"

"I'll go," Gilly said.

But Mary wasn't as easily convinced. "Are you sure you are only going to oil his swords?"

"Yes," Flora assured her, neglecting to mention the kind of oil she would be using. But clearly Mary was still vacillating. "You don't even need to come in," Flora said. "All you need to do is watch for Odin."

A soft pink flush rose to Mary's cheeks. "You shouldn't call him that. His name is Allan."

Flora lifted her brows. So that was the way of it. Mary was harboring a tender for the captain of the castle. "I know his name," Flora said. "But you have to admit, he's got the look of the Norse god of war." She liked to make up nicknames. The laird was Thor—the Norse god of thunder—due to his expression.

"Flora's right, Mary," Gilly said. "He's always terrified me."

"You don't know him," Mary defended staunchly. "He's really very . . . sweet."

Flora let out a burst of laughter. "Don't let your brother hear that. I don't think he'd like to hear one of his fiercest warriors described as sweet."

Mary blanched. "You won't tell him—"

"Don't be silly, I was only jesting." But Mary looked so worried, Flora felt awful for teasing her. She took her hand and gave it a gentle squeeze. "Why don't you stay here? Gilly can watch for Od—Allan—and we'll be back before you know it."

Mary shook her head. "I'll come."

Flora smiled. "Good. To the armory, ladies."

Lachlan was itching for a fight. Even the hours spent in the yard training had barely taken the edge off. He felt like a caged lion, restless and agitated. The source of his discomfort wasn't hard to identify.

The wee hellion had been here less than a week and had already managed to turn his keep upside down. She was a born troublemaker. Or his personal tormentor, he wasn't sure yet. To think, he'd actually been happy at first, believing her interest in his castle was a good sign that she was becoming involved. He grimaced. One look at the termagant's face and he knew exactly what she was up to. But he'd be damned if he'd give her the satisfaction of losing his temper. Countless times over the past few days he'd been forced to bite back his anger, although every instinct clamored to put her in her place. Too much depended on wooing the recalcitrant lass.

But her mischief was only half the problem. He couldn't seem to look at her without getting hard. And Lachlan was not a man used to keeping his passions in check. Although some of the tension could be relieved with a long visit to his leman, he told himself that he refrained for Flora's sake—not wanting to flaunt the woman before her. But there was another explanation far more troubling: The lovely and talented widow Seonaid held little appeal.

Not when all he could think of was big blue eyes in a delicate elfin face. It was a case of wanting what he could not have. Not yet, anyway.

The years of constant fighting and fending off attack had taught him to be careful. To plan. To appraise the situation before rushing in. He was doing his best to give her time to adjust to her presence at his keep, but he'd been patient long enough.

It was time to make his move.

As she hadn't been in her tower room or the hall, he'd made his way to the *barmkin*. It was a fine day, and he thought she might have decided to take a walk around the courtyard. He looked across at the armory and noticed his sister Mary talking to Allan.

Lately, whenever he saw Mary or Gilly, Flora wasn't far away. His sisters were enthralled by Flora's sophisticated grace and refinement—which was obvious even without the fashionable wardrobe. He felt a twinge of regret. His sisters had suffered along with the rest of his clan. There hadn't been the time or money to see to their instruction. At least Flora's tocher would help with that. Two thousand merks. It was a bloody king's ransom. He'd be a fool not to marry her for that alone.

He frowned, watching Mary converse with Allan. His captain was . . . hell, he was smiling. Mary's eyes were sparkling, and her cheeks were pink. She was looking at Allan with . . .

Damn. He strode across the courtyard, intending to put a stop to it immediately. He had other plans for Mary. What was Allan thinking? He should know better than to encourage the attentions of an impressionable young lass, barely out of the schoolroom—or what would be the schoolroom, if there had been money for such luxuries. Allan might be his most trusted guardsman and his fiercest warrior, but he was not for Mary.

As he drew closer, his sister caught sight of him and froze. Her eyes widened, and he swore a look of guilt swept across her features.

"What are you doing out here, Mary? And where's Gilly?" He ignored Allan. He would have a wee talk with his captain later.

"Uh . . . I . . . ," Mary mumbled. Instinctively, she'd

taken a step toward the door. Almost as if she were hiding . . .

The armory. Flora was in the armory. He let out an oath. "I'll kill her."

After moving his sister gently out of the way, he opened the door. The smell almost made him keel over. Both women looked up.

Gilly jumped up and came rushing toward him. "Brother, we were hoping to surprise you."

Lachlan looked right at Flora. "I'm sure you were." God help her, the wee banshee looked as if she were going to burst out laughing. Anger whipped around inside him like a tempest. The carefully constructed façade of patience he'd built up over the past few days shattered.

The lass had oiled his swords—including his claymore—in fulmar oil. The birds spat the fishy-smelling oil on anything that drew too close. The damn odor lingered and stank like hell. He'd imported the oil from St. Kilda for lamps—which was no doubt how she'd known what it was. The remote isle of St. Kilda was part of her brother Rory's lands.

Lachlan looked at the pile of gleaming weapons scattered across the floor. She hadn't left a surface uncovered, including the horn hilt and leather grips.

Gilly wrinkled her nose. "It certainly does have a strong smell. But Flora said this type of oil is the best." She sensed something wasn't right. "Did we do wrong, brother?"

He turned to his sister, trying to control his fury. "Gilly, you and your sister go inside the keep and ready yourself for the evening meal. I would like to speak with Mistress MacLeod for a moment."

When the door had closed, he was on her in a second flat, pulling her from the bench and jerking her hard against his chest. Blood pounded through his body. No one had ever brought him so close to losing control.

She tried to push away. "Let go of me."

Anger and lust converged as she squirmed against him, and his body thickened with the heavy rush of heat. He didn't know whether to shake her or drag her to his chamber and release the pent-up desire raging inside him. He couldn't think straight. She was the most stubborn, willful woman he'd ever met. Yet when he held her in his arms, and she gazed up at him with those wide, defiant blue eyes, he was deeply conscious of her fragility. Of how easily he could hurt her.

She was just a lass. And from what he'd surmised, a scared and lonely one at that.

He let go of her, struggling to cool his rage. "You've gone too far. You will wipe these swords until every last bit of that oil is removed."

"Did I do something wrong?" She gazed up at him from under her lashes. Lashes that curled thick and feathery against the ivory softness of her pale cheek. Despite its calculation, the sweetly feminine gesture was not without effect. But the twitch of that naughty little dimple near the corner of her mouth almost pushed him over the edge.

He leaned closer to her, inhaling the sweet fragrance of her hair. His body shook with restraint, and his erection throbbed hard against his stomach. Every instinct clamored to take her. To kiss the taunt from her lips, to sink his fingers through the long silk of her hair and devour her until she yielded to him. "Do not play with me, Flora. I'm not one of your pet courtiers. Poke me and I'll bite."

He saw the glint of satisfaction in her eyes. As if she'd wanted him to lose control. She'd thought she was safe from him. God, he ached to prove her wrong.

"I don't know what you are talking about. I was only

trying to be helpful. Didn't you say that I should keep myself busy?"

"I know exactly what you are trying to do. Simply because I chose to tolerate your mischief doesn't mean I don't know why you're doing it. But mark this: If I decide to have you, a little salt or a few flowers would not stop me from doing so."

She sucked in her breath, her spine rigid. "Your threats do not worry me. If you want your castle back, you will not lay a hand on me."

"I never make threats, my sweet. Only promises. You will obey me."

"You're a tyrant."

"No, I'm chief. And while you are in this keep you will follow my rules. No more of your tricks, Flora. And do not think to involve my sisters again in your wee games."

"Your sisters are bored. It was time they had some fun. This is no place for young women. Gilly should be getting some schooling, and Mary should be at court. They should be dancing, meeting others of their own age, wearing beautiful gowns."

He stiffened, hearing the judgment in her voice. She didn't know when to stop. "When I want your advice, I'll ask for it. I would not see my sisters corrupted or turned into spoiled courtiers. They belong here, with me."

He was furious both that he was defending himself to her and that she'd spoken aloud thoughts he didn't want to acknowledge. His sisters did deserve more.

He stepped back and raked a hand through his hair. How did she manage to do this? He'd come to find her with the best intentions of wooing her, yet here he was arguing with her. But he wasn't used to being disobeyed, and Flora was a beguiling termagant who defied him at every turn. Aye, and who confoundingly challenged and intrigued him in a way no woman ever had before.

"Is that what you think?" she asked. "That court is corrupting? How would you know? I've never seen you there."

"Like every other Highland chief, I travel to Edinburgh yearly to present myself at court and account for my 'good behavior.' " Leaving as soon as he could.

"In your case, it doesn't seem to have worked," she said dryly.

He chuckled. She froze, staring at him as if he'd just parted the Red Sea. Their eyes locked, and he felt a strange jolt—a charged connection.

He knew by the way she held his gaze that she felt it, too, but not wanting to acknowledge it, she shifted her gaze, started to fumble nervously with the leather gloves she wore to protect her hands, and finally removed them. "Did you want something?" she asked. "Has my brother responded?"

"He has not. But after you have cleaned up this mess, you will dine with me tonight."

Her eyes narrowed suspiciously. "Why?"

He fought to contain his irritation. "I thought you might enjoy some company."

"No. I'm quite happy taking my meals in my room."

He bit back the angry retort. With what she'd done to his swords, he was in no mood for her defiance, but he had a job to do. He'd never had to woo a woman before—women came to him. And wooing this one was like extracting a tooth. "I've arranged for some entertainment."

She crossed her arms, digging in. "I don't wish to dine with you. The circumstances of my being here hardly make for friendly conversation."

Her mulish expression did it, sending his good intentions right out the window. He took a step closer. She stood tall before him, not giving an inch. He had to admire her fortitude, given that the top of her head barely reached his shoulders and he was at least twice her weight.

He lowered his voice. "It wasn't a request."

"You can't force me."

"The hell I can't."

He could see the rigid, uncompromising set of her chin and recognized that he'd made a mistake. Flora didn't like to be ordered or forced to do anything. It might be the wrong approach, but right now he didn't care. He was a man used to giving orders and to being obeyed. They might be destined to clash. But he would win.

"You are a brute. A gentleman—"

That was it. He snapped. He'd heard enough of her opinions on Highlanders. Before she could get out the offending words, he pulled her into his arms. His body reacted with swift force, stirring hard against her. He savored the erotic sensations coursing through him as he looked deep into her eyes. Eyes that widened apprehensively as his arousal pressed firmly against her.

Good. He wanted her to feel him. To know what she did to him. To know just how far from civilized he really was.

"How many times must I tell you that I am not one of your damn gentlemen?"

"Please—"

His mouth fell on hers, covering any objection with the force of his kiss. This was what he'd wanted to do from the first. The relief was so intense, he nearly groaned. Heat welled up inside him, threatening to erupt. His mouth moved over hers hungrily, possessively. Tasting.

He felt her shock. And then, blissfully, her innocence. *God, she was sweet.* Her lips were so incredibly soft and warm. Her skin smelled of roses, and her mouth tasted like heaven. He wanted to devour her. To slide in his tongue and delve into the honey recesses of her mouth. To unleash the maelstrom of his desire and force her to acknowledge the heat sizzling between them.

He was hard as a rock, every inch of his body taut and primed for passion. He should be ravishing her, kissing her hard and thoroughly. Giving way to the lust that had been straining inside him from the first moment he'd seen her. Lust such as he'd never felt before.

But something held him back. It wasn't just the knowledge that he couldn't force her. Never had he so wanted a lass to respond to him—at a base level that not even she could deny. He wanted it with an intensity that should have troubled him. Enough to tame the fires of his own desire. All he could think about was the vulnerability of the innocent young woman in his arms.

He forced his blood to cool and ignored the aching pressure in his loins.

The kiss that was intended to punish turned soft and coaxing. His mouth brushed against hers, demanding a response with gentle persuasion, not force. He brought his hand to her face and stroked her cheek with his thumb, stunned by the velvety softness of her skin. His fingers cupped her chin, gently urging her lips apart.

She opened for him, making a tiny sound.

A primal roar of masculine satisfaction swelled inside him. She did want him. He swept his tongue inside her mouth, feeling her surprise and then her response. She stretched against him, wrapping her arms around his neck, and returned his kiss with an innocent fervor that nearly undid him.

An unexpected wave of tenderness gripped him. He'd never felt like this before. Protective. Possessive. *Moved*. By a simple kiss.

* * *

Flora's heart hammered in her chest. He was kissing her. She wanted to pull away, should have pulled away, but God help her, she could not. She was awash in sensation, drowning in his seductive masculine heat. Nothing else mattered but the exquisite feel of his mouth on hers.

His lips teased and implored, coaxing her response with a gentle caress that was so achingly sweet, it almost hurt. His mouth was so soft, the dark spicy taste of him intoxicating. She melted against him, savoring the wicked sensation of her body molded against the hard wall of his broad chest and the strong muscular arms that held her so protectively.

How could he do this to her? It was all wrong. He should be savage, rough, forceful. But he was none of those. This powerful Highlander kissed her with more tenderness and finess than she'd ever dreamed possible. And with a poignancy that frightened her. Men had stolen kisses from her, but no man had ever kissed her in a way that made her want to weep, her heart slam against her chest, and her knees go weak all at the same time.

He was everything she'd ever dreamed of and nothing he was supposed to be.

And if it didn't feel so perfect she would stop him. But it did feel perfect.

His kiss grew more insistent. More demanding. When his tongue slid in her mouth, her heart seemed to stop beating. She was shocked but also deeply aroused by the long, languorous strokes of his tongue. Strokes that set off wicked sparks in her body and made her heart tug with longing.

She silenced the roar of questions in her head and allowed herself to feel. He tasted her deep and slow. Delving into the farthest reaches of her mouth. Her body flooded with heat, building with an urgency that she could not describe and a hunger that would not be denied. So she gave herself over to his kiss, to the raw sensuality. Responding the only way she knew how, with eagerness and enthusiasm.

She kissed him back. Entwining her tongue with his. Tasting him as deeply as he did her. Soon, the gentle touch of his mouth was not enough. She wanted it harder. Faster. Deeper. She wrapped her hands around his neck, wanting to get closer. Wanting to feel the hard strength of his body under her fingertips. Wanting to press her body against him. Wanting to dissolve into his heat.

He moved his arousal firmly against her. Big, bold, and threatening. A dangerous reminder that shattered the brief spell of insanity. She felt a flicker of excitement before the cold splash of reality. And fear.

Oh, my God, what am I doing? He's my captor. She pushed him away in horror, as if she could push away her own treacherous desires. "Stop!"

They stood in silence, both breathing hard, staring at each other. It was all there between them in that one glance. Everything she was feeling in the look that stretched between them. For a moment his implacable expression shifted, revealing a flash of surprise.

She covered her mouth with her hand, feeling the heat and gentle throbbing of her lips.

When he finally spoke, his expression had again become unreadable. "You will join me tonight."

Whether it was a request or an order, she was too overwhelmed to notice. Her entire body pulsed with a strange sensation. All she could manage was a nod.

He turned and left her without a backward glance, his stride as determined and powerful as the man himself. Leaving Flora to stare at the door, wondering what had just happened. And why she felt as though everything had just changed.

Chapter 5

❖

By time she'd returned to her room, Flora was ready to collapse. Exhausted from the struggle of removing as much of the pungent oil from his swords as possible. If she wasn't sure that he would come up to her room and drag her down himself, she would beg off from the evening meal.

She started to remove her clothing, eager to sink into the tub that had been filled with steaming hot water and sprinkled with dried lavender. The soft floral scent floated through the air, drowning out the stench of fulmar oil that had seemed permanently lodged in her nose.

Despite the apron she'd worn to protect her gown, the residue from the oil had penetrated the linen into the wool. She sighed, recognizing that it was her own fault. But it had been worth it, even if the skirt of her only gown smelled a bit. Perhaps Mary would be willing to lend her another?

Or maybe she should leave it be, in the hope that the smell would keep him away.

She'd driven his kiss from her mind while she worked, but the memories returned the moment she sank into the warm, soothing water. Her fingers went to her still tender lips.

Had he really kissed her like that?

And had she really responded so completely, melting against him in a soft pool of heat? That, of course, was the far more troubling question. Thank God she'd caught herself in time.

It was difficult to believe that the fierce warrior who'd abducted her could kiss her as if she were a fragile piece of porcelain. Evoking feelings she'd never experienced before. Deep feelings of longing and contentment. In his arms, she felt protected, cherished, cared for.

She tapped the water with her hand, scattering the dried leaves like dust to the wind. She was being ridiculous. It wasn't like her to be so fanciful, though neither was it like her to fall into the embrace of a barbarian.

No, she corrected. He wasn't a barbarian. If she'd learned anything since the night he'd upset her elopement, she'd learned that. There was an inherent streak of nobility and strength in him that could not be denied. He was hard and uncompromising, but he could also be thoughtful and considerate.

She slipped under the water to clear the soap from her hair, wishing it were as easy to erase the memory of his mouth on hers. She didn't think she'd ever forget the feel of him or the rich masculine taste of him.

But it didn't matter. She'd made a mistake in allowing him to kiss her; she would not make it again. She was his prisoner. And she'd do best not to forget it. To him, she was simply something to leverage over her brother. A means to an end. She could never care for a man who saw her as such. A kiss, no matter how sublime, wouldn't change that. Flora knew her worth, not as a prize of marriage or to end a curse, but as a woman. And she would accept nothing less from a husband.

She'd thought Lord Murray different. Instead he'd served as a powerful lesson in trusting the wrong man. She wouldn't make that mistake again.

She stood up and stepped carefully from the tub, wrapping the drying cloth around her shivering body. Where was Morag? She'd promised to return to light the fire and help comb out her hair. Flora drifted to the small window, seeking the last amber rays of sun to warm the chill on her skin.

A soft knock at the door signaled the woman's arrival. She bade her enter, thinking that if she did one thing before she left, it would be to make the humorless old woman smile—a laugh would undoubtedly be expecting too much.

She heard a sharp intake of breath, followed by a muffled curse. Slowly, she turned around.

The blood drained from her face. It wasn't the maid.

Lachlan Maclean stood stone still in the doorway. His eyes bore into her with an intensity that made her every nerve ending stand on edge.

She couldn't breathe.

For the first time in her life, Flora felt truly vulnerable. Not because she thought he would hurt her, but because of the undeniable intimacy of the moment. No man had ever seen her like this.

She was nearly naked. The thin piece of linen was wrapped around her and slung low over her breasts. She struggled to hide behind the damp piece of fabric, but it was useless. It clung to her, revealing every inch of her body to his smoldering gaze.

He looked impossibly handsome. His hair, still damp from bathing, slumped across his face and curled roguishly at his collar. He'd shaved, but the rough stubble of his beard still shadowed the hard lines of his jaw and chin. The thin scars that crossed his nose and cheek emphasized his rough warrior's appeal. Rough, but not brutish. A fresh linen shirt stretched over the broad, powerful chest, and a silver brooch secured the plaid that he'd wrapped over his shoulder. He was tall and strong and unbearably masculine. But all she could think about was how he'd tasted and the seductive heat of his mouth on hers. A shiver swept over her.

She wanted to order him to leave, but her words strangled in her throat. For a moment she'd passed into a dream realm, where nothing seemed real.

"God, you're beautiful." His voice was deep and ragged. It wasn't the most poetic compliment she'd ever received, but it pleased her more than any that had come before. And it was the only one that had made her body tingle and then hum with awareness.

His eyes darkened, and the muscle in his jaw began to twitch. She felt a prickle of alarm, realizing he was holding himself by a very thin thread. No man had ever looked at her like this. Hungry. Starving. As if she were a succulent dish and he'd like nothing better than to gobble her up.

"Get out," she finally managed, though her voice shook. "You don't belong here. This is my room." *My sanctuary.* And he was invading it, making it his. Leaving her nowhere to hide. "You must leave." Her voice rose in panic. "Now!"

Lachlan's mouth went dry. He'd lost the ability of rational thought. Leave? He couldn't move his feet, even if he wanted to. Which he didn't.

The body he'd fantasized about had been revealed in full naked splendor. Or as good as naked, with the little that swath of linen did to hide her from his gaze. Her skin was creamy perfection. She was lean and soft in all the right places. Her breasts rose full and high above a tiny waist and curvy hips. Her legs were long and slim, with gently defined muscles. He could even see the peak of her pale pink nipples. Small and tight and begging for his kiss.

And before she'd turned . . .

He'd been mesmerized by the long golden tendrils of damp hair tumbling down her back. He'd wanted to use his tongue to catch the rivulets of water that slid down the sleek curve of her spine to the soft swell of her perfectly round bottom. A bottom that would nestle against his groin perfectly as he slid into her from behind.

He couldn't tear his gaze from her.

The response of his body was visceral, a primal urge so intense it made every muscle in his body clench with restraint. His hands were fisted into tight balls at his side, his shoulders tensed, and sweat gathered on his brow. He was pulled as tight as a bow, ready to spring.

First the kiss, now this torture. His control had never been put to such a test. Made all the worse because he knew she was his.

In one swift motion, he could remove the cloth and put his hands on all that creamy soft skin. Bury his face between her heavy round breasts and slide his tongue over the soft peak of her nipple until it tightened in his mouth.

He wanted to run his tongue down the flat plane of her stomach, put his hands on that soft round bottom, and sink his head between her legs. Tasting the very essence of her. Licking and sucking until she exploded against him in helpless abandon. Aye, he wanted her helpless. Helpless for anything but him.

"Please," she repeated. "Go."

He didn't answer, but dropped the box that he'd been carrying and took a step toward her.

She took a step back, but with her back to the window, there was nowhere to go.

She eyed him warily. For the first time, he saw uncertainty in her gaze.

The air was thick and heavy between them, his desire almost palpable, but she was shivering from cold and was still wet from her bath. He thought of how hot he could make her. And how much wetter. Instinctively, he reached out.

He heard her sharp intake of breath as his fingers

trailed down the smooth expanse of her throat, over her collarbone, to the lush swell of her breast. With the back of his finger he outlined the heavy curve of her breast. Her nipple hardened, and he felt a surge of blood to his loins so strong, he nearly jerked.

Mine. The voice was loud and clear as a wave of possessiveness gripped him hard.

Her cheeks flooded with heat. He'd embarrassed her. He could see the confusion in her gaze. She didn't know what was happening to her body. He might be ready for this, but she wasn't. He knew her reaction to their kiss had scared her. Hell, it had scared him.

"Please . . . ," she whispered, her voice raw.

He could take that soft plea either way . . . please yes or please no.

God's blood, she was the devil of temptation.

He dropped his hand and stepped away, knowing he had to stop. His body hammered with need, but he didn't want to frighten her. She was a damn virgin. And what he wanted to do with her right now would put a blush on a hardened harlot.

Lachlan was a man of prodigious appetites, and he believed in holding nothing back. When they came together, it would be hot and hard and raw. There was not a part of her that he would leave uncovered or unexplored. Patience in matters of lust was not something he was used to. Soon.

Shifting his gaze, he motioned to the box. "I brought you something for this evening. We do not have much occasion for such finery at Drimnin. But it is yours; I thought you should have it."

Flora glanced at the box beside the bed. She momentarily forgot her embarrassment, and her eyes lit up. "My gown!" She turned back to him with confusion in her gaze. "But how?"

He shrugged. "I suspected what it was and thought you might have need of it."

She studied him keenly, as if he'd unwittingly revealed something. "That was very thoughtful of you. Thank you."

"I'll send Morag up to help you. But do not dally," he said gruffly, uncomfortable with what he saw in her eyes. It suddenly felt as if he were the one naked.

He turned and strode to the door, not trusting himself to look at her again. If he did, he didn't know if he'd be able to leave. Flora MacLeod's virginity hung by a very thin thread. He had more reasons than ever to hasten the wedding. Sooner or later, she would be his. But any more run-ins like this one, and it would be sooner.

Where was she?

Lachlan took a long drink of *cuirm*, his gaze fixed on the entry. From his seat at the high table—though there was nothing as formal as a dais—he could keep his eyes fixed on the door opposite him and still have a good view of the rest of the festivities. The room was crammed full, every available seat filled with his clansmen clad in their colorful plaids. The entire castle—depleted though it was by the absence of so many of his people who remained trapped on Coll—had gathered tonight for the first feast in a very long time. Since well before his brother had been imprisoned, he realized. The pipers were piping, the ale was flowing, the hall was blazing with candles. But they were still waiting.

He'd left her room almost an hour ago, and despite his warning, she'd yet to appear. He wouldn't put it past her to tarry just to spite him.

God's blood, the woman was proving an unexpected challenge. In more ways than one. He'd expected a spoiled, headstrong girl and discovered instead a complex woman unlike any he'd ever met. Confident, determined, and strong, yet also oddly vulnerable. One whose kiss roused strange feelings in him and whose body . . . He took another swig, trying to dull the vivid picture that sprang to mind. Of legs that went on forever, a bottom made for cupping, and breasts sculpted for a man's fantasies. He tried to thrust the image away, but he knew the sight of her sumptuous form wrapped in transparent linen would be imprinted on his consciousness for a long time.

He dreaded sleep. The long, dark hours stretched out endlessly before him, with nothing for relief but his hand to combat the taunting erotic images of her naked above him, those lush breasts bouncing with the frantic rhythm of their lovemaking as she rode him hard. He got tight and heavy just thinking about it.

Damn, he needed a woman. He was tempted to seek out his leman tonight after all. Seonaid sat across the room, staring at him with reproachful hurt in her gaze. He owed her an explanation, at least. And perhaps more.

He was wound so tight, he needed a little release.

But all thoughts of another woman fled when Flora entered the room. The breath left him as he caught sight of the achingly beautiful woman heading toward him. She possessed such a regal grace; she seemed to be walking on air. Her golden hair caught the flickering light, shimmering like an ethereal haze around her.

The room, boisterous and raucous before, suddenly hushed.

It was at once clear to him, as it was to every person in this room, that she did not belong here. The humble keep of Drimnin was a poor backdrop for such magnificence.

She wore a gold brocade French gown with a low square neckline and tight bodice. The contrasting sleeves and forepart were of ivory silk embroidered in gold and encrusted with hundreds of tiny pearls. The farthingale was relatively tame by court standards, as was the soft ruff that framed her face. Her long blond locks had been twisted into some complicated arrangement that he was sure Morag had never attempted before. The overall effect was stunning—heightened by the fact that he knew exactly what was hidden underneath.

But it also served to illustrate the wide gap between them. The cost of her ensemble probably could have fed his entire clan for months.

For the first time, Lachlan experienced a moment of uncertainty. Convincing her to marry him might be a bit more difficult than he'd anticipated. She was one of the wealthiest women in the kingdom, and a woman used to the splendor and riches of court. He was a Highland chief who'd been under constant attack since he was a lad. His clan had had to struggle through more lean years than he'd like to recall. He was a fighter, a warrior. Nothing like the polished popinjays she was used to. He'd been too busy fighting to attend Tounis College in Edinburgh, as many of his Highland counterparts had, and he'd avoided court like the plague. How was he going to convince her to forsake such riches for the simple Highland way of life?

But as quick as the flash of uncertainty came, it went. Replaced by renewed determination. The battle would not be easily won, but it would be won. By him. There was no other choice. Just as he'd fended off her brother's attacks for years, he would use the tools he had at his disposal. What he lacked in wealth and education, he made up for in wit and cunning.

She was not indifferent to him. He thought of her response to his kiss, the way her body had instinctively reacted to his touch. No, not indifferent at all. Attraction could be a powerful weapon. If wooing didn't work, seduction just might. Whatever it took, just as long as she agreed.

He stood as she neared. Their eyes met. The memory of that heated moment in her room flared full force between them. She was remembering it, too. The sudden pinkening of her cheeks gave her away. With a slight gesture of his hand, he indicated for her to take the seat beside him.

Gilly, who was seated on his other side, spoke first. "You look beautiful, Flora."

The longing in his sister's voice hit him hard, angering him. A resplendent Flora forced him to confront what he could not give his sisters.

"Thank you, Gilly." She gave him a sidelong glance, as if seeking his approval.

He looked her over appraisingly. "We've been waiting."

Her cheeks flushed hotter, and he could swear he saw a flash of disappointment in her eyes. "I came as fast as I could. Morag is not experienced with this type of clothing, and I usually have two maidservants to help me dress." Before he could respond, she added, "I'm not criticizing, simply pointing out that donning a gown like this is not a simple matter."

He eyed her carefully. "I can see that."

A delicate frown marred her lovely features. Tiny lines appeared between her brows. He felt a strange urge to rub them away with the pad of his thumb. But his finger would be too rough and unwieldy on such baby soft skin.

"Perhaps I shouldn't have worn it. The gown you provided for me upon my arrival is more appropriate."

She was self-conscious, he realized. Lachlan felt a stab of guilt. It wasn't her fault he couldn't provide such finery for his sisters.

"You look fine," he said gruffly.

Her eyes danced with amusement. "Why, that sounded almost like a compliment," she exclaimed with exaggerated surprise. "If you go on like this, that silver tongue of yours will make the bards weep with envy."

His mouth twisted in a wry smile. The lass had a dry wit. "I'll remember that and try not to get carried away." She returned his smile, and he was surprised by how much he enjoyed the shared moment of camaraderie.

She glanced around, looking down the table. "Where's Mary?"

His smile fell. "She wasn't feeling well. She asked to take her meal in her room."

Flora's eyes lit with concern. She put her hands on the table as if she intended to stand up. "Is she ill? Perhaps I should check on her?"

He covered her hand with his, immediately conscious of how small and soft it was under his. He'd acted unconsciously but realized it was a possessive gesture. And a strangely intimate one. The simple touch of his hand had forged a surprisingly strong connection.

"She's fine," he assured her. "I'm sure she'll be recovered by tomorrow." At least he hoped she would be. He thought of the tearstained face that had stared at him as if he were the cruelest person on earth. As if he'd just stepped on the tail of her favorite puppy. He shook it off. Mary was young, she would recover.

Flora stared at his hand, a strange expression on her face. Did she feel it? This odd connection between them?

She gazed up at him. "That reminds me. Who's John?"

He tensed but recovered quickly, removing his hand. The connection was severed. "My younger brother."

She smiled. "I thought so. I overheard a few men on the staircase on the way to the hall, but when I asked, they refused to say. Strange, isn't it?" She looked around. "Why have I not been introduced to him?"

His heart thumped. "He's not here right now."

"Oh. Will he return soon?"

"Yes." *As soon as we are married.*

Brought harshly back to reality, he lifted his hand to signal the beginning of the feast and an end to their conversation. Platter after platter of food made its way through the crowded hall. Food he could ill afford, since Hector had stolen a great number of his cattle—and thus his ready source for silver. But foolishly, he'd wanted to impress her. But all it had taken was one look at that gown to realize how difficult that would be. Still, he'd take a Highland *fèis* over a masque at court any day.

But would she?

He watched her as they ate, talking animatedly with Allan on her other side and Gilly, who sat beside him. She seemed to be enjoying herself. But who could read the mind of a lass?

"You're glad you came tonight?"

Flora's gaze slid to the handsome man beside her. She'd been achingly aware of him all throughout the meal. The powerful physical effect he had on her was disconcerting. A simple brush of his wide shoulders or muscular arm against her as they ate and her heart went into palpitations. One look at that wide mouth, implacable jaw, and rugged, battle-scarred face and her stomach flipped. She'd seen many handsome men before, but none had ever affected her so . . . completely.

He wasn't classically handsome by most measures. His features were too hard, his jaw too square, his nose crooked from having been broken more than once; but the overall result was of roughly hewn masculine beauty. There was something decidedly threatening about that raw power. Her attraction stemmed from a place inside her that she'd never felt before. A deep, sensual place.

She dropped her eyes from his penetrating gaze, afraid he would realize what she was thinking, and considered his question.

Truth be told, she was enjoying herself. It was difficult not to. Although the feast had lasted for many hours, the room still buzzed with the festive sounds of celebration and easy laughter. There was something comforting and relaxed about it. Homey. She couldn't help but compare it with the rigid formality of court.

They'd been entertained by the magical sounds of the pipers and the fanciful tales of the *seannachie*. But watching the warriors—and Mary's Odin in particular—perform the intricate sword dance had been the high point for Flora. The ill-prepared food was perhaps the only complaint, but the people seemed to be having too much fun to notice. And with the copious amounts of ale flowing through the hall, most were too soused to mind.

Then there was the laird himself. At dinner he'd been attentive, but not obtrusively so. He'd kept the conversation light and deftly brought her in by asking her opinion on the music, or the bard, or the dancing—she was relieved he hadn't asked her about the food. He hadn't set out to charm with false flattery like most men, but had really talked to her. And listened. She'd never noticed before how rare that was. He was interesting and smart and appallingly adept at getting her to talk without revealing much about himself.

Thankfully, he'd appeared to have forgotten about her trick with the fulmar oil.

But watching him interact with his clan was perhaps the most illuminating. At one point or another throughout the long meal, it seemed as if most of the castle had approached the table to exchange words with their laird. Seeking his advice on such far-reaching subjects as a dispute between two men over a small plot of land, the weather, or the price of cattle. They treated him with deference and respect, but also with something else: love. He had the utter command of a chief, but he'd clearly earned it with respect and not fear.

One man in particular stood out. A young warrior she'd never seen before, probably not much older than her four and twenty years. With tears in his eyes, he thanked the laird for the news of his babe. A son born by his wife, who was being held at Breacachadh. Flora imagined it was no small matter to get word of the child. If it surprised her that the laird would concern himself with the lives of his men, it did no one else. And that, she supposed, spoke volumes.

She'd noticed quite a few of the women staring at him with interest. One raven-haired woman in particular didn't bother to hide her inviting glances. Actually, the look she cast him was more than an invitation, it was possessive. And it bothered Flora more than it should have.

Unexpectedly, she found herself drawn to this gruff chief who watched her with a disarming intensity. Who looked at her like a woman and not a prize.

The Laird of Coll was undoubtedly a hard man. He didn't smile often, but when he did, it was as if the sun broke through the clouds. And he was smiling right now as she considered his question, knowing very well that she was enjoying herself.

But she hadn't quite forgiven him for forcing her to come here tonight.

"If you mean am I happy that you ordered me to dine with you, no. But your pipers are wonderful . . . and the dancing was magnificent. So, yes, I'm enjoying myself." He stared at her with that hard, impenetrable expression on his face—the expression she was becoming quite used to. Perhaps she was even becoming good at deciphering it, because she thought he looked pleased. He wanted her enjoyment. But why? Could he be . . . wooing her? The thought didn't offend her as much as it should. She leaned closer and lowered her voice conspiratorially. "You know, you might get more bees with honey."

Something sparked in his gaze. His eyes fell to the low bodice of her gown and to her breasts, of which she'd unwittingly given him a very good view. Though he'd had more than a view earlier, and the realization that he was thinking the same thing made her nipples harden and her body tingle with awareness.

"What kind of honey do you have in mind, Flora?"

Her body heated, responding to the unmistakable innuendo of his tone that she didn't fully understand. "Anything not phrased as an order."

He leaned back, a wry set to his lips. "I'll keep that in mind. But I'm used to giving orders." His mouth moved into a full-fledged grin. "I'm just not used to being disobeyed."

The impact of his jaunty smile slammed straight into her chest. "You should smile more often." She spoke her thoughts aloud.

He looked at her intently. "Why?"

She shrugged and tried not to blush. She could hardly tell him how handsome and how much younger it made him look. Initially, she'd thought him in his late thirties, but now she suspected he was quite a few years younger. "It doesn't make you look so . . . imposing."

He sat back in his chair and crossed his arms, a perplexed expression on his face. Flora tried not to gape at the way the muscles in his arms bulged. Or how his shirt stretched across his broad chest. *Dear Lord, he was strong.* There was not one inch of him that did not appear to be chipped from stone.

"I'm a Highland chief. I *am* imposing."

She grinned, realizing he was half teasing her. Then a

shadow crossed his face. "There has been precious little reason for joy of late." He looked around the hall meaningfully. She didn't need to look to know what he was thinking. The lack of ornamentation, the threadbare clothing of his clansmen, the sorry state of the castle. But she also saw the happy faces and inherent pride of the people around her. And of their leader. "The floods and the feud with your brother have taken their toll," he finished.

"Because Hector has captured your castle?"

She saw him tense, almost imperceptible, but she'd been watching him closely. "Yes."

But she sensed there was something else. The feud with Hector was about more than just his lands and castle.

His finger slid over the silver-encrusted goblet. The silver plates and cups were the only visible signs of wealth in the otherwise sparse keep—she couldn't help thinking a few hangings and flowers would do much to lighten up the place. The soft motion of his finger entranced her for a moment. His hands were like the rest of him: big, rough, and strong. Scarred by battle, they were a warrior's hands. A man's hands. Lord Murray's hands had been pale white and as soft as hers.

She swallowed, remembering the gentle touch of those rough, callused fingers on her breast. She'd been shocked when he'd touched her through the drying cloth, but also undeniably aroused. Her body had softened with a wave of shimmering heat and an indescribable heaviness that had made her legs weak.

The way he'd been looking at her . . . still looked at her. As if he could see beneath her clothes. There was an intimacy between them that had been created in that room tonight. He'd wanted her and hadn't bothered to hide it. The only question was whether he would do something about it.

She didn't want to think about her own reaction if he did. She couldn't deny her attraction to him, but she would not be seduced by her jailer, no matter how handsome—or how tender his kiss. "How did the feud with Hector begin?" she asked.

"You know so little of your brother?"

She felt her cheeks go hot and fought the instinctive defensiveness roused by his question. She'd never wanted to become involved in the endless bickering and shifting alliances of the Highlands, but he had a way of making her feel ashamed for having ignored a part of her heritage for so long.

"We were never close. He's over twenty years older than I." She paused thoughtfully. "My mother didn't talk about him much. I think she blamed him for something, though they reconciled at the end." Before she died. Flora looked down at her plate so that he would not see the emotion in her eyes. When the wave of longing passed, she looked back up to find him still staring at her. So he wouldn't think her disloyal, she added, "But whenever our paths have crossed, Hector has always been kind to me."

He looked as though he wanted to say something, but he held his tongue. "What do you want to know?" he asked.

"Why did he take your castle? Why do you hate each other so much?"

"There has been bad blood between the clans for years. I was not yet ten when my father died. Hector saw my father's death as an opportunity to try to take the lands that they have coveted for some time. He chose the day of his burial for an attack. What he didn't count on was my uncle defeating him. Soundly, I might add." And bloodily, she realized. "Even though we were greatly outnumbered and admittedly ill prepared. The people blamed the curse for your brother's loss," he finished.

"But that doesn't make any sense. Macleans fought on both sides. How do they account for the fact that it was Macleans who won the battle?"

He shook his head. "The invocation of the curse isn't rational. You'll find that it is a convenient scapegoat whenever something goes wrong. Like the unusual years of heavy flooding we've had on Coll."

She gave him a long, steady look. "You haven't had an easy time of it, have you."

Her observation had surprised him. He appeared almost uncomfortable. "I never expected being chief to be easy. It is my birthright and my duty." And an integral part of his identity, she realized. "I will do anything to protect and preserve it."

It sounded like a warning, but she let it go, returning to the feud. "And so after his defeat at the hands of your uncle, I assume Hector sought revenge."

Lachlan nodded. "My uncle was murdered seven years later."

"And you blame Hector?"

His jaw clenched. "I do, though I cannot prove it. But the men who were responsible for the deed were punished."

Flora didn't need to ask what he meant. They'd been killed. By his hand. He was watching her as if he expected her to challenge him for brutality, but she didn't. Nor would she. Justice was justice. And in the Highlands, it was meted out swiftly and succinctly.

"And so he took your castle? But wouldn't that be admitting complicity in the death of your uncle?"

"Hector doesn't need a reason for treachery. But justice for my uncle's murders took place many years ago. No, he's raided my lands and stolen my castle to try to force me to his bidding. Something that will never happen."

He said it with such loathing and steely determination

that it took her aback, giving her a glimpse of the ruthless Highlander her mother had warned her about. Gilly's admonition about his single-minded resolve also came back to her.

Flora felt torn. Her loyalty belonged to her brother, not to this man who'd kidnapped her. But she couldn't ignore what she'd learned of Lachlan Maclean. He seemed fair. Except, apparently, when it came to her brother.

"Why?" she asked.

"I wouldn't join his feud against the MacDonalds. He expected me to bow to him as chief. I refused."

Flora wrinkled her brow. She knew enough to know that the Duart branch of the clan was descended from an older brother, the Macleans of Coll from a younger. "But he's right. Duart is the chief branch of the Clan Gillian. It is your duty to bow to him. It's the Highland way."

His entire body went rigid. This time, his steely control could not mask his fury. "And you're an expert on the Highland way? A girl who avoids her kin and her home? Coll has been a barony for over two hundred years. I will not pay him *calps*, nor will I send my men to fight his battles. I'm the *Laird* of Coll, a free baron. A chief in my own right. I don't owe allegiance or anything else to Hector."

"So you choose feudal law over the Erse Brehon Law? That is an unusual position for a Highlander to take."

"Feudalism has been a part of the clans in Scotland for centuries. The Macleans of Coll haven't considered themselves a part of Clan Gillian for a long time. We are our own clan. It was my father's position. Now it is mine."

Pride. Was that what this was about? Her mother's words of warning came back to her: *Never trust a Highlander. They are hard men with tender pride who solve problems with their swords.* Was her mother right? Had there been years of feuding and killing because of pride?

"But all of this between you and Hector could be settled if you acknowledged him as chief?"

"It is more complicated than that."

"But is it? Is the feuding worth it? Hector is one of the most powerful chiefs in the Highlands. With at least four hundred fighting men. You probably don't have a third of that. It's foolish to battle him. How can you think to defeat him?"

The muscle in his jaw flexed, signaling a warning. She was treading a dangerous path. "Have care who you call a fool, lass. You don't know what you speak of."

Her temper flared. "Perhaps not, but I can see the toll it has taken on your clan." Her gaze swept the hall, this time ignoring the warmth of the revelers and lingering on the crude furnishings and lack of ornamentation. "Take a look around. Your clan is suffering. If you weren't so busy fighting Hector, perhaps your sisters could be at court."

His withdrawal was swift, his expression icy. Her words had struck a blow, one that she hadn't intended. Too late, she realized how she must sound. Criticism to a proud man who'd had to fight since he was a lad for survival. But she'd been thinking only of his sisters— and the poverty of his clan. If Lachlan Maclean had a weakness, it was his pride. But perhaps, she admitted, it was well earned.

She put her hand on his arm, feeling the tension, the rigid muscle pulled tight as steel. "I'm sorry. I spoke out of turn. I did not mean to anger you."

His blue gaze turned flinty. "Then don't speak of matters you do not understand."

"I only wanted to help."

"You will."

The coldness of his reply stung. As did the forced reminder of her presence at Drimnin. Her spine straightened. "By helping you get your castle back?" she asked bitterly.

He hesitated, leaving her feeling that there was something more. "Yes."

"But why me? Didn't you appeal to the king for help?"

His face was like granite. "I did. Through his Lowland toad—" He stopped. "His privy councillors."

"Surely Hector has no valid claim to Coll—its castle or its lands."

"No legal claim whatsoever. I took sasine to my lands many years ago, receiving the symbolic earth and stone."

"Then the king has done something about it?"

His eyes were flat. "He has."

Flora was relieved. King James would see justice done. "Then perhaps you will not have need of me after all?"

He held her gaze. "I need you, my sweet. Make no mistake of that."

Chapter 6

❖

Early the next morning, Lachlan strode purposefully across the courtyard toward the small garden on the south side of the *barmkin*. The promise of spring hung in the salty sea air, a natural foil for his wintry mood. He was vaguely aware of the bright sun and cloudless sky, but not even the promise of an unusually warm day could douse the fires of his discontent. He needed to find Seonaid before beginning his training. What he had to do couldn't wait.

He'd spent a restless night. But not solely for the reason he'd anticipated—though it was asinine how his body could ache for a lass who so infuriated him.

He knew better than anyone the toll the feuding had taken on his clan. He didn't need it pointed out by a naïve chit who'd never gone hungry a day in her life. Yes, pride and the honor of his clan were at stake in his battle with Hector, but so was the very preservation of his clan. If Lachlan accepted Hector as his chief, Hector would drive them into the ground with his feud with the MacDonalds. Lachlan would be duty bound to send his men to fight for Hector. Hector could call on them at will. And he was unrelenting. He'd been feuding with the MacDonalds for years.

Lachlan was protecting his clan the only way he could. He wanted the fighting with Hector done more than anyone.

Yet Flora dared to question him. In fact, it seemed

never to occur to her to temper her tongue. She'd been encouraged to speak her mind—a rarity in the Highlands for a woman. Not many people dared to challenge him openly. But Flora did.

He found it maddening, but also oddly refreshing.

Her faith in the king, however, was laughable.

A few months ago, angry over the resumption of feuding between the two clans, King James had attempted to bring Lachlan and Hector to heel by ordering them to appear before the Privy Council under promise of safe conduct to Edinburgh. Not trusting Hector to abide by the king's directive, Lachlan sent his brother, John, in his stead, so that he could stay and defend Breacachadh from attack.

He'd expected treachery from Hector and found it with the king. Instead of hearing the merits of the dispute, King James had summarily tossed John into prison— trying to force Lachlan to end the fighting and cede to the jurisdiction of the Privy Council. Lachlan went to Argyll to help seek his brother's release from Blackness Prison, and it was cold comfort to know that he'd been right to fear an invasion when Hector had immediately taken the opportunity to capture Breacachadh.

Hector was a harsh and brutal leader—Lachlan could only imagine the suffering of his clan under Hector's dominion. And with both his clan and brother suffering, there was no time to lose.

He would take his men and storm Blackness himself— were it not for his sisters and his people. He couldn't risk it. Not if there was another way. Flora was that way. He would not shirk from doing what was necessary to convince her to marry him, even if it meant deceiving her. A prospect that had seemed a whole hell of a lot simpler when he'd thought she was a spoiled girl. But there was nothing simple about Flora MacLeod. Or the riotous feelings she roused in him.

She would never agree to marry him if she learned the truth. The *whole* truth of the devil's bargain he'd struck with her cousin Argyll to ensure his brother's release from prison. And it disturbed him to realize how much that prospect bothered him.

Lust had obviously addled him. Flora would help secure John's release, and Hector would pay for all he'd done—that was all that mattered.

Seonaid was right where Morag said she would be, collecting herbs from the garden. She had some skill with herbs and served as the clan's healer. That the sight of her softly rounded bottom perched in the air didn't give him a flicker of hesitation proved that he was doing the right thing.

She heard him approach and stood up slowly to greet him with a wide smile. "My laird. What a pleasant surprise." She sauntered toward him, her hips swaying in the sensual way that had originally caught his eye. She stood right in front of him, her soft, plump breasts poking his chest, and glanced up at him coyly. "Is there something you need?"

Yes, but unfortunately not from her. He wasn't even tempted. But it wasn't Seonaid's fault. "Not today, lass."

She gazed at him hopefully. "Tonight, then, perhaps?"

He shook his head. "I'm afraid not."

"Oh," she said softly. "I see."

He could tell from the crushed look on her face that she did. He hadn't intended to hurt her, but he'd been honest from the start. "I thought you understood."

She tried to smile, but he could see the tears shining in her eyes. "I did. I just hoped . . ." She looked down. A lock of hair slid across her face, and he reached down to tuck it behind her ear. But she read more into the gesture than he'd intended. He could see her hope swell before she turned her blame from him to Flora. "It's her, isn't it?" Her voice grew angry. "She was watching me last night. She told you to be rid of me."

Lachlan frowned, not liking the venom he saw on Seonaid's face—or the inference that he would be dictated to by a lass. "The decision was mine."

She reached up, sliding her arms behind his neck, pressing her soft and very willing body against his. "She'll never satisfy you. A woman like that. You'll terrify her." She trailed her hand down his stomach and wrapped her fingers around him intimately. "I know what you like." She breathed against his ear. "How you like me to take you deep in my mouth."

One long pull of that talented mouth, and Lachlan could release some of this restless energy. But it wasn't Seonaid's mouth that he pictured. His body stirred at the image of Flora's red lips stretched taut around the heavy head of his cock, milking him.

Seonaid misunderstood, and a satisfied gleam appeared in her eyes. "Do you think your fancy court lady will do that for you?"

Her words bothered him more than they should have. The differences between Flora and him had not gone unnoticed. But Seonaid had overstepped her bounds.

Lachlan removed her hand and stepped away from her. "It isn't your concern."

"I thought we had something more."

He didn't want to be cruel, but he didn't want there to be any doubt. "What we had was sex. From the start I made that very clear. You were my leman."

"And she will be your wife."

Lachlan's eyes narrowed. Only his guardsmen, Morag, and his sisters were aware of the true purpose for Flora's presence in Drimnin. He'd thought it best to keep the matter of John's imprisonment quiet; there would be fewer questions to answer and less likelihood she would discover her cousin's involvement. Was Seonaid merely speculating, or had someone spoken out of turn? He'd have to make damn sure that none of the talk reached Flora's ears.

"You forget yourself, Seonaid. Whether I take a wife is no concern of yours." She flinched at his blunt words. He knew the lass spoke out of jealousy, but he would not tolerate disrespect. Nor did he like the calculation he saw in her gaze. "I'm sorry if I've caused you any pain, lass. But I warn you. Do not interfere."

I need you, my sweet. Make no mistake of that.

Echoes of last night's conversation still sounded in her head, even as Flora sat down to break her fast. Why did he need her if the king was involved? Without a legal claim to Breacachadh Castle, surely Hector would be ordered to return Coll's castle. It didn't make any sense. Was there another reason? But when she'd asked him, he'd brushed aside her questions.

Flora had learned something of the dark, enigmatic Laird of Coll, but a great deal remained unexplained. And she was surprised by how much the prospect intrigued her. *He* intrigued her.

But right now, she had other concerns. She washed down the last bit of dry bread with a spoonful of barley gruel, anxious to go in search of Mary, who had not come downstairs to break her fast. Gilly had assured her that Mary was simply tired, but Flora had a horrible feeling that it might have something to do with polishing the swords yesterday. The laird had been furious. Had he blamed his sister?

Flora should not have involved Mary in her plans; the sweet girl simply didn't have the temperament for mischief making—or, more specifically, for the repercussions of mischief making. It wasn't just that she was quiet, which she was, but Mary took things too much to heart. Flora should have realized how it would pain her to disappoint her brother.

Excusing herself, she stood up from the table to go in search of her when she happened to glance out one of the windows.

Her heart stalled, and a startled gasp escaped from between her lips. The flash of hurt was swift and hard, like a mule kick in the chest. She wanted to turn away, but her eyes were glued to the scene taking place below.

Lachlan Maclean stood at the southern edge of the courtyard in what appeared to be a small garden, locked in an embrace with the woman she'd noticed staring at him last night. The woman had her arms around his neck and her body plastered against his broad chest. Flora's gaze slid down. Her stomach turned. If she wasn't mistaken, the woman had her hand around his . . .

The laird quickly removed himself from the woman's grasp, but it didn't stop the squeezing in Flora's chest. She might be a virgin, but she knew enough to recognize that this woman had enough familiarity with his body to suggest an intimate relationship.

She tore her gaze from the window and turned back to Gilly, who was still seated at the table, finishing her meal. "Gilly, who was that dark-haired woman staring at your brother last night?" Though she tried to make it sound like an afterthought, the hollowness in her chest extended to her voice.

Gilly's eating knife slipped from her fingers and clattered on the table. "What woman?"

Her reaction proved that she knew very well what woman. It was not as if there were more than a dozen to choose from. The castle was not a large one, and most of the women and children of Coll's warriors were trapped at Breacachadh. "The pretty one with black hair. Is she the laird's intended?"

Gilly looked like a hare caught in a trap. Eyes wide, she shook her head furiously. "My brother is not presently engaged."

Flora's heart pounded. There was another possibility, one that was a common enough practice in the Highlands. Such arrangements were quite open. "His leman, then?"

Gilly looked down at her plate, her cheeks bright pink, giving Flora all the answer she needed.

It shouldn't surprise her. Many Highlanders had lemans, and Lachlan Maclean was a strong, virile man. His raw sensuality was one of the first things she'd noticed about him. What she didn't expect was how it made her feel. Hurt. Disappointed . . . She bit her lip. Maybe even jealous.

Ridiculous.

"Flora, it's not—"

She held up her hand. "You don't need to say anything, Gilly." Drawing up her shoulders, she ignored the unaccountable burning in her throat. "I shouldn't have asked. It's none of my business."

But it didn't make the disappointment any easier to swallow.

She hurried for the doorway, her steps falling into almost a run. "I'm going to check on Mary," she called over her shoulder, not wanting Gilly to see her face.

Once safe in the darkness of the stairwell, Flora took refuge in the solitude. She rested her back against the cool stones, closed her eyes, and took deep, even breaths. Her pulse raced, her chest ached, and her eyes prickled with heat. If she didn't know better, she'd think she was close to bursting into tears.

She was being a fool. Lachlan Maclean was nothing to her. He was her captor. Her brother's enemy.

But she'd thought . . .

What had she thought?

That he wanted me.

He'd kissed her with such tenderness, touched her body as no man ever had before, and charmed her with his brusque honesty and lack of false flattery. And, she was forced to admit, it had been effective. Somehow, he'd managed to sneak beneath her defenses.

She must be mad. He was everything her mother had warned her against.

Or was he?

The fierce beating of her heart returned to normal. She was overreacting. Flora had no claim on him. She was only an unwilling guest, nothing more.

Putting the Laird of Coll out of her mind, she pulled herself together and started up the stairs in search of Mary.

On the second floor, she came to the door of the chamber that Mary shared with Gilly and knocked. She could barely make out the soft voice that answered. The door creaked as she opened it, but Mary didn't turn. She sat in a small chair, her gaze fixed out the window. The food that had been sent up sat uneaten on a small table beside her. Her pale cheeks were streaked white with the salty remnants of her tears.

Mary looked impossibly forlorn. There was something so hopeless in her gaze, it touched a part of Flora still tender from her mother's death. She knew such sadness. Knew what it was like to feel lost. Had she been the cause of this poor girl's grief?

She moved across the room and knelt beside her.

"Mary," Flora said gently, not wanting to startle her. "What is it, child? What is wrong?"

Mary flinched. She turned, her eyes red and stark. "I'm not a child."

Realizing that she'd unwittingly hit on a tender subject, Flora hastened to correct the error. "Of course you're not. Forgive me. But what has happened to make you so sad? Is it your brother?"

Mary nodded, and Flora felt a sharp stab of guilt. It *was* her fault. "I'm sorry, I never should have involved you. Everything will be fine, you'll see. I'll tell him it was all my fault."

Mary looked at her, obviously confused. "What are you talking about?"

"Why, the swords, of course." Flora blushed. "I assume your brother was angry with you for my wee jest with the fulmar oil. But, truly, I do not think he is mad any longer."

Fresh tears streamed down her cheeks. Mary shook her head. "I wish it were the swords—" She sank her face into her hands. "If only it were the swords."

Flora was at a loss to see Mary like this. She didn't know what to do, having had little practical experience with sisters. She hesitated only a moment before gathering the poor weeping girl in her arms. Stroking her silky head, Flora whispered soothing words until her shoulders no longer shook and the tears had at last run dry.

When Mary had calmed down enough to speak, Flora said, "Tell me what he has said to make you so upset."

She watched as Mary struggled with the words, trying not to dissolve into tears again. "It's Allan."

Flora cursed, realizing at once what had happened. Apparently, she hadn't been the only one to notice Mary's tender feelings for her brother's captain. "Let me guess. Your brother has discouraged your feelings for his captain."

Mary's face crumpled. "It's worse than that. He's forbidden Allan from speaking with me in private. Making it clear that he would not permit a match between us."

"But why? Allan is the captain of his castle, one of his guardsmen, and a chieftain in his own right."

Mary lowered her gaze. "My brother has other plans for me."

Bigger plans. Flora wondered what he intended. A match between Mary and Allan, although not a good one, was not a bad one, either. From the look of this place, she'd wager that the girl didn't have much of a tocher. "Well, surely he will take your feelings into account. Perhaps he can be persuaded to change his mind?"

Mary shook her head. "You don't know my brother. He's determined. Once he's made a decision, nothing could turn him from his course. He's been like that since he was a lad. He'll never change his mind."

Flora could barely contain the sudden eruption of anger. This was precisely the situation she'd fought against her whole life. "Are you saying he would force you into a marriage you do not want?" She didn't want to believe that the man she'd unwittingly grown to admire could be so callous.

He's a Highlander.

"It's not like that. He's only doing what he thinks is best for the clan. He wouldn't need to force me. I could not refuse him my duty. I just wish—" Her voice hitched, and a solitary tear slid down her cheek. "I just wish circumstances could be different."

Flora couldn't believe Mary would defend him. Of course, this sweet, good-natured child would do his bidding. Her "duty," as she called it. Mary would never think to defy her brother. But Flora would. In a heartbeat. She'd seen the alternative. Doing your "duty" for a woman all too often meant a future of suffering and sadness. If Mary had a chance at happiness, she needed to take it.

"Could your brother John help?"

With her arm still slung around Mary's shoulder, Flora could feel her stiffen. "No." She gazed at Flora with something akin to guilt in her eyes. "You've been so kind."

"It's not your fault your brother abducted me."

"Don't blame him too harshly. Lachlan had no choice."

Flora's expression hardened. "There is always a choice." She took Mary's hand and gave it an encouraging squeeze. "Do not despair, Mary. I will speak to him. I'm sure I can knock some sense into him."

Her words were prophetic, but not in the manner she intended. Instead, it was she who was knocked senseless.

After making sure that Mary had eaten some food, Flora set about fulfilling her promise. She knew from the time of day that the laird would be seeing to his men's battle skills on the practice yard. She'd seen the swirl of dust and heard the clatter of swords often enough in the past week but had purposely stayed clear of the half-naked men wielding their weapons of death—perhaps subconsciously trying to avoid a visual affirmation of her mother's warnings.

They're primitive, brutal men who are happy only when they are at war.

But as she left the shadow of the castle behind her and approached the raucous sounds of swordplay, the sight that met her eyes shook her to the core.

My God, he was magnificent, blazing in the sun like a tawny lion.

She might have made a mistake in avoiding the practice yard. The laird wasn't just supervising his warriors, his skills were on display today. But skills weren't all that was on display.

She let out the breath she didn't realize she'd been holding. With only a pair of leather trews that stretched over his powerful thighs, the smooth, tanned skin of his bare chest gleamed like polished granite in the sunlight.

Every inch of his powerful torso had been chipped from stone, the heavy slabs of muscle cut and built by years of battle. His shoulders were broad, his arms thick, and his waist narrow. Tight bands of well-defined muscle layered across his flat stomach. A smattering of small scars had left their warrior's mark, but it was the one long slash across his side that drew her gaze. The one that had yet to heal. She felt a stab of regret. Her mark.

But the scars did not detract from his rugged perfection. Not an ounce of spare flesh padded his form; he was rippled and strong and impossibly masculine, every inch a powerful Highland warrior. She wanted to touch him, to run her hands over his hot skin. The urge was so strong, it frightened her. Her mother had been wrong. There was some appeal to the Highlander's warrior way of life. Now that she had seen a man such as this, a man of such physicality, of such raw power, how could a delicate courtier possibly compare?

They couldn't. Lachlan Maclean was a man built for protection. And there was something almost intoxicating about watching him demonstrate his skills and strength.

Her senses flared. She couldn't tear her eyes away, though she knew she was treading dangerously. No longer could she deny it, even to herself. She wanted him. And seeing him like this would only make him that much harder to resist. What would it be like to be held in his strong arms, cradled against that muscular chest and kissed passionately? Would she dissolve in heat again? Would she ever want to leave the shelter of that protective embrace?

He raised his arms, holding the two-handed claymore high above his head, wielding it with an ease and grace that belied its weight. Only when he met the powerful blows of his opponent did the long cords of muscles flex and ripple with exertion.

At first, she was mesmerized by the sheer power of the display before her. There was a beauty to the thrust and swing of each powerful stroke. Beauty in the way he moved to evade and then attack.

Then she realized something strange was going on. There was an intensity to his movements, a ferocity to his strokes, that seemed odd. It seemed . . . real.

About a score of his warriors had gathered around. She looked at their faces, so transfixed that no one had yet to become aware of her presence. It was more quiet than usual—barely a sound above the heavy clashing of the swords and the exertions of the two men exchanging blow after powerful blow. The ground seemed to shake with the force of each stroke. There was a subtle undercurrent that permeated the air, thick with tension and the sultry scent of sea tinged with sweat.

For the first time, she glanced at the laird's opponent. Physically, they were well matched. The other man was perhaps an inch or two taller than Coll and also heavily muscled, albeit bulkier. His movements were a bit more ponderous. She paused. There was only one man with that build and white blond hair. Odin. Mary's captain.

A chill of unease slid down her spine as understanding dawned. This *was* a battle.

Allan swung the mighty steel blade in a deadly arc, bringing it down with such force that Flora gasped and took a step forward as if she could protect him. She need not have worried. The laird blocked the fierce blow with barely a grimace. But he'd heard her. She felt the swift jolt when his eyes bored into her with piercing intensity. Marking her. A look that made it clear he didn't want her here; that she was intruding. But how could she leave? She was rooted to the fierce drama unfolding before her.

Back and forth they went, exchanging blow after blow until Flora didn't think she could take it anymore.

Anxiety twisted in her stomach. She wanted them to stop. But it was clear they were almost evenly matched. This could go on forever. Or until they both collapsed from exhaustion.

Allan seemed to find a burst of strength. Her breath caught when he attacked with renewed vigor, driving the laird back until he neared the *barmkin* wall. She covered her mouth with her hand, muffling the cry that slipped out. She feared he was still weak from the stabbing.

Her heart pounded. *Dear God, he was going to be hurt.* Allan had homed in for the kill. He swung the blade down again with deadly force, and the laird managed to block it with his sword high over his head. But Allan had leverage. He used his formidable size to lower the sword, blade to blade, in a silvery cross, until it inched ever closer to the laird's head.

"Yield, damn you," Allan urged through clenched teeth.

Coll's reply was too low for her to hear. But from Allan's enraged expression, she could tell it hadn't been pleasant.

The laird was straining under the weight. The muscles of his arms bulged and shook as he fought to prevent the blade from crashing down on him. She had to do something.

She made a move toward them. But in one smooth motion, the laird dropped to the side, laced his foot around Allan's ankle, and brought the bigger man down to his knees. Before Flora could blink, Coll had his sword poised at Allan's neck. She halted midstep, stunned by the quick turn of events.

"Yield," he said raggedly. And in a voice she could just make out: "She's not for you."

Allan wasn't going to surrender. She could see it in his eyes. Not defiance, but resolve. He would never outright challenge his chief in his decision, but neither would he yield. Not in this. Not for the woman he loved. Without thinking, Flora rushed forward, putting herself between the two men. The anger surging between them was palpable. Neither would look away as their eyes engaged in an interminable battle of wills.

She reached up, gently placing her palm on the laird's naked chest. It shocked them both. His skin was hot to the touch, and her senses reeled from the heady masculine force of him. She was immediately conscious of the raw power surging under her fingertips, radiating from him like an invisible shield. She must be mad. What in the world was she doing? She felt as though she'd just placed herself in the mouth of a lion. How could she expect to harness such strength?

He hadn't moved the sword from Allan's neck, but his gaze had locked on hers.

He swore. "What the hell do you think you are doing?"

"Please, my laird." Her voice trembled. "I need to speak with you."

"Not now, Flora," he growled.

She leaned her body closer to his and moved her hand in a light, soothing caress over his hot chest. "Please," she begged. And under her breath she added, "Don't do this. It's gone too far already."

She looked deep into his eyes, and something passed between them. Something that made her heart flutter hard in her chest. Something intense and . . . significant.

Slowly, he lowered his sword.

The hot rage of battle that had welled inside him eased back, dampened by Flora.

His men dispersed, fading away quietly as Lachlan stood in the hot sun, staring at the fey creature before him, not quite sure what had just happened. Hell, he knew what had happened. After their conversation about Mary, he and Allan had taken their anger to the battlefield. Lachlan didn't want to think what might have occurred had Flora not stepped in and defused the situation.

Allan had shot him a quick glance before he left. His captain had looked equally taken aback by what had transpired. By how quickly their practice had turned into something altogether different. Damn. This thing with Mary had gotten out of control. How could he not have realized what was happening? Allan might be his friend, but Lachlan was chief, and he had to make his decisions as such—for the good of the clan. Even if those decisions went against his personal feelings.

He glanced down at her tiny hand, still resting on his chest. He couldn't describe what he felt the moment she had touched him. It was as if her hand had plunged through ice, reaching a part of him he hadn't even known existed. She'd drawn him back into the light from a dark place. All with a simple touch.

Seeing the direction of his gaze, she dropped her hand self-consciously. He felt the loss acutely, the severing of a connection the significance of which he was only beginning to comprehend. This woman did something strange to him.

He bent down, picking up the shirt and plaid that he'd tossed over a rock, feeling suddenly exposed. Though he knew it wasn't his state of undress that bothered him. He folded the clothing over his arm and held out his hand. "Come."

She looked at him uncertainly. "Where are we going?"

"To the water. Then you can tell me what you wished to speak to me about."

Steeling himself for rejection, he was surprised when she wordlessly slid her hand into his. He ignored the sudden hitch in his chest and led her down the rocky pathway to the water's edge. Rather than step on the white sandy beach, she pulled back with almost an aversion that he found odd and found a low rock to sit on.

Once again he relinquished his shirt and plaid to a rock, then pulled off his boots and dove into the waves of the sound, allowing the cool water to wash over him and rinse away the sweat and grime of the fight. His muscles burned, and he could have used a long, cold soak, but he was acutely aware that she was waiting. Reinvigorated nonetheless, he stepped up the rocky bank, feeling her big blue eyes on him the whole time, traveling over his chest and arms, unable to hide her interest. His body hardened. He wanted more than her eyes on him. Her hands . . . for starters. And then that naughty red mouth. She could drive a man wild with erotic images of those softly curved lips.

The heat of battle had left him and been replaced by a different heat. A raw one. For her. Even sitting there in that simple gown, she looked beautiful. Soft and sweetly feminine. Her hair tumbled in loose waves around her shoulders like a silky golden veil. Her pale cheeks flushed with a hint of pink from the heat of the sun. But it was the taunt of his vivid memories that drove him to distraction. Memories of lush breasts with tight nipples, curvy hips, a round bottom, and long, lean legs.

Completely unaware of the direction of his thoughts, she pointed behind him across the sound. "Is that the Isle of Mull?"

He nodded, reluctantly pulling on his shirt. "The northern edge."

"And Coll?"

"It lies just beyond Mull to the west."

She thought for a minute. "So Hector is close?"

"Yes." He could hear the unspoken question. Then what was taking Hector so long? Wringing the remaining water from his hair with a squeeze of his fingers, he changed the subject. "What is it that you wanted?"

Hands twisting, she gazed up at him with wide, uncertain eyes. Eyes that were the same startling blue tinged with green as the sea he'd just sunk into. Mesmerizing eyes. Her long dark lashes shone iridescent in the sun like the edge of a raven's wing. She took his breath away.

"Mary is unwell," she said.

His head cleared immediately. "What's wrong with her?"

She raised her chin to him defiantly. "Her heart is broken."

He stiffened, the tension returning to the back of his neck and shoulders. "It will mend." He hadn't intended to sound so harsh, but damn her for interfering. His sisters were none of her concern.

"You can't mean that."

She sounded so certain. He didn't know what she *thought* she knew about him, but she was wrong. "I assure you, I always mean what I say."

"Then you don't know what you are doing."

"I know exactly what I'm doing." Mary's marriage was important to the survival of his clan. He'd already had discussions with Ian MacDonald, son of the Chief of Glengarry and brother to Rory MacLeod's wife, Isabel. Ian was a good man. His sister would be well cared for, with liferents in some important property in Morvern. And his clan would have another important ally in the feud against Hector.

Her mouth pursed with annoyance, a sentiment he well understood. "You have nothing more to say?" she asked indignantly.

"I'm not accustomed to explaining myself." He gave her a long, hard look. "To anyone."

She disregarded the warning. "But surely you can see that she *loves* him."

Love. Love wasn't part of the marriage equation. It

was the same for Mary as it would be for him. That was
the way of it. "She *thinks* she loves him," he said. "But
Mary is young. With the romantic notions of a girl."

He started to turn away, indicating that he was finished with the conversation, but she grabbed his arm.
Her tiny fingers pressed into the thin linen of his damp
shirt. The soft, imploring touch sent waves of heat rippling through him. She was ardent in her beliefs, and he
wrestled with the strange urge to please her, though in
this, he knew he could not.

"I think you are wrong," she said flatly. "Mary truly
cares for him. You must have seen how she looks at
him." He had, which was why he'd put a stop to it.
"Talk to her. Not as a chief, but as her brother."

She was talking nonsense. "I'm both. But it is the chief
who must make the decision for the clan."

"But she needs a brother. I know you care for your sisters, but you act more like their father than their brother."
A wry smile twisted her lips. "It's something I'm familiar with. Take the time now to get to know them, before
you come to regret it."

She was wrong. He was very close to his sisters. Not
as close as they once were, perhaps, but not by his choice.
"I've nothing to regret."

"Not yet. Don't force her into an unhappy marriage,"
she implored, her eyes soft and pleading. "I've seen what
it can do."

"My sister isn't your mother, Flora."

"Are you so sure? My mother was once a biddable girl
who did her duty, and look what it got her—four husbands with varying degrees of cruelty and a lifetime of
unhappiness." He could hear the bitterness and pain in
her voice. Dropping her hand, she looked away from
him, as if trying to hide the tumult of emotion. But it
didn't work. He could see the toll her mother's death
had taken in the stiff carriage of her shoulders. Here, on

the windswept beach, with the harsh sea crashing behind her and the tower keep standing guard like a lone
sentinel across a desolate land, she looked unbearably
alone. Her refined beauty was a stark contrast to the
rugged landscape of the Highlands. A delicate white
rose among the hearty Highland heather. A sharp pang
pricked his chest. *She didn't belong here.*

Would this harsh life destroy her, too? *No,* he tried to
convince himself. Flora was strong.

"What was she like?" he asked quietly.

Flora reached down to pick up a flat stone and tossed
it across the water, just as the wave pulled back flat from
the shore. She managed two skips before it sank sharply
into the retreating water. It was something his sisters
might do. And hinted of a carefree girl not unaccus-
tomed to the sea. A remnant of her past from Dunvegan,
perhaps?

"Sweet," she said finally. "Gentle. Loving. But always
shadowed by sadness." She paused to look at him. "She
was all I had." The look of misery on her face hit him
hard. She glanced back to the water. "When I was
young, I used to spend hours devising ways of making
her laugh. Little plays, dances, funny costumes. Anything to make her smile." A wistful look transcended
her face. Her skin was flawless. Not a single freckle to
mar the ivory perfection. He remembered how soft it
was under his fingertips.

Unaware of his scrutiny, she continued. "I thought she
was the most beautiful woman in the world when she
smiled. And when she laughed, I would hear echoes of
the happy girl she'd been before she was locked away.
My mother was like a caged bird who'd forgotten how
to sing. She was beautiful and delicate, a gentle creature
who was tossed into a world that was utterly foreign to
her."

"You mean the Highlands?"

Flora nodded. "Yes, but it was more than that. Her husbands were much older and harsh, forbidding men constantly waging war, who didn't know what to do with a young girl accustomed to gentler pursuits. Her father and brothers should have known better. But she trusted blindly. Trusted that doing her duty was the right thing. But it wasn't. Not for her. She was never allowed to make decisions for herself. She resented her every move being controlled, and resented the domineering men she was married to. Eventually they broke her."

He could understand why Janet Campbell had wanted a different life for her daughter. But not all men were like her husbands.

"I know something of the men she was married to." The stories of Hector's father were legendary. He was a revered chief, but unquestionably a brutal one. Much like his son.

"You probably know more than I do," she said wryly. "My father was her last husband, and I don't remember him much—except that he seemed ancient and remote. My mother never talked in specifics about the men she was married to, but they left a lasting impression on me. I saw what they did to her. So you see what a forced marriage can bring? Do you really want your sister consigned to such a fate?"

"Of course not. Nor do I think she will be. Not all arranged marriages end up the way of your mother's. My parents were happy enough. And unlike your mother, my sister was raised in the Highlands, this is her home. Besides, the man I have chosen for her is a good man. But I will not force her. If she does not wish to marry him, there are others."

"But she *loves* Allan." Her expression turned fierce. "If I loved a man, nothing could force me to marry someone else."

Her words chilled him to the bone. The thought of her so passionate about another man made his insides twist. Even though he knew there was nothing to worry about. Nothing would stand in the way of their marriage.

He met her gaze. "I've made my decision."

"And your decisions are always right?"

"They are the only ones that matter," he snapped, not liking the scorn he heard in her voice. That was what he did. As chief, he made decisions that had broad ramifications for hundreds of people. He had to be decisive and confident. A leader. A man whom men would willingly die for. He damn well better trust himself to be right.

And Flora would have to learn that as well. She seemed to have no understanding of duty and responsibility—or of how difficult it could be to make the hard decisions. Her impulsive decision to take her marriage into her own hands and elope was proof enough of that.

She took a step closer to him. The wind whipped through her hair, sending silky tendrils streaming in wild abandon across her face. "Is there nothing that will change your mind?" she asked.

The world shifted. Day suddenly turned to night. Her innocent plea played tricks on his mind, on the desires of his body, taunting his tightly wrought control. Lust fired his blood. The subtle floral scent of her rose up to trap him in its hypnotic embrace. He couldn't move. Every instinct clamored to gather her in his arms and take what she offered. It was there between them, crackling with erotic promise.

He knew how good it would be.

God, he was tempted. He wanted to kiss her so badly, it hurt. His fists clenched at his sides as her lips parted. Soft and achingly sweet. Beckoning. Only inches away. His body drummed with need. The urge was so strong, he could almost taste her.

He knew what she was doing, even if she didn't. Unconsciously using her feminine wiles on him. She'd already proved how much she could affect him, by putting herself between him and Allan earlier. But she was doomed to failure. He would never allow a woman to control his actions. It was a lesson she needed to learn.

The air was thick with tension. He leaned closer, towering over her, letting her feel his heat. "What are you offering?"

The color slid from her cheeks, and she tried to back away. But she stumbled on the uneven rocks, and he reached out to catch her, wrapping her in a fierce embrace. He felt the furious flutter of her heart against his, like a bird caught in a trap. His trap.

"You m-misunderstand," she stammered.

He traced his fingers down her throat and over the frantic pulse. "Do I?" He held her gaze. "I don't think so."

He'd waited long enough. Whatever control he had over his passion had been undone by the exquisite feel of holding her in his arms. His hand snaked behind her neck, and he plunged his fingers through the silky waves of her hair, warmed from the sun, bringing her mouth hard against his with a deep guttural groan. The relief was overwhelming. Her scent. Her taste. The sensation of her soft lips under his. The tightness inside him burst in a slow gush of heat that spread through his veins, and his cock swelled hot and hard against her. He'd been waiting for this for too long.

This time, he did not hold back. It was no gentle wooing, but an explosion of passion. His mouth moved over hers with swift possession as he kissed her with all of the raw hunger raging inside him. He pulled her closer, his fingers caressing the baby soft skin of her neck as he urged her jaw open with his thumb.

And she melted against him. Opening her mouth. Taking him in. Making sweet little sounds of pleasure that drove him wild.

He sank into her, kissing her harder, trying to quench the impossible lust that would not be sated. His tongue delved deep into her mouth, stroking, tasting, devouring, until her tongue entwined with his and she returned his stroke with a parry of her own. It was hot and wet and wickedly carnal. And a little bit rough. Just the way he liked it.

God, it felt good. So damn good. He'd known how it would be between them, but never could he have imagined the powerful feelings surging through him— unfamiliar feelings of possession, tenderness, and longing.

He couldn't get enough. His lips trailed over her mouth, her jaw, her neck, tasting every inch of her fevered skin.

She sagged against him in sweet surrender. Her hands were on his shoulders, his arms, his back. Feeling him. Clutching him. He felt her passion rise up to meet him, returning his passion with a fervor of her own.

Her kisses were sweet and innocent and utterly potent, but he wanted more. His tongue was in her mouth, deep in her mouth, and his hand was on her breast, squeezing her gently in his palm as he thrust with his tongue. Her breasts were magnificent; he cursed the fabric and stays, wishing he could feel the soft, full weight of all that naked flesh in his hands. His thumb caressed the hard peak of her nipple, and she moaned, arching against his hand.

It was too much. It wasn't enough. Her soft whimpers of pleasure sent a bolt of lust straight to his groin. He slid his hand down to her bottom, lifting her against him. His erection was rock hard and throbbing as their bodies came together. She rubbed against him, and his knees almost buckled.

He wanted to open her up and fill her. To make her

tremble. To make her come as she cried out his name. To make her his. He wanted it more than anything he'd ever wanted in his life.

So much so that it shook him. This clawing need for her.

When she melted against him, touched him, kissed him, she could make him do almost anything. She could bring him to his knees with one kiss.

Hell. He wrenched away with a growl, his body pounding as he fought for control. Never had he felt more threatened, by anyone. "What do you want from me?" he said hoarsely, wanting to take back the words as soon as they were uttered.

"I . . . ," she gasped, her face stricken as he watched her grapple with what had just happened. Of how they'd come together in a hot burst of flames. And of how easily she'd succumbed. Her eyes rounded. "I don't know."

There it was. The crack that he'd been waiting for. He should be happy. She wanted him. He'd won. But it didn't feel like a victory. He felt like the one who'd lost.

She spun around and started to climb up the hill toward the keep, but not before he saw the look on her face. The truth horrified her. As it did him. She wanted him as much as he wanted her—with an uncompromising intensity that could not be denied.

He'd wanted to teach her a lesson, but it was he who'd been cautioned. Passion worked both ways. In using it against her, he'd been the one burned. She'd gotten under his skin, and he didn't like it. But it wouldn't change anything. He wouldn't let it.

She scrambled up the shore, moving purposefully up the rocky crags.

"Flora," he called out. She stopped but didn't turn. "Next time you make an offer like that, I won't refuse."

She flinched, and then she ran.

Chapter 7

❖

"Ouch, you stepped on my toe, you big oaf."

Flora bit back a smile. The outrage on Gilly's face was really quite comical. As was the look of fury on her partner's face. Poor Murdoch. It had taken quite some convincing to get him here in the first place, and now Gilly was about to make Flora's prodigious efforts come to naught.

Though the lad could still barely look Flora in the eye without blushing, he seemed to take delight in tormenting Gilly. Not to mention ungraciously lording his two additional years over her.

"I warned you, my lady," Murdoch said. "Court dances are not for warriors. Men don't dance like we have a rod up our ars—" He stopped at her frown.

After witnessing the sword dance last week, she tended to agree with him, but if the girls were going to go to court, they needed to learn to dance appropriately. Thus she'd gathered a piper, Gilly, Mary, and Murdoch for dance lessons. Mary needed some cheering up, and right now she was stifling a giggle watching her sister spar with Murdoch.

Though Flora had told herself not to get involved while at Drimnin, the temptation had proved too much. She could hardly sit idly by while so many things cried out for her attention. In addition to dance, she'd begun instructing the girls in reading and writing Scots and a little Latin. The most challenging aspect of her project thus far had proved to be the woefully inadequate handful of folios scattered about the keep. As there was no library per se, she'd taken over the laird's private solar located behind the great hall for her purposes. Her friends at court would be so amused to hear of the Holyrood hellion acting as tutor, but Flora had never felt so useful.

Mary and Gilly weren't the sole focus of her attentions. She'd also had a few delicate conversations with Morag about improvements around the keep and, despite being banished from the kitchens, about the preparations of the food.

"Warrior. Ha!" Gilly muttered with a snort, just loudly enough for Murdoch to hear.

He took an intimidating step toward her, looking as if he'd like nothing more than to throttle her. Though he was young, Flora saw a shadow of the formidable man he could become. But right now he was still too full of youthful pride, and Gilly had just trampled all over it.

"Nonsense, Murdoch, you are doing very well." Flora stepped between them, trying to smooth things over. "It was Gilly who got in your way." She gave her a reproachful stare. "Wasn't it, Gilly?"

Although she clearly wanted to disagree, Gilly seemed to realize that she was about to lose her partner—and they were horribly shorthanded as it was in that department. Conscripting men to help with Gilly's and Mary's dance lessons had proved next to impossible. Flora had never heard so many excuses. The only reason Murdoch was here at all was because Alasdair had volunteered him to avoid coming himself, grumbling that he'd rather clean the garderobe than prance around like a Lowland peacock.

Murdoch looked as though he felt the same way, but they weren't finished with him yet. They'd already been through some of the popular court dances, including the lively galliard, a modified lavolta—without the scandalous lift—and the coranto. Now she was trying to teach the girls a reel, and they had to have at least four people, though eight would have been better.

"Yes, I'm sorry, Murdoch, it was my fault," Gilly said sweetly, though her eyes sparked with mutiny. Flora had a feeling she was only biding her time before unleashing a wicked sting of barbs on the poor lad. It's what she'd have done in Gilly's place.

"I still don't see why you're going to all the trouble, my lady. It's hardly likely that this one will ever go to court—" He motioned to Gilly. "And it will take more than dancing to make a man forget about a sharp tongue—although I suppose they are Lowlanders," he said disparagingly.

Flora's mouth quirked. Apparently, she need not have felt sorry for him. Murdoch could take care of himself.

Gilly's face flamed, and she looked ready to explode in a tirade, but Flora shot her a staying glance.

"As sisters of a laird, the girls should go to court," Flora said. "So when the opportunity arises, I want them to be prepared. Shall we try again?" She motioned to Duncan, the piper, who was doing his best to hide his laughter. "Mary?" The girl had drifted off again. Flora walked over to gently turn Mary away from the window, giving her an encouraging squeeze when she saw the look of anguish on her face. The situation with Mary gave her pause. How could the laird do this to his sister? He was wrong. Mary would not outgrow her feelings for Allan. Flora would have to convince Lach—the laird—of it. "Come," she said to Mary. "Don't give up," she urged, not referring simply to the dance. Mary met her gaze and nodded. Flora smiled. "This time you will partner with Gilly."

As she took them through the steps of the dance again, Flora knew she was treading on dangerous ground. She was becoming too attached. To the girls. To the dreadful old keep. And, to be truthful, to the enigmatic man who was its laird.

She was no less confused today than she had been a week ago. What *did* she want from him? She no longer knew. He evoked a thousand different emotions in her, none of which she wanted to analyze too closely. And never far from her consciousness was the memory of that kiss. Of his mouth. His tongue. His big hands on her body. He'd cupped her breast, and heat had poured through her. She'd come apart in his arms, yielding to him without hesitation.

How could she have reacted like that? She didn't understand what had come over her. She'd felt his passion and her own. It made her anxious. On edge. For something. Something that made her skin prickle whenever he was in the room with her. Indeed, she found it difficult to concentrate when he was around. He was big and strong and smelled incredible. She wanted to curl up against his chest and never leave. She'd never had such strong urges. But then again, she'd never met a man who made her feel so protected simply by his solid presence and his confident command of everything around him. His strength was strangely soothing. She couldn't remember a time in her life when she'd felt so . . . content. And given the circumstances of her presence at Drimnin, that was strange indeed.

Though her attraction to him was undeniable, she couldn't forget that she was his prisoner. Her thoughts should be of escape. That day at the beach, she'd noticed a small boat moored close to the shore. The Isle of Mull was tantalizingly close. At night, she could probably get to it without being seen. But something held her back, something other than the obvious danger. She'd never liked boats, with good reason. Though Morvern was part of the mainland of Scotland, stealing a horse would be near impossible; the stables were too well guarded.

She told herself she was waiting for Hector, but the longer it took, the more she knew it for a lie. As the days went by with no word from her brother, she realized she'd been right: Hector wouldn't exchange her for Breacachadh Castle. She barely knew him. It shouldn't matter. But "should" didn't prevent the kernel of disappointment and hurt.

The laird must realize that his plan hadn't worked. The past week had made her even more confident that he was ever so subtly wooing her. And she was forced to admit, it was not without effect. Though it was an unusual wooing, devoid of compliments and heartfelt declarations. None of the social niceties she'd grown accustomed to. Accustomed to and bored with, she realized. Lachlan Maclean was not just rough around the edges; he was rough through and through and every ounce the proud Highland chief.

All her life she'd been brought up to never trust a Highlander and to despise their way of life. But he was different. Watching him with his clan, she admired his leadership, his strength, and his protectiveness toward his men and his sisters. Especially given what she now knew about his past. Of how he'd had to fight and struggle to provide for his clan. They looked at him as nothing less than a hero.

She wanted to trust him, but how could she when he held her prisoner? She still couldn't reconcile the man who'd abducted her—and prevented his own sister from marrying the man she loved—with the chief she'd grown to admire and the man who'd kissed her at first tenderly and then with such passion.

At times, she felt as if she could be happy here. Mary and Gilly were wonderful, and the laird . . . for all his rough ways, he held a strange appeal. She could almost believe he might make a good husband.

Husband. Could she really consider such a thing? Marrying a Highlander, forsaking all she knew to live in this harsh, remote landscape? Drimnin didn't have the luxuries she was used to, but never had she been more comfortable—even, she thought with a wry smile, without silk bed linens, silver candelabra, and gold-encrusted plates. She would miss the pageantry of court, but it wasn't as if she were being banished—she could always return. And her tocher would go a long way toward helping to update the dilapidated old keep. She would miss her former life, but the prospect of living in the Highlands didn't appall her as it should. And she knew the reason why: Lachlan Maclean.

But why had he brought her here? He'd sworn he would not force her into marriage, and desperately, she wanted to believe him.

They stumbled through another attempt at the reel before Gilly collapsed, exhausted, on a chair. Murdoch was actually quite a good dancer—when not partnered with Gilly.

"I don't know why we're bothering," Gilly said woefully. "As much as I hate to say it, Murdoch is right. Lachlan will never let us go."

"He can hardly object if you are my guests. When I return to Edinburgh, you will come and stay with me in my cousin's lodgings. I will take care of everything." For once, she was grateful for her wealth.

"You are being so kind and generous. . . ." A shadow crossed Mary's face. A shadow that looked like guilt. "But it won't matter. Lachlan despises court. He says it's a place of intrigue and deception. And corruption."

Flora thought about it for a moment. There was truth to Mary's words, but court was also the center of power and a place of excitement and energy, with all the modern conveniences and advantages of society. "There is some truth to what your brother says. But it is not all bad." She gave Gilly a sidelong glance. "There are balls, dancing, masques . . . and plenty of handsome young men to partner with."

Gilly practically jumped out of her chair, her energy suddenly renewed. "I think we should have another go at it."

Flora laughed. "Let's try the lavolta again."

Murdoch groaned, and Flora couldn't help but chuckle at his much put-upon expression. She took his hand and led him into position. "Come, it won't be that bad. And this time we'll try the lift that had all England on its ear when Queen Elizabeth first performed it with Robert Dudley, Earl of Leicester."

When Murdoch mumbled something about the foolish Englishmen, Flora hid her smile and pretended not to hear him.

Lachlan had a mutiny on his hands, and he needed to do something about it. Or, rather, about someone. He shook his head. He didn't know why he was surprised; trouble followed Flora MacLeod like a lovesick pup.

He climbed the narrow staircase up to the first floor, his shoulders banging against the hard stones as he went. The stairway hadn't been built to accommodate men of his size; it had been constructed as an additional defense against attack, intended to prevent enemies from storming the keep. Though no enemy had ever caused as much trouble as Flora. How did one wee lass manage so much upheaval?

Part of him was pleased. Her involvement with his sisters, his keep, and his clan proved that she was softening. Whether she'd realized it or not, she'd assumed the role of chatelaine. The role that belonged to his wife. He'd noticed the subtle changes she'd made—fresh wildflowers in the hall, the addition of some old hangings to the walls, and the unmistakable improvements to the food. And he'd noticed the interest she'd taken in his sisters as well.

But this time, she'd gone too far.

He strode past the great hall to the small antechamber beyond. The private solar served as the chamber where he held council with his guardsmen. One such meeting had taken place this very morning, which was why he was here now instead of where he should be—training his men for the battle that was sure to come.

He paused outside for a moment, enjoying the joyful sounds of the pipes. Then he opened the door and started through, but the gurgle of laughter stopped him in his tracks. Mary and Gilly stood clapping their hands to the beat of the music as Flora and Murdoch spun and stepped in an energetic dance. All four were smiling and laughing. He hesitated to intrude. It was the first time he'd seen Mary smile in a week. The extent of his relief told him how much her unhappiness had weighed on him. He'd even begun to think that Flora might have been right. Did his sister truly care for his captain? And if so, did it change anything?

Lachlan wasn't a man used to second-guessing himself. He supposed he had Flora to "thank" for that as well.

His gaze shifted to the source of his troubles. God, she was beautiful. His chest tightened just looking at her. And never far behind was the memory of that kiss. Of how damn much he wanted her, with an intensity that had penetrated deep into his bones.

He should have taken her that day on the beach. But his own reaction and the depth of his emotion to the kiss had disconcerted him. He'd been lost in the haze of a desire so strong, it went well beyond mere lust. And that realization had taken him aback—and held him back.

But no longer. The latest news smuggled out of Brea-cachadh warned that the situation on Coll had grown dire. As he'd feared, Hector was stripping his land and ill-treating his clan. At the council earlier today, his guardsmen had clamored to do something. But his hands were tied. If they attacked Hector right now, they would lose. They needed support. Argyll's support. And Lach-lan couldn't attack Hector while his brother was in prison and subject to the whims of an angry king. But the waiting was driving him crazy. Every instinct urged him to attack, but his clan would never have survived this long if he were one to act recklessly.

He needed to marry Flora . . . now. He didn't have the time to let nature take its course. In this case, it might need some prodding. And there was one way to assure that it happened right away.

Flora's cheeks flushed pink, and her eyes sparkled with laughter. He'd never seen her look so radiant. *This* was the girl he'd heard about at court. This was the girl who could break a thousand hearts.

She wasn't what he'd expected. She was headstrong and stubborn, but confident and compassionate as well. She was also lonely, scared, and emotionally scarred by her mother's death—or, perhaps more so, by her life. But what stunned him most was her passion. She might be a sophisticated courtier, but she burned as hot as he did.

He knew she'd softened toward him, but would the attraction between them be enough for her to forsake her life in the Lowlands? To put to rest her fears of being used as a political pawn, of not having control? Though he was all too aware that when she found out why he'd brought her here, she'd realize her fears had been justi-fied. The thought was deeply unsettling.

Not for the first time, he wished there were another way.

"Now be ready this time when I jump," Flora said with mock severity to Murdoch.

"I'll try," the lad said. "But I don't know where to put my hands." When Murdoch realized what he'd said, his face turned scarlet. They danced in a circle, and then Murdoch took her by the waist and started to lift her.

Lachlan froze. He knew this dance. He hadn't recognized it at first because it wasn't usually danced to the pipes. He crossed the room in three long strides. The music stopped, and he felt four sets of eyes on him. Five, actually, including the piper's.

"Brother," Gilly said, clearly surprised by the interruption. And enormously pleased. He rarely appeared during the day; usually he was training his warriors or attending to the administration of the clan. Lachlan couldn't tear his eyes away from Flora, but he spoke to Murdoch. "You'll drop her like that, lad."

"I know," Murdoch said miserably. "I've done so three times."

Lachlan heard Gilly snicker, but he would reprimand her later. Right now, he had eyes for only one person. He stepped in front of Murdoch and took Flora's hand. "May I?"

Eyes wide, she nodded.

"Duncan," Lachlan said, indicating for the music to begin again.

It had been a long time since he'd been to court and stayed long enough to dance, and it took him a moment to remember the steps. But after a few minutes it came back to him, and he relaxed, allowing himself to enjoy the subtle flirtation of the dance. And of touching her. Holding her so close to his body, he could feel the gentle warmth surrounding her and smell her delicate floral scent. With shouts of encouragement from the enthusiastic gallery, he and Flora executed the intricate dance steps of the galliard with smooth precision.

Never had he been so aware of the movements of another. He felt tied to her, bound by some invisible cord. Each time their hands touched, he felt a shock run through him. The quickening of her breath and the race of her heart were like an elixir. From her expression, he could tell that she was just as affected.

They moved to a close position. She shuddered when his hand slid around her waist to her hip, and her hand came up to rest on his shoulder. They were so close now, their bodies almost touching. It was torture, holding her like this and not kissing her.

They stepped forward in a turn, and when the moment came to lift her, their timing was perfect. Just as she sprang into the air, he lifted her up with his hands, using his thigh for support. He held her there for a long beat and slid her down, tight against his body, savoring every moment of the physical connection. His body responded instantly to her sweet femininity. Never once did he take his gaze from her, unable to turn away from what he saw in her eyes, even though it made his chest ache.

It took him a moment to realize that the music had stopped and that his sisters were cheering. Hell, he'd forgotten they weren't alone. Releasing her, he took a step back, breathing heavily from the exertion of the dance. And from something else.

"That was wonderful, brother," Gilly said. "Why have you never told us you knew these dances?"

He turned to his sister and shrugged. "There's not much opportunity for court dances in the Highlands."

"No, there's not," Flora argued, "which is why—"

He didn't let her finish, anticipating what she might say. "I need to speak with Mistress MacLeod," he said to the others. "In private."

"But . . ." Flora stopped her protest when she saw how quickly they moved to do his bidding.

When the door clicked shut, she swung back around on him with her hands on her hips. "We weren't done. Do you know how hard it was for me to find someone willing to help?"

"I can imagine," he said dryly, knowing his men.

She sighed and then shot him a curious glance. "So you *have* spent some time at court."

He shrugged. "Long enough to learn a few dances."

Her gaze turned probing. "What else are you hiding?"

He stiffened. Inadvertently, she'd hit precariously close to the truth. He steered her away with a jest. "Not a gold silk peascod and slops, I assure you."

Her mouth twitched. "Somehow I can't quite picture you in anything but Highland garb. Though I'm sure you would look magnificent in anything—"

She stopped, her cheeks flaming with color.

He warmed, not at the compliment, but at the underlying sentiment—and at what it had revealed. Aye, she was softening. And it made him happy for more reasons than it should.

Trying to cover up her mistake, she turned, intending to replace the chairs she'd moved for the dancing.

"Don't." He took her by the arm. "I'll have some of my men see to it."

She stared at his hand wrapped around her arm as if he'd branded her. "Was there something you wanted?" she asked tightly.

Yes, damn it. You.

But that wasn't why he'd come. Hell, he'd almost forgotten. He dropped her arm. "I've been informed of some disturbing threats being issued against some of my men. Threats that have my men very angry and tired. And when my men are angry and tired, it becomes my problem."

"I don't know what you are talking about," she said, trying to flounce away.

But he took hold of her again, stopping her. "I think you know exactly what I'm talking about." He brought her a little closer, took her chin in his hand, and forced her to look at him. "Do you deny giving instructions on private matters, such as the sleeping arrangements of a man and his wife?"

She shrugged indifferently. "I don't recall."

He didn't buy her innocent act for one moment. It sounded exactly like something she would do. He'd heard an earful from his men about her interference all morning. She'd damn well better explain herself.

He brought her closer still, his anger overriding his good sense. She wasn't as blithe as she seemed; he could see the nervous pulse in her neck—right below her tiny soft ear. If he put his mouth . . . God, he wanted to make her come apart in his arms.

"You encouraged the women to ban the men from their beds?"

A telltale blush stained her cheeks. "I did no such thing."

Minx. Why must she always challenge him? "Let me refresh your memory. Do you recall discussing my men's bathing habits?"

She lifted her chin defiantly. Always so damn defiant.

The air between them felt suddenly charged. Every inch of his body was primed to take her in his arms and bring her to submission. To bring her to him. He'd had enough. He hadn't planned on this, but his patience had just run out. He wouldn't force her, but then again he wouldn't need to.

For more reasons than one, it was time for this dance to end.

Flora didn't know what made her persist in flirting with danger. She knew she was pushing him, knew that she was making him angry, but somehow it didn't matter. She liked him like this. Liked the glimpse of emotion. For the past week, he'd been unfailingly attentive, polite, patient—not objecting to anything—and remote. She hated it. Where was the man who had kissed her with such fiery passion?

The steely control that she admired also served to keep a part of him away from her. But when he was angry, he didn't hold back. And there was something exciting, and more than a bit thrilling, about that.

She purposefully feigned boredom, flicking at a ball of fuzz off the shoulder of his plaid. "I may have said something about a man bedding down with dogs if he smelled like one."

He was furious, though she suspected it was more her attitude than her words.

"And don't you think that might have been interpreted the wrong way?"

"How so? I think they interpreted it precisely as I intended it. I see no reason why a man can't wash before he comes home to his wife." She looked at him pointedly. "You always smell clean. I wouldn't kick you out—"

She put her hand over her mouth, mortified by what she'd been about to say. But in truth, with him standing so close she couldn't think about anything other than how amazing he smelled. And of nestling up and resting her cheek against that warm, broad chest.

His eyes darkened, and his voice was dangerously low. "You wouldn't kick me out of where, Flora?"

He was looking at her as if he wanted to ravish her, but it didn't frighten her at all. It actually sent a thrill of anticipation shooting through her veins. She swallowed hard, her throat suddenly dry. "I was speaking metaphorically."

His arm slid around her waist. The way it had been when they'd danced. That dance . . . She shivered. He could put any courtier to shame. Who would have thought a warrior of his size would dance so beautifully? Graceful, but strong. When he lifted her, she'd felt as light as a feather. It was different dancing with him. She'd never been so aware of a man's hands on her. She'd never noticed how seductive a dance could be. How each little touch could shock with tiny tremors of awareness.

She'd never wanted a man before. Not like this. Not with every fiber of her being. The truth hit her square in the chest. She cared for him. He *was* different. He had to be. She wouldn't feel like this otherwise. That was what had held her back from trying to escape.

"Where, Flora?"

The dark promise in his voice made her tremble. His mouth was so close. She wanted him to kiss her again. But he knew that. "Bed," she said softly. "Out of bed."

With a growl, he kissed her. Nay, not kissed—he devoured her. His mouth was hot and hard, and his lips demanding, as he took her in his arms and kissed her as though he would never let her go.

She wanted to believe it. Wanted to think that the wave of emotion swelling inside her meant something. That the passion between them was special. Because it was to her. No man had ever made her feel this way. Made her blood heat and her limbs go weak with the press of his lips against hers.

All she could think of was getting closer to him. It felt so good, it almost hurt. To be in his arms again. Kissing him. Feeling the familiar hard press of his body against hers and the rapid beat of his heart that did not lie.

His warm masculine scent surrounded her, engulfing her senses. He kissed her harder and deeper. His mouth moved over hers, branding her, searing her with his heat. But it wasn't enough. Wrapping her hands around his neck, she leaned her body closer, dissolving. Moaning as the passion welled inside her. She opened her mouth, wanting the wicked press of his tongue against hers. Wanting the dark, rich taste of him filling her mouth.

With a groan, he complied, sinking his tongue deep into her mouth. She opened to him, returning the sensual thrusts of his tongue the way he'd taught her. The subtle erotic rhythm increased the strange restlessness rising inside her, struggling to break free. He bent her farther back, taking her even deeper as his hands slid down to her bottom and he lifted her firmly against him.

She melted in a pool of heat, feeling the power of his erection pressing against her, hot and demanding. He was big and hard, just like the rest of him. She shivered, this time not with fear, but with desire, and felt a wicked urge to rub up against the solid length of him. She might be a maid, but she was well-enough versed in the details of mating—courtesy of the more profligate women at court.

He pressed against her again, this time more insistently, setting off a thousand little explosions of awareness. Unconsciously, her legs opened around him, wanting to feel him closer.

He froze, every muscle in his body taut. She could almost feel the blood surging through his veins under her palms. "Do that again, lass," he whispered against her mouth, "and having care for your innocence will be the last thing on my mind."

Heat stained her cheeks. "I'm sorry—"

But he pressed his finger over her mouth, stopping her. "Your instincts are perfect, my sweet. I just want you too much." His eyes were dark and stormy. "I want to give you pleasure."

He already was. Unimaginable pleasure.

She relaxed, closing her eyes as his warm mouth trailed down her neck, making her shiver. His hands were on her breasts, squeezing gently as his mouth slid over the sensitive flesh of her chest. She didn't know what he was doing, but she didn't care. Deftly he worked the fastenings of her gown and kirtle loose enough so that with a gentle tug her breasts popped over her stays. He didn't move, staring at her until her skin flushed pink under the smoldering intensity of his gaze.

"God, you're beautiful," he said hoarsely. He glanced up at her, perhaps sensing her embarrassment. "You have nothing to be ashamed of, lass. Your breasts are perfect. Big and round. I can't wait to taste you."

She shivered.

He weighed her in his hands, sliding his thumb over the taut tip of one nipple, and her legs turned to jelly.

She grasped his broad shoulders to prevent herself from collapsing, savoring the feel of the hard, bulging muscles in her hands. God, he was strong, every inch of him as tightly wrought as steel. Just touching him sent a thrill surging through her. Though the linen of his shirt was fine, she felt a violent urge to rip it off him and splay her hands across his hot skin, recalling all too well the hard, sculpted ridges of his magnificent chest.

When he began to caress her breasts with his big rough hands, she lost all coherent thought. He pinched her nipples lightly between his fingers, and heat spread between her legs.

Scooping up her breasts with his hands, he sank his face into her, nuzzling her skin with the scratch of his beard. God, it was amazing. His mouth was hot and wet as he kissed her nakedness, sliding his tongue achingly close to the very tip of her. Her nipples throbbed, aching for the soft press of his mouth.

She moaned when his tongue flicked out to tease her.

"Do you like that?" he asked softly.

She arched against him.

"God, you're hot," he groaned. "So lush and responsive." And then he was sucking her, his tongue circling the hard tip as he took her nipple deep into the warm recesses of his mouth. A cry of pure pleasure escaped from between her lips as a needle of white hot heat surged through her.

Her body was on fire. She was pressing against him, moving, unable to release the building tension. Wanting more. Wanting the friction of his body. Frantically, her hands roamed over his back and her hips circled against him.

She felt the change. Felt as he succumbed to the heat. He sucked her harder, using his teeth to gently nibble and pull as his hands moved over her bottom and down her leg with clear purpose. He was done teasing. Done talking. He wanted this as badly as she did.

His hand was under her skirt, sliding up her leg as he increased the pressure on her breast, laving her with his tongue and sucking her deep and hard. The warm spot between her legs began to clench.

She didn't understand what was happening, her body felt so strange. She was trembling and quivering all over. His fingers skimmed the sensitive skin of her inner thigh. She tensed, embarrassed by the sudden gush of dampness near his hand. She tried to close her legs, but he stopped her with a stroke, the barest graze of his finger against her core.

She froze in shock and wonder.

"Don't be frightened," he said soothingly, lifting his head from her breast. "I promise this will feel good."

His finger reached out to sweep against her again, this time lingering to cup her and massage her gently. What was he doing? And why did it feel so incredible? No one ever told her it would be like this. So warm and silky and overwhelming. Her shock abated as she succumbed to sensation. Wallowing in the wet heat building where he touched.

Sensing her surrender, he caught her lips with his, sliding his tongue in her mouth just as his finger slid inside her. Oh God, it was perfect. She'd never felt so wanton, so free. He was cupping her, his finger sliding in and out, faster and faster, until her hips started moving against his hand. She couldn't breathe. Her mind focused on the pulse between her legs that was concentrating and building in intensity. She was frantic, writhing against him. Something magical beckoned just out of reach. She wanted desperately to leap, but something was holding her back.

A knock on the door shattered the fragile moment like glass. The flood of heat turned to shards of ice.

He swore, stepped back from her, and struggled to control the primal lust she saw raging in his gaze. Every inch of his body seemed tense and rigid. No man had ever looked at her with such raw desire. She felt as though she'd unleashed a lion, a lion that would not be tamed. A twinge of unease fluttered in her chest.

What had she almost done? The truth hit her hard. The ramifications of what had nearly happened poured down on her in an unforgiving deluge. She'd almost given herself to him. Her captor. The man who intended to use her for his own ends.

But it had seemed so right.

Flora moved to the other side of the room, trying to get as far away from him as possible, and adjusted her gown as quickly as she could manage with shaking fingers, giving thanks that the simple gown could be easily slipped back over her shoulders and tied at the front. But there was little she could do about her swollen lips and mussed hair.

In a rough voice, Lachlan bade the intruder—or perhaps her savior—enter.

The door opened, and she recognized the man who entered as one of the laird's young guardsmen. His gaze flickered between the two of them cautiously. Flora's cheeks heated as she realized he'd guessed what he'd interrupted. No doubt she looked as if she'd just been ravished—which she had. Nearly, anyway.

After a heavy pause, he cleared his throat and spoke. "My laird, I'm sorry to disturb you. But it's important."

The change that came over Lachlan was instantaneous: All vestiges of passion disappeared, and his expression was once again hard and impenetrable. Remote. The air of invincibility once again surrounded him, and too easily, she'd been forgotten. She felt a hard pang in her chest. The commanding chief had returned with a transformation so complete, it shook her.

"What is it?" he asked in clipped tones.

"A letter, my laird." The messenger gave Flora an uneasy glance. "From Duart."

Chapter 8

❖

Flora's heart plummeted to the floor. She couldn't breathe. Here it was, the response she'd been waiting for. Dread crashed over her. Not because she feared that Hector would not exchange her, but because she feared he would. Would Lachlan let her go? Would he trade her for his castle?

Her pulse raced as she awaited the answer.

Wrapped in her own jumble of emotions, she almost missed the fleeting look of surprise on Lachlan's face. He took the missive from the man, broke the seal, glanced at it briefly, and slid it in his leather sporran. His eyes turned black and cold as onyx. Clearly, something had angered him.

"That will be all," he said, dismissing the guardsman, who, from the awkward way he shuffled his feet, obviously couldn't wait to leave.

As soon as the door clicked shut, Flora turned to him. Fists clenched at her side, she took a deep breath and prepared for the worst. "What does it say?"

His jaw clenched forbiddingly. "We will discuss it later."

There could be only one explanation for his anger. "Hector refused?"

The look he shot her made her take a step back. His expression was as fierce as she'd ever seen it. He'd never looked at her with something akin to . . . resentment. "I said not now. Return to your chamber"—his hard gaze fell to her breasts and then lowered—"unless you'd care to resume where we left off?"

She flinched, his words as effective as a slap. The crude taunt after the intimacies they'd just shared stung. Something was wrong. Why was he lashing out at her like this? She'd thought him hard and forbidding, perhaps even ruthless, but never cruel. Was it something Hector had said? A lump settled low in her belly. Or had she done something wrong?

Mouth trembling, she stood her ground. "Why are you treating me like this? I deserve to know. Tell me what the letter says."

Hard blue eyes bored into her. There was something raw in his gaze that made her heart tug. She made a movement toward him and then stopped self-consciously. His shoulders were so stiff, she yearned to put her hands on him and rub away the tension from the thick slabs of muscle. Only moments ago she'd been in his arms, and now he seemed untouchable. An insurmountable fortress had sprung up between them; she wondered if she'd only imagined the moments of intimacy.

"Please," she urged.

He stared at her for a long moment, looking as if he were going to explode in rage; then, inexplicably, the fight seemed to leave him. "Damn you," he swore.

She reached for him then, placing her hand on his chest, feeling the tension under her palm. "What did he say?"

"I don't know." His voice sounded oddly hollow.

Her brows furrowed. She didn't understand. She'd seen him open it. "But why . . . ?"

All of a sudden, it hit her. *He couldn't read it.* She nearly sighed with relief. He wasn't angry with her. But he'd wanted to hide it from her. God, did he think she would ridicule him? She cringed inwardly, realizing that she might have—at one time. But not now. Not since she'd grown to know him. And respect him.

Having to fight for his clan rather than attend Tounis College in Edinburgh, as most of the Highland chiefs' sons now did, including her brothers, in no way diminished her opinion of him. Though she couldn't deny that many would feel differently. Her mother, for one. One of the things Janet Campbell had deplored in the men she'd married had been their lack of education. Learning had always been important to Flora as well. But Lachlan had made her realize that schooling did not necessarily equate with intelligence. Any man who could defend himself against attack from her powerful brother for so many years had more than proved himself in that regard.

"You didn't attend Tounis?"

He held her gaze stiffly, as if bracing himself for her scorn. "No, there was not the opportunity or the means. I can read Erse, but not Scots. A fact of which your brother is well aware."

Flora frowned, not liking what that said about Hector. "May I see it?"

He hesitated. For some reason, he still seemed reluctant to give it to her. Then he slipped it out of his sporran and placed it in her hand. The stiff piece of wrinkled parchment crackled as Flora unfolded it carefully. She read it over quickly, trying to prevent her relief from showing.

Lifting her gaze to him, she saw the harsh flex of his jaw. "Shall I read it?"

He nodded.

" 'Release my sister or suffer the consequences. Consider this a warning. The only one you shall receive.' "

"Strange," she said, her gaze narrowing on the piece of parchment. "He doesn't address your demands at all."

His expression went blank. "I think we can assume a refusal."

Ignoring the stab of hurt, Flora schooled her features into a mask of indifference. "I feared as much. Perhaps you will believe me now. Hector will never willingly relinquish the castle. Not for me, anyway."

This time, he didn't argue with her.

There was no reason to hold her now. "You will release me, then?"

"No."

The flat refusal reverberated through her, shaking her to the core. Until this moment, she hadn't realized how important it was to her. She needed him to let her go so she could make her own choice on whether to stay. "But there is no other reason to keep me here."

He didn't say anything, just stared at her. Ruthless and determined.

Apprehension coiled inside her. There was only one reason to keep her. One that would confirm her worst fears. "You've changed your mind," she said dully, barely able to get out the words. "You'll force me to marry you."

He gave her another penetrating stare. "A few more minutes, and I would not have needed to force anything."

Flora gasped. Was that what he'd intended? To seduce her so that she would have to marry him? The blood drained from her face. She'd almost let him. "You bastard. How could you?"

"I want you," he said bluntly.

"You don't want me, you want what I can bring you," she replied bitterly, unable to hide the despair in her voice. Her wealth, her connections, an end to the curse were all too tempting. He saw her not as a desirable woman, but as a marriage prize. Just like everyone else.

He held her gaze steadily, and didn't deny it. "When will you realize that none of this is your choice?"

She flinched. How could he say something so cruel? She'd begun to trust him. She'd actually thought he might be someone she could . . . marry. Hot tears gathered behind her eyes and thickened her throat. "It is my choice. I've made it so."

"You are who you are, Flora. You can't change that."

He didn't understand. She grasped for a shred to hold on to, not wanting to believe she could have been so wrong. "Please don't do this. Just let me go." She might as well have been trying to melt granite. She wrapped her fingers around the hard muscle of his arm and squeezed. It didn't give an inch. Impenetrable. Just like the rest of him.

His face was a stony mask. "I can't."

"Why?" Her voice broke.

He looked away, and she could see the tic in his neck. The only sign that he was not completely unaffected.

"Please." She was begging now and trying to hold back the tears that threatened to storm at any moment. "Don't hold me here. Let me go home."

"And where is home, Flora?"

She made a strangled sound in her throat as his poisoned arrow struck its target. She didn't have a home. She didn't have anyone. Certainly not this cold, emotionless stranger. "Anywhere but here," she whispered.

His eyes softened for an instant. "Is it really so bad being here with me?"

No. That was exactly the problem. She'd allowed herself to believe that he was different. Like a fool, she'd begun to trust him. The lessons of her mother's life had been in vain. She'd thought she was impervious, but she was wrong. When she thought of what had nearly happened between them, how she'd nearly succumbed, her stomach turned. She had to get away from here, before she traded her soul for a moment of pleasure in his arms.

"Let me go to Hector."

His eyes narrowed. "Your brother will not protect you."

"And you will?"

"With my life."

He said it so matter-of-factly, she almost believed him. *Fool.*

"Have care of Hector, Flora. Do not trust him."

Again she tried not to laugh at the bitter irony. "He is my brother. And unlike you, he doesn't want anything from me."

Loathing for him, for herself, banished the hurt, leaving an aching emptiness in her chest. The cold residue of disillusionment.

"A minute ago, you wanted me as much as I wanted you." He slid his thumb across her mouth. "Has anything really changed?"

And curse her traitorous body, she trembled. The rippling effect of his touch shuddered through her. Heart pounding, she jerked away, knowing that he knew exactly what he did to her. Her body wanted him. "You might succeed in seducing me." For if she stayed much longer, it seemed inevitable. She gazed deep into his eyes so there would be no mistake. "But I will never agree to marry you."

He hardened himself against the urge to reach out to her again and simply let her go. This time. Though he was tempted to prove to her just how wrong she was.

She was already his. She just didn't know it yet. The moment he'd touched her, her fate had been sealed. If she thought she had any control over this undeniable force between them, she was only fooling herself. She didn't know how powerful the yearnings of the body could be.

But he did.

Never had he wanted anything as badly as he wanted Flora. And he'd almost had her, but he'd been well caught in a trap of his own making. All thoughts of seduction, of coercing her into marrying him, had fallen to the wayside the moment he'd held her in his arms. When she'd pressed her soft body against him and opened her mouth to him so sweet and eager, something had imploded in his chest. His only thought had been to please her.

He thought of how wet and hot she'd been, how her sweet little hips had pressed against his hand, how preciously close she'd been to release.

He cursed the sudden rush of heat to his groin, his cock brought to quick life by the memories. His body still throbbed from the abrupt curtailment of their passion.

Damn Hector.

His heart skipped a beat at the sound of the door opening, thinking foolishly that it might be Flora coming back. But it was only his sister.

"What happened?" Gilly asked anxiously. "I saw Flora rush out of here, looking close to tears."

"There's nothing to worry about, Gilly. Go back to your chamber."

"Does it have something to do with the messenger I saw arriving earlier?"

He frowned. It wasn't like Gilly to ignore his instructions. Flora was having more of an influence over his sisters than he realized. And he didn't like it. He was about to repeat his directive when Gilly placed her hand on his arm, an affectionate sisterly gesture—and also, he realized, a rare one. When had his sisters stopped touching him? As girls, they always climbed all over him, giggling with some jest or prank.

"Please, I'm not a child. I only want to help."

He gave her a long look, seeing the adorable face—no

longer of a child, but of a young woman almost six and ten—and felt a sharp pang of melancholy. Of longing. How had it happened? How had his sisters grown up without his realizing it? He knew there was nothing he could have done to change it; he'd been consumed with fighting and protecting his clan. But that didn't mean he did not regret that circumstances were not different. That he'd not had more time for his brother and sisters. Regret made all the more poignant by his brother's imprisonment. But he would get him back.

"Please," Gilly repeated.

Lachlan didn't discuss clan business with his sisters, partially out of consideration for their innocence. He thought he was protecting them by keeping his troubles from them. But this time, he relented. A wry smile turned his mouth. His sisters, it seemed, weren't the only ones affected by Flora MacLeod. "It was a message from Duart."

"Flora's brother? But I didn't think you *really* intended to write to him and propose the exchange?"

"I didn't." He hadn't sent Hector a letter at all. It had all been a ruse to buy him precious time for wooing his recalcitrant bride.

"Then how did he find out so quickly that Flora was here?"

He'd been wondering the same thing. He could only hope that Hector wouldn't alert Rory. There would be hell to pay if the MacLeod discovered what Lachlan had done before he secured her agreement.

"I don't know," he answered. "But I intend to find out." He didn't want to consider that one of his own people could betray him. But who else would know? He'd have to think on it.

"What did the note say?"

He felt the anger flare inside him again. Hector's jabs were petty but struck hard nonetheless. He pulled it out and handed it to her. Gilly unfolded it and handed it right back to him, her brows furrowed. "It's in Scots."

"Exactly."

She thought for a minute, before a look of disgust appeared on her face. "I see."

"Yes, wasn't it fortunate that the only person in the castle who could read it happened to be standing right beside me?" he said bitterly, unable to hide his sarcasm. The timing couldn't have been worse. Normally, he didn't react to Hector's barbs, but Flora's presence had caused him to lash out. Without intending it, she had a way of making him feel somehow lacking.

"You let Flora read it?"

He shrugged. "I didn't have much choice."

"What did it say?"

"Hector's typical threats, nothing more. No doubt the main purpose was to shame me in front of his sister." Hector never wasted an opportunity to prod Lachlan for his so-called barbarity. "I'm sure he'd be pleased to know how well it worked." He would pay for that. As if Lachlan needed any more reason for revenge. He'd been looking forward to the day he would destroy Hector since he was nine years old.

Gilly scrunched up her nose. "That doesn't sound like Flora."

He hadn't thought so, either. But why else would she ask to leave right after she'd discovered that he hadn't been educated? Even after what had happened between them.

"Flora was raised in the Lowlands," he said tensely. "With their biases."

Gilly shook her head. "She's not like that. She would not ill judge you for something that could not be helped. You forget, she's been giving Mary and me daily instruction in Scots and Latin. Not once have I ever felt her pity or scorn. I don't think your lack of education would in any way change her opinion of you."

Lachlan shook his head, amazed how quickly Flora had won the loyalty of his sisters. Still, there was a ring of truth to what Gilly said. He looked at his young sister with increased estimation. Was she right? Had he misinterpreted Flora's reasons for wanting to leave?

If so, his misplaced anger might have caused more damage than he'd realized.

Gilly studied him, clearly puzzled. "I still don't understand why she was so upset."

"She wanted to leave. I told her it was impossible."

Gilly was watching him with a strange look on her face. "You care for her."

His jaw clenched. "No."

"Would it be so bad if you did?" she asked softly.

It would make it harder. And doing what needed to be done was already difficult, with each day as he learned more and more about her past and started to understand that beneath the headstrong exterior was a deep-seated fear of ending up like her mother, of helplessness, and of being at the mercy of those who might seek to control her. *Like me.* Justified or not.

And now she was aware of his intentions for marriage. It definitely made his job more difficult, but having one less secret between them gave him some measure of relief. But his goal hadn't changed. For more reasons than one, he couldn't let her go.

"Nothing has changed," he said. "If anything, the situation has grown graver."

Gilly nodded, sobered by the reminder. He watched as the conflicting emotions crossed her face. He could commiserate. He felt the same way, but unlike his sister, he'd become adept at masking his thoughts and feelings.

Finally, she lifted her gaze to his hesitantly. "You won't hurt her?" she asked in a small voice.

"No." A flash of Flora's luminous blue eyes shimmering with unshed tears, staring at him accusingly, swam before his eyes. He was no longer sure it could be avoided. "Not if it can be helped," he amended.

"What will you do?"

"What must be done." His options were few.

They stood there for some time in shared silence. The direness of the situation held them both in its solemn thrall.

How could one wee lass hold so many lives in the palm of her tiny hand?

Hector Maclean grunted deeply with each thrust, but he was finding little pleasure in the act. Not even the lush body spread out naked before him helped. His mind kept straying to the latest outrage committed by his nemesis.

He was not a patient man by nature, and the nearly twenty-five years he had waited to destroy Lachlan Maclean had taken their toll. The Laird of Coll had been a thorn in his side for years, but Hector vowed this latest insult would be the last. Abducting his sister. He thrust harder. Interfering with his plans. He ground his hips against her roughly. Coll would pay for the insult. With his life.

Damn bitch, he was losing his erection. "Move," he ordered.

The whey-faced little maid did as ordered and began to sway back and forth on her hands and knees, reaching back with her plump bottom to meet his thrusts. He could still feel her reluctance, but at least in taking her from behind, he didn't have to see her face.

He reached around to squeeze her enormous breasts, which hung so low that they almost touched the ground, pinching her flat nipples to a peak.

He stopped and reached for his goblet. But even the

whisky suddenly tasted bitter. Thinking he was done, the lass tried to crawl away, but he gave her a sharp slap on her bottom and pulled her hips angrily against him, letting her know otherwise. He jabbed her harder, showing his displeasure, and she made a pathetic little yelping sound.

A hot surge of lust filled his groin. That was more like it. Normally he wasn't so rough, but the anger inside him had festered like an open wound. Violence was its only release. If not against Coll, then . . . He slapped her again, leaving a flat angry handprint on her pale skin.

He slammed into her harder and harder, his frenzy only increasing with her muffled sounds of distress. *Oh yes.* That was it. He felt the pressure building and slapped her again. She cried out, and with a few rough pumps, he spewed his seed deep inside her.

He pulled out, and she collapsed on the bed, curling into a tiny ball, whimpering. The sound infuriated him. He pushed her roughly from the bed and tossed her a coin. Which was more than she deserved. Even coming had left him strangely unsatisfied. It was probably the chit's fault. These people of Coll were a surly bunch.

They blamed him for their circumstances when it was their laird who should feel their wrath. It was *his* defiance that had put them in this position.

The girl reached for her gown, but he wrenched it from her hands and used it to wipe himself before handing it back to her. After gathering the rest of her clothing, she left, never once raising her eyes. At least she knew her place.

Which was more than could be said of her former laird. Anger and resentment returned in full force, not softened by his release one whit. Coll's continued refusal to bow to him as chief ate at him like acid. It was a blow to Hector's pride that could be satisfied only by Coll's death.

He needed a plan. A way to get his sister back and destroy Coll at the same time. Poor little Flora. He had fond enough memories of the girl to regret that she'd become involved. But the willful lass had brought it on herself.

If Coll had touched her, Hector swore that he would not live long enough to regret it.

Chapter 9

❖

Flora fought to control the panic rising in her chest. But it was dark and cold, and danger seemed to permeate the night like a heavy wet plaid. The knowledge that it was likely all in her mind drew little comfort. She knew well what she risked.

A sharp wind blew across the rocky crags, peppering her face with droplets of sea spray and filling her nose with the sharp salty tang of the ocean, though the blustery wind wasn't strong enough to keep the mist at bay. As gray and soupy as gruel, it was a double-edged sword. The mist would help cloak her escape from the watchful eye of the guards, but it would also make navigating the treacherous sound even more perilous.

I can do this, she told herself. The Isle of Mull was close enough to see the heather and bluebells carpeting the hillsides; the boat—really more of a skiff—was small enough for her to manage on her own.

She had no choice. She had to leave this place. After what had happened today in the laird's solar, she could not stay another day. Disappointment still burned in her throat. He was just like everyone else, wanting to use her for his own ends. Her chest tightened, leaving her amazed by how much it still hurt.

She was a fool. No man would ever be able to see beyond the prize.

She took another step down the path and felt the rocks give way beneath her foot. Her arms reached out wildly in the night air for something to hold on to. For a long, hair-raising moment, she thought she might slide off the cliff. Somehow she managed to regain her balance, but she couldn't prevent the small landslide of rocks from tumbling down the hill.

A dog barked. And then another.

She stood stone still, ears cocked, heart pounding in her chest as she waited to see whether the noise would draw the attention of the guards. Not for the first time, she cursed the flimsy satin slippers that would have been perfect for a wedding but had little traction on the slick pathway. With few women at the castle, more appropriate shoes had not been available. For the second time, those once beautiful shoes could ruin everything.

A minute passed, and finally, hearing no voices, she exhaled.

Although it was well past midnight, a castle never slept. Guards were always stationed around the *barmkin* wall, ready for an attack. It was her luck that they hadn't anticipated an escape. Hiding in the shadows of the keep, she'd lain in wait for her opportunity. It had taken some time, but finally, with the changing of the guard, she was able to slip across the courtyard and through the gate before the porter had made his rounds, locking it for the night.

Now with even greater care after her near disastrous tumble, she worked her way slowly down the steep path to the small inlet where she'd noticed the skiff. Every detail of that day was forever branded on her consciousness. It was the day he'd kissed her with such passion and awakened her desire from its innocent slumber. The day she'd allowed herself to hope.

She shook off the memory. That was before she'd learned the truth.

Her feet sank deep into sand as she stepped onto the beach. The mist had dissipated enough to make out the shadow of a large object a short way down the beach. Exactly where she remembered it. She sighed with relief.

Her pulse quickened as she drew nearer. Tentatively. Every nerve ending set on edge. Wishing there were another way. But the sea was her only hope of success. The laird stabled a small number of horses within the *barmkin* in a small enclosure built against the north side of the wall, but she'd never be able to steal a horse without being seen. On foot, she would never be able to outrun them. Not across the rugged open terrain of Morvern. A place of endless vistas of barren moorland and dangerous peat bogs, without the cover of trees in which to hide.

It had to be the boat.

She swallowed the well of panic rising in her throat as, unbidden, the memories assailed her. It was a long time ago, but the memory of her near drowning was as strong as if it had happened only yesterday.

She'd been seven, staying at Inveraray for the summer with her aunt and uncle, the former Earl of Argyll. The occasion had been a wedding feast for her cousin Archie, the present earl, and the first time all of her brothers— and even a few of her sisters—had all been in the same place at the same time. She'd wanted desperately to impress them, so when she saw them going to the loch for a swim one morning, she'd traipsed along after them. When Rory had asked her whether she knew how to swim, knowing they wouldn't let her go if she said no, she'd nodded confidently.

Everything had been fine. She'd taken off her stockings and slippers and plunged her toes in the cool water. The rest of the group was in the middle of the loch, splashing and diving and laughing. Curious to hear what they were saying, she'd taken a few more steps

toward them. And then a few more. And then . . .
promptly dropped into a black void.

She'd never forget the feeling of the dark, suffocating
water closing over her, filling her nose, her mouth, her
lungs. There was a moment where the world stilled—
where what was happening didn't seem real. Where
every second extended for a minute. She paddled her
arms and for a moment bobbed near the surface, before
the weight of her body dragged her down like a rock.

She remembered thinking how dark and murky it was
and how she couldn't even see her hands in front of her
face. She remembered thinking how angry her mother
would be that Flora had lied. But most of all, Flora remembered not being able to breathe.

She was lucky. Her struggle, the single splash that
she'd managed above the surface, had been witnessed by
her brother Alex. Her brothers, all four of them—for
William had still been alive then—reached her just in
time. The water had been over ten feet deep, and Rory
said later that she'd been lying on the bottom, curled up
like a mermaid—or the *Maighdean na Tuinne,* as he
called them.

She'd never forget her mother's tears or her brothers'
collective anger. She'd never seen them so unified. To a
one, they'd been furious that she'd lied to them. Even
Alex had yelled at her. Her excuse that they wouldn't
have allowed her to come if they knew the truth had
been met by deaf ears.

The next time the group went to the loch, she stayed
at the castle.

A pattern, it seemed, that was repeated ever after.

Her gaze fell to the skiff, resting peacefully on its side
a few feet up from the water's edge.

She steeled herself against the sudden flash of panic. *I
can do this.*

Her fear of the water wasn't usually an issue, since

she'd been raised mostly in the Lowlands. Not the way it would be in the Isles, where Highlanders ruled the vast seaways on their *birlinns* like their Norse ancestors before them. Their prowess on the water was part of their way of life. Yet another reason she didn't belong here.

Indeed, the journey a few weeks ago was the first time she'd been in a boat in years. She'd been fine. She'd hoped that maybe her fear had lessened, but now she knew better. It was *Lachlan* who'd abated her fear. His presence had made the difference. Even then, she'd intuitively trusted his strength.

But not any longer.

Now she trusted only herself.

God, how she missed her mother.

Her fingers were stiff and awkward with the cold as she worked the knot of the rope, but eventually she managed to untie the mooring. After checking to make sure the oars were inside, she pushed the boat as quietly as possible to the water. The scrape of the hull against the sand and stones sounded unnaturally loud, but in a few minutes the water caught it with its natural buoy.

This was it. After sliding on the pattens she'd brought for this purpose, she took her first tentative step into the water. A black wave of nausea gave her a moment of dizziness, but she fought it back. She forced her feet forward until the water lapped around her knees. Taking a deep breath for courage, she climbed in. The skiff rolled sharply to the side, and she bit back a scream. Lying prone across the bottom, she gripped the sides until her knuckles turned white as the small craft rocked back and forth with her weight. Eventually, it steadied. Only then did she carefully adjust her position to sitting. Not giving herself time to think, she took one of the oars in her hand and began to paddle—her confidence increasing with each stroke.

It was slow, difficult work. Though the sea appeared

calm, the current was surprisingly strong. After a few minutes, she paused and turned around to check her progress, dismayed to see that she'd traveled only fifty feet or so beyond the beach.

It was going to be a long night. But she could do it.

God, she was cold. She tried to adjust her cloak, but her wet fingers were like ice. Her feet were completely soaked, not just from dragging in the skiff, but also from the few inches of standing water in the bottom of the hull. She should have been more careful when she paddled not to splash water in the boat.

Not giving herself time to think, she plunged the oar in again and pulled hard, wanting to put as much distance between her and the beach as possible. Fighting the current that seemed intent on pulling her back.

Something called to her.

A voice hovering on the edge of the wind. A longing deep in her soul. An invisible force that compelled her to turn around. She gazed up to the keep looming in the darkness, barely able to make it out through the shadowy haze. An overwhelming sense of sadness hit her. She thought of how much she'd miss Mary, Gilly, Murdoch, Alasdair, and even the crotchety old Morag. She regretted not being able to say good-bye to the girls but swore that as soon as she was able, she would send for them. No matter what *he* said.

Lachlan Maclean. She hoped she never saw him again. Even now the memory of him tormented her. He'd confused her, evoking a maelstrom of emotions that she didn't begin to understand. Except that it hurt.

A single tear slid out of the corner of her eye. Furious, she brushed it away with the back of her hand.

She'd waited too long. She should have tried to escape as soon as he'd allowed her freedom to move about the castle. Before she'd grown attached. Perhaps then she could have prevented the burning ache located precariously close to her heart.

With one last look behind her, she faced forward, a determined set to her shoulders, and resumed paddling.

The thought that he might have been wrong about Flora's reaction haunted Lachlan throughout the day. After what had happened, he wasn't surprised when she begged off from the evening meal. He'd thought about searching her out but decided to leave her in peace. For now.

Unable to sleep, he sat sprawled out in a chair beside the fire, gazing at the bright orange flames until his eyes hurt.

Hell.

He slammed the goblet he'd been holding onto the table beside him with a curse. The strange disquiet prickling inside him could not be washed away with *cuirm*. He stood up, paced around his chamber for a few minutes, and decided he'd had enough. Before he could think better of it, he left his room and climbed the two levels to the top of the tower. Standing outside her door, he braced himself, knocked—and heard only silence in response.

Thinking she might well be sleeping, he knocked again, this time louder. A vague uneasy feeling began to take hold of him. His fingers closed around the handle, and slowly he pulled the door open.

The first thing he noticed was the chill. And then the emptiness. The fire had gone out long ago, and the familiar floral scent that seemed to permeate the air had faded. Though the shutters were closed, the lantern from the niche in the corridor outside filled the room with soft light. His gaze fell to the bed. But he already knew. The sinking feeling had penetrated to his gut.

She'd run.

After what had happened this afternoon, he should have anticipated this.

The door to the guard's room opposite her door opened, revealing Alasdair, who'd obviously just been roused from his bed by the noise.

"Is there a problem, my laird?"

Lachlan tried to control the sudden explosion of rage. Or cold fear, he wasn't sure which. He clenched his fists to his sides to prevent himself from grabbing the man by his shirt and shaking him. "Yes. Damn it. The lass is not in her room. When did you last check on her?"

The old guardsman's face paled. "About an hour ago. Before I went to bed, as you ordered."

His orders. It was his fault she'd escaped. He'd grown too lax. He'd trusted her word. He should never have removed the permanent guard from her door. If anything happened to her, he had only himself to blame. She was headstrong. Willful. And scared. A dangerous combination.

"She couldn't have gone very far, my laird."

But Lachlan was already storming down the stairs. He focused on the task at hand, blocking out everything else. His only thought was to find her. The military tactician took over, and his mind immediately went to work analyzing her most likely escape routes, methodically sorting through the possibilities and prioritizing the more likely scenarios. Relying on the skills honed by years of battle. But with the realization that no battle had ever affected him so acutely. Her life might well depend on his ability to think and plan quickly and clearly. There was no room for mistakes.

"Rouse as many men as you can find," he yelled behind him to Alasdair. "And check the stables," he added, though he knew it was unlikely that she would have been able to sneak a horse past the guards. *Nothing* should sneak past his guards. There would be hell to pay if he discovered otherwise.

The castle had two points of entry: the sea-gate and the landward-gate. As the sea-gate led directly to the dock where his *birlinns* sat, well guarded, he realized that she must have left by the other. Still, he'd have someone check the sea-gate and dock, just to make sure.

He exited the keep and strode down the forestairs two steps at a time. A few torches lit the courtyard, enabling him to take quick appraisal of the situation. Nothing appeared amiss, which was a bad sign. If she'd escaped, she'd done so without being noticed.

His arrival immediately drew the attention of the guardsmen scattered around the perimeter of the *barmkin* wall.

The porter appeared. "My laird, is something—"

"Are the gates locked?"

The man looked confused. "Yes, my laird. A short while ago at the changing of the guard, as usual."

By now, a few more men had gathered round. "Mistress MacLeod is missing. I want every available man looking for her." His voice was firm and surprisingly calm. Detached. Emotionless. He'd always possessed an unnatural calm under pressure, but his iron control had never been stretched so close to the snapping point. "Did any of you hear anything unusual? Anything at all?"

A stream of "No, my laird" came back to him. But for one man. He stepped forward. "The dogs barked not long after I came on, my laird."

Lachlan fought to stay calm, but he knew. That's when she'd left. Castigation would come later, once they'd found her. "How long ago was that?"

"A half hour. Maybe a bit less."

She didn't have much of a head start. They would find

her. Unless the bogs or the cliffs found her first. Bile crept up the back of his throat. *Don't think about it.*

"From what direction did the dogs bark?"

The man shook his head. "I can't be sure, my laird. North, perhaps?"

Consistent with his theory that she'd departed from the landward-gate, as the sea-gate only led west. Alasdair had returned with more men. Lachlan was vaguely aware of the sounds of the castle stirring behind him and of the increased brightness as more and more lanterns and torches were lit.

"All of the horses are accounted for, my laird," Alasdair said. "She's on foot."

Anticipating his next request, Alasdair had ordered his destrier led out of the stable.

Lachlan started issuing orders. Sending a man down to the sea-gate to account for all the *birlinns*. Sending others both north and south along the rocky seashore. But most of the men would come with him, on horseback and on foot, to roam the moors.

Within minutes, the courtyard was crowded with men and horses. Mary and Gilly had come down the stairs, dressed in their nightclothes with only a plaid for warmth. He could see the worry in their faces, but he didn't have time to soothe their fears. Not now. Not when every second he delayed might make the difference between life and death.

He mounted his horse and turned back to them. "Search every corner of the keep." Just to be sure. But he *knew* she'd fled.

"We will," Mary said.

"Find her," Gilly said.

He nodded, his face grim. "I intend to."

The gate opened, and Lachlan led the rest of his men through in a thunderous stampede. Once outside, they disbanded like the spokes on a wheel, radiating out in all directions.

He'd ordered the men to ride for a half hour, then turn around and head back by a slightly different route. Those on foot, he'd sent in a zigzag pattern, hoping to cover more ground. The mist would make it hazardous for all involved. But most of all for Flora, who had no knowledge of the countryside.

Senses honed, Lachlan rode hard for a few minutes, playing everything over and over in his mind to make sure he hadn't missed something.

Had she learned nothing from her failed elopement? How could she behave so recklessly?

Fear, he realized. Of him.

He couldn't believe that she wouldn't recognize the danger in traversing unfamiliar territory in the misty darkness. She'd been outside the gates only once. When he'd taken her down the pathway to the beach.

The scene came back to him so vividly, he recalled every detail. She was seated on a rock by the edge of the beach with her golden hair streaming in the wind, the crystal-clear view to Mull, the white sand, the—

His heart crashed to his feet. *Oh God. The old skiff.* It had belonged to a fisherman who'd had a hut at the end of the beach. He'd died a few years back, and the boat hadn't been used since. By now, the wood would be dried out. It would leak like a sieve.

Why hadn't he thought of it? It made perfect sense. But she wouldn't realize . . .

He pulled hard on the reins, turning his mount in one smooth motion. A strange emotion gripped him—a fear so strong, it could only be panic. He lowered his head to the thick, powerful neck of his destrier, and he rode. As fast as he'd ever ridden in his life.

*   *   *

By the time Flora realized what was happening, it was too late. But she turned the boat around back toward shore anyway. Thoughts of escape had given way to a fight for survival.

At first, she'd thought it was her inexperienced paddling filling the skiff. Soon, she realized it was something else. In the darkness, she hadn't been able to see what was happening, but she could feel the water rising. Slowly but surely, it climbed farther and farther up her leg.

Her boat was leaking.

She tried paddling, hoping that the current she'd fought against so determinedly only moments before would take her back to the beach. But the skiff had grown so heavy, it was barely moving. The shore that had only minutes ago seemed so close now seemed infinitely far away. She hadn't traveled more than a few hundred yards, but it didn't matter. She couldn't swim a foot, let alone the distance to safety. When it was clear that she would never make it back to shore by paddling, she started bailing. Scooping the icy seawater with her hands and tossing it out as if her life depended on it. Ignoring the obvious fact that it did. So focused was she on her task, for a while she forgot to be scared.

She gave a valiant effort, but it kept filling. Higher and higher. The skiff, in turn, began to sink lower and lower. The sea had claimed it, and it would not give it back.

But she wouldn't give up. Not as long as there was a chance.

She didn't want to die.

Still bailing, she glanced back toward shore. And blinked, thinking her eyes might be playing tricks on her. But no. Her pulse leapt. There was no mistake. Peering into the haze, she could see the castle glowing brightly in the darkness. Even from here she could see the unmistakable signs of life. Perhaps someone had noticed her gone and they were looking for her? Hope swelled in her chest. He would find her. She knew it deep in her heart. Knew it with a certainty that could not be assailed. If it were humanly possible, Lachlan Maclean would save her. She just had to hold on long enough for him to reach her.

She wanted to stand up and wave her arms, but she dared not stop bailing. "Help me!" she cried out in the darkness over and over until her voice grew hoarse. Someone had to hear her.

With a renewed burst of energy, she bailed, scooping out the water as fast as she could. Not wanting to acknowledge the futility of her efforts. The orange glow of a torch appeared upon the shore. A horseman. A feeling of euphoria crashed over her.

They've found me. Tears of joy streamed down her cheeks, and she yelled again. Yelled as loud as her voice could carry.

"Here! I'm *here!*"

The skiff had drifted back toward shore, but it was clear the rider couldn't hear her. She cursed the mist, the darkness, and everything else she could think of.

A few minutes later, the orange light that had seemed a beacon of life faded. Taking with it her last ray of hope, leaving only desperation and despair in its black wake.

The cruel disappointment almost killed her. Her weary body screamed to just give up. She was freezing, and her arms and back ached with the effort of paddling and then of bailing.

She wanted to cry out with frustration and rage and the unfairness of it all, but the scream lodged in her throat. There was no one to hear.

Only that much maligned streak of stubbornness kept her scooping the icy seawater with her frozen hands.

*   *   *

Lachlan intercepted a few of his men near the castle and sent them back with instructions to launch the *birlinns* and search every inch of the sound between here and Mull—in case he was right. With most of the men roaming the countryside, it would take time to find others to man the boats. And time was something he didn't have.

Never had he so badly wanted to be wrong.

He calculated how long it would take the skiff to fill, and fear gripped his chest.

Once he'd reached the rocky precipice above the inlet, he dismounted and raced the rest of the way down the narrow path to the beach. His worst fears were realized when he looked down the white spans of sand and saw that the old skiff was indeed gone.

His breath lodged in his throat as he scanned the horizon above the sea through the fog. *Be there, damn you. . . .*

Nothing. Damn it, where was she? He ran into the water and tried again. Peering hard into the darkness, cursing the mist that shrouded the moonlight, blurring night and sea into one murky cauldron.

His eyes moved purposefully, intently, back and forth over the waves. . . .

There. His gaze caught a movement perhaps a hundred feet from shore. A shimmer of something silvery. His heart stopped and then raced full force. Her hair. The boat was all but sunken under the water, which was why he hadn't seen her at first.

Why was she still holding on to the boat? Why hadn't she just started swimming? The answer hit him. She didn't know how to swim. How could she be so reckless to try to escape in a damn boat? Understanding eviscerated the tenuous hold he had on his control. She'd been that desperate to get away from him. Apparently, a watery death was preferable to the idea of marriage to him.

"Flora!" he yelled, running farther into the sea toward her.

He thought her head turned, but he couldn't be sure. Without thinking, he dove into the waves and started to swim as if his life depended on it, every stroke strong and determined. He'd grown up swimming in the waters around the Isles and usually won the speed events when his clan participated in the Highland games, but the current of the sound was ruthless. The time it was taking to reach her seemed interminable. He checked her position every time he lifted his head to take a breath.

He was about halfway there when he heard her voice. "Lachlan . . ."

It was so soft, he thought he'd imagined it. He paused for only a second, then heard it again. "Lachlan . . ." The plea in her voice cut through him like a knife. He heard her hope. Her trust. She believed in him. And it ate at him. He couldn't let her down.

"Hurry. I can't—"

The choking sound stopped his heart. Her head bobbed once with the waves and disappeared.

"Flora!" The voice that tore from him was not his own. He felt as if his heart were being ripped out of his chest. She was only about fifty feet away. His body exploded with uncontrollable rage. He wasn't going to be able to reach her in time. "Hold on!" he yelled, even though he knew she couldn't hear him, right before he dove into the water.

He swam to the place he'd last seen her. Swam until his lungs were about to explode. Only knowing that hers were doing the same kept him going. He tried opening his eyes underwater, but the salt burned and it was too damn dark to see anything. Swimming near the bottom, he reached around blindly, grabbing for anything.

His lungs were burning, screaming for air. He couldn't hold his breath much longer. *Think of her. She's drowning, damn it.* He was frantic now. Reaching wildly around him. Suddenly, mercifully, he felt something. His fingers tangled in something too fine to be kelp. Her hair. He could have cried with relief. He'd found her. Pulling her harshly against him, he wrapped his arm around her stomach, holding her snuggly under her ribs, and shot to the surface.

When his head broke through the water, he gasped in air. But she still fell limply against him. Lifeless. "Flora!" He heard the raw panic in his voice. Panic that had shred the last bit of his reserve. He couldn't lose her. Instinctively, he jerked her hard against him, hitching his arm against her stomach. The swift movement caused her to spasm, and she choked, seawater gurgling from her mouth. He turned her around to face him. Cradling her face in his hands, he urged her with his voice. "Flora. God. I've got you. Can you hear me?"

Her eyes fluttered and closed. But she was alive.

He pressed his lips on her forehead, tasting only salty seawater. She was like ice. He brought his face to hers, cheek to cheek, and felt the unmistakable wisp of her breath on his neck. Shallow but true. His skin prickled, every nerve ending flared at the sweet sensation. But he could not savor it for long.

The danger wasn't over.

Rolling her around so that she floated on her back, he swam her to shore. A much easier proposition than on the way out. Reaching the safety of the beach, he lifted her in his arms, wrenching her from the steel jaws of the sea that had tried to claim her.

He carried her a few feet up the beach and set her down carefully, kneeling beside her.

"Flora." He shook her shoulders gently. "Wake up."

She looked so still. So horribly still. "Flora." He shook

her gently, his chest squeezing painfully. "Please wake up. I need you to wake up." *I need you.*

Her eyes fluttered again and then—blissfully—opened. And he found himself looking into the achingly familiar fathomless depths. He felt a rush of relief so strong, he could have wept. Instead he kissed her.

He knew there wasn't time, that he had to get her back, but he couldn't help it. He needed to know that she was alive.

His mouth covered hers in a searing kiss, as if he could warm the cold from her lips with the heat of his passion. He kissed her with a raw desperation born of fear. With all the intensity of the emotions she'd exposed inside him. He told her with his lips what he couldn't admit to himself.

In that one brief instant, he told her so much. When he lifted his head, her eyes met his and he could see her surprise.

"Lachlan, I . . ." Her eyes fluttered again, then closed as she slipped back into unconsciousness.

For a moment, he thought she'd died. Fear gripped him again as pressed his hand against her chest, relieved to feel the precious beat of her heart. He swore, still breathing hard as he gathered her in his arms again. The currents of the sound had sapped him of his strength, but he knew that if he did not get her back to the keep, to warmth, she would die.

There was nothing more he could do for her until he got her back to the castle. Her shallow breath against the open V in his shirt would be all the assurance he would have. He held on to it like a precious talisman. A lifeline that gave him strength where there was none.

His breath came hard and heavy between his lips. His legs burned with each dragging step across the sandy beach. Her normally insignificant weight grew heavier and heavier as he climbed swiftly and steadily up the rocky path. Pressing on. Using every last reserve of energy.

He wouldn't let himself think about how cold she was. How long she'd been in the freezing water. He swallowed. How long she'd been underneath. He wouldn't think about the pallor of her skin resting against his sopping shirt. Her bloodless lips. The dark shadows under her eyes. It was just the moonlight. . . .

God take him, she wouldn't die. He wouldn't let her. As if by the sheer force of his will, he would defy anyone, God or man, who sought to take her from him.

She was his. She'd belonged to him from the first moment he'd seen her. And not because of his devil's bargain with her cousin Argyll that would ensure his brother's safety and his clan's future. No, the truth was far more elemental than that.

The fierce pounding in his chest did not lie. Gilly had been right. He did care for her. For the first time in his life, he couldn't deny an emotional attachment to a woman—he'd thought himself dedicated to his family and clan alone. He was wrong.

Finally, he'd reached the top of the path and his horse. Beyond exhausted, he was moving mechanically, instinct, forged by years of pushing himself to the limit of endurance, taking over. He needed every last ounce of it right now. After laying her across his saddle, he mounted behind her and nestled her in his arms again, then rode hard for the keep.

He didn't take the time to explain to the men he passed along the way but simply ordered them to spread the word that he'd found her and to return to the castle.

No longer able to feel her breath against his skin with the wind of his ride, he held his hand against her chest, needing the surety of her beating heart, but terrified by how soft and faint it was—and how dangerously slow.

He entered the gate to a flurry of activity. Activity that

stopped as soon as he came galloping inside, soaking wet with his precious bundle limp against him.

Gilly and Mary must have been watching by the door, because they appeared beside him before his feet hit the ground. Some of his men, appraising his condition, moved to help him, but he held them back, his whole body shaking with effort. No one else would touch her. She was his.

"You found her, thank God," Gilly said. Drawing nearer, she gasped and voiced the fear that had made the courtyard as quiet as a tomb from the moment he entered. "What happened? What's wrong with her?" Her voice broke into a sob. "Is she dead?"

"No!" he said savagely. "She still breathes. But I need to get her inside and warm." He plowed up the forestairs, savoring the blast of heat as he entered the keep. Not hesitating, he headed straight for the stairs.

"Where are you taking her?" Mary asked, hustling along beside him.

His face was grim as he gave his sister a fierce stare. "To my bed."

Chapter 10

❖

Lachlan didn't think about the symbolism or the propriety of having Flora in his bed. All he knew was that it was warmer in his chamber. The fire would still be burning. And he knew exactly what had to be done.

Mary's eyes widened, but she didn't argue, though clearly it worried her. Not because she feared that he would do something untoward—she knew him better than that—but because she knew what it said. Taking Flora to his room, rather than any other, amounted to a public declaration of his intentions. She was his, and he was saying as much.

Lachlan didn't give a damn what anyone thought, he wanted her with him. It was as simple as that.

Though in the back of his mind, he realized that when it came to Flora, nothing was simple. It hadn't been since the first day he'd laid eyes on her.

Taking two steps at a time, he quickly reached the second floor. Since the moment he'd entered the castle, he'd been focused on one thing: getting her warm and dry as soon as possible. Moving from the stairwell into the corridor outside his chamber, he turned back to his sister. "Bring me blankets, fresh clothes, anything to make her warm."

Mary nodded, keeping step with him. "Oh, Lachlan, why did she do this? Was she so unhappy here?"

He felt a sharp pang in his chest. *Yes*. But seeing the guilt on his sister's face, he said, "I don't know, lass."

"I thought she liked us."

"She does." He glanced down at Flora's face, cold realization shuddering through him. "It has nothing to do with you or Gilly," he said firmly. "She left because of me."

Mary gave him a long, tormented look before hurrying to do his bidding.

It seemed half the castle had followed him up the stairs, including Gilly and Morag. Shifting Flora's weight to one arm, he opened the door with the other, immediately feeling the welcome blast of heat.

Until that moment, he hadn't realized how cold he was himself. So attuned was he to Flora's needs, he hadn't noticed his own shivering. Dread engulfed him, knowing that he hadn't been in the frigid water nearly as long as Flora.

He had to move fast.

Forcing himself to relinquish her, if only momentarily, he carefully laid her down on his bed. And for the first time, he examined her in the light.

He felt a stab of fear so acute, it gave him a vicious jolt. If he hadn't just felt her heart beating against his hand, he would have thought she no longer lived. Not a touch of color warmed her pale skin. Her long, thick lashes lay in tiny icy spikes against her pallid cheeks, her normally red lips were a deathly shade of blue, and her golden hair seemed frozen, plastered in long sheets to her head.

He gazed at her with his heart in his throat. She looked so small and fragile. And so horribly still. Like a wax doll he'd once seen.

To leave him, she'd risked her life. That she would take such a risk to be rid of him hit like a lead ball in his chest.

He checked her still, damp cheek with his hand. God,

she was cold. If he didn't do something drastic, she was going to die.

After unfastening the wool cloak from around her neck, he quickly started working the ties and hooks of her gown.

Hearing a noise behind him, he turned to see Morag adding another block of peat to the fire. But a roaring fire wouldn't be enough. He needed a way to bring her body temperature up fast. Very fast.

Lachlan exchanged a meaningful look with his old nursemaid. Morag moved to help him, but he shook her off. They both knew what had to be done, but he would do it himself.

"Is there anything I can do?" Gilly asked.

His gaze flicked to his sister standing hesitantly in the doorway, a few of his men—including Alasdair and Allan—behind her.

He shook his head, forcing himself to stay calm, though panic welled in his chest. "Not right now, lass."

Mary bustled in, setting down the extra plaids and clothing at the foot of the bed. Seeing what he was about to do, she blushed with understanding.

"Come," Morag said to Gilly and Mary, "there is nothing we can do for her now. The laird will do what needs to be done."

"But what—" Gilly broke off as Morag shuffled her out of the room, her question and Morag's response lost behind the firmly shut door. Though bold and adventuresome, in many ways his youngest sister was still an utter innocent.

Cursing his large, cumbersome fingers and the intricacy of even a simple gown, he started tearing off her clothes, doing his best to preserve her modesty. Though he knew there was no other choice, he also realized she would be embarrassed at best and furious at worst. Perhaps he should have let Morag help, but he couldn't stand aside. She was his.

He paused, catching sight of the amulet hidden under the layers of clothing. Though part of him wished it had fallen to the bottom of the sea—taking the curse with it—the other part of him was happy for Flora because he knew how much she treasured it. He removed it from her neck, attributing the tingling in his fingers to the cold. He made quick work of the rest of her wet garments, removing them piece by piece until she wore only her shift. And then he took that off, too.

He drew in his breath, unable to completely ignore the exquisite details of the naked beauty he'd revealed. Details that would be stored for later. Her honor would be preserved this night, but he wasn't blind. He'd yearned to strip off her clothes and to see her naked in his bed for a long time. But not like this. Right now she needed his body not for pleasure, but for survival. And he would give it to her gladly. With no conditions.

But hell, she took his breath away.

The next time he took off her clothes, he swore he would savor every gorgeous inch of her.

With one last glance that warmed his blood more effectively than any fire, he forced his mind back on the task at hand. Realizing the damp had soaked through the bed linens, he slid one of the blankets Mary had brought underneath her. The rest he layered on top of her.

Standing up from beside the bed, he started to tear off his own wet clothing. First the plaid he'd worn as a cloak, and then the linen shirt, and finally his trews and boots.

Then, before he could think about what he was about to do, he slid into the bed beside her and pulled her gently into his arms, immediately shivering, shocked by the touch of her icy skin against his. Damn, she was freezing. Dangerously so. Bracing himself, he snuggled her firmly against him and felt a fierce wave of tenderness swell hard against his ribs.

Tenderness that spoke of just how much she meant to him.

The thought that he could lose her tore a gash across his chest. Right now, he'd give anything to have her fully clothed, eyes flashing, defying him as usual.

If only she would move. Though he'd nestled her firmly against his body, she felt so rigid. And she was still so deathly cold.

The removal of his own wet clothing and the heat from the fire had rejuvenated him almost immediately, but even ensconced in the heated blanket of his body, she'd barely warmed. The chill had penetrated bone deep.

Warm, damn you, he swore, as if he could command her temperature back to normal. He had enough determination for both of them, but Flora was a fighter—he knew she would not give up. It stunned him how long she'd managed to stay afloat in the leaky skiff. Yet perhaps it shouldn't. Her tenacity and strength were two of the qualities he most admired about her.

Though right now she seemed anything but. She seemed fragile and vulnerable—as if with one false touch, he might break her. He couldn't believe how small she was in his arms. Or how sweetly feminine. He'd lain with many women—done much more than lain, actually—but none had ever felt so significant. Simply holding her moved him more than any previous sexual liaison.

With her nestled up against him, her bottom tucked against his groin, he was acutely aware of everything about her. From the blond tendrils of hair that were springing into soft waves as they started to dry, to her narrow shoulders and slim hips, to the tips of her tiny frozen feet. To every incredible inch of her flawless naked skin.

She smelled of seawater and salt, and nothing had ever smelled so wonderful. Because she lived.

He could no longer pretend that she was just a means to an end. Not once when he'd discovered she'd gone had he thought about his devil's bargain with Argyll. He'd thought only about her safety.

Her attempted escape and near drowning had forced him to realize that he wanted her not just for his plan, but for himself. It didn't change what he had to do. If anything, his feelings only complicated matters. Damn it, his duty should be his only consideration. His brother needed him to be ruthless. But Flora had engaged his conscience. Doing what must be done was no longer a simple proposition. If it ever was.

He pulled her a little closer and held her a little tighter, reacting unconsciously to the sudden amorphous threat that seemed to have invaded the chamber.

For hours he lay like that. Holding her close, a ball of emotion lodged firmly in his throat as he waited for the danger to pass. Slowly, the harsh bite of cold faded as his body warmed her and she softened against him, breathing steady.

It was near dawn when she finally stirred. She turned to him in her sleep. Burrowing her head under his chin and placing her hand on his chest. A hand that was as searing as a brand. His chest hitched. Raw emotion surged inside him, ignited by the instinctive trusting movement. Trust that tore him apart. He wanted to deserve that trust.

But in doing his duty, he was manipulating her in a way that he knew would hurt her, yet he couldn't risk telling her the truth. It wasn't his life at stake, but his brother's.

Two months ago, he'd gone to Argyll for help. Lach-

Ian recalled standing inside the great hall of Inveraray Castle and staring with a mixture of admiration and loathing at one of the most powerful—and wily—men in Scotland, Archibald "the Grim" Campbell, Earl of Argyll.

Argyll sat on a raised dais near the fireplace in a gilded chair with a large scarlet velvet cushion. It looked remarkably like a throne, which probably wasn't a coincidence.

Argyll peered down the length of his long nose with dark eyes, the sharp angles of his features lending credence to the clan's claim of Norman ancestry. "So the king has seized your brother. What do you expect me to do about it?"

Lachlan fought to control his temper. "I thought our bond of manrent included protection in return for the *calp* duties I've paid to you."

The earl's eyes narrowed dangerously. "I do not need to be reminded of our agreement, or my duty thereby. But what do you suggest I do? Storm the king's castle to free your brother?"

"You have influence with the king and the Privy Council. The king's actions were unjust. Hector has raided my lands and illegally stolen my castle, he has no legal claim to Coll."

"Duart claims otherwise, since you refused your duty to him as chief."

Lachlan held his anger in check. "He is not my chief. And Hector is hardly a friend to you," he reminded him. Argyll and Hector had been feuding since Hector married without the earl's consent.

Argyll gave him a hard stare, surprised no doubt by Lachlan's refusal to play toady to his despot. Lachlan pandered to no man, powerful or not.

Argyll turned his attention to a man who entered the hall and handed him a missive. Annoyed by the interruption, Lachlan attempted to wait patiently as Argyll scanned the letter. The earl's face darkened with fury. He let out a long string of expletives, displaying a temper completely incongruous with the stoic unflappability that had earned him his epithet—the Grim. He stood up, crumpled the letter into his fist, and tossed it into the fire.

"That chit will be the death of me."

"My lord?" Lachlan asked.

Argyll turned back to him as if he'd forgotten he was still there. He studied him hard, giving him a long, calculating look. Some of the anger left him, and he sat back down on the chair. Lachlan thought he detected a hard glint in Argyll's black eyes, so he was surprised when Argyll said, "I believe I might be able to help you."

He nearly sighed with relief. He needed Argyll's influence to get his brother freed, and he hadn't allowed himself to think about the possibility of failure.

"But . . ."

Lachlan tensed, not liking the sound of that.

"In return, I need you to handle a little problem for me," Argyll finished, reaching for a large crystal glass of claret. He took a long drink, sat back in his throne, and propped his fingers together in a triangle before him.

Lachlan's instincts flared. "What kind of problem?"

"My young cousin Flora MacLeod. It seems she's decided to run off with Lord Murray."

Lachlan arched his brow. Lord Murray, though young, was a fierce political rival of Argyll's. No wonder he'd been furious. Lachlan vaguely recalled Rory MacLeod's youngest sister, Flora. She was a renowned heiress, he remembered that much.

"You want me to stop her?"

Argyll's mouth curved in what was supposed to be a smile, but it actually looked more like a grimace. "In a matter of speaking." He paused. "I want you to marry her."

Lachlan froze. It was the last thing he'd expected to hear. Having caught the gleam of calculation in Argyll's eyes, he thought at first to refuse. But though he had no intention of taking a wife for some time, an alliance with Flora MacLeod could not be summarily dismissed. In marrying her, he'd ally himself not just with Argyll, but also with Rory MacLeod. And with Hector, he supposed, though that weighed in the negative.

Lachlan's expression gave no hint of his thoughts. "Why? What's wrong with the lass? Is she addled?"

A bark escaped from Argyll, nearly causing him to spew his claret. The sound was so out of character, it took Lachlan a minute to realize it was laughter. "No. She's quite beautiful. And very rich. Her tocher is two thousand merks—in addition to the lands she brings."

His heart stopped. It was a bloody fortune. Money like that could restore his clan's fortunes in one fell swoop. She was a prize indeed. His gaze sharpened. "Then why me?" Lachlan might be an unmarried Highland chief, but with a tocher like that, Argyll could have his pick of Lowland toadies.

Argyll tapped his fingers together in his lap. "Because you might have a chance. You seem to be the sort of man that would make an impression on a young girl."

Lachlan frowned. "I don't understand." Why would her impression matter? It was her duty to marry where her guardian demanded. "Don't you control her marriage?"

He shrugged. "Technically, the right belongs to her brother—though he would not marry her to anyone without my approval." The MacLeod and Argyll also shared a bond of manrent. "The MacLeod has refused to force the gel to marry, so he would not agree to a match if she is not willing. You and he are friends. He will not object to your suit. You must convince her to marry you. But be forewarned, it is not a simple matter. The lass is trouble. Her mother spoiled her and gave her some rather unusual notions of duty."

Trouble. Vague recollections of conversations with Rory suddenly came back to him. Of his headstrong young sister who was always getting into some sort of mischief or another. The last thing Lachlan wanted was a spoiled brat for a wife. But he also knew that this marriage was more than he could hope for. Not only was there the money to consider, but it would also cement the ties with both Argyll and Rory with blood. He'd made his decision, although with his brother and clan suffering, he'd never really had one.

"Convincing her won't be a problem."

"You haven't met her yet. Contrary doesn't begin to describe the gel."

Lachlan wasn't worried. He could handle one willful lass. But he also knew Argyll well enough to know that he would not be granted such largesse without something in return. "What else?" he asked, not bothering to hide his suspicion.

The earl smiled, not at all offended by Lachlan's obvious distrust, especially since it was warranted. "Your cooperation."

He didn't pretend to misunderstand. Argyll wanted to bring him in line with the king. He asked much, after what the king had done by imprisoning his brother. But Lachlan was pragmatic enough to realize that he was in better standing with Argyll than without. He would never trust King James again, but perhaps he shouldn't have in the first place.

"My dispute was never with the king, only with Hector. It is the king who has broken faith with me. I will need your support not only for my brother, but also in my dispute with Hector over the return of my castle. If the king intercedes on my behalf, I will have no cause to disagree with him."

Argyll's brows shot up. "You bargain with your brother's life at stake?"

"As much as you do with your wee cousin racing to the altar with Lord Murray." Lachlan knew how to bluff. He would have married anyone to release his brother. But he would not bargain from a position of weakness.

The earl studied him thoughtfully. Lachlan held himself perfectly still, to all appearances calm despite the unrest churning inside him.

Finally, Argyll nodded. "Done. But remember, don't think about forcing the lass. As she angers me, Flora is a bewitching little minx, and I would not see her harmed. You'll not get my support if you do."

"And the release of my brother?"

"Once I am assured of Flora's agreement, on your wedding day I will see to his release."

And thus the devil's bargain had been struck.

Marrying Argyll's cousin had seemed a small price to pay for the release of his brother and the return of his castle. He hadn't realized the heavy toll it would exact.

Unconsciously, he pulled her closer. A soft, contented sound escaped from between her lips. She opened her eyes. He stilled, heart pounding in his chest, looking into those fathomless blue depths. She was only half-conscious, but the look in her eyes was so soft and yielding—without pretense of wariness—that it cut him to the quick. It gave him a glimpse of a future that he'd never dreamed of. Of a connection so powerful and strong, it didn't seem possible.

But it was nothing compared with the effect of the wide smile that turned her lips when she looked at him. His chest squeezed painfully with longing. Longing for something that wasn't his. But what would it be like to hold her in his arms like this for real? To make love to her and have her smile at him with such boundless happiness?

It would be perfect.

He watched confusion traverse her face.

"I must be dreaming," she murmured, her voice cracking from the rawness of her throat. She closed her eyes, giving way to unconsciousness once again, and snuggled against him. Her fingers gripped him tightly, and her soft cheek rested over his aching heart.

He couldn't move. Every inch of his body was taut with desire. Desire for something that he'd never wanted before, but that now hovered just out of his reach.

While she was deathly cold, it hadn't been hard to dissociate himself from the sensation of her naked body molded to his. But as she warmed, so had he. All that soft, pliant skin plastered against his became impossible to ignore. He slid his hand down her spine from her nape to the small of her back, savoring the velvet under his fingertips, and the soft curve of her bottom. Wanting desperately to bring her against him. To slide deep inside her with long, slow strokes and make her his.

All vestiges of her icy swim were gone. Unconsciously, she rubbed against him, her nipples hardening. Raking his chest and making him instantly hard.

He caressed her again, cupping her bottom, his entire body drumming with temptation.

God, he couldn't do this. He wanted to touch her all over. Run his hands over every inch of her nakedness and kiss her until she cried out.

But honor held him back. He wouldn't take advantage of her like this. Not when she was weak. Her body might want him, but she didn't.

Flora had run from him because she was scared. Scared by what had nearly happened in the laird's solar. But their bodies were made to come together. Just holding her against him, he could feel it. He knew how good it would be.

With a soft groan, he tore himself from her seductive grasp. Not wanting to be in bed with her when she woke, knowing that his presence would only upset her.

He'd done what he needed to do; the danger had passed. She no longer needed him.

He pulled on a clean shirt, wrapped a fresh plaid around himself, and secured it with his chieftain's badge. Turning back to the bed one more time he took in every detail, his heart swelling hard in his chest. Unable to stop himself, he bent down and brushed a gentle kiss on her lips. "Rest, my sweet," he whispered.

The pale light of dawn stirred her awake. A soft warmth surrounded her. Flora opened her eyes, feeling as if she'd been wrapped in a blanket of sunshine. She felt safe. Protected. Burrowing her face into the pillow beside her, she savored the warm scent of myrtle . . . and something else oddly familiar.

Indeed, she felt the strangest sensation of being somewhere that was both unfamiliar and familiar at the same time. Stretching her arms above her head, she noticed the twinge of aching muscles in her back and arms. She raised her head to look around, but it was so heavy. Everything was a little foggy, and it took her a moment to realize that she was not in her chamber.

The bed was bigger, for one. A large chair was positioned before the fireplace. She looked around, noticing the rough, stark furnishings, similar to those in her room. Unlike her room, however, there was an aumbry for storing clothing, in addition to a large, heavily carved wooden chest before the bed. The window was much narrower than hers, suggesting that she was perhaps on a lower floor of the keep.

Why wasn't she in her room, and why was she so

thirsty? Her lips were cracked, her mouth dry. She ran her hand along her bare arm, her skin felt so gritty . . .

All of a sudden, she realized three things at once. She hadn't drowned, she was in *his* bed, and she was completely naked. Each was shocking enough, but together they were enough to toss her into a panic.

The sound of the door creaking open didn't help matters. When she saw who it was, the riot of emotions swirling inside her grew much worse.

"I see you're awake," the woman said. "I brought you some broth."

Flora had the most appalling urge to hide under the covers. Instead, she forced herself to respond. But what did one say to the leman of the man's bed you'd just woken up in? "Thank you," was all she could think of.

Seeing the question in Flora's eyes, the woman explained, "The laird asked that I look in on you."

"You're a healer?"

She shrugged. "I have some skill with herbs."

Among other things, she thought uncharitably.

Bending over Flora, she started her examination. Putting a gentle hand on Flora's forehead, feeling the pulse at her neck. All of which seemed very strange. Eventually, curiosity got the better of her. "What is your name?" the healer asked.

The woman gave her a long look. "You know who I am?"

Flora nodded.

"Seonaid," she answered.

She started to lift the plaids covering her, but Flora held them tightly, her cheeks on fire. "I'm fine."

The woman lifted a perfectly arched brow. "Your modesty is wasted on me. You don't have anything I haven't seen before. It is your decision, but you nearly drowned, and then nearly froze to death."

Flora's blush intensified. "You don't understand." Her voice lowered. "I don't have any clothes on."

Seonaid shook her head as if Flora were addled. "You were freezing to death." At Flora's obviously perplexed expression, she continued, "You needed the heat of another against you to warm you quickly. 'Twas the only way."

Flora's brows gathered together across her nose. "I don't understand. . . ." Her voice fell off, and her eyes widened as comprehension dawned. The blush was nothing to the mortified heat that spread across her face as her embarrassment got much worse. Dear God. It *was* him. It hadn't been a dream. How could he take advantage of her like that?

Seonaid must have read her thoughts. Her face flooded with anger. "He saved your life. You should be thanking him instead of worrying about your precious maidenly modesty."

Flora flinched at the venom in the woman's voice. And at the knowledge that Seonaid was right. Flora's moment of misplaced outrage subsided. "I'm sorry, you must think me very ungrateful." She bit her lip. "It's just that I don't remember much of what happened."

Seonaid peered at her intently. Then apparently deciding that Flora was in earnest, she nodded. "I'm sure the laird will answer your questions when you are feeling better."

Flora swallowed. The laird. Dear God, what would she do when she saw him? How could she ever look at him again, knowing what he'd done? What he'd seen?

Faint recollections came back to her, making it worse. Images that seemed hazy like a dream, but which she now suspected were very real. Big, strong arms surrounding her. Her cheek pressed against a warm, hard, and very masculine chest.

This time, Flora didn't argue when the woman continued her examination. She even made Flora wiggle her toes and fingers, and Flora didn't say a word in protest—though it seemed very silly indeed.

Finally, Seonaid finished her ministrations, handed her a sark that had been left at the foot of the bed, and declared her surprisingly well.

Flora quickly pulled it over her head. The thin linen gave her no small measure of relief.

"I will send up a posset for you to drink. And then you should rest."

"Thank you," Flora said, and meant it. Given the circumstances, she was surprised by the woman's kindness.

Seonaid turned and walked to the door, then hesitated and looked back at Flora. "You have nothing to be ashamed of. The laird did nothing more than warm your body."

A point she seemed happy to make.

"I know." And she did. Flora recognized that despite his determination to have her, Lachlan Maclean was too honorable to prey on the weak and helpless. And last night she had been both.

With her hand still on the door, Seonaid asked, "So you'll be marrying him now?"

Flora drew back, shocked. "No!" She calmed. "I have no intention of marrying anyone."

Again, Flora got the impression that the woman thought her a fool. As if no woman of sound mind would ever refuse Lachlan Maclean.

"Even after what happened?"

Flora shook her head emphatically. "As you said, it was an emergency. It changes nothing."

Seonaid gave her an appraising look. "He wants you."

Flora blushed. "Well, I don't want him." But the woman's sharp gaze read the lie. Flora lifted her chin. "Even if I did, I still would not marry him."

"I don't think it's that simple," Seonaid said mysteriously.

Neither did Flora. Still, it was odd to have this woman echoing her own thoughts. There was something strange about the laird's wooing of her. From the beginning, she'd sensed both a calculation and an urgency. "What do you mean?"

"I've never seen the laird pursue a woman with such intensity. Let alone one who claims not to want him. You are very beautiful, but he has had many beautiful women. I wonder if there is another reason, that is all."

Initially, she thought the woman felt sorry for her, but now Flora wondered whether Seonaid might have another motive for voicing her suspicions. "Why are you telling me all this?"

She shrugged. "He wants you, but he will not wait forever. He is a very virile man." The authority in her voice made Flora's chest ache. "And when he's done chasing what he cannot have, I'll be waiting."

Long after the woman left, Flora heard her voice. And the warning that had twisted Flora's heartstrings in knots.

Chapter 11

❖

Seonaid's posset proved as potent as her warning, and it was another day before Flora felt well enough to rise from bed and return to her room under Morag's watchful eye. The first thing she did was request that a tub be sent up. The salt from the seawater was irritating her skin, which had begun to itch.

By midmorning, clean, fed, and dressed in a gown that had appeared on the chest the day before while she slept, she almost felt like a new woman.

Almost.

But not everything could be washed away with lavender-scented bathwater. The knowledge of what he'd done to her, for one. Snippets of memories haunted her, teasing the edges of her consciousness with an unexpectedly powerful tug of emotion. She'd lain naked with a man. Even if she couldn't recall the details, it was hardly something she could forget—though she desperately wished she could.

But he'd saved her life. That was one thing she'd never forget. She owed him . . . something.

She tapped her fingertips in a rolling motion on the stone sill as she gazed out her window to the sound. From this vantage point, escape looked like such a simple proposition. The water appeared placid and the distance to the Isle of Mull barely a stone's throw away. How had it gone so terribly wrong?

Since neither the laird nor his sisters had been to see

her, she still didn't know exactly what had happened. Their absence disturbed her more than she wanted to admit. Even though he'd abducted her, and she had every right to escape, she felt in some way as if she'd let them down in her attempt to do so.

It was irrational, but true nonetheless.

Turning from the window, she sighed, more confused than ever. If anything, her attempt at escape seemed to have made the jumble of emotions tangled inside her even worse. Lachlan Maclean had kidnapped her, wooed her with curious intensity, sparked her passion, refused to release her, and then rescued her. She didn't know what to think. In some ways, she feared him more than any man she'd ever met. He held a strange power over her that she couldn't dismiss or ignore.

There was, however, one thing she knew she had to do. No matter how uneasy the prospect of confronting him made her, she needed to thank him. He'd saved her life.

Opening the door, she expected to see Alasdair back at his post, but was surprised to find the corridor empty. If anything, she'd thought the guard would have been doubled. She frowned, not knowing quite what to make of it, and hurried down the corridor.

Considering the ordeal she'd been through, she felt remarkably well—until she started to go down the stairs. A wave of dizziness overtook her, and she had to grab the stone wall to keep from taking a tumble. When it had passed, she resumed stepping down the stairs, suitably chastened and a bit more careful.

Focused as she was on the narrow stone steps, it wasn't until she reached the great hall that she noticed how unnaturally quiet it seemed. The boisterous sounds of life that she'd grown accustomed to over the past few weeks had dimmed to silence. She passed a few serving women, but they quickly turned their heads to avoid her gaze.

It soon became apparent why. Exiting the keep, she glanced into the courtyard and saw a gathering of what looked to be every man in the castle before their chief. Though she heard only the tail end of his speech, it was enough for her to realize what was happening. The men were being reprimanded and punished for allowing her to escape. "Fail duty," "possible attack," and "confinement in the dungeon" left no doubt.

A not insubstantial pang of guilt needled her. No wonder no one would meet her gaze. It was because of her that these men were being punished. And she'd learned enough the past few weeks to understand that the worst punishment of all was for a Highland warrior to be shamed before his chief.

But the dungeon . . .

She shivered. Her attempted escape had far greater repercussions than she'd realized.

She'd never seen him disciplining his men, and it was more than a little intimidating. His expression was hard and implacable, and his voice resounded with absolute authority. To his people he was lord, master, judge, and jury all in one. Her mother was right. A Highland chief was like a king of his own small fiefdom. Such absolute power was disconcerting, making Flora realize just how vulnerable she was. If he'd wanted to, he could have done almost anything to her—forced her to marry him, ravaged her, imprisoned her—and no one would have lifted a finger. It took a strong man to hold such power, know when to wield it, and do so nobly and with honor.

She didn't think he'd noticed her standing atop the forestairs, but as soon as the men had dispersed, he pinned her with his gaze. Heated awareness rippled through her, and then a deluge of powerful emotion and all that had happened that night came back to her in full force. She could remember everything.

The first glimpse of him on the beach. The surge of hope that had given her strength to keep fighting as water poured into the skiff. Watching him swim toward her, the powerful strokes cutting across the heavy current. Knowing how hard he'd fought to reach her in time. Hearing his voice. The steady, soothing tones that had staved off panic as the boat finally succumbed to the waves and tried to take her with it. The comfort of knowing that he was out there as the water dragged her under. Holding on to the image of his face before blackness overtook her.

She remembered everything.

The raw intensity of his kiss when he'd pulled her from her watery death. How she'd felt in his arms. How safe. How protected. *How right.*

And then later, waking to find him beside her. The gentle warmth that seemed a balm to her soul. Reaching for him. The erotic sensation of his naked body molded to hers. His hands on her skin. Her breasts pressed against his chest. His powerful, muscular legs entwined with hers.

He's a very virile man. Seonaid's words rang in her head like a taunt. Yes. She'd felt evidence of that snuggled up against her. He wanted her. Yet from his leman's words, Flora gleaned that he hadn't been visiting Seonaid. The relief she felt upon learning that told her much. But how much longer would he wait?

Finished with his men, Lachlan strode purposefully across the courtyard and up the stairs. The timber shook with the angry force of his step. She took a few steps back, not knowing what to expect. Would she be punished as well? She swallowed hard against the sudden lump in her throat.

"Get back to—" He stopped himself, then continued more gently. "You shouldn't be out of bed."

Flora lifted her brow at his attempt to curtail his natural proclivity toward issuing orders. "I'm feeling much better," she assured him.

He pretended not to hear her, took her elbow, and steered her right back into the keep. So much for the attempts at niceties, she thought. The new leaf hadn't lasted long.

She halted outside the great hall and tried to shrug off his hold. "Really. I'm fine."

His gaze narrowed. She yearned to wipe away the frown with a caress of her hand, wanting him to look at her the way he had that night. Softly, and with tenderness in his gaze.

"You almost drowned and then nearly froze to death. You lost consciousness for hours. You need to rest."

He was concerned about her. The realization settled over her like a warm, fuzzy plaid. Perhaps she could forgive his heavy-handedness—this time. Putting her hand on his arm, she said softly, "I'm fine. Please, I'd like to speak with you."

He held her gaze, as if to assure himself that she spoke true. Finally, he nodded and led her through to the laird's solar behind the great hall. The place where she'd nearly succumbed . . .

She shook off the memories. "I couldn't help overhearing some of what you said out there." She bit her lip, uncertain of how to proceed. It was because of her that those men were being punished. She had to do something. "Is imprisonment really necessary for those men? They were only turned away for an instant, and they weren't expecting anyone to leave."

He closed the door behind him and turned to her, his expression hard and impenetrable. "Too barbaric for you, Flora?"

She heard the bitter undertone and knew he'd misread her intent. She'd accused him of such, but no longer. "No, of course not," she said hastily. "I just—"

"You think I like punishing my men? I've known most of them since they were lads. But no one may pass through the gate in either direction without being seen. No one. The men who allowed you to do so must be punished. Standing guard is one of the most important facets to the security of a keep. Need I explain to you the importance? Any lapse could leave us vulnerable to attack. Two days in the dungeon will be unpleasant, a hard lesson, but they will not be harmed. The alternative is flogging. Would you have me do that?"

She shook her head miserably. "No, of course not."

He paused to study her face. "I think it's not whether the punishment is justified that bothers you, but the reason for it."

He was right. She was feeling guilty for her part in the debacle. She understood that he did not have a choice, there had to be consequences for such a serious breach. And from the vehemence of his reply, it was clear he did not relish the prospect. But he was chief. He had to make the difficult decisions and enforce them—even if he didn't like it. That was part of his strength, she realized.

"Am I to be punished as well, then?"

She saw the spark of surprise in his gaze. He cleared his throat and turned away from her, focused on the cold fireplace. "I think you have been punished enough."

There was something in his voice that gave her pause, a depth of emotion that hit her square in the chest. Her hand still rested on his arm. She took a step closer. "Thank you."

He glanced down at her uncertainly.

"Thank you," she repeated, "for what you did. Saving

me from drowning." Her cheeks warmed. "And what you did to warm me."

His wide mouth lifted at one side, a strangely boyish look that made her chest squeeze.

"Believe me, it was no hardship. Although I wasn't sure you would want to thank me."

She lowered her gaze. It was all too clear what he was thinking. The same thing she was: their naked bodies pressed intimately together.

"I don't remember what happened," she lied. "But I'm not so prudish that I would rather die than preserve my modesty."

For a moment, his gaze heated and he looked as if he wanted to challenge her supposed lapse in memory. Her pulse raced nervously as his gaze lowered to her bodice; her nipples hardened, and she knew exactly what he was remembering. With one touch, she would fall apart. Desire simmered between them, so thick and heavy that it was impossible to ignore. He appeared to waver, but in the end, he decided not to press her.

"Why did you run, Flora? Why were you so desperate to leave—" *Me,* he left unsaid.

But she heard the unspoken question. "You wouldn't let me go."

"I *couldn't* let you go."

His gaze met hers, for once unshielded. The stark longing she read there set off a fierce fluttering in her chest.

"Why?" she asked, not daring to hope.

He didn't say anything for a moment, merely stared at her, the depth of his emotion for once unveiled. "Do you need to ask? I told you I want you."

"But not why."

The words did not come easily. "I care for you, lass." He put his hand on her face, cradling her cheek tenderly with his big rough hand. "You must realize that," he said, stroking her chin with his thumb in a gentle caress.

She did. But hearing it made all the difference. She didn't know what reason there was for the subterfuge or what had made him decide to marry her, but he did care for her. And the knowledge set off a shower of effervescent joy bursting inside her.

"I couldn't risk losing you," he finished.

She leaned closer to him, so that their bodies were almost touching. Inhaling the heady masculine scent of him. Drawing closer to the warmth that surrounded him like a seductive shield. "You won't. But I could never come to you as your prisoner."

Lachlan finally understood. She hadn't been rejecting him, she'd been reacting against her confinement. By abducting her, he'd taken away not just her freedom, but her sense of control.

He had to set her free.

He knew he was taking a risk. He just prayed it wasn't a catastrophic one for all involved. He put his hands on her shoulders and took a step back, needing to think straight, something he could never do when she stood so close to him. With her soft, feminine scent coiling around him. When all he could think about was pulling her into his arms and kissing her until she could no longer refuse him anything.

His hands flexed at his sides, every inch of his body taut with what he risked. With what he'd known he had to do since he realized how desperate she'd been to leave him—enough to risk drowning. He drew a deep breath and prayed he was not about to make a huge mistake. "Very well. You are free to leave."

She gasped, covering her mouth with her hand. "Do you mean it?" He heard her incredulity. "I'm no longer a prisoner?"

"I will convey the instructions to my men that you are not to be prevented from leaving."

It was his turn to be shocked when she threw herself against him, wrapping her arms around his neck, her sweet, irresistible little body stretched against his. "Oh, thank you! You don't know how much this means to me."

He smiled ruefully. "I think I can guess."

She tilted her head, looking at him with a question in her eyes. "Do you want me to go?"

He resisted the sudden urge to close his eyes and beg for mercy. He would never understand the mind of a lass. Hadn't he just been telling her how much he wanted her?

His hand slid around her waist, and he held her tight against him, savoring the heady sensation of the feminine curves that had haunted him for so long. Remembering every detail of that lush naked body. The brush of her nipples. Her round bottom in his hands. He felt the sharp pull in his groin, the heaviness and throbbing tightness. "I want you to stay," he answered. "As my guest."

She lifted her gaze to his. He could see her hesitate. Why had he done it? It was a ridiculous suggestion to willingly stay with the man who'd abducted her. Of course she'd say no. But she surprised him.

She smiled, a shy, adorable grin that cut him to the quick. The happiness in her eyes took his breath away. "I'd like that, too."

Relief converged with desire. He groaned, unable to resist the urge to taste her. Lowering his head, he covered her mouth with his. Drawing her hard against him in one long, languorous kiss. A kiss not to punish or possess, but to savor and honor. The scent of flowers was intoxicating. Her lips were incredibly soft and yielding, her skin like velvet under his hand as he urged her mouth open with his fingers.

His tongue slid into her mouth as the hot flow of emotion welled deep inside him, threatening to erupt. The taste, the sensation, had become achingly familiar—and essential. He kissed her more deeply, circling his tongue in the warm recesses of her mouth. Long, languid strokes that stretched from the deepest part of him. His need for her was both poignant and crushing.

She swayed in his arms, her knees buckling.

He swore and wrenched away. Seeing the dizziness swim in her eyes that she fought to hide. "You aren't well. You should be in bed."

Before she could protest, he swept her up in his arms and started to carry her upstairs. Instead of arguing, she snuggled her head against his shoulder and sighed with contentment. It was a sound that stole into the deepest part of him.

He settled her in her bed, wanting nothing more than to slide in beside her. The most difficult part was that he was almost certain she would not refuse him. When she recovered, she was his.

He propped a pillow under her head and bent to give her a soft kiss on the forehead. "Rest. I will have Morag check on you later."

She nodded, a look of concern crossing her face. "Lachlan, are Gilly and Mary very angry with me?"

He shook his head. "No. Though I do think they were disappointed that you did not say good-bye."

"I planned to send for them."

He would never have let them go, but the thought that she truly cared for his sisters warmed him.

"Have you reconsidered the situation with Mary?"

He frowned. "My decision hasn't changed. Why would it?"

Her cheeks heated. "You said you cared for me. I thought you might have understood—"

"It doesn't change anything." For Mary or for him, he realized grimly. Duty came first. But Flora wouldn't see it that way. Given the limited ties to her family, he supposed he shouldn't be surprised.

"Please. Won't you at least reconsider? As a sign of goodwill, perhaps?"

He tensed. "Don't ask me to choose between you and my duty or doing what I think is right as chief." It was a warning. Whether to himself or to her, he didn't know.

"I'm not. All I'm asking is that you reconsider. I don't think revisiting the matter impinges on your duty."

He stroked his jaw. He could give her that. But she would give him something in return. "Very well, I will reconsider the matter." He smiled. "On one condition."

Chapter 12

❖

A few days later, Flora was having second thoughts about accepting her erstwhile kidnapper's offer to stay as his guest. If she'd refused, as she ought to have done, she wouldn't be in this predicament.

She almost regretted her decision . . . almost.

She could blame her acceptance of his invitation on shock, but that wouldn't be truthful. Admittedly, she'd been surprised by his request, but she *had* given the matter some deliberation.

In truth, there was nowhere she would rather be than the dilapidated old keep that was now fading into the distance behind her. Even though Lachlan had brought her to his castle against her will, she'd grown fond of the place. More than fond. With Lachlan and his sisters, Drimnin was as close to a home as she'd felt in a long time. Maybe ever. She'd never lived with her sisters, and for the first time realized how much she'd missed. As her mother had always been chatelaine, she'd also never had the opportunity to make her own improvements on a place.

She supposed she could have returned to her cousin's lodgings in Edinburgh or gone to Hector or Rory, but for all she knew, they would force her into a marriage of their liking. She gazed at the handsome man riding beside her, ignoring the self-satisfied look on his face. Although Lachlan wanted to marry her, he gave every indication that he would not force her to do so—which was more than she could be assured of from her brothers. Marrying him was one way of getting a reprieve from her brothers' agendas, she thought with a wry smile.

But Flora knew the real reason she'd agreed to stay was that she couldn't bear the thought of saying goodbye to him.

But that was before he'd tricked her. The wretch. She looked at him again, this time taking in the expression on his face.

On one condition. She should have known better.

Lachlan glanced at Flora as she rode beside him, her blond hair shimmering like a diamond in the sunlight. The sky was a wide swath of endless blue stretching to the hills rising in the distance. He smiled, feeling lighter than he had in quite some time.

It was a perfect day for a swim.

His companion, however, did not share his enthusiasm. Her expression landed somewhere between peeved and furious.

"Now, lass, don't look so sour. You did promise. And wasn't it you who told me that I would get more bees with honey?"

The look she turned on him was scathing. "I don't think you understand the concept. Honey is not the same thing as blackmail."

He shrugged unrepentently, trying to hide his smile. "You wouldn't have agreed otherwise. Besides, it won't be so bad. The water is shallow, and I won't let go of you. I used to swim at this loch all the time when I was a boy. Actually, it's more of a small pool. It's private and sheltered by a thick copse of trees. There will be no one there to see you."

"You'll be there," she said pointedly.

Aye, and he couldn't wait. Just the thought of her all

wet in a thin linen sark made his blood heat. Teaching her to swim would definitely have his rewards. "But I'm harmless," he said with mocking innocence.

She didn't even dignify that with a response, simply snorting her disavowal.

They rode a few minutes longer, and he broached the subject that had been bothering him. "Why did you never learn to swim?"

She eyed him carefully, drew a deep breath, and recounted the episode at Inveraray when she was a child. The story made his blood run cold. Twice she'd nearly drowned.

The chilling episode also explained more than her inability to swim. He could almost see the lonely girl— much younger than her siblings—so eager to belong that she was willing to do anything. And he also saw what it had cost her, leaving her firmly entrenched on the outside looking in.

"And you've avoided the water ever since?"

She nodded. "Not an easy prospect in the Highlands, as I'm sure you can appreciate."

That was an understatement. Especially in the Isles, where both her brothers resided. He wondered if that perhaps explained some of her reluctance to travel to Dunvegan Castle on Skye, or to Duart Castle on Mull, for that matter.

He frowned, remembering something. "You did not seem unusually nervous on the boat ride to Drimnin." And as he recalled, the sound had been particularly choppy that day.

His observation appeared to fluster her. He thought a touch of pink heightened her color, but it could have been the effects of the warm day and the vigorous ride.

"I think I was more concerned about the immediate threat of having just been abducted."

He held her gaze. "You were never in any danger, lass."

"I wasn't so sure of that then." A soft smile turned her lips. "Or now, for that matter."

It was clear that the prospect of learning how to swim truly frightened her. Perhaps if he'd been aware of the circumstances, he would not have been so forceful in his method of persuasion. But then again, she wouldn't have agreed. And in this case, the end justified the means.

The lass had every right to her fear, but she could not let it control her. "Trust me, Flora. I won't let anything happen to you."

He saw a slight shiver run across her shoulders and wished she were closer so that he could gather her in his arms and soothe away her fears.

"You don't understand. I've tried. Truly, I have. But something comes over me in the water. My pulse races so hard that my heart feels weak. My mind goes blank. My entire body goes rigid and my blood runs cold. My hands start to sweat and I feel queasy and light-headed."

He'd seen men with similar symptoms in battle. It was a type of extreme panic. "Your reaction is certainly understandable under the circumstances. But holding on to your fear has only made you more vulnerable to the very thing that frightens you. And I know you are no coward, Flora." He held her gaze, telling her with his eyes that he meant what he said. "I won't lie to you, lass. Teaching you to swim will not make you invincible. I've lost too many men to the sea to make such a claim. But it will give you a fighting chance. And believe it or not, there is also great pleasure in it."

She nodded, but he could tell that she wasn't convinced.

The copse of trees appeared beyond the hill like an oasis. He hadn't been to this place in a long time, and unexpected memories of his father came back to him, re-

calling a more carefree time in his childhood. His father
had brought him here one summer when repairs were
being done on Breacachadh and the family had moved
to Morvern. Only a few years before the death of his
mother and then his father only a year later. When there
had been time to ride across the moors and to fritter
away a long summer day swimming in a loch. It seemed
a fitting place for teaching Flora, as this was where he
himself had learned to swim. Of course, his father had
unceremoniously tossed him in and told him to figure
it out—Lachlan had a slightly more civilized method
planned for Flora.

He led her through the trees to the small loch. It was
exactly as he remembered it. Surrounded by jagged
rocks and filled by a burn that led from the mountains,
the circular pool was no bigger than a hundred feet in
diameter. There was something magical about the place.
Without a doubt it was picturesque, with its clear blue
green waters, black jagged rocks, and lush emerald
green backdrop; but there was more to it than that.

He heard Flora draw in her breath. She turned to him.
"It's beautiful. What is it called?"

"The Faerie Pool."

He half expected her to laugh at the superstitions of
the Highlanders who'd given the loch its name, but instead she nodded in agreement. "It suits. I feel like I'm in
another world."

Her response pleased him in a way he couldn't have
imagined. The acknowledgment of the beauty of his
land seemed of strange importance. It was as if she were
finally relinquishing her old prejudices about the Highlands. She could be happy here. He told himself he
would do whatever it took to make her so.

After helping her down, he tended to the horses, giving her time to accustom herself to the place. When he
was finished, he removed a loaf of bread, some cheese,

and a flagon of claret from his pack, spread out his plaid
on the ground, and invited her to sit. She eyed him nervously but did as he instructed. They ate in comfortable
silence, listening to the sounds of nature blooming all
around them. The song of the skylark, the rustle of the
wind through the leaves, the gentle trickle of the burn
over the rocks as it drained into the loch. He lay on his
side, propped up on his elbow, watching her. Entranced
by the way her hair curled around her temple in the
heat, the way the sun warmed her pale complexion, the
dainty way she ate, and the way she held the flagon to
her lips for just a moment too long, betraying her increasing nervousness.

It was time.

He dragged himself to his feet and held out his hand.
"Ready?"

She looked up at him, the green flecks in her sea blue
eyes even more prominent in the stark sunlight. "I
haven't finished—"

He gave her an encouraging smile. "It won't get any
easier by delay. Come. There is nothing to be scared of."
He looked around meaningfully. "What could go wrong
on a day like this?"

A number of unpleasant things came to mind. But
rather than voice them, Flora took a deep breath and
slid her icy hand into his, drawing immediate strength
from the warm, callused palm.

She trusted him. The truth was undeniable. Enough to
brave the water and face her darkest fears.

He helped her to her feet and indicated a large boulder
near the mouth of the burn. "You can change over
there."

She did as he instructed, making sure to take her time.
Her fingers were stiff and shaky as she removed the simple stays that tied in front and the wool gown, both of

which she'd borrowed from Mary, grateful for the way it untied at the sides to lift over her head. She couldn't have done it by herself otherwise, and she didn't think she could take the feel of his fingers on her right now. She was ready to jump out of her skin. And it wasn't just the prospect of getting in the water that was putting her on edge.

It was Lachlan.

Something new and poignant had sprung up between them. An ease, a familiarity . . . an intimacy that had filled her with a deep sense of contentment. By giving her freedom, he'd changed everything. Turning from jailer to suitor in the bat of an eye. Opening up a world of possibilities.

He cleared his throat impatiently. Realizing he was going to come looking for her if she delayed any longer, she stepped out from behind her impromptu dressing chamber.

His brow lifted when he saw her.

She glanced down at the trews and linen shirt that she'd worn under her gown, relieved to see that she was decent. Mostly. "Murdoch borrowed it from your squire," she explained.

His gaze traveled down the length of her, lingering at her breasts stretching against the tight linen, her hips in the wool trews, to her naked calves and the tips of her bare toes. She saw the heat in his gaze for an instant, before he doused it with a chuckle. "Those clothes don't look quite the same on you."

A flush rose to her cheeks at the obvious admiration in his voice.

Admiration that she returned wholeheartedly. He'd removed his shirt and boots and wore only his trews, which hung low on his hips, emphasizing the hard lines of his impressively muscled stomach. A warm, sultry feeling came over her just looking at him. She didn't think she'd ever get used to the sight of his naked chest. The vast array of finely sculpted muscle. The strength and overwhelming masculinity. The sheer beauty of his form.

Realizing that she'd been staring, she shifted her gaze to the loch. "It looks cold," she said, rubbing her arms. "Perhaps we should wait a little while. Until it warms up a bit."

"It's one of the hottest days of the year, the water will be as tepid as a bath," he said patiently. "It will be fine." He offered her his hand. "Come now, lass. No more delays."

His voice was adamant but surprisingly gentle. She could try, but she knew in the end he would not be gainsaid. She placed her hand in his and allowed him to lead her to the water's edge. Her feet felt weighed down with lead, each step on the rocky dirt path a battle against the overwhelming urge to turn and run. Sensing her building trepidation, he gave her hand an encouraging squeeze.

Too soon, they reached the soft muddy bank. Not letting go of her hand, he took a few steps into the water and turned around to face her. "Breathe, lass," he said softly. "One step at a time."

She shook her head, the breath stuck in her throat. She couldn't. Fear had taken hold. It was just as she'd described before. The panic had wrapped itself around her like a vise. "I d-d-on't think I can do this," she stuttered, looking at him wildly.

"The Holyrood hellion admitting defeat? Is this the same girl who once scaled parapets?" he teased. "What would your friends at court say?"

She scowled at his attempt to prick her pride. "I know very well what you are doing. It won't work."

He shrugged none too innocently. The look on his face was so out of character, she nearly laughed. Nearly.

Until she looked down at the water looming only inches from her feet.

"Don't look at the water. Look at me."

She did as he directed, gazing deep into the steady strength of his piercing blue eyes. *God, he was incredible.* So handsome that he made her insides flip.

The distraction worked. Her pulse slowed, and the tightness constricting her chest released a little. Clasping both her hands, he coaxed her gently into the loch.

At the first touch of the cool water on her toes, she gasped, pulling back instinctively.

He murmured soothing words in lilting Erse, the confidence in his gaze and voice giving her much needed courage.

She shivered as they waded waist deep into the water. Her skin prickled, the tiny hairs on her arms standing straight up. Chilled not from the water, which was pleasantly cool, but from the fear surging through her veins.

He sensed her distress and brought her closer against his chest, wrapping her firmly in his arms and allowing the heat of his body to take the chill from her skin.

"You are doing beautifully, my sweet."

It didn't feel like it; she felt like a quivering mess. But she had made it this far.

"I'm just going to lower you a bit more into the water. Are you ready?"

"Isn't this deep enough?" Her voice quivered noticeably.

"We won't go any deeper, but you can't learn to swim standing like this. My arms will be around you the entire time, all right?"

She nodded, and he slowly lowered them into the water, cradling her against him, until he was on his knees and the water lapped around her shoulders. He'd positioned her so that he held her by her waist and chest and her feet floated out to the side. She fought the nausea as the memories took hold, of the suffocating darkness, of the water filling her nose and mouth.

She couldn't do this. She had to get out of here.

Panic erupted, and she flailed wildly, trying to stand up. But his arms held her close.

"Let me go!" she gasped.

"Shhh . . ." he said softly. "I have you. You are perfectly safe."

Tears sprang to her eyes. He didn't understand. Look at him—he was a rock. He'd probably never felt a moment of fear in his life. This was so humiliating. She didn't want him to see her like this.

She buried her face against his warm neck and clasped his broad shoulders, her entire body shaking, his solid strength an iron tether to hold on to. He simply held her, easing her panic with the soft caress of his hand on her back. His hand slid down her side to her hips. To her bottom. And achingly close to between her legs. His touch was feather soft and deftly arousing. She stopped shaking. He stroked her until her body softened and the water no longer felt like a pool of lead, but lighter and freer—like a cloud. Until the panic receded and she couldn't think of anything but his hands on her skin.

They were so close, his mouth was only inches from hers. She was achingly aware of her breasts plastered against his chest. The drenched fabric of her shirt was an insignificant barrier to the wide expanse of powerful muscle.

There was nothing decent about her garments now. Nothing of her shape was hidden from his view. And though he was taking pains not to make her self-conscious, she knew he was very aware of it as well.

"Is that better?" he murmured against her ear, the warmth of his breath making her shiver again.

She wanted nothing more than to dissolve against

him. Her body felt warm and languid, but also aroused and aching for his touch. Which was exactly what he'd intended. She eyed him. *The rogue.* But there was some consolation. If the strain on his face was any indication, he was not unaffected.

"Yes," she answered. "It is better. Your teaching method is somewhat unconventional, but effective." She shifted against him, not surprised to feel the hard length of his erection nudging her bottom. Good, he was just as aroused as she. "And dangerous."

His fingers trailed down the curve of her spine. A teasing stroke when she wanted pressure. "Aye," he admitted. "Very dangerous."

Realizing she'd best put an end to this perilous game, she lifted her gaze back to his. "What's next?"

The passion still burned in his gaze. A simmering threat or a promise, she didn't know.

"The next part you must do on your own. I want you to dip your chin in the water, up to your nose, keeping your mouth closed. You will still be able to breathe through your nose. Like this." He demonstrated.

Her eyes widened. She wanted to refuse, but he was right: She would never learn to swim and always be vulnerable if she kept allowing fear to win.

Which, of course, was easier said than done. She tried three times, but each time the water started to close over her mouth, her head seemed to jerk up of its own volition.

He held her hands, murmuring little encouragements, but it didn't help.

She looked at him hopelessly. "It's no use. I can't do it."

He tipped her chin with his finger so that he was looking right into her eyes. "Your fear will not go away in one day, lass. Don't be so hard on yourself. You've already made great progress."

"You're not disappointed in me?" She bit her lip. "I know you're busy, and I haven't proved a very apt student."

A lazy smile curved his wide, sensual mouth. A mouth that teased and spoke of so many unknown pleasures. "Rather the opposite. I look forward to more lessons. I can't imagine a more"—he slid his hand down the curve of her hip—"delightful pupil."

Flora's cheeks warmed. "You're enjoying this."

"Every minute," he admitted unabashedly. "Would you like to try one more time?" His mouth moved just a fraction of an inch closer. She felt the warm spice of his breath on her cheek. The tiny hairs on the back of her neck rose. Her pulse spiked, but not with fear. Every nerve ending was ragged with anticipation. She would agree to anything, if only he would kiss her.

"What did you have in mind?" she breathed.

"Another wee distraction."

His dark voice seeped into her bones. She shivered as his hand slid achingly close to her breast. He could reach out and stroke her with his thumb.

He was driving her mad with his touch. With his gentle teasing. All she could think about was his mouth on hers, his hands covering her body and appeasing the wicked sensations firing through her body.

"Concentrate on my mouth."

I am. Dear God, I can think of nothing else. She could almost taste the warm spiciness of his breath. She nodded, her body drumming with desire.

He covered her mouth with his, and her heart slammed into her chest. Slowly, he lowered her under the water and then back up. It was just for a moment, but it worked.

He broke the kiss and she opened her eyes right into his. Her face lit with accomplishment. "I did it!"

He returned her smile. "You did. Well done, lass. It

won't be long before you are swimming like one of the
Maighdean na Tuinne."

She wrapped her hands around his neck, looking deep
into those incredible blue eyes. She loved the way the
light reflected off the rare strand of gold hidden deep in
the chestnut of his hair. "I don't know how to thank
you," she said softly.

He pulled her to her feet to stand before him, so that
she was stretched against the long length of him. The
evidence of his desire pulsed hard against her stomach.
His hand slid up to cup her breast, and a wave of delicious heat poured through her. He rubbed his thumb
over her nipple, and a rush of sensation spread between
her legs. She felt as though she were breaking apart, just
from his touch.

"A kiss," he said, his mouth a hairbreadth from hers.
"You can thank me with a kiss."

A kiss wouldn't be enough. Not for her. Her body
ached for his touch. For his possession. She wanted him.
Enough to throw caution to the wind. She knew well
what she risked. But her virginity had never been a sacred object for her. Indeed, it only made her a more valuable marriage prize. In truth, she'd do well to be rid of
it. But until she'd met the Laird of Coll, there had never
been a man she'd wanted enough to risk the censure.

By rousing her curiosity, he'd already shattered her innocence. Since that day in the laird's chamber when he'd
stroked her body, bringing her to the point of something
cataclysmic and beautiful. Something that set her body
on edge every time he touched her. Something that
needed to be satisfied. Maybe then she could think
clearly.

Flora had never been one to allow consequences to
rule her actions. She wanted him, and there was nothing
to prevent her from having him. She wanted the culmi-
nation of the closeness she'd felt in his bed. The intimacy

of sharing her body with this man. Instinctively, she knew he was keeping something from her, holding back a part of himself. This would bring them closer, and then maybe he would confide in her.

Rising on her tiptoes, she offered herself with a kiss. Never having attempted to seduce a man before, she acted solely on instinct. A slow drag of the lips, a wicked dart of the tongue along the seam of his mouth, a soft nuzzle of her cheek against the coarse scrape of his jaw. She pressed her body against his enticingly and ever so slightly brushed up and down against him, circling her hips against his erection and raking her nipples against his naked chest. Telling him in every way possible—except with words—that she wanted him.

He stood stone still, seemingly unaffected. But she could feel the furious pounding of his heart against hers.

She drew back and looked into the violent maelstrom of his gaze. "Will that suffice?"

She could see the pulse in his neck as he fought for control. "Yes." His voice was strained and ragged. "That will do just fine."

But it wasn't enough for her. Emboldened, she brought her hand between them and trailed her fingers across the ridges of his stomach muscles, the heel of her hand brushing over the heavy round head of his erection, which just broke through the edge of the water. "Are you sure?"

"Flora," he hissed. But she ignored the warning and covered him with her hand, wrapping her fingers firmly around his thickness. He swore. She could see the strain in his body, the tautness of his shoulders, the flex of his arms at his side. She felt empowered, relishing the exquisite sensation of harnessing such powerful masculinity in her hand. She felt bold and wicked as she touched him with her fingers. He allowed her to explore him, but she could see the toll it was taking on him. Every muscle in his body pulsed with restraint. But when she squeezed him lightly, dragging her hand down the long length of him, he snapped.

He pulled her against him and kissed her with the passion that had struggled to break free, sliding his tongue in her mouth, claiming her in the most basic way. He kissed her long and hard, with a dark carnality that hinted at the erotic pleasures to come.

She was drawn to the dangerous intensity that threatened just under the surface of this man. Sensing in him something similar in herself. The very thing that had made her touch him so boldly. A wild, base sensuality that was only waiting to be unleashed. Making love with Lachlan Maclean would be raw and powerful. And like a moth to the flame, she was helpless to fight the pull of attraction.

His mouth was on her neck, her breasts in his hands. Cupping her. Pinching her nipples lightly until she writhed in innocent frustration against him. The scratch of his beard on her skin as his mouth trailed down her neck drove her mad. She felt ready to explode. Impatient to discover all the pleasure he had in store.

Her hands splayed across the muscles of his back, feeling the tension waiting to be unharnessed. Her legs went weak with her need of him.

He'd untied her shirt, and his mouth had found the tops of her breasts. Her skin was so hot, every kiss blazing a fiery path in its wake. His tongue flicked her taut nipple, and the teasing, gyrating movements increased her frenzy. When he finally took her in his mouth, a sound of raw pleasure escaped from between her lips. She arched her back as he sucked her harder. Plying her nipple with the gentle tug of his teeth and tongue. She writhed helplessly, pressing urgently against his erection. Cradling him between the apex of her legs. At her very core.

He groaned, a deep guttural sound that hinted of danger. He was holding her against him, taking her with his mouth and hands, but it wasn't enough. She wanted more pressure, more of everything. She wanted to feel the weight of him on top of her. She wanted him inside her.

She wanted everything he had to give.

Blood pounded in his ears. The urge to explode in her hand was crushing. He'd never been this close to losing control. Never been so damned aroused as when she'd circled him in her hand and milked him so innocently—and so perfectly. He'd fought the urge to come and hadn't been completely successful. His stomach clenched as he fought the pull, but a few drops escaped nonetheless.

He wanted to strip her down and caress every inch of her with his mouth and tongue. She was driving him insane with her innocent touch. With her eagerness. With her open desire.

The heavy haze of lust had crashed over him so completely, it took every ounce of his will to pull back.

She was offering herself to him, and the hardest thing he'd ever had to do was not take her.

He hadn't known until this moment to what lengths he would go to see her bound to him. But his sense of honor, at least as far as she was concerned, went deeper than he'd realized. He might not be able to risk telling her the whole truth about Argyll's complicity in arranging their marriage, but he would not seduce her and take her virginity. Not until she agreed to marry him. He just prayed that she didn't wait too long. His body raged with pent-up desire. The fullness in his loins had long passed the point of pain.

Mindful of her fear in the water, he held her firmly but nonetheless pushed her away. "We have to stop now," he said through clenched teeth. "I won't take your innocence. Not without marriage."

Her mouth was swollen and red from his kiss, her eyes hazy with passion. "I don't want to stop."

His heart paused for one long beat, not daring to believe what he'd heard. She would marry him. He looked deep into her fathomless blue eyes. "You know what you are saying? You would come to me of your own free will? You will not try to claim later that I seduced you into agreement?"

His voice was fierce, refusing to allow for the possibility until he heard it from her own lips. But every muscle strained. He wanted this more than he'd ever wanted anything in his life.

"I understand the consequences." She took a step toward him and put her hand firmly on his chest. "I want you."

Blood surged through his body, and he shook with the last threads of restraint. He clasped her hand and brought it to his mouth. His lips pressed against her damp fingers. "There will be no going back. If you give yourself to me, I want all of you."

A flash of uncertainty flickered in her gaze, but she nodded.

Elation spread through him. The significance of this moment would be forever etched on his memory. Of this sophisticated, beautiful woman giving herself to him. A thick ball lodged in his chest. He was overwhelmed by the force of emotion swelling inside him.

He swept her into his arms and carried her to shore. God, he would make this perfect for her. With what she'd given him, he could give no less.

Carefully, as if she were the most precious treasure in the world, he laid her down on the plaid.

He sensed her uncertainty and, now that it was agreed, her rising embarrassment.

Bending over her, he took her chin in his hand and placed a tender kiss on her lips. "There is no shame in what we will share, Flora."

She nodded shyly and circled her hands around his neck, bringing his mouth down to hers.

He drank her in. Sliding his tongue in her mouth, he circled her slowly, delving into the deepest recesses as his fingers stroked the velvety softness of her neck.

Her tongue entwined with his, meeting the sensuous thrust with her own and making urgent little sounds that tore to shreds his intention to take it slowly.

His hands were on her. Cupping the heavy weight of her breasts, squeezing the fullness in his hands, as his tongue thrust against hers in the slow rhythm of lovemaking.

Her skin was on fire, her nipples tight and pebbled in his palm. He pinched her with his fingers until she arched against him, her need painfully clear.

Breaking the kiss, he slid his hands under the damp fabric of her shirt and lifted it to expose her breasts. The ivory perfection took his breath away. Her waist was flat and thin, in contrast with the very womanly curves that rose and fell enticingly with the quickening of her breath.

"God, you're beautiful." She shifted her gaze shyly, but he turned her face back to his. "Do not hide from me, lass. I've waited for this for too long. This time, I intend to savor every naked inch of you."

He leaned down and placed a gentle kiss on each delicate pink tip, then helped her shimmy the shirt over her head. And then he worked the trews she wore. Deftly, he untied the wet knot and slid his hands around her hips. She was so slim, he could almost span her with his hands.

She sucked in her breath as he slowly slid the wet wool down her long legs.

He wanted nothing more than to take off his own trews and lay naked on top of her. But not yet. He didn't want to frighten her.

He drew in his breath, allowing his gaze to roam over her nakedness. The sun drenched over her; she radiated golden warmth. Her hair had begun to dry and glistened like a golden crown around her head. He skimmed his hands over her, memorizing every flawless inch of her.

She shifted uncomfortably, and his hand turned from reverent to caressing. He stroked her breasts and nuzzled his face between them, inhaling the sweet floral scent of her skin.

She was so sweetly restless against him. So eager for pleasure that he chuckled, murmuring for patience.

Finally, he took the ripe tip of her breast in his mouth, sucking hard as she arched her back against him so urgently that he could feel her body shudder in his hands.

He knew how close she was to falling apart. Never could he have imagined her responsiveness. Her deep sensuality.

Ignoring his own frantic need, he took it slowly. Drawing every ounce of pleasure from her as he brought her to the very brink just by sucking her breasts.

What would happen when he touched her?

He slid his hand down her flat belly and cupped her mound. She let out a cry of such pleasure, his erection jerked hard against her hip. He was so hard, he strained painfully against the damp fabric of his trews.

Her hips pressed against him, and he fought the fierce surge of heated pressure to his loins. He ached to thrust up high inside her, feeling her damp heat surround him like a tight glove. But damn it, he would make this good for her if it killed him. He slid one long finger deep inside her. She was deliciously wet and responsive. He kissed her again, probing her mouth with his tongue as he probed her core with his finger. She writhed against him, pressing her breasts against his naked chest. Lifting her hips to meet the frantic rhythm.

God, she was going to come. She was killing him. He slid his mouth over her jaw, down her neck, and down her velvety soft belly until he'd positioned his face between her legs.

Her skin was flushed and pink with their lovemaking. He would picture her like this always, he thought, feeling a surprisingly sharp tug in his chest. Never had she looked more beautiful. She was his.

She eyed him warily. Not knowing what he intended, but perhaps guessing. "What—"

"All of you, Flora," he reminded her. "I want all of you." He held her gaze as his tongue flicked out to taste her. It was the most darkly erotic moment of his life. Looking into her eyes, seeing her surprise, tasting her on his tongue, and feeling her body quiver with a surge of damp pleasure.

Any objections she'd been about to make were lost as he cupped her soft bottom and lifted her fully to his mouth, sliding his tongue deep inside her.

He heard her moan, felt her shake, and watched as her body gave over to the pleasure he was bringing her. Watched as every last veil of modesty dissolved under the skilled movements of his mouth and tongue.

She fought it. Not wanting to succumb so completely. Not wanting to lose control. But he was merciless— teasing her, bringing her to the very peak, and forcing her over. He murmured encouraging words as he laved, nibbled, and sucked. And then he felt it. The contraction. The sweet spasm of her climax. She tensed as the power of her release took her and cried out, pulsing against his hungry mouth.

It wasn't enough. He brought her hard to her second orgasm, finding the sweet spot of her pleasure with his lips sucking and entering her with his finger again, until she came again hard on the heels of her first.

She was soft and hot and finally ready for him.

His erection throbbed. He couldn't wait any longer. Quickly, he unfastened his trews and slid them off.

Flora thought she'd died and gone to heaven. Twice. Never could she have imagined anything so wonderful. Slowly the ebb faded, and she became intensely aware of the naked man beside her.

Unable to resist, she ventured a curious glance. Her eyes widened as she took him in. He'd removed his trews, and he was even more impressive than she'd imagined.

Though what she'd imagined she didn't know, except that it was nothing close to the reality. Of course, she'd known he was large from touching him. But there was something quite different in seeing him for herself. There was something inherently beautiful about the evidence of his desire, but also threatening. Her courage faltered. Knowing what he planned to do, but not exactly how it would work. How could her body accommodate a man of his size? Given the length and girth, it didn't seem possible.

"Don't worry, lass, your body will stretch," he said, reading her mind with frightening accuracy. "It will hurt for but a moment. Only once."

She nodded but still didn't quite believe him.

"Touch me, Flora," he whispered, his voice hoarse with need. "The way you did before."

She lifted her hand between them, grazing her fingers across the hard planes of his stomach before brushing her hand across his tip.

He jerked in apparent pain. She started to withdraw, but he shook his head. "Don't. It feels good. Too good."

A warm feeling ran through her, and she touched him

again, this time taking him fully in her hand. Her fingers were barely able to close around his thickness. He felt amazing, the soft surrounding his rigid length. Like a velvet glove over a pillar of steel.

He groaned when she touched him. Clenching his jaw and closing his eyes as she watched the sensations coursing through his body.

She explored him with her fingers, relishing the way every touch seemed to increase his pleasure. She traced a line with her fingertip down the long length of him, rubbed her thumb over the soft head, wondering at the drop of liquid that seeped from him.

He swore and pulled her hand from him. Dropping his head to kiss her passionately. She felt the heat build, felt the desire build, as he slid his finger inside her again.

She could see the effort it was taking him to go slowly. If his release was anything like hers, she could only imagine the instincts clamoring in him to find his pleasure. She'd been almost mindless in her need for him. Not caring about anything but the powerful sensations racking her body.

God, his mouth had been on her most private parts. And it had been amazing.

He'd placed his hands on either side of her shoulders, the shadow of his broad chest cast over her possessively. The muscles in his shoulders and arms bulged with the effort of restraint. She ran her hands over his back, savoring the heat of his skin and the hardness of his body.

He positioned himself between her legs and slowly started to enter her. Nudging her wider with each inch that he sank into her. It was the oddest sensation. She felt stretched and full and possessed at the same time.

His face was tense and strained. He held her gaze as he slid into her inch by wicked inch.

It started to pinch. Her body tensed. He was wrong. She couldn't do this. He wouldn't fit.

Maybe this wasn't a good idea after all.

He sensed her sudden misgivings. "Only a minute, Flora." He looked into her eyes. "Trust me."

Their eyes locked, and something intense passed between them. She nodded, too moved to speak. He held her gaze as he pushed a little deeper.

Her heart hitched. The poignancy of the moment blocked out the pain for an instant. Finally, with one thrust he sank deep inside her—so deep that it felt as though he'd touched her heart.

She winced with the knife of pain and resisted the reflexive urge to push against him. He held perfectly still, allowing her body to adjust to the invasion.

He kissed her again, tenderly and with such raw emotion that the pain was all but forgotten.

And when he started to move, all she could think of were the exquisite sensations rocking her body.

He started slowly, pulling in and out of her body in a sensuous rhythm, allowing her to savor every powerful inch of him. Each stroke was like a caress. He made love to her with a heart-wrenching tenderness that was all the more surprising coming from this rough, rugged Highlander. Never could she have imagined this.

But soon it wasn't enough. She knew he was holding back, and like him, she wanted everything.

She kissed him harder, the way he'd taught her to do. She clenched his back as her legs wrapped around his buttocks and she lifted her hips to meet his thrusts.

Relishing the increased frenzy of his thrusts, knowing that it was working. His hands were rough on her body, the hard calluses providing exquisite sensation as he crushed her breasts in his hands. He was losing control. Mindless with passion. For her.

It was rough and raw and absolutely perfect. He

slammed into her harder and deeper. The intensity shook her to her core. She felt the pressure build inside her, felt the quivering that was even deeper and more powerful than before.

She started to shatter, breaking apart in thousands of tiny pieces like glass. And then, amazingly, so did he. With one last thrust he sank deep inside her and cried out as the force of his release surged through him and into her.

He collapsed on top of her. But Flora was so weak, her body so heavy, she barely noticed the added weight.

He rolled to the side and was so quiet for a moment, she thought he'd fallen asleep.

She didn't know what to say. Their bodies, it seemed, had said everything.

He took a lock of her hair and slid it through his fingertips. Suddenly self-conscious, she felt her cheeks heat. Feeling oddly vulnerable, she didn't trust herself to look at him. Not sure what it would reveal.

"We'll be wed as soon as the banns can be read."

Chapter 13

❖

"What?" Flora asked, shock surely written all over her flushed face.

Lachlan rose up on his elbow to look at her. A lock of hair slumped across his forehead. Her heart squeezed. He was so incredibly handsome and strong. His rugged face was relaxed for once, although the slightest hint of a frown had appeared between his brows. "Our marriage, of course. It was understood."

Recalling his words, she could see how he might have misconstrued her agreement.

When she didn't respond, he added, "I suppose there wasn't much of a proposal." He held her gaze with a moving intensity, a look that was possessive yet tender. A look that made her breath hitch. He lifted her hand to his mouth and pressed a gentle kiss on her knuckles. "Flora MacLeod, would you do me the honor of becoming my wife?"

She couldn't prevent the reflexive spike of happiness. For a moment, she was tempted. She'd tried to guard against it, but she could no longer deny her feelings for the gruff Highlander. He was nothing at all like the sort of man she'd imagined herself marrying, yet his appeal was undeniable.

He seemed in earnest, but all was not as it appeared; of that she was sure. He wanted her, if only she could be sure *why*. Her mother's warnings and the situation with

Lord Murray had conspired to make her proceed with caution.

She swallowed hard, her throat suddenly dry. "I . . . I don't know what to say."

" 'Yes' would seem appropriate."

His voice held the slightest hint of an edge. She studied his face intently, wishing she could see inside his head. He seemed to be waiting patiently for her answer, but he wasn't patient at all. He was tense, held too still, though he wanted her to think otherwise. "Why is marriage so important to you?"

"I took your virginity. I hardly think you need to ask."

But she did. And his response proved achingly disappointing. There was no more talk of caring for her, and certainly not the declaration that perhaps she was secretly hoping for. For a moment, she wished for a little more of the insouciant courtier prone to flatter, rather than the implacable Highland warrior. She didn't know what she expected, except that it was more.

A wry smile hid her disappointment. "You don't need to marry me for that."

He bridled, and a fierce expression obliterated the joy of only moments before. "My honor demands otherwise."

Honor. The soft blow hit with a forceful impact. "And that is all?" she asked quietly. "That is the only reason you wish to marry me?"

His eyes shuttered, and he hesitated a moment too long. "I told you before that I cared for you."

He swept his finger along her jaw in a soothing caress, but she turned her head away.

He doesn't trust me, she realized. *And maybe I don't completely trust him.* Not enough to risk her future or, she feared, her heart.

She felt the bond they'd just shared unraveling. "No," she said tonelessly. "I won't marry you."

Incredulity warred with the sudden flare of anger that appeared on his face. "But you agreed."

She lifted her chin. "I did no such thing. You asked me if I understood the consequences. I did. I do."

"You gave yourself to me." The hard look in his piercing blue eyes sent a chill through her bones. "You are ruined."

She flinched. Never had she more resented that term. It seemed to sully everything about what they'd just shared. "I hardly think my loss of virginity will be a bar to finding a husband. Not that I would mind if it did."

Something pained flickered in his gaze before anger smothered it. The fingers caressing her jaw stopped and held firmly. "Am I to understand that you were using me for your own ends, Flora?" His voice was deceptively calm, though nothing had ever felt so dangerous. "To make yourself less appealing as a bride, perhaps?"

She couldn't deny that the thought had crossed her mind, but she never would have given herself to him for that alone. She shook her head. "That was not my intent. No more than you were using me for your own, I'm sure." He held perfectly still. He might have masked his reaction, but there had been one.

Had she simply wounded his pride by refusing, or was there something more? She didn't want to hurt him, but she needed to be sure that his motives for wanting her were what they appeared—surety that so far he'd been unable to provide. But there was no denying the magic of what had just occurred between them. Magic that she didn't want to lose in unwarranted suspicion.

She held the wrist of the hand on her face and leaned up to place a tender kiss on his lips. "Please, don't be angry. I don't want to let this misunderstanding ruin the beauty of what just happened. Your honor is intact. I came to you willingly, and with full understanding of the consequences. I would do so again, if you asked."

* * *

Lachlan couldn't believe it. *What could she be thinking?* He didn't want her as his leman, but as his wife. He bit back a crude retort and the spur of anger unleashed by her refusal.

Did she think him simply a stud, good enough to fuck but not refined enough to marry? He'd never asked a woman to be his wife before. And never had he anticipated a refusal, let alone one that would sting so badly. Coming as it was on the heels of the most incredible sexual encounter of his life. Making love to Flora had been unlike anything he'd ever experienced. Deep. Raw. Powerful. Life-changing.

It was as though he'd waited his entire life for something he hadn't even known was missing. And now that he'd found her, he sure as hell wouldn't let her go. Not without a fight. She belonged to him, she just didn't know it yet.

They'd made love. She'd given him her innocence, he had every right to expect that she would marry him. Under normal circumstances, she wouldn't have a choice. But he couldn't be sure that Rory would compel her to marry him, even now. Nor did he want to force a marriage between them that way—not if there was a chance he could convince her.

And he intended to do just that.

He ran his finger down her collarbone and over the lush tip of her bare breast. Her nipple tightened immediately. He'd prove to her that despite their different backgrounds, they were alike in the only way that mattered.

"No one else will ever make you feel like this."

She eyed him warily, the soft flush of desire working its way across her body as fingers skimmed the soft naked velvet of her belly to reach between her legs and probe her intimately. She was wet and soft and responded to his touch with a sensuous press of her hips.

He loved the way she closed her eyes and squeezed her legs against his hand.

He surrendered to the sultry haze for just a moment, reveling in the completeness of her response. Leaning over, he gave her a hard kiss on the lips and slid his finger from her damp heat. His body, stirred by her response, throbbed its objection.

Her eyes opened in surprise at the swift curtailment of pleasure.

But if he had to wait, so would she. "Not again, Flora. I won't make love to you until you agree to be my wife."

Her eyes flashed with anger. "That was a rotten trick."

He shrugged, not disagreeing. "I would do right by you this instant. Say the word and I will give you more pleasure than you can stand."

She turned away, her long blond hair spilling over his plaid like a silky golden veil. He wanted her so much, it hurt. Her continued refusal—her rejection—gnawed at him. As did another possibility.

He took her chin and turned her back to face him. "And what if there is a child, Flora?" he said, his voice deceptively flat. "What of that consequence?"

She let out a small gasp of surprise. Her hands unconsciously covered her naked stomach.

"Apparently you did not consider all of the ramifications."

"I'm s-sure the likelihood is small," she stammered.

"If there is a child, you will marry me, even if I have to drag you to the door of the kirk myself. Do you understand?" The fierceness of his tone left no doubt that he meant every word.

Eyes wide, she nodded.

He stood up, donned his clothes, and left her without a glance to ready the horses for their return. In truth, he didn't trust himself to say another word. He was still too damn angry by her refusal.

But anger wasn't the only emotion tying him in knots. His reaction when she'd nearly died should have warned him, and now that they'd made love . . . he'd gotten in too deep.

He wasn't as detached as he needed to be in the situation. Hell, he wasn't detached at all.

He raked his fingers through his hair, wondering how a simple plan had become so complicated. Two months ago, he'd wondered whether he'd made a bad bargain. He remembered thinking that Argyll had agreed too easily, and now he knew why. Flora MacLeod was trouble. He just hadn't anticipated how much. Or that the trouble would impact him so personally. Balancing her feelings with his duty was no easy feat.

He'd finished readying the horses and returned to find her dressed, the plaid folded, and the remainder of the food packed away. All signs of what had transpired not a quarter of an hour ago were gone.

"Are you ready?" he asked.

She nodded and gave him a hesitant look. "Are you still very angry?"

He was, but not only at her. The situation had spun out of control. Mistakenly, he'd thought that once they made love, she would agree to marry him. He'd admitted that he cared for her, but it wasn't enough. She wanted something more from him. More than he could give. He was a chief, he had responsibilities—too many people were counting on him.

Just looking at her, seeing the vulnerability on her face, tore at his heart—and at his conscience.

He drew her into his arms and pressed a tender kiss on her still swollen lips. Tempted to take more, but too cognizant of the danger—at how quickly the fire between them could flare out of control.

Lifting his mouth from hers, he looked into her confused eyes. "I'm not a man used to taking no for an answer, Flora. Be forewarned, I intend to convince you otherwise." He put his mouth close to her ear, nibbled lightly on the sweet lobe, and breathed softly, savoring the way she shuddered against him. "No matter what it takes," he whispered. His hand moved to cup her breast, rubbing his thumb over the fabric of her gown. She softened against him, her body responding to his seductive stroke.

His cock hardened, and his body flooded with heat. He wanted her, but not just the response of her body. He wanted her heart. He wanted to bind her to him, so that nothing, even the truth, would tear them apart. "I'm not a patient man, my sweet. Don't make me wait too long."

Chapter 14

❖

Flora's resistance was crumbling. Lachlan Maclean was nothing if not true to his word. Over the past few days since their return from the Faerie Pool, he seemed to have made it his mission to drive her mad with longing.

He took every opportunity to touch her, to stand too close, to whisper in her ear—his mouth achingly close, but never close enough.

And never far from her consciousness was the memory of what he'd done to her. The passion that, once unleashed, wanted to run free. He'd kissed her mouth, her breasts, her . . . Heat crept up her cheeks just thinking about it. She couldn't believe he'd kissed her *there*, but neither could she forget the shattering sensation that followed. Never had she felt such pleasure, until he'd thrust deep inside her—filling her—and started to move.

He held his experience over her, teasing her with the promise of what he could do to her. Hinting at pleasure she could only imagine, but which she wanted—badly. "On edge" didn't begin to describe her state. She felt as if she were walking around ready to explode at any moment.

Her only salvation was the mornings she spent with Mary and Gilly at their lessons. Only then did he offer her a brief respite from his seductive attentions.

She sighed, knowing her temporary peace of mind was coming to an end. Mary and Gilly had just left their makeshift schoolroom to dress for the midday meal, leaving Flora to finish tidying up. The girls had readily accepted her apology for leaving without saying goodbye and seemed to have understood her attempt to leave without demanding the specifics.

She'd just slid one of the folios they'd been using— *Songs and Sonnets,* a collection that included works by the former Earl of Surrey and Sir Thomas Wyatt—back onto the shelf when a tanned muscular arm wrapped around her waist from behind. She felt the subtle press of his hard body, the heat, and the impossible strength. His fingers gripped her hips, pulling her closer—molding her body to his.

When he pressed behind her like this and nudged his hips, it made her wonder . . . was it possible? She shook off the image. What had he done to her?

Like a powerful magnet, he drew her in. His touch, his scent, the warmth of his breath on her neck. The force of his presence shattered her resolve. Awash in heat, she melted against him. Her body, which had been in constant deprivation for the past few days, felt aroused to the point of bursting—reveling in any opportunity for contact, no matter how brief.

He dug his face in her hair, nuzzling along her neck, his lips as soft as a feather along her skin until she shivered, but never giving her the friction she craved.

"Miss me?" he whispered near her ear.

The warmth of his breath tickled, and the tiny hairs on the back of her neck stood up. The dark, rich brogue was like molten lava that had seeped into her bones. But she heard the mockery and wanted to curse him, almost as much as she wanted to sink against him and beg him to take her again.

"N-no," she answered, her voice shaking.

"Liar." He let go of her, backing away. It took a few

moments to compose herself and for her pulse to return to normal before she turned around to look at him.

"What are you doing here?" she asked. "I thought you said you would be away this afternoon." *To give me time to recover from this morning's teasing.*

He quirked his brow, amused, as if he knew exactly what she was thinking. "I am. I'm leaving right now. I just came by to remind you of our lesson tomorrow."

How could she forget another swimming lesson? She smiled sweetly. "I'm looking forward to it."

"So am I."

She didn't miss the naughty innuendo and bit back a giggle; she could well imagine what he had planned. But his plans would come to naught. "Oh, by the way," she said offhandedly, "I've invited your sisters to come along."

One corner of his mouth lifted. "Afraid of being alone with me, Flora?"

She straightened her back. "Of course not. Don't be ridiculous."

He chuckled, knowing the lie for what it was. She *was* scared of being alone with him. Of what she might agree to if pushed. And he'd been pushing hard, very hard.

She lifted her gaze to his. "I just thought the girls might like a day away from the monotony of the castle. It will be fun." She paused. "Perhaps Allan could go as well." His eyes narrowed, guessing what she was up to. "You did promise to reconsider your decision about Mary."

He gave her a long look. "I have."

"And?"

He shook his head. "I'm sorry, lass, but my decision stands. The alliance with Ian MacDonald of Glengarry is too important."

Flora didn't bother to hide her disappointment. "I see." But she didn't. He still didn't understand. Still didn't see that his sister should have a choice. He saw only duty.

"And what about you, Flora? Have you reconsidered?"

"How can you speak of our marriage when your sister is so unhappy? You would force her to a marriage she doesn't want." She let the implication fall. She could never marry a man who had so little regard for his sister's wishes. It was too similar to what had happened to her mother.

His gaze hardened almost imperceptibly, but she recognized the small changes in his expression that weeks ago would have seemed nothing.

"I am not forcing her. Mary understands that we all must make sacrifices for the good of the clan, why can't you?"

But marriage shouldn't be a sacrifice she should be asked to make. Flora knew he was right: Mary would go through with it out of some warped sense of duty. In that they were very different. "I would never marry a man in that situation."

He tensed. "But this isn't about you. It's about Mary. This isn't your fight, yet you've turned it into your personal crusade."

Flora bristled. "You're wrong. I only want to give Mary a chance at happiness. I thought you would understand."

"I do understand, Flora. But my sister's feelings are not the only issue."

"But you said—"

"I did not promise to change my mind, only to reconsider. I did so."

"But—"

"Do not try to manipulate me to your bidding, Flora."

"Are you sure it is not the other way around?" she asked, referring to his seduction.

A strange expression crossed his face, and not for the first time she wondered if there was something else behind that look. She studied his face, wishing she could see through stone. "Why did you really bring me here?"

He hesitated. "To get my castle back from your brother."

"And to marry me?"

His gaze flickered over her face. "It seemed a good idea."

Her instincts flared. He was clearly choosing his words with care. "Why?"

He shrugged. "Many reasons."

"Such as?"

Her persistence was getting to him, and his annoyance was evident in the flex of his jaw and the white lines around his mouth. "What would you like me to say, Flora? I know how you feel about your situation as a marriage prize."

She lifted her chin. "The truth." *I can take it. I hope.*

He held her gaze. "You are beautiful, rich, powerfully connected, and"—he gestured to the amulet—"a symbol to my people as an end to an eighty-year curse. I'd be a fool not to want to marry you."

She flinched. She'd asked for the truth, and he'd given it to her. But why did it have to sting so much?

He must have sensed the pain his frank words caused, because in the next instant she was in his arms. "Just because I recognize your value as a potential bride doesn't mean I can't want you for myself."

She heard it in his voice: He was telling the truth. Her eyes flickered across his face, looking for signs, anything that would point her in the right direction. "And there is no other reason?"

* * *

Why did she always have to push him? Couldn't she just leave well enough alone?

It was the question Lachlan didn't want to answer. If there was ever a time to tell her the truth, this was it.

He felt as if he were being torn in opposite directions, forced to choose between two undesirable ends. He could tell Flora about his bargain with Argyll and risk his brother and clan if she refused him, or lie and tell her there was no other reason he wanted to marry her in the hope that it would impress her enough to accept his suit.

He knew she was wavering—warring with desire and her fear of being used like her mother. If he told her, it would only confirm those fears. He could guess how she would react. He was using her—for honorable ends—but using her nonetheless. And now that he knew her, he understood what that would do to her. She cared for him, of that he was certain; but would it be enough to forgive his manipulation? For that was how she would see it.

Who was he fooling? Any choice he had was illusory. He needed Argyll's help, and he must do what was necessary to get it. He might be able to retake his castle by siege or subterfuge, but at what cost? He'd lost too many men already, and the fighting would only further infuriate a king who wanted an end to feuding. But then there was his brother, imprisoned at Blackness Castle— the king's impenetrable stronghold. He'd never be able to secure his brother's release from Blackness without Argyll's influence, and attempting to break him out by force would be a suicide mission.

If only there were another way. Any attempt to free John would have to be undertaken with cunning and trickery, and thus far, Lachlan had been unable to think of a suitable plan—one that would not unduly risk more men.

He also realized that if he told her about his bargain

with her cousin, he could very well lose her. And that was something he couldn't risk. Once his brother was safe, he swore he would explain everything.

It was an untenable situation, one that he wanted to end.

He felt her scrutiny as she waited for his response. Scrutiny that only increased his frustration with the entire situation. "Why must you persist in denying what is between us?" he said almost angrily. "Are you so worried about ending up like your mother that you would rather end up alone?"

Flora recoiled as if he'd struck her. "Of course not. You don't know what you are talking about."

She started to spin away, but he grabbed her arm and swung her back toward him. Close enough to feel the flutter of her heart and inhale the intoxicating floral scent that surrounded her—taunting him. His body grew taut with anger and desire. "You know what I think, Flora? I think you are scared. Scared to take a chance. So scared you'll make the wrong decision that you reject everyone who comes too close. Your brothers. Your sisters. Me. Your life has been as much a reaction against your mother's life as it has been your own. You are too busy fighting everyone to recognize those who only want the best for you."

Her cheeks flushed an angry red. "How dare you! You have no right—"

"I have every right," he growled. He heard the fury in his voice, but damn it, she pushed him, prodding parts of him that had never before been exposed. "The moment you gave yourself to me, I earned that right. What does it matter other than I care for you and you care for me? Does it matter how it came to be? Or why I want you, other than the fact that I do?" He knew he was trying to convince himself, almost as much as he was trying to convince her, skating precariously close to the truth.

"It matters to me," she said softly, her eyes bright.

She looked so proud and vulnerable at that moment, he wished he could take her in his arms and wipe away her fears with his mouth. "It shouldn't. I would never hurt you, lass. Not intentionally. I want to protect you. Cherish you. Take care of you. Surely you know that?" It was the truth. He'd never wanted a woman the way he wanted her—completely. Body and heart.

"I don't know what to think."

He buried his face in the warmth of her silky hair, nuzzling the baby soft skin of her neck, aroused to the breaking point by the erotic sensation of her responsive body pressed against his. "Maybe you are thinking too much."

He felt her softening, melting against him . . . wanting him.

Blood surged through his veins. "I should go," he said, pulling back forcibly. "Unless there is a reason for me to stay?"

Eyes wide, she shook her head. "Y-you never said where you are going."

He stiffened at the reminder. He thought about telling her exactly where he was going and the reports of abuse against his people by her brother Hector on Coll, but without proof he wasn't sure she would believe him. He didn't need any more barriers between them. "To attend to some of my lands. I will return later tonight. I should be going." He started to pull away, but she stopped him with a hand on his arm.

"Lachlan."

He looked down at her, surprised—and pleased—to hear the intimacy of his given name on her tongue. For a moment, he actually thought she might have changed her mind.

"You never answered my question."

No, he hadn't. Nor would he. He cupped her chin in

his fingers and lowered his face, keeping his gaze locked on hers, wanting nothing more than to cover her mouth and taste her. To feel her tongue slide in his mouth, entwining with his. "I said all that was important. Now it's for you to decide. Take a chance or live in the past, it's up to you." Unable to resist, he dropped a soft kiss on her lips, lingering as his mouth moved over hers in a possessive caress. The urge to deepen the kiss was primal, but he couldn't. Not yet. He lifted his head, seeing desire mirrored on her face. "Let me know what you decide."

And without another word, he left her to ponder their future.

Hector stormed through the gates of Breacachadh on his destrier, more furious than he'd been in some time—since the last time the Laird of Coll had gotten the best of him.

He dismounted and tossed his reins to the waiting stable lad. Sweat poured off his forehead from behind the metal helmet, and his body shook with rage.

Lachlan Maclean had been right under his nose and had escaped. And not alone. He'd absconded with half a dozen men and a few market-ready head of cattle as well.

Men and cattle that belonged to Hector.

When word had come of Coll's presence on the isle, Hector couldn't believe his luck. He'd raced to reach him, but by the time he'd arrived, the skirmish was over.

A score of his warriors had been bested by a mere handful of Coll's. His fists clenched with the urge to thrash someone.

Damn Coll! He would pay. Not only for the loss of men and source of silver—both of which he needed in his war with MacDonald—but for daring to abduct his valuable sister.

He pushed through the entrance into the great hall, paying no mind to the mud and muck he tracked across the rugs strewn over the wooden floors.

Where was that bloody woman? "Mairi!" he bellowed, in no mood for recalcitrant servants. The dour old maidservant finally appeared in the doorway, moving with the speed of an aged tortoise.

"Get me my claret and be quick about it."

"Yes, my laird."

There was nothing outwardly mocking about the response, but Hector heard it nonetheless. Blood pounded in his ears. He was fed up with morose and belligerent servants. These people would learn respect. They would learn who was laird.

He tossed his claymore to the squire who'd followed him in. "Clean this. And if it's not sharp this time, I'll cut off your incompetent hand."

The fear he saw on the lad's face was a soothing balm to his anger. That was better. If they didn't listen to reason, they would listen to his iron fist. But they *would* listen.

Mairi returned with his drink. God, he was thirsty. His mouth was as dry and parched as a desert. He took a long drink and nearly choked, spewing the dark liquid across the floor. His eyes narrowed at the stubborn old biddy. "How dare you serve me this swill. Bring me another flagon." He met the woman's defiant glare. His fingers tightened around the goblet. "And while you're at it, find your daughter." The woman's eyes widened with horror. He smiled. "What was her name? Janet? I'd like to . . . talk to her."

He'd finally gotten her attention. The woman's hands fluttered anxiously like the wings of a bird. "I'm afraid my daughter is gone, my laird."

"You'll find her and bring her to me," he said with

deadly calm. "Or if you'd rather, you can bring me your other daughter."

The defiance sagged right out of her, but the broken expression on her face failed to move him one inch.

"But my laird, she's just three and ten."

He shrugged. "It makes no difference to me." He gave her a hard look. "You choose. But I'll have one of them. If you defy me, I'll have them both."

The old woman's eyes took on an unnatural brightness. "It was the devil that brought you here. A curse you are. But our laird will return—"

"Hold your tongue, woman, or I'll cut it out." She shot him an evil glance before she moved to do his bidding. Fools. He didn't want to hear any more about damn curses. He was tired of the crazed superstitions of these people. He knew they blamed him for the failure of the crops this year, which was ridiculous considering the wind and rain that had pummeled the small isle.

The wrath of the lady, they claimed. Hector had forgotten about the curse until the old witch Beathag, Coll's healer, had mentioned it. And with his mother dead, he realized who now wore the amulet—Flora.

Why hadn't he thought of that before?

Rumors of Coll's courtship of his sister worried him more than he wanted to admit. His sister wouldn't betray him by marrying his enemy. But how well did he know her?

If Coll married Flora, Hector knew that the "end" of the curse would be a powerful symbol against him, silly superstition or not. But it was the alliance with Argyll that worried him. Under no circumstances could a marriage between them be allowed to happen.

Just one more reason to want Coll dead. He sat in a chair set before the fire and began to plan. His enemy's daring foray had given him an idea.

Chapter 15

❖

The party that traveled to the Faerie Pool was larger than Lachlan had intended and included himself, Flora, his sisters, and a handful of his guardsmen. They arrived before noontide and spent the better part of the day eating, drinking, and frolicking in the water. Perhaps it wasn't the sort of frolicking he'd originally planned, but he admitted it had been an enjoyable day—particularly coming on the heels of his victory yesterday against Hector.

Though he was happy to have some of his men back, he could not forget the suffering he'd seen and those he'd left behind. Rain had destroyed the crops, and the fields were bare; the people were forced to give Duart what little they had left. And the stories of Duart's abuse—especially the womenfolk—filled him with rage. But he needed men to retake his castle against Duart's much larger force, men he didn't have. Not yet, at least. But he would. Waiting for the king to decide in his favor was no longer an option; he needed Rory MacLeod—and his fighting force. And that would come with a marriage alliance.

His gaze fell to Flora, who stood knee deep in the water, laughing with Mary and Gilly—both of whom had followed Flora's lead in borrowing clothing from his men. Gilly had just splashed Murdoch in the face, and the lad was doing his best to ignore her.

After the skirmish yesterday, Lachlan had thought

it prudent to bring along half a dozen guardsmen—including Allan, though now he wished he hadn't. Observing the heartbreak on his sister's face when her gaze fell upon his captain was enough to convince him that he'd severely underestimated his sister's sentiments. Allan's refusal to meet Mary's gaze—following his laird's instructions—only made it worse. He could see the flicker of pain in his sister's eyes each time Allan's gaze swept over her.

Damn.

"What's wrong?" Flora had emerged from the water to stand before him on the rocky shore. Deeply conscious of the wet shirt that clung to her body and his own naked chest, he forced his gaze not to drop below her shoulders.

"Nothing." He leaned over and plucked his shirt from the rock, not wanting to talk about Mary. It was a subject they could not agree upon. Her mother had raised Flora with no sense of obligation or familial duty. To her it was a simple matter, but to him it was complicated by his responsibility to his clan. "It is getting late, we should be leaving." He started to pull the shirt over his head, but Flora stopped him with a touch. He flinched, the press of her cool fingers a shocking brand against his skin.

"What happened?" she asked, tracing the outline of the mottled bruise on his ribs. "I noticed it earlier."

He sucked in his breath as her fingers dipped to his waist. Just a simple touch was enough to fill him with heat. "Studying me closely, Flora?"

She blushed. "Of course not. It's hard to miss, that's all." Her gaze locked on his. "You were in a fight."

"It was nothing."

"It doesn't look like nothing. It looks like you took a heavy blow with a sword. Won't you tell me what happened?"

He'd been dispensing with one of Duart's men when another had surprised him from behind. The man had managed one blow, but it had been his last. He took her wrist to stop the dip of her hand; she was driving him mad. She gasped at the contact, and he made the mistake of looking down. The shirt was plastered to her skin, revealing the lush shape of her breasts to his hungry gaze. God, he ached to touch her. The memory of what had taken place on this very shore was too fresh. Too vivid. The hard evidence of his arousal grew between them. It was nearly impossible to stand beside this woman he'd bedded, inhaling her perfume, knowing how she felt in his arms, and not being able to claim her. A woman he wanted for so many reasons. She'd invaded his senses, his thoughts, his dreams.

"You'll stop touching me, my sweet, unless you'd care to finish what you started with an audience."

Her eyes dropped, widening as she took in his condition. She looked at him a second too long, the weight of her eyes more erotic than a harlot's trick.

"Well?" he repeated.

She shook her head.

"Then take my sisters with you while you change."

She started to walk away but turned back to him. "Lachlan, I . . ."

"Yes?"

"I'm sorry. I didn't mean . . ."

She looked so flustered, he had to smile. "I know. Now hurry. It grows late."

He watched her hurry to do his bidding and felt warmth spread over him that had nothing to do with the heat of the sun. It felt odd to have someone concerned about him. He could get used to it.

Mary and Gilly had finished changing out of their wet clothing and rejoined the men, but Flora lingered behind the welcome shelter of the rock, needing the time to collect her thoughts. Thoughts that had been in a jumble after her exchange with Lachlan a few minutes ago.

For a moment—standing so close to him, seeing the strength of his arousal, remembering the feel of him inside her, craving the intimacy of those moments—she'd nearly succumbed. She forgot everything except her need for him.

The magnitude of her response had hit her hard. She'd stared at him, wanting him . . . needing him. And if it hadn't been for his reminder of where they were, she feared she might have reached out and touched him.

It was like fire between them, igniting with the barest spark. A touch. A look. A word.

What was holding her back? Was Lachlan right? Was she so scared of ending up like her mother that she would toss away a chance at happiness? She didn't want to think so, yet his words had stung far more than she cared to admit. She told herself she was only being cautious, but what if he was right? Was she imagining deception where there was none?

She sighed and finished lacing the front of her gown. After pulling back her long damp hair, she secured it at her nape with a scrap of ribbon. Her swimming lessons were helping. Today, she'd managed to go completely under without panicking—though she never would have done it without Lachlan right beside her.

With her wet clothes secured in a bundle, she took a last look around to make sure they hadn't forgotten anything.

Noticing one of Gilly's hose on the ground, she bent to pick it up and heard the crack of a twig behind her. Before she could react, someone grabbed her from behind. A dirty hand covered her mouth, muffling the scream that tore from her throat.

Fear gripped her; she knew right away it wasn't

Lachlan—and that this was no game. The man, though large and strong, was not nearly as tall and solid as Lachlan. Also, he smelled—not of myrtle and soap, but of sweat and horse.

He was suffocating her, his fetid fingers digging into the tender skin of her mouth and cheeks.

His mouth fell to her ear. "Make no sound or we'll kill them all," he whispered, and the stench of his breath filled her nose, making her stomach turn. "It's you we want."

Flora could hardly believe it—she was being abducted again. She would laugh if she weren't so terrified—and if she could move her lips.

The man started to drag her into the trees. She wanted to twist and stomp on his foot the way she had with Lachlan, but she dared not risk it. Not with Mary and Gilly so close. She prayed they were far enough away.

"Flora, I . . ."

God, no! It was Gilly. She'd come around the rock, no doubt to check on what was taking her so long. Frantically, Flora tried to warn her with her eyes, but it was too late.

She heard the man holding her let out a vile explicative just as Gilly screamed. "*Help!* Oh, my God, Lachlan, *help*! A man has Flora!"

Her captor gave up trying to drag her and lifted her off the ground, eliminating her ability to attempt her favored method of escape. Knowing Gilly's screams had alerted the group and that it was too late to avoid danger to the others, she twisted and thrashed against him.

He only gripped her harder. His fingers tore into her cheeks as his hand tightened like a vise around her mouth and nose, cutting off her breath. The other arm was coiled around her ribs. She stopped struggling, pulling his hand instead as she fought for air.

They'd reached a clearing beyond the circle of trees,

perhaps a hundred feet from the Faerie Pool, when he released her, pushing her toward another man. She bent over, gasping for breath, hearing the sounds of fighting coming from where they'd just left. Her heart dropped as she realized what must be happening.

The other man rushed toward them, leading a horse. "What happened?" he asked.

"A girl saw me taking her."

"Who are you?" she gasped. "What do you want with me?"

"We've come to help you," said the man with the horse. He was about forty years of age and had a pleasant weathered face. "My name is Aonghus. Your brother sent us to rescue you from your abductor."

Her brother? "Which one?" she demanded.

The man looked confused for a minute before he said, "The Maclean of Duart."

Hector. The sounds of the fighting were growing louder. A sharp scream tore through the air, and she spun around. *Oh, dear God, that was Gilly.* She started to make a move back toward the fighting, but the restraining grip of her initial captor held her. For the first time, she got a good look at him. Her first thought was of hair. It blanketed most of his face with his heavy dark brows, a beard, and thick sideburns. His eyes were dark as well and none too friendly.

"Get your hands off me."

Her tone startled him, and he let her go.

"I apologize for Cormac, my lady," the other man, Aonghus, interjected. "But we did not want to take a chance that you would alert them to our presence."

"I think it's too late for that." Her eyes kept darting to the trees. She could hear the thrash of men coming toward them. Flora didn't know what to do. She just didn't want anyone to be hurt on her account. A few weeks ago, she would have leapt at the opportunity to escape, but now . . . now everything had changed. "You must call off your men. There has been a misunderstanding. I am no longer a prisoner." She took a step toward the sounds when her captor moved to block her.

"You have been deceived. Coll is not what he seems—"

But he never finished because at that moment all hell broke loose.

Lachlan had sensed something was wrong. He'd motioned for his men to form a perimeter, getting into position only moments before the attack started from the west. The sound of Gilly's scream sent ice shooting through his veins. And then he realized that someone had Flora—and that they'd just been outflanked. He'd recognized a few of the men and knew retaliation for yesterday's foray had been swift, but he quickly realized it was more than that. This wasn't just a raiding party, they were after Flora. Hector wanted his sister back. Or more likely, he didn't want Lachlan to have her.

They must have been scouting for an attack and come upon them by chance. Thank God he'd had the foresight to bring extra men.

He fought like a man possessed—with only two thoughts, the safety of his sisters and reaching Flora in time.

They'd easily repelled the initial attack, and he immediately ordered Allan and a few of the other men to see his sisters home to safety. Then, having gathered the rest of his men, he went after Flora—his chest twisting as he realized he didn't know whether she wanted to stay or go. The thought that given the chance she might leave him wormed its way into his heart.

But he wouldn't let her go without a fight.

Flora had never been more happy to see anyone in her life.

Men poured from the trees, Lachlan in the lead, with at least four men hard on his tail. He looked around, his gaze locking on hers. She saw the relief and realized that he'd been worried—for her. She counted at least a dozen of her brother's men and only three of Lachlan's—Murdoch was the only one she knew by name. He must have sent Allan and the others back with Mary and Gilly. She prayed they were safe.

She'd seen Lachlan training with his men, but nothing could have prepared her for witnessing him in battle. He wielded his claymore with unbelievable strength and agility, swinging it in a high arc with one hand to force back an attacker, thrusting his dirk with the other. It was brutal and graceful at the same time, and undeniably powerful. This was the fierce edge to him that she'd always sensed lurking under the surface.

Highlanders are barbarians, nothing more than bloodthirsty killers. Her mother's words came back to her. If Flora didn't know Lachlan, watching him right now, she might think the same. But she did know him. And the hand that held his claymore with deadly purpose could also caress with tenderness. The hard blue eyes that killed ruthlessly could also be soft and gentle. Yes, he was a formidable warrior, but he was so much more.

The danger he faced set her heart racing. But despite the odds against him, Lachlan appeared completely in control—almost eerily calm and more dangerous than she'd ever seen him. He looked like a man who'd spent a lifetime on a battlefield. *He had*, she realized. But until now she hadn't understood what that meant, of what it must have been like. Her admiration only increased. She couldn't imagine what it must be like to face death constantly.

His skills were dominating. He dispatched two of his

attackers with relative ease, purposefully making his way toward her.

The odds were improving. It was perhaps only eight to four now. Plus the two men who guarded her, she realized.

"Come, my lady," Aonghus said. "It's not safe for you here, we must leave."

"But I can't . . ." Flora hesitated, looking back at Lachlan. She couldn't leave him. Or, more accurately, she didn't want to leave him.

Cormac must have read her hesitation, because he pushed her toward Aonghus. "Take her, I'll take care of Coll." He drew his sword from the baldric at his back. The deadly blade sent a shiver rippling through her. She sensed this man was a threat.

Aonghus tried to lead her off, but she jerked out of his hold. Though the brutality of battle horrified her, she couldn't turn away. Not while Lachlan was in danger. Her heart rose in her throat as the brute who'd captured her attacked Lachlan.

She felt the force of every heavy strike reverberate through her bones as the two men exchanged blows. How could they stand it? Even the sound was horrible.

Out of the corner of her eye, Flora saw one of Lachlan's men cut down. A strangled sound emerged from her throat, and from the fury in his gaze, she realized that Lachlan had seen it, too. He struck harder against his opponent, lowering the sword with such force, it would have cut Cormac in two had he not blocked it.

Though her brother's man didn't have the strength or skill of Lachlan, he was an able warrior—with surprising agility for a man of his size and weight—which was considerable. The brute continued to block stroke after stroke and didn't seem to be tiring.

Lachlan's arms and torso flexed with his exertions; she didn't know how much longer he would be able to keep it up. The relentless attacking had surely sapped his strength—not that you would know it from looking at him. He barely seemed to be breathing hard.

She chanced a glance at the others. Her hand covered her mouth. Murdoch was in trouble—he was being forced back against the trees with nowhere to go. Lachlan's remaining guardsman tried to get to him to help but was set upon by three of her brother's men.

With his men in danger, something came over Lachlan. He moved with cold purpose. Not frenzied, but strong and sure. Cormac sensed it as well. He tried to swing his blade, but Lachlan nearly plucked it from his hand with a hard twist of his wrist. The moment of surprise was all the opening he needed. He plunged his dirk into Cormac's gut, and Flora looked away.

Aonghus swore. The death of the other man had clearly rattled him. He kept shooting furtive glances toward the trees. Flora had the horrible suspicion that he was waiting for reinforcements. No longer content to watch the battle unfold before them, he urged her away with renewed vigor. Though not much taller than she, he was wiry and strong.

"Let go of me," Flora said, ripping her arm from his hold. "I'll not leave—"

"Forgive me, my lady, but I'm afraid I must insist." He took hold of her and forcibly pulled her toward the waiting horse. She wanted to shout to Lachlan for help, but he'd gone to Murdoch's aid and was engaged with three of her brother's men—she dared not risk the distraction. Instead, she used all her strength to resist him, all the time keeping her eyes pinned on the fight.

She muffled a cry, seeing Lachlan surrounded. He warded off blow after blow, but they kept closing in on him. *Dear God, they were going to cut him to shreds.* At least Murdoch was holding his own now that one of the men pinning him back had turned to Lachlan. The remaining guardsman from Coll—a man she recognized as one of Murdoch's friends—was trying to stave off two others, but he stumbled on a root. Flora sucked in her breath and turned her head, unable to watch as one of her brother's men plunged a dirk into his heart. She knew he was dead when the two men he'd been fighting joined the others against Lachlan.

Panic rose in the back of her throat. He was fighting five men. He would not be able to hold them back forever, no matter how superior his fighting skills. Her fears were soon realized. A scream strangled in her throat when one of her brother's men slashed high across Lachlan's arm. The gash that tore through his shirt was horrifying. Bile rose in her throat as blood flooded the white sleeve crimson.

Aonghus was still dragging her from behind toward the horse, and she stomped down as hard as she could on his foot, as she'd done with Lachlan, and twisted out of his arms. Then she ran toward Lachlan.

In that moment, nothing had ever been clearer. She didn't want to go with her brother's men; she didn't want to leave Lachlan.

She loved him.

The intense initial attraction she'd felt for him had grown stronger as she came to know him. Behind the implacable façade, she'd discovered a man of surprising tenderness. With him she felt safe, protected—and, most of all, wanted. She'd been lost after the death of her mother, and he'd given her a home with a family. He was a rough and brutal Highland chief, but pure of heart and honorable. He was a survivor. A man who'd had to fight for his heritage and his clan not only with brute strength, but with cunning.

He was the first man not to be intimidated by her in some way, whether by her wealth, her supposed beauty, her connections, or her so-called willfulness—which

Flora simply considered confidence. Lachlan challenged her and didn't back down. And she respected him enough to heed the warning. She admired his fortitude, his calm under pressure, and his physical strength.

She loved him more than she'd ever dreamed possible. If only she'd realized it sooner. Not now, when it might be too late.

She raced toward him. But with so many men surrounding him, she'd temporarily lost sight of him.

She searched frantically through the circle of tall, imposing men, to no avail. Hearing the heavy breath of Aonghus as he closed in behind her, she ran faster. A branch snagged her cheek, but she was barely aware of the stinging pain. One of the men surrounding Lachlan fell, and she caught a glimpse of him before the circle around him closed again. The sight of him at that moment would stay with her forever. Swinging his sword with deadly grace, fending off blows from all around, standing proud and strong, as confident as if he faced only one man and not four. No matter his rough ways and his lack of schooling, she would be proud to have this man stand beside her. She would be proud to call him husband.

Thankfully, Murdoch had managed to get the best of his attacker and had moved to help his chief—engaging the man closest to him. Though there were now only three men left, she could see that Lachlan was tiring, his movements slower and more laborious. Sweat poured off his forehead, and blood now soaked his entire sleeve and part of his chest. It was his sword arm, she realized, and blood was running down his arm, soaking his hand.

Holding off five men had taken its toll. She experienced a fleeting moment of hope when another of the men surrounding him fell. Now numb to the horror, she did not turn away. Her primal instincts for survival—his survival—had flared. She knew it wouldn't be over until the last man fell.

What happened next seemed to pass in slow motion. Lachlan's blade flashed above his head as he blocked a blow from his right. He then moved his hands to block a nearly simultaneous blow from the left, but the sword landed with a resounding thump on his head. Lachlan dropped to the ground like a rock, and a scream tore from her throat. *"No!"* she cried. He couldn't die.

Felling their enemy had stunned the two men for a moment and stopped the fight between Murdoch and his attacker. Hector's men recovered quickly, and one lifted his sword for the death blow across Lachlan's still body. She didn't think, just threw herself on top of him.

"No!" She glared up at the men through tear-filled eyes. "Don't touch him." She peered up at them with her arms around Lachlan, relieved to feel the beat of his heart.

Aonghus was right behind her. "Get out of the way, my lady."

The look she gave him could have started a fire. "I'll not leave him."

Murdoch had moved to stand behind them. "The lady said she wanted to be left alone," he said.

Her brother's men were clearly at an impasse. She could see the indecision on their faces as they grappled with her surprising resistance.

"Come, my lady," the man tried to persuade her. "Your brother only wishes for your safety."

"Tell him that I appreciate his help, but I'm perfectly safe and content where I am."

Lachlan regained consciousness, feeling as if his head had shattered into a thousand pieces. But he was also aware of the sweetly soft body pressing against his.

When he heard her words, proclaiming before her

brother's men that she wanted to stay with him, he thought his heart would explode as well as his head. Relief, happiness, and amazement crashed over him.

"Are you sure, lass?"

He felt her startle, and then those beautiful blue eyes locked on his. What he saw there answered his question, even as her words confirmed it. "I've never been more certain of anything in my life."

The conviction in her voice was like a song from the gods.

His gaze darted to Murdoch, and reading Lachlan's intent, the lad moved around to stand between him and Hector's men. Ignoring the pain in his head and arm, he sprang to his feet, hauling Flora up after him.

He addressed their leader, an old warrior he recognized—they'd crossed paths before. "You heard the lady, Aonghus. She does not wish to leave."

"I have my orders."

Lachlan caught the other man's glance toward the trees. Guessing the direction of his thoughts, he said, "The rest of your men won't be coming back." He shifted Flora behind him and lifted his sword, which thankfully was still in his blood-soaked hand. "There has been enough death for today. Leave now or the next will be your own."

"You speak boldly for a man with one arm and a lad against three."

He heard Murdoch's grumble of outrage and quieted him with his hand.

He wouldn't need more, but pointing it out would only force Duart's men to fight to defend their honor. So instead he said, "Aye, but I have good reason to fight." He gave a meaningful glance toward Flora. "Can you say the same?" He paused, giving them time to realize he was right. "Return to your chief and tell him the lass refused his . . . gracious invitation. She is happy where she is."

Aonghus held his gaze for a long beat before turning to Flora. "If you change your mind—"

"She won't," Lachlan said with cool finality.

Aonghus looked as though he wanted to say more. Instead, he nodded to his men and they moved to the clearing, where they gathered the horses of the fallen men and rode away.

But Lachlan knew they would be back—for their dead, and for the battle that was brewing between him and Hector.

Flora was in his arms before the others had faded from view. It was as if a dam had broken free and the deluge of emotion poured from her body, racking her shoulders with violent sobs. Silently, she sought comfort from him, and he gave it to her. He'd never seen her cry before, and it left him feeling strangely helpless.

Murdoch had moved away to give them privacy and see to the dead. Allan, he knew, would return soon with reinforcements, but instead they would carry home their dead. Though it was the plight of a warrior, the pain of losing men never lessened. He took each loss personally. These men would be honored for their valor and sacrifice.

Flora emitted another sob. She didn't seem to mind that his sleeve was staining her gown, though he couldn't release her even if he wanted to. Just holding her was a balm to his soul. The heat of battle still roared through his blood, but with such softness pressed against his body, calm descended over him.

He'd never realized before what had been missing. His life up to this point had been one battle after another. Never had there been someone special to hold on to. Someone to care for. Someone to . . . love.

I love her.

Of course. It was what he'd known for some time but hadn't wanted to acknowledge. Perhaps he'd realized how much it would hurt not to have his feelings returned. But she wanted to stay with him. He'd heard it for himself, but he still couldn't believe what she'd said.

He'd thought himself immune to such emotion—he was wrong. From the first, she'd been different. She was the only woman who'd ever been able to get under his skin. The only woman ever to make him think of his own needs—needs that had nothing to do with his duty to his clan.

He loved her spirit and the streak of wildness in the proper lady that left him wondering what she'd do next. He loved her strength and confidence, as well as the vulnerability she sought to hide. He loved the way she made him feel.

He tipped her chin and looked into her watery eyes, strikingly blue from her tears. "What's this, lass?" he asked, wiping her tears with his thumb and noticing the scratch on her cheek. "Did he hurt you?"

She shook her head. "No. It's just that . . ." She sniffled and hiccupped. "I thought you were dead. When I saw the sword hit your head . . ." She shivered, and a wave of fresh tears sprang from her eyes.

"And the thought of my death distresses you?"

She thumped him hard on the chest—a surprisingly hard blow for such a wee lass. "Of course it did, you foolish man. How could you think it would not?"

"Maybe it has something to do with your refusal of my offer of marriage?"

She bit her lip. "Oh yes, about that. I didn't realize then . . ."

He stilled, seeing in her face his heart's desire. What he wanted with a soul-wrenching intensity that squeezed like a vise around his heart. "Realize what?" he asked carefully.

She slipped her arms around his neck and looked up at him with such depth of emotion in her face, it took his breath away. Her eyes seemed to dominate her tiny face, and her cheeks were flushed pink as she peered up at him hesitantly.

"Realize that I love you."

A wave of incredible happiness crashed over him. His heart seemed to swell in his chest. It seemed impossible that this beautiful, amazing woman could love him. That a woman who'd known such privilege and had the most powerful men in Scotland at her feet had chosen to give her heart to him was humbling. It was hard to find the words, but he knew what his response had to be, it was what was in his heart. He lifted her chin and looked deeply into luminous blue eyes. "And I love you, you stubborn lass."

She looked stunned. "You do? But why did you not tell me before?"

His mouth twisted in a wry smile. "As this is a unique experience for me, I didn't realize that this overwhelming irrationality I was feeling for you was love."

She grinned. "Overwhelming irrationality? I suppose that is a good way of putting it. I didn't realize it, either—until I thought I might lose you."

He pulled her tighter, ignoring the stab of pain in his arm. "Never."

She pressed her cheek against his chest and sighed. "Just try to get rid of me now. I have a reputation for being a touch headstrong, you know."

He tensed suddenly, not daring to hope. "Does this mean you will agree to marry me?"

She raised her head and nodded, a wide smile breaking through the sparkly remnants of her tears. "Yes, I'll marry you, Lachlan Maclean."

Relief, happiness, and disbelief intersected in a moment of pure happiness. More moved by the moment than he could believe, he did not trust himself to speak. Instead, his mouth found hers in a long, hungry kiss. A kiss that spoke the truth of his heart far more eloquently than words ever could.

Chapter 16

❖

He loves me. Flora thought her heart would burst each time she thought about it—which in the hours since the attack near the Faerie Pool was constantly.

With Gilly and Mary safely ensconced in the castle, Allan had returned with reinforcements—interrupting their kiss. And while he gathered the bodies of their fallen, Flora had tended to the wound on Lachlan's arm. The blade had cut a deep gash in his shoulder that needed stitching, but she cleaned it and wrapped it with a swatch of linen from his ruined shirt until it could be tended to. Although he claimed it did not pain him, Flora had the distinct feeling that he was enjoying her fussing over him. Always grateful for an excuse to touch him, she made good use of the opportunity to do so.

Indeed, after the terror of the attack, she didn't want to let go of him. Perhaps he sensed her need for the strength of his presence beside her, because he offered to have her ride with him on the return journey to the castle. An offer she willingly accepted. As she basked in the glow of her newly discovered feelings and the comforting embrace of the man she loved, the horror of the attack faded under the healing power of joy.

It seemed a sin to be so happy.

Even now, as she stood in her tower room preparing for bed, it didn't seem possible that such fortune had found her. That which had eluded her mother for a lifetime, Flora had found in the most unexpected place—in the arms of a Highland chief who'd abducted her. It was ironic how things turned out. The thought that right now were it not for Lachlan she could be married to Lord Murray was nearly inconceivable. To think what she might never have known. The wonder, the magic of knowing that she loved and that love was returned.

She would have settled for a loveless marriage because she never thought she'd be able to find a man who could look beyond the prize and want her for herself. She'd been fighting for so long to protect herself from her mother's unhappiness that she'd erected barriers around her heart, barriers that had taken a formidable man like Lachlan to topple. But now that she'd let go of her fears, she gave herself to him completely.

Flora never did anything by half, and in this it was no different.

Taking one last glance in the looking glass, she adjusted the tie of her silk dressing gown and blew out the candle.

Lachlan stood before the smoldering fire in his bedchamber, strangely restless. He took a long drink of *cuirm,* hoping to ease the burning in his shoulder and the burgeoning sense of unease stirring inside him. Unease that had started the moment they'd returned to the castle and he'd been forced to release her. Only when he held her in the protective enclosure of his embrace did he feel that nothing could come between them.

Damn. He paced across the room, trying to burn off some of this restless energy. Like the calm before the storm, his entire body felt on edge. He usually felt like this after battle, as though he needed a woman. He did, but it had nothing to do with the fighting earlier and everything to do with Flora.

All he could think about was taking her in his arms and making love to her. The only thing that kept him from going to her tonight was the knowledge that she needed to rest after the shock of witnessing her first battle—he could see by her reaction to the killing that it was so. He had to remind himself that in a few days she would be his forever.

The kiss today had left him wanting. A mere morsel for a man who was starving. Part of him just wanted to take her, to lay claim, and to seal the promise of their love in the most basic way. But another part of him, the honorable part, knew that he should wait until she knew the whole story.

The realization that their newly discovered love would soon be tested only contributed to his unease. Would knowing about the bargain he'd made with her cousin Argyll crush their love before it had a chance to bloom, or would it be strong enough to weather the storm? He did not delude himself: There was a storm brewing, and it would be a torrential one.

Now that he'd recognized his own feelings for what they were, he knew exactly what he had to lose—everything.

That realization had prompted him to take a dangerous gamble. In return for marrying Flora, Argyll had promised to help restore his castle and secure the release of his brother, John, from Blackness Prison. With Rory's fighting men, he might not need Argyll for the former, and if he could find another way to get John out of Blackness, he wouldn't need him for the latter. Without the bargain, an ulterior motive for marrying Flora would no longer exist.

Upon returning to the castle earlier, he'd convened a meeting of his most trusted *luchd-taighe* guardsmen to discuss not the attack by Hector, but an attempt to free his brother from Blackness Castle—the impenetrable royal stronghold that served as the king's prison. A possibility that had seemed untenable until he'd received an interesting piece of information.

John was being held in the sea tower—aptly named, as it was built on the edge of the Firth of Forth. Although his brother was being held in the tower apartments—a privilege afforded prisoners of noble blood—the doors were steel and the staircases so narrow as to be virtually inaccessible.

The windows, however, were not.

If they could smuggle in some rope, John might be able to scale the tower wall and drop to a waiting *birlinn*. The problem had been how to get him the rope. Although they had a man positioned inside the castle, as a mere stable hand he would never make it past the tower guards.

His plan had been at a standstill until the last report, when a small but significant piece of information caught his attention. The prisoners were sometimes visited by a local minister.

It was just what he needed.

He had the final piece of his plan. A handful of men would detain the minister and "borrow" his vestments. One of the men would then pose as the minister and smuggle in the rope hidden under his robe. When night fell, John could make his escape.

They had surprise working in their favor. Sir James Sandilands, the keeper of the castle, wouldn't be expecting a rescue attempt. For good reason, not many would be so bold—or foolhardy.

The most difficult part was deciding who should go. Lachlan had initially planned to go himself, but his guardsmen had argued against it. And as much as he hated it, he knew they were right. As chief, he could not risk capture—his clan would be left unprotected and ripe for pillage by Hector. Allan would go in his stead, and Hugh, one of Lachlan's older warriors, would pose as the minister.

If something went wrong and he needed to rely on Argyll's influence with the king to secure his brother's release, Lachlan figured the news of the attempt would not reach either Argyll or the king in time for either to change his mind.

But now that his plan was in motion, it weighed on him. Though it was relatively straightforward, it was fraught with risk. Risk he would not take if he weren't looking for any way out of his bargain with Argyll.

The alternative had become untenable.

The knock barely registered. His back was to the door as he was still gazing out the window to the darkened sea. Knowing that it would be Morag checking to make sure he had what he needed, he bade her enter.

"Bring me another flagon of *cuirm,* and then that will be all for the evening."

"Not yet married and already you are ordering me about? I hope this is not a harbinger of things to come."

At the sound of her voice, he tensed, his already frayed nerves flared.

He turned, fists clenched at his side, steeling himself against the shock of seeing the object of his desire materialize as if out of a dream. But no fantasy could have prepared him for seeing the woman he loved clad only in an ivory silk dressing gown, her long golden hair tumbling in heavy waves around her shoulders, her tiny feet bare. *Bloody hell, what was she trying to do, torture him?*

"What are you doing here?" His voice came out rougher than he'd intended. "You should be abed."

She moved toward him, the fire illuminating her lush figure so that he could see . . .

His heart stopped, and everything went perfectly still. *Everything.* God help him, he could see everything. She was naked under the thin swath of silk. Blood surged through his veins as his body went rigid—as every part of him went rigid.

"I couldn't sleep," she said. "And"—she glanced pointedly at the half-empty cup—"it seems neither could you."

"What are you doing here, Flora?"

She kept moving toward him, hips swaying seductively, until she stood right in front of him. Close enough for her sweet feminine scent to flood his senses and make him crazed with desire.

"I would hope that was obvious."

His heart pounded in his chest. It was, damn it, it was. She was giving herself to him—and God, how he wanted her.

She slipped her hands around his neck and pressed her body against his bare chest. The softness of the silk, her breasts crushed against him . . . heat, all he could think about was heat. The sensation was so intense, he nearly groaned. Hell, why hadn't he put on a shirt? Because his arm hurt. But the only pain he felt right now was the agony of restraint. "I thought since we will be married in a few days that you might want to wait until we are man and wife," he said, fighting to hold on to his good intentions.

A tiny furrow appeared between her brows. "But it takes two weeks to proclaim the banns."

"I've written to your cousin about dispensing with banns." They would pay a fine instead at the time of recording for the irregular marriage.

She arched a brow, clearly amused. "That was fast."

He shrugged, masking the stab of guilt. "I didn't want to give you a chance to change your mind." And if his plan didn't work, he wouldn't wait another day to free his brother from the hellhole of Blackness Prison and his people from Duart's suffering. To that end, he added, "I've written Rory as well."

She smiled, nestling against him, the hard press of her nipples an erotic tease. "I'm flattered, but there is no reason to rush. I won't change my mind. Though I'm sure my brother and cousin will be so eager to see me wed they will do whatever is necessary to ensure it is done quickly. I'm afraid my cousin has been rather annoyed with me lately."

"With good reason, I'd wager."

A naughty smile played upon her lips. "Perhaps." Her nose crinkled adorably. "You don't think there will be any problem in securing their agreement, do you?"

The irony of her question was not lost on him—it was all but decided. "I was very persuasive. They will have no objection." Argyll would see that Rory agreed; there was no reason for him not to.

She gazed up at him with all the trust in the world. He had to look away.

"I know how persuasive you can be." Her hand caressed the muscle of his uninjured arm, sending heat rippling through him. "Did you tell them . . ."

He knew what she was thinking. That she was no longer a virgin. "Not unless it is necessary."

She nodded, relieved, and continued her stroking. Touching him. Her hands skimming over his body like the softest feather. A feather that singed a fiery path wherever she went.

"But surely we will need more time to prepare for the celebration?" she asked.

He could barely think; his senses were overwhelmed with the scent, the feel, and the touch of her. "I won't wait a moment longer than necessary to make you my wife. I'd do it today if it were possible. As it is not, we will be married on Sunday." Four days hence. He could wait four damn days.

Her hand slid over his stomach and dipped. Or maybe not.

"Hmm. It seems a long time to wait." Her fingers traced the taut muscles, skimming dangerously close to his erection. He couldn't breathe. "For no real reason."

Was there a reason? None he could think of right now. She had him so damn aroused, lust was doing his thinking. All he could think about was making love to her until they collapsed in an exhausted heap. Until he bound her to him so that she could never deny their feelings. Maybe making love again would help.

She gazed up at him, her expression suddenly uncertain. He knew she was confused by his apparent reluctance when he'd been doing everything in his power to seduce her the past few days. Hell, he was confused by it, too.

"You meant what you said, didn't you?"

He smoothed the lines of worry between her brows with the soft press of his lips. "Aye, lass. I meant it." That was what was making this so difficult.

"You love me?"

"With all my heart."

Her eyes sparked. "Then show me."

He would, damn it. It was a challenge he could not resist. Lachlan wasn't a man used to spouting pretty words to express his emotions—and even if he were, there were no words for what he was feeling right now. When he looked at her, he felt as if he'd been given the greatest prize in the kingdom—her love. She made him feel invincible. He wanted to tell her what he was feeling, but he didn't know where to begin. Words were not his way, but he could show her.

He would make love to her until she could never doubt it.

She was his.

He slid his hand behind her neck, savoring the warmth

and the heavy drape of her silky soft hair, and brought
her mouth to his in a hungry kiss—a kiss that had been
too long denied. There was nothing poignant or teasing
about this kiss; this time he took her with a savageness
that only hinted at the raging passion burning inside
him. Passion that was part abstinence, part fear, part
frustration, and all desire.

He groaned against her mouth, savoring the exquisite
softness of her lips and skin, the subtle fragrance that
surrounded her, the sweet taste of her . . . God, it had
been too long. He kissed her harder, clasping her against
him as his tongue delved deep into the honey recesses of
her mouth. She opened against him, taking him deeper,
returning the thrust of his tongue with her own—her response every bit as carnal as his. The little sounds of
pleasure escaping from her lips urged him on. Her body
seemed molded to his, every curve, every crevice, dissolving all that came between them.

He kissed her mouth, her chin, her neck, savoring the
delicious taste of her skin. But it wasn't enough—he
wanted her naked on his bed so he could devour every
luscious inch of her.

He scooped her up in his arms and carried her the few
steps to his bed, laying her down gently. Then, slowly, he
slid off her robe, stopping her when she tried to pull a
sheet over herself.

"No. Let me look at you." He wanted to hold on to
this moment forever. To remember exactly how she
looked lying on his bed, ready for him to take her. She
was achingly beautiful—her blond hair shimmering in
the candlelight, her flawless ivory skin as smooth as al-
abaster, her delicate, heart-shaped face dominated by
those luminous blue eyes.

He slipped his fingers through the silk of her hair
fanned out behind her head on the fluffy feather pillow
and then traced her swollen lips with his thumb. His

gaze moved down the length of her body, and a swift kick of lust hit him hard. Her body was incredible. Built for a man's pleasure with her lush round breasts, the pale nearly transparent skin tipped by nipples the mouthwatering pink of ripe berries. Unable to resist, he leaned over and took one luscious tip in his mouth, rolling it gently between his teeth. She moaned with pleasure, and he forced himself to release her, not yet done with his study.

Her stomach was flat and her hips softly curved. He slipped his hand around her waist, almost spanning her. And that bottom . . . He moved his hands around to cup her. He'd been pressed against that soft bottom too many times this past week, he knew exactly how she felt against him. Later, he would appease her curiosity and show her exactly how it worked. How he could fill her from behind.

Her legs. Damn, her legs went on forever. Long and lean, with perfectly sculpted calves. Even her feet were small and delicately arched, with adorable pink toes.

He'd seen many naked women in his life, but none had ever affected him so. It wasn't just her beauty that overwhelmed him, or the lust he felt for her, it was something more fundamental. Something that went to the very core of him and filled his chest with an incredible warmth. Something he hadn't even known he was looking for, but now that he'd found it, he couldn't imagine being without. Losing her would be like cutting himself in half. How had it happened so damn fast without his realizing it?

"Lachlan . . ."

He saw the embarrassment flooding her face pink. Her natural spirit and confidence sometimes made him forget just how truly innocent she was. "You're so beautiful. It gives me pleasure to look at you."

Her gaze slid over his naked chest and down his stomach to the heavy bulge in his trews. "I can see that."

He smiled. "You're a bold lass."

She returned his smile. "Only with you."

A fierce wave of possessiveness swept over him. The enormity of what she'd given him hit him hard.

"You humble me, *mo ghradh*." My love.

She reached up and tucked a lock of his hair behind his ear; the happiness sparkling in her eyes made his chest ache.

"I'm so happy. I love you so much. I can't believe that you feel the same."

"Never doubt it," he said fiercely. "No matter what happens, Flora, never doubt my feelings for you."

The vehemence of his voice startled her; he saw the sudden flash of uncertainty in her gaze. "What could possibly happen?"

He cursed his uncharacteristic display of emotion. "Nothing," he assured her, and started to unfasten his trews. "But after tonight, I promise you will never doubt my love for you again."

Flora shuddered with anticipation. The sensual promise in his voice set her blood aflame. She had no doubt he meant every word.

But it was his eyes that touched her heart. No man had ever looked at her with such all-consuming intensity—with raw hunger, possessiveness, and reverence all at the same time. His eyes caressed her nakedness, making her feel special—loved—as if she were the most beautiful, most precious woman in the world.

When she'd first entered his room, she'd felt a moment of uncertainty, sensing his reluctance. It was really quite sweet, his wanting to wait until they were wed. She smiled. Who would have thought her wild Highlander would be beset by sudden propriety?

But she didn't want to wait until they were married. She couldn't wait a moment longer. His reverent touch and devouring gaze had made every inch of her tingle with need. The shattering sensations he'd awakened in her the last time teased the edges of her memory but were still too new to be fully recalled. She felt that strange restlessness building inside her, the powerful urgency. She ached for his mouth, his hands, his fullness inside her. For the fulfillment of his promise.

His naked chest gleamed like polished bronze in the candlelight. The rock-hard muscles of his arms and stomach were so clearly defined, they could have been chipped from slate. She would never cease to be impressed by his size and strength. Noticing the fresh bandage, she frowned.

He'd started to unfasten his trews, but she grabbed his wrist, stopping him, realizing there might have been another reason for his reluctance tonight. "Your arm. It is not bothering you?"

"It's fine."

"You had it stitched?"

He nodded. "The healer tended to it after the evening meal."

"Oh." The healer. He meant Seonaid. She bit her lip, knowing she was being ridiculous but unable to resist the surge of jealousy that his leman had touched him and admired the same chest she did. He might claim to love her, but he'd never made any promises of fidelity. Nor would such an arrangement be expected, except that she found she did—very much so. The thought of him with another woman tore her heart out. She vowed to do everything she could to ensure he never wanted anyone else but her. But how?

"Why the frown, my sweet?"

She shook her head. "It's nothing." She released her hold around his wrist, encouraging him to continue.

He laughed and kissed the frown from her mouth. "Jealous, Flora? You have no reason."

"I'm not jealous."

He smiled, the familiar handsome features devilishly sharp and angled in the shadows.

Her eyes narrowed, not appreciating his expression. "It's not the least amusing. How would you like it if I were alone in a bedchamber with a man with whom I'd shared intimacies?" It gave her no small amount of pleasure to see his eyes turn black.

"I'd kill him. And since I am the only man you shall ever be intimate with, the issue shan't arise."

"And does the same hold true for you, my laird? You'll find I won't be a very accommodating wife."

It took him a moment to get her meaning, and then he chuckled. "Lass, your fears are unfounded. When I make a vow, I keep it."

She stilled, not daring to hope. "You will not take a leman?"

He held her gaze. "I would never dishonor you."

Flora didn't think she could be happier, but she was wrong. At that moment, it felt as if the world were at her feet. Forgetting her state of undress, she leaned up and threw her arms around his neck.

The shock that coursed through her was as powerful as lightning. The heat of his skin drove all other thoughts from her mind but the wicked sensation of her bare breasts pressed against the solid strength of his naked chest.

She moaned and snuggled against him, wanting to dissolve into him, loving the delicious friction of rubbing against his smooth, warm skin.

His mouth was on hers again, hot and demanding. She opened against his determined onslaught, taking him deeper and deeper. She splayed her hands against the taut skin of his back, digging in her fingers as the kiss intensified. An inexplicable urgency rose up inside her.

His hands covered her, cupping her breasts, squeezing as his tongue circled and thrust in her mouth. The sensual rhythm sent shards of white hot pleasure shooting through her body. She felt her body dampen as desire spread between her legs.

He released her mouth and slowly kissed his way down to her chest. Taking his own sweet time, drawing out every sensation as his lips and tongue blazed a path across her fevered skin. His mouth was so warm and the night air so cool, her skin tingled in his wake. He kissed her ear, her neck, the hollow at her throat, and finally he dipped between her breasts, licking and nuzzling with the gentle scrape of his beard as he teased her mercilessly with the deft stroke of his tongue—coming achingly close to the sensitive tip, but never close enough.

He was killing her. Her nipples were so tight that they hurt, straining for the pleasure of his mouth. He circled the taut peaks with his tongue, and the warmth of his breath blowing across her chest made her shiver. Finally, when she didn't think she could take it a minute longer, he took her in his mouth and sucked. She moaned, arching against him. The bolt of pleasure that went through her seemed to link his mouth to her heart. She plunged her fingers through the soft wave of his hair, pulling him closer. He sucked her until she writhed against him. Until she felt the place between her legs start to quiver.

She experienced a moment of disappointment when he released her, his mouth sliding down the length of her belly. But then she remembered what he'd done to her last time. How he'd kissed her in the most intimate of places.

Perhaps, knowing what he intended, she should object. Surely such a kiss was wicked? But she found herself unable to fight the virulent demands of her body.

Demands made all the more pressing as he sank lower and lower, until his head rested between her legs.

He kissed the top of her thigh, and she shuddered. His finger swept her, as if testing her readiness. She'd never been more primed for anything. She was wet and hot and aching for the soothing press of his mouth. It was all she could think about. How it felt to have him kiss her, slide his tongue inside her, and suck. Desire pooled low in her belly with a fiery intensity that would not be denied. His hands slid around to grip her hips, lifting her to his mouth.

She couldn't wait. Her body wept for his touch.

Their eyes met as his tongue swept over her. The shock made her cry out as intense bolts of pleasure racked her with tremors. He licked her again, pressing a little harder against the now frantic pulse. *God, it felt amazing.* So warm and hot and deliciously erotic. She melted as a heavy warmth descended over her.

And then he was sucking her, slipping his tongue deep inside her until she thought she would die from the intensity of sensation building inside her. Until the quivering turned into spasms. Until the pressure inside her started to shatter. The force of her release was so intense, she cried out, lifting her hips and dissolving into his mouth. He held her there, wringing every last bit of pleasure from her. Only then did he release her.

Flora was utterly spent, her body warm and heavy, as though she could slip into a deep slumber. But she knew this was only the beginning. Lachlan had risen to his knees and started to unfasten his trews again when she stopped him.

"Let me." She needed to touch him and feel the sheer power harnessed under her fingertips.

He lowered his hands. The heat in his eyes made her feel warm and tingly all over again.

Sitting up, she let her eyes roam over the powerfully

sculpted chest that loomed before her—a warrior's body. The wide shoulders, the heavily muscled arms from years of wielding the claymore, the scars that peppered his torso giving proof of the battles he'd fought—and won. Never would she have imagined the strength of her attraction to such raw physicality. But there was no denying the primal response to his muscled body and the warm shiver of anticipation running through her. But the powerful physical attraction paled in comparison with the love she felt for the man.

She traced the tight bands of stomach muscle with her fingers and noticed how he tensed as she drew closer to his arousal, straining against the leather confines of his trews. Slowly, teasingly, she began to work the ties, allowing her hands to brush over him, lingering as if she might mold her hand around him. He drew in his breath at her gentle teasing. Now loosened, the trews slid down past his waist, revealing the enormity of his desire.

If she didn't know it for fact, she would have thought it impossible that he could fit inside her. She ran her finger down the long length of him, still amazed by the softness of the skin that covered hard steel. He groaned as she explored him, tracing the ridges and rolling her thumb over the thick head, feeling his impatience. Finally, she circled him with her hand. He tightened as she pumped him long and hard as he'd shown her, gradually increasing the speed as she felt the passion inside him build. She could feel the throbbing under her fingertips, the force of his desire straining to break free.

His face was tight and his eyes dark with burgeoning passion. He looked impossibly fierce and not a little dangerous, but she knew it was all for her—frantic desire that could not be chained. She loved that she could give him such pleasure, as he gave her.

Her mouth was level with him, and she caught the inkling of an idea. An idea that she would have been far too embarrassed to voice, but the need to hold on to him, to make it so that he would never think of wanting another woman, gave her courage to be bold.

He was watching her, his jaw clenched in a hard line, as if he knew what she was thinking.

She wet her lips. "Could I . . ." Somehow the words would not form. She peeked up at him from beneath her lashes and saw the sudden flare in his eyes. "Would it—"

"God, yes," he said roughly.

She leaned forward and tentatively placed her mouth on him.

His reaction was instantaneous. The surge of lust that powered through Lachlan was as hot and heavy as molten steel. Never had he felt such an intense rush of pleasure. Pleasure so powerful, it penetrated every part of his body. His knees nearly buckled when she pressed her moist, soft lips on the head of his cock. He jerked against her, the pressure nearly unbearable. The blood roared in his ears, and he could barely think.

It wasn't supposed to be like this. He'd wanted tonight to be about her, so that he could show her the depth of his love for her. But Flora had completely surprised him. Her instincts hinted at a sensuality that, once given flight, would rival his own. He'd sensed she would be adventuresome and spirited, but he hadn't expected it so quickly. The streak of boldness, the fire he admired in her character, just might prove his undoing.

She already had him on his knees.

Her kiss was tentative at first. It took every ounce of his strength not to guide her warm, inviting mouth around him. She let her soft lips trail down the length of him and then drew up her tongue, licking him in one long stroke.

He watched her through half-lidded eyes, her blond

hair shimmering in the candlelight, her feathery lashes fluttering against her pale cheek. But it was the sight of that sensuous mouth around him that gripped his heart. She would do this for him. Never had a woman wrought such emotion and pleasure from him.

His body strained against the base demands she was calling with her innocent kiss. All he could think about was being inside the hot cavern of her mouth.

She circled him with her tongue, and a fresh surge of lust hit him hard. He beaded, the pleasure too intense to deny. But nothing prepared him for seeing her tongue flick out to lick the drop that seeped from him.

He groaned and, unable to take it anymore, guided her mouth over him.

His mind went black as he drowned in the chasm of her moist, hot mouth surrounding him, taking him deeper and deeper. He clenched his body, forcing himself not to thrust, giving her time to adjust to the feel of him in her mouth.

The haze cleared when she released him, but then only for a moment.

"Tell me what to do."

His heart pounded. His muscles, too long flexed, were feeling the pain of control. It took him a moment to get out the words. "Suck me with your mouth the way you do with your hand."

She scooted up a little closer and tentatively placed her hands on his backside, before lowering her mouth around him again.

This time he didn't think, just surrendered completely to the erotic satisfaction she was giving him. The soft pull of her mouth was as close to paradise as he would ever come. He couldn't take it, watching her lips stretch around him, the way she took him so eagerly into her mouth, the way her hands grabbed his buttocks to pull him deeper. The pressure was so intense, the need to explode primal. His entire body went rigid, and knowing he was about to come, he pulled himself from her mouth.

She looked at him with surprise.

"I need to be inside you, right now."

Realizing his trews were still bunched around his knees, he pulled them off and tossed them on the ground beside the bed as his body came down hard on top of her.

He kissed her mouth, her neck, her breasts, as his hands slipped between her thighs. He realized how much she'd enjoyed pleasuring him; she was wet and hot and ready for him. He placed his hands beside her shoulders and lifted his chest so he could watch her as he entered her.

He rubbed the head of his cock against her, and her legs opened around him. He pushed into her gently, wanting to draw out the moment, savoring the sensation of sliding in inch by inch. She gripped him like a tight glove, enfolding him into her body. He groaned, the wave of pleasure so hot and sweet.

She was everything to him, and he wanted her to feel the significance of their joining. Of how their bodies came together in perfect symmetry. When he was fully inside her, he held her gaze, telling her with his eyes everything he was feeling. Still holding her gaze, he pushed a little deeper and stilled. Her soft moan of pleasure, the pure poignancy of the moment, touched the deepest part of him.

For the first time in his life, he felt complete.

Flora didn't think that she could feel any closer to him than when she'd taken him in her mouth, tasting the salty masculine essence of him.

At first, she thought all she would do was kiss him, but the more she kissed him, the more she understood that he was holding something back. She never realized . . .

It had never occurred to her to take him in her mouth—there was simply too much of him. But her mouth stretched around him, and knowing the pleasure she was giving him, she relaxed and took him deeper. She still wasn't convinced she was doing it right, but he hadn't seemed to mind. It was the oddest sensation, using her mouth to give pleasure to such an intimate part of his body. But it made her feel closer to him than ever before.

Until he slid inside her, looking deep into her eyes, and touched a part of her she hadn't even known existed.

He'd opened up her heart, revealing everything she'd held safely inside. Emotions so intense, it almost scared her. Because she realized what she'd done. She'd given him the most important part of herself—not her body, but her heart. He held power over her that no man had before. A power she trusted him with completely.

But the most wondrous part was that everything she was feeling, she could see mirrored in his eyes. The tender way he touched her and made love to her said in every way that was important how he felt. Lachlan Maclean was not a man who would write sonnets or make heartfelt declarations about his emotions. She suspected those words had not come easily, and she would wager that before today, he'd never told another woman he'd loved her.

But she knew as he gathered her against him, cradling her in his arms, simply holding himself inside her, that he did.

Lachlan had never known what true desire was. It wasn't simply lust, but wanting someone with every fiber of his being and wanting to prolong the experience for as long as he could. With Flora it wasn't just about finding release, but about savoring every sensation and every moment leading up to it. He stroked her long silky hair, sliding his hand down the curve of her spine to cup the soft flesh of her bottom, lifting her even closer to him.

She moaned, rubbing her lush breasts against his chest, melting against him.

He caught her mouth with his, kissing her slowly and deeply as he began to move inside her with long, languid strokes, stretching every second of connection between them.

Legs entwined, he taught her how to lift her hips to meet his thrust, how to tilt her hips to take him deeper, how to clench her body around him and draw out the pleasure.

God, it felt good. She was so tight and hot around him. He watched where their bodies joined as he slid out of her almost completely, felt the cold emptiness grab him, and then sank right back into her warm, delicious heat.

With each deep thrust he felt her squeeze around him, milking him with her body.

He'd never made love with such deliberateness and purpose. Or with such tenderness. It was incredible. Less wildfire and more a controlled burn, but the results were the same—utter physical devastation.

He saw the wonder in her eyes and heard the startled cry catch in her throat as her climax took hold. Holding her gaze, he plunged inside her full hilt and gave over the most powerful climax of his life. It gripped not just his manhood, but every part of his body. Not in a sudden cataclysmic explosion, but in a slow building eruption that seemed to go on forever, wringing every bit of energy from his body.

But even as the last twinges of passion faded away, he still could not bring himself to leave her. He gathered her in his arms and held her against him, feeling the beat of her heart against his.

They stayed like that for some time, both too moved to speak.

It was Flora who broke the silence. "I still can't believe it."

Lachlan groaned, knowing to what she referred. "If I have to try to prove my feelings to you again, I might not survive."

"Not that." She swiped at him playfully. "How could I doubt it after that? I just never thought that something like this would happen to me." Her mouth twisted in a wry smile. "I never thought I'd meet a man who wanted me just for myself. It was something my mother was never able to find and I thought would never be for me." She brought her hand up to his face and cradled his cheek in her hand. He could see the unshed tears glistening in her eyes. "I feel so lucky."

Lachlan felt his chest squeeze, the reality of the situation brought back to him full force. He held her a little tighter in his arms. His plan to rescue his brother would work.

Chapter 17

❖

Three days later, while practicing with his men for the coming battle to reclaim Breacachadh, Lachlan had his answer.

"I'm sorry, my laird," Allan said, standing before him, his face streaked with dirt and sweat. Lachlan knew he'd just arrived—the smell of the moors and wind still clung to him.

Disappointment sank through him like a rock. *The rescue hadn't worked.* "What happened?" he asked, steeling himself for the worst.

"Everything went as planned. Hugh made it past the guards and smuggled in the rope to John. We were waiting for him in the *birlinn* below the tower as he started his descent. He was about halfway down when all hell broke loose. He'd been seen. We waited as long as possible and barely escaped without being captured ourselves."

They were fortunate in that. It might be suspected who was behind the rescue, but at least it couldn't be tied directly to him.

"And John?" His hands clenched. "What happened to my brother?"

"They pulled the rope back up. We feared they might let him go and the fall would have killed him."

Thank God. He could have been the cause of his brother's death. "I don't understand how this could have happened. John was supposed to descend on the side opposite the watchtower—where no one could see him."

"He was. We found out later a guard on watch left his post to relieve himself. He happened to look up and noticed a movement."

Lachlan clenched his jaw. He couldn't believe that their plan had worked only to be foiled by a man who couldn't hold his piss.

He could tell by Allan's expression that there was more. Lachlan's fingers tightened around the hilt of his claymore. "What else?"

Allan met his gaze. "Our man inside the castle did as instructed if something went wrong and found us in the village of Kinneil near the port." He paused. "John has been taken to the pit."

Lachlan swore, tossing down his sword before he flung it out to sea in frustration. His brother had been moved from the tower to the pit prison—a place usually reserved for lowborn criminals. Blackness Castle had a particularly macabre feature. At high tide, the water from the sea poured through a grate, filling the bottom of the pit with icy water.

John wouldn't last a week.

He wouldn't have to. Lachlan's fear of losing Flora had made him grasp at any straw. And now he'd made it worse. He hardened his heart and knew his options had just run out. He needed Argyll. Flora would have to understand that he had no choice.

Marriages were arranged all the time; theirs was no different. Except they were luckier than most, for they'd found love in the bargain. He loved her. That was all that mattered. No matter how it came to be.

Lachlan caught her in the laird's solar from behind as he had before—except this time he did not leave anything to Flora's imagination. After three nights of making love to him for hours on end, her body immediately filled with liquid heat.

The days had spun by in an excited whirl and the nights steamed in passion. But as the day of the wedding drew closer, there seemed to be almost a desperate edge to their lovemaking, as if the fire that consumed them both might burn out of control. Tender and slow or rough and wild, it didn't matter. Flora couldn't get enough of him.

His strong hands clasped her around her waist. She felt the granite wall of his chest against her back. Being surrounded by all that muscle and the warm masculine scent never failed to make her breath catch.

She could feel the warmth of his breath at her ear, and she closed her eyes, allowing the familiar tingling sensations to wash over her as her body opened like a flower at his touch. He cupped her breasts and slid hot kisses down her neck. She stretched against him, savoring each exquisite sensation that he wrought from her as his hands moved over her body in swift possession.

The rock-hard press of his erection at her bottom sent a shiver of desire running straight between her legs. The sensual haze descended around her, blocking out everything but the touch, the feel of the man behind her. She was aware of every movement, every press of his finger, every breath, every beat of his heart. He nudged her again, and she pressed her bottom against him, teasing him right back.

She felt him work the ties of his trews, and then the cool air hit her legs as he lifted her gown over her hips. Leaning her slightly forward so that she could rest her hands on the wooden cabinet against the wall, he spread her legs.

She could barely stand, so strong was her need for him. She could feel her own dampness gathering between her legs. She throbbed, so ready for him, she wondered if she would last before he could . . .

Oh God. She groaned as she felt the heavy head of his erection sliding against her, setting off wave after wave of shaking desire. He was so wonderfully thick and hard, and she wanted him inside her. She arched her back, trying to catch him. But he was merciless, rubbing against her until she'd already started to shatter, until the sharp spasms rocked her hard against him. Only then did he slowly push himself inside.

The feeling was incredible. She felt so full, holding him tight between her thighs. But she wanted him deeper. She bent a little more and lifted her bottom higher to accommodate him.

He swore.

She smiled, did it again, and all teasing was gone. Taking her hips, in one smooth motion he guided himself fully inside her, filling her to the hilt as he started to pump. He loosened her gown so he could cup her breasts.

He sank into her faster and faster until Flora thought she was going to explode.

"Oh God, I'm going to come," he said tightly.

She loved when he was like this, out of control with need for her. When he told her exactly what he was going to do to her—in every wicked detail.

He did it right now, whispering in her ear with his rough, ragged voice as his hand slipped between her legs, pressing her most sensitive spot, sending her over the edge again, just as he started to explode inside her.

Lachlan slid his hand down her naked breast, lingering on the precious tip as the last vestiges of their shared climax ebbed.

He hadn't meant to take her so roughly. Indeed, he'd sought her out for another reason altogether. But Allan's news had shaken him, and he'd needed the soul-cleansing balm of her love.

Sliding out of her, he leaned forward to whisper in her ear again. "I have a surprise for you."

She took a moment to collect her breath, before turning to face him. "Another one like that?"

"Jade." Though he wished divining new ways of making love to her were all he had to worry about. The failed rescue and his brother's fate in the pit haunted him. In his effort to avoid hurting Flora, he'd made the situation worse. He knew he had to go through with his original plan, but knowing didn't make it any easier.

Sometimes, like right now, with her eyes bright with happiness as she looked at him as if he were some kind of heroic knight in shining armor, it hurt just to look at her. Her innocent happiness ate at him. More than once, it had been on the tip of his tongue to tell her everything about his brother and the bargain he'd made with her cousin—usually at moments like this in the afterglow of their shared passion, when it seemed their love was the most indestructible. But no matter how many times he made love to her over the past few days, he still he couldn't be sure of her reaction. Her natural stubbornness coupled with her unreasonable fear of ending up like her mother were wild cards. And he couldn't risk his brother's life or the safety of his clan, not when it was in his power to do otherwise.

So the frustration and anger built inside him. Some of which, he knew, was coming out in his lovemaking. Like now, when he took her hard and rough in a maelstrom of reckless need. He knew she sensed it, not understanding what drove him to such extremes of passion. All too soon, she would know why.

He brushed a golden wisp of hair from her face and tucked it behind her ear. She smiled and nuzzled her cheek into the palm of his hand.

He felt a sharp pinch in his chest and had to look away. "Come," he said, dropping his hand to step away from her. "But you'll have to straighten your clothes first."

She blushed and began to work the ties of her gown that he'd nearly ripped apart in his efforts to free her breasts. Just the thought of being inside her made him hot all over again. His need was insatiable. Drowning in her heat, he could forget everything else. For a while.

"What kind of surprise is it? Where are we going?"

He shook his head and turned away from her naked chest. "Patience, little one. It wouldn't be much of a surprise, now, if I told you, would it?"

When she'd seen to her clothing, he took her hand and led her from the solar through the great hall and up the tower stairs.

"You're taking me to my chamber?"

"Yes, though it won't be for very much longer." He grabbed the handle and pushed open the door, then led her through. "We'll have to move it all over again tomorrow."

She gazed around at the stack of trunks piled high around the small room. "What . . ." Her gaze shot to him in sudden comprehension. "My clothes," she said, stunned. "You sent for my clothes."

"And shoes," he added. "Don't forget the shoes." Two trunks' worth of shoes. His back still ached just thinking about it. Who knew a woman's slippers could be so heavy? By the third level of stairs, he would have sworn the trunks were loaded with stones. "I thought you might be weary of Mary's old gowns and—"

But he didn't finish because she'd hurled herself in his arms and started pressing kisses over his mouth and jaw. He knew she'd be pleased, but he hadn't expected this effusion of sentiment. She must have missed her finery more than he'd realized. He'd never understand women's fascination with fashion. Not that he minded right now, when he was reaping the benefits.

"Oh, you are the most wonderful man!" She beamed. "How shall I ever thank you?"

His mouth crooked. "I can think of a few ways."

She pursed her mouth playfully, her eyes bright with mischief. "I'm sure you can. But that will have to wait. At least until I've unpacked." She opened the nearest trunk and started pulling out gown after gown and different parts of gowns—sleeves, foreparts, skirts, and ruffs—as fast as she could, making little sighing sounds of pleasure whenever she came across one that she particularly liked. She was like a bairn in a room fool of sweets. There were silks, velvets, wools, brocades, and satins in every color embroidered with jewels, metallic threads, and lace. He'd never seen such a wardrobe; it was fit for a queen.

Lachlan was pleased that he'd made her so happy, but he couldn't resist the twinge of unease when faced with such obvious signs of wealth. It had been some time since she'd worn that elaborate bridal gown to dinner; attired in Mary's castoffs, it was easy to forget the world from which she came. Where would she wear all of this? For the yearly journey to Edinburgh when he was forced to present himself before the king?

Watching the pile on her bed grow higher made his next surprise seem woefully inadequate.

He walked toward the fireplace and picked up the small box he'd placed on the chair earlier. "I'll leave you to your unpacking, then, but before I go, I have one more thing for you."

She placed the stack of fine linen sarks she'd removed from the trunk on the bed and turned to him. "What more could you possibly give me? You've already given me so much."

" 'Tis but a small token. A gift to mark the occasion of our marriage."

Her face fell. "But I have nothing for you."

"I have all I want." He held out the box. "Please, take it."

Eyeing him hesitantly, she took the box and then sat on the chair to open it. He held still as he waited for her to untie the string and lift off the top. She was looking down, so he couldn't see her face, but he heard her gasp. Carefully, she slid one of the slippers from the box and held it up to the light. The tiny pearls and diamonds that lined the heel of the delicate silk shoe caught the flame of the fire and sparkled. "Lachlan . . ." Her voice was full of wonder. She turned to him with wide blue eyes. "But how?"

He tried to hide his pleasure that his gift had pleased her. "I know it's a tradition for the father to present shoes to the groom, but I thought since . . . I thought you could wear them on our wedding. I had them made in ivory since I didn't know what color gown you would wear."

She slipped her delicate arched foot into the shoe and straightened her leg to admire it. *It must be innate,* he thought. His sisters did exactly the same thing whenever they had new shoes.

"They fit perfectly," she marveled. "How did you do it?"

"I was able to salvage one of the slippers you lost in the sea; it washed up on shore the next day."

"But you must have ordered these some time ago. How could you possibly have known?"

He shrugged. "I didn't. I hoped that I would eventually succeed in convincing you. Since it was a shoe that brought you to me, I thought it a fitting way to mark the occasion."

Her smile reached all the way to her eyes. "Why,

Lachlan Maclean, behind that hard-as-steel warrior's exterior, you are a romantic."

He frowned. "Don't be ridiculous." But his disgruntled response only seemed to amuse her further. "If you'd rather have jewelry—"

"Absolutely not!" She tucked her feet under her protectively, as if daring him to try to take them away. "They're the most beautiful shoes I've ever seen."

He grinned at her fearsome expression.

"But . . ." She paused, and her gaze turned questioning. "They must have cost a fortune."

They had. Money he didn't have. But how could he marry her without giving her something worthy of her? And it was important that he buy her something without her tocher. He took her hand and dropped a kiss atop her knuckles, staring into her eyes. "They are a gift. I just wanted to show you how much you mean to me."

Flora's heart swelled in her chest, touched by the sentiment and thoughtfulness of Lachlan's gift. She never would have imagined the harsh, forbidding man who'd abducted her would turn out to be so thoughtful. Not that she'd try telling him so. Just thinking about the way his mouth had curled with distaste at the mention of him being romantic made her chuckle. No, this was something she would keep to herself. This side of him was all for her.

She draped her arms around his neck, stood up on her toes, and kissed him softly on his mouth. "Thank you," she whispered. "I will cherish them always. I only wish that I had something for you. If there is anything you desire, anything you want, name it. If it is in my power, I shall give it to you."

His arms had wrapped around her waist, and he pulled her a little closer. "Flora, I . . ."

There was something strange in his voice. She cocked her head. "What is it?"

His gaze bored into her intently, as if searching for something.

"You've seemed preoccupied the past couple of days," she said. "Is something bothering you?"

"No." He dropped his arms and shook his head, taking a step back. "The guests will be arriving soon, we won't have much time to be alone again before the ceremony tomorrow."

The guests would be few, she thought with a stab of disappointment. Her cousin Argyll, her brother Rory, and only a few neighboring clan chieftains and their families. There simply hadn't been time to send for the rest of her brothers and sisters—or her cousins Jamie and Elizabeth Campbell, for that matter.

"I'm sorry, lass," he said, reading her mind. "I know you wished more of your family could be here."

She shook her head. "It doesn't matter. I know you are eager to have this finalized." She frowned, realizing there was still one person unaccounted for. "Will your brother John arrive in time? I'm anxious to meet him."

He went unnaturally still, a reaction that seemed to occur whenever the subject of his brother arose. It was strange that Lachlan never talked about John. Perhaps they'd had a falling-out, but given how close Lachlan was to Gilly and Mary, it seemed out of character.

"I'm afraid not," he said. "John's been unavoidably detained."

"You never said where he was."

He paused, and she thought his jaw hardened. "Near Edinburgh."

"Truly?" She smiled. "I wonder if I met him at court?"

"No." He shook his head. "I don't think so."

Clearly, the mention of his brother had upset him. He

seemed remote, distant. Taking a step toward him, she said, "Lachlan, I—"

"I'll leave you to your gowns," he said roughly. "As soon as your brother and cousin arrive, I'll send for you."

And before she could move to comfort him, he'd gone. Flora knew something was wrong. What she didn't know was why he wouldn't share it with her.

When Flora answered Lachlan's summons a few hours later, she felt like her old self. She wore a French gown of dark blue velvet embroidered with tiny seed pearls across the stomacher and a matching pair of shoes. Since her arrival at Drimnin Castle, she'd become accustomed to simply tying her hair back with a scrap of ribbon to hang loose down her back, but tonight she'd asked Morag to help arrange it in a complicated twist secured by a matching velvet-and-pearl cap.

Though nowhere as extravagant as the wedding gown she'd worn a couple of weeks ago, the dress was elegant and finely made, giving her courage a much needed boost. Something she would need to face her formidable cousin and brother. Taking a deep breath, she entered the laird's solar.

Lachlan stood before the fire, facing her. The two other men rose as she entered. Surprisingly, the normally dour expression on her cousin's face that had earned him his epithet, Archibald the Grim, was absent—he actually appeared to be smiling.

She turned to the other man and drew in her breath. Though it had been years since they'd last met, she recognized him at once. Rory.

She'd forgotten what impressive men her brothers were. He stood at least half a foot over six feet tall—a couple of inches taller than Lachlan, who was himself an unusually tall man. Like Lachlan, Rory was broad-shouldered and exceedingly well muscled. His hair was dark golden brown, his eyes an unusually striking blue, and his perfectly chiseled features well tanned. The combination was striking, and something was oddly familiar. It took her a moment to realize why. His eyes were the exact same color as hers. The obvious blood connection moved her more than she would have thought possible.

Realizing she was staring, she shifted her gaze back to Lachlan, who seemed amused by her study of her brother.

She grinned sheepishly and, remembering her duty, greeted one of the most powerful men in Scotland, the Earl of Argyll. "Cousin, I hope your journey was a pleasant one."

"Uneventful, at least. We had to travel with uncomfortable speed to arrive in the time allotted by Coll's messenger." Seeing Flora's contrite expression, he added, "Not that I mind." He gave her a sharp look. "I'd begun to think you would never wed."

Rory stepped forward to greet her with an unexpected hug. "It is good to see you, Flora. It's been too long."

Not used to such brotherly displays of affection, Flora held herself awkwardly for a moment before she allowed herself to relax. It felt strange . . . but nice. When he released her, she was able to say with all sincerity, "It has indeed, brother."

"I'm sorry for the loss of your mother, lass."

Flora felt the familiar wave of sadness, stayed by the sudden comforting press of Lachlan's hand at her waist. "Thank you," she said. "I miss her greatly."

Rory glanced meaningfully at Lachlan's hand. "Coll was just explaining how this all came about. I admit it was a bit of a surprise. I was under the impression from the missive you sent refusing my invitation to Dunvegan that you were with Duart."

Luckily, she and Lachlan had anticipated this question and were prepared. Indicating for the men to sit, Flora took the seat beside Lachlan. Folding her hands in her lap, she turned to her brother and tried to stay calm under his intense scrutiny. Something she'd had plenty of practice with the past few weeks, thanks to Lachlan.

"On my way to see Hector, we suffered a carriage accident on the road near Falkirk." She left out the fact that she'd been eloping with Lord Murray and that the accident was a result of being waylaid by kidnappers.

"I happened to be returning from Edinburgh," Lachlan continued. "And was able to offer Mistress MacLeod assistance."

"How fortunate that you were there to help," Argyll said. "Brigands and thieves have made the roads so dangerous, who knows what might have befallen you, Flora."

She looked at her cousin quizzically. It wasn't like him to be so accommodating. She'd expected some rather pointed questions from her demanding cousin.

Rory studied her so intently, she felt a strange urge to squirm. Then he turned his scrutiny on Lachlan. "Fortunate indeed." It was clear from his tone that he was skeptical. He looked directly at Lachlan. "Why did you not return my sister to Edinburgh?"

"I was needed here."

"She should have been returned to her family as soon as was possible," Rory pointed out, his voice holding an ominous edge. "Even if you could not do so yourself, you should have sent for me. Immediately."

Lachlan met his gaze. "I discovered I liked having Mistress MacLeod here—with me."

Rory's eyes flared, and Flora could see his hand tighten on the wooden arm of the chair. Lachlan noticed but didn't seem to show any indication of backing down. The tension between the two men was palpable. Realizing she'd better do something before this deteriorated further, she stepped in. "It was my wish as well, brother. Please, don't be angry. Can't you see that it has all turned out for the best?"

Rory broke his glare at Lachlan long enough to look at her and see that she was in earnest.

"Are you sure that this is what you want, Flora? You wish to marry Coll? He has not coerced you—"

"No," Flora said firmly, putting a restraining hand on Lachlan, sensing his anger. "I came to this decision on my own. I assure you, Rory, I wish to marry him." She smiled at Lachlan. "More than anything I've ever wanted in my life."

Lachlan took her hand and held it in his, an almost symbolic gesture. "You've heard it. We have agreed to marry. It is done."

Flora looked at him questioningly, noting the odd turn of phrase.

"Not if I withhold my permission," Rory said.

"Are you doing so?" Lachlan challenged.

"Of course he isn't," Argyll said. "He's already agreed."

But Rory looked as though he were having second thoughts. What would she do if he withheld his permission? She had to make him see.

"Please, brother," Flora said softly. "I love him."

Rory looked into her eyes. Flora waited, holding her breath. Finally, a wide smile spread across his handsome face. "Ah, then how can I object? It is your decision." He leaned over and gave her a peck on the cheek. "Congratulations, little sister."

Once the situation was under control and the tension between the two men had dissipated, Flora excused herself, leaving the men to their whisky. She needed to check on Mary and Gilly and make sure everything was ready for tomorrow.

The meeting had gone much better than she'd expected, she thought with not a small amount of relief. Rory had been suspicious. Rightfully so, she admitted. What had been more surprising was her cousin's reaction—she'd expected more resistance from him. He must be more anxious to see her wed than she'd realized.

She didn't have to look long, finding the girls in the kitchens' vaults beneath the great hall. Gilly was giggling with one of the young serving girls, and Mary was giving last minute instructions to the cook. Her eyes were bright and her face unusually animated. It was the happiest she'd seen her in some time, Flora realized.

"Is everything ready?" she asked.

Both girls turned to her at once.

"Flora!" Gilly said. "You look beautiful. Wherever did you get that lovely gown?"

"Your brother sent for my clothes."

"He did?" Gilly said, obviously surprised. "What have you done to him? Gowns are the last thing he thinks about. You should see his face when I tell him my dresses are too short or out-of-date."

Flora laughed. "I couldn't believe it myself. But that's not why I'm here. I have a surprise for both of you."

Gilly's eyes lit up. "What kind of surprise?"

"Gilly," Mary said patiently, "it wouldn't be a surprise if she told us."

Gilly shot Mary a look of sisterly annoyance. Flora bit her lip to keep from laughing aloud. Instead she said, "You'll have to go to your chamber and find out." She'd never realized how many gowns and shoes she had until confronted with the sight of all her trunks stacked about in her small tower room. After living so many weeks with a limited—to put it mildly—wardrobe, such superfluity embarrassed her. So she'd gone through her gowns and chosen a number that would be perfect for Gilly and Mary. When she returned to Edinburgh, she would have an entire new wardrobe made for each of them.

Gilly took off running at once, and Flora and Mary watched her disappear up the stairs with a smile.

"Gilly has never been one for patience," Mary said.

"I can see that," Flora replied. "Though I have to admit, I'm much like her." Her gaze fell on Mary's happy face. "It's good to see you smile again, Mary."

Mary lowered her eyes and blushed. "I have good reason."

"You do?"

Mary nodded. Flora could see she was struggling to contain her excitement. "I wasn't supposed to tell you until tomorrow . . ."

Flora held her breath, hoping. "Tell me what?"

Mary met her gaze, and Flora could see tears of happiness shining back at her. "My brother has changed his mind. He's agreed to let Allan court me, and if we both still feel the same in a year, he will give his permission for us to marry."

Flora wrapped her arms around the younger girl in a big hug. "Oh, Mary, that's wonderful. I'm so happy for you."

"Yes, it is, isn't it?" Mary laughed. "And I have you to thank for it."

Flora shook her head. "No. Your brother would have changed his mind eventually—once he realized your feelings were in earnest. He would never force you into a marriage you didn't want. He loves you."

Mary looked at her skeptically. "He was quite determined. He loves us, but the good of the clan comes first. I know you spoke to him and urged him to reconsider, he said as much to me."

"He did?"

"Yes. And don't you see, when you agreed to marry him and he gained your family connections, garnering an alliance with my marriage became much less important."

"Well, however it came about, I'm so happy for you. You look radiant. Allan won't be able to take his eyes off you." She grinned. "Especially when he sees what I've left you. Now hurry, up to your room, there isn't much time left to change."

Mary's eyes widened with comprehension. She gave Flora another quick hug before following her sister up the stairs with only a slightly more dignified speed.

Flora was so happy, she thought she could burst. After tomorrow, it would be perfect.

Lachlan felt the tension dissipate with Rory's agreement. After the declaration he'd made with Flora and with what he had planned tonight, he didn't need it, but for Flora's sake he was glad. It would make tomorrow much more pleasant.

Marriage law in Scotland was open to interpretation, to say the least. Although the kirk frowned on irregular marriage and tried to discourage them by levying fines and the like, it did not take much to make a valid claim of marriage. A statement of intent to marry followed by consummation would suffice. And Lachlan intended to make sure he had such a claim, not wanting to take a chance that Rory would change his mind.

Clearly, Rory didn't believe their story of a chance meeting, and Lachlan expected to be under some intense questioning as soon as Flora left the room—which she did not long after to attend to the evening meal.

He wasn't disappointed. The door had barely closed before Rory turned on him. "Now you'll tell me what really happened."

He considered lying, but he respected his old friend

too much to do so—even if it meant facing the wrong end of Rory's fabled claymore. He wouldn't tell him about the bargain he'd made with Argyll, but he would tell him enough of the truth to forestall any more questions.

He gave Argyll a quick glance before turning back to Rory. "It wasn't an accident. My men stopped her carriage."

All signs of conviviality vanished. There was only so far he could stretch the bonds of friendship, and he'd just hit the limits.

"You abducted my sister?"

There was no good answer to that question, so he stayed silent.

Rory's jaw hardened, holding back his fury by a very thin thread. "Why?" he asked.

Lachlan met Rory's angry gaze, knowing that it was only their long friendship that had prevented him from challenging him first and asking questions second. "I wanted her."

"If you forced her, you are a dead man." The cold fury in Rory's voice resonated in the small room.

"You know me better than that."

"I thought so. Why not come to me? You know I would have pressed your suit."

"That is the very reason I did not. I'd heard she was strong-willed and opposed to the idea of an arranged marriage. I thought the direct approach would be more effective."

Rory must have acknowledged the truth to that, because he did not argue. Instead he said, "How did you know where she would be?"

Lachlan explained about the elopement, leaving out how he'd come to be aware of it.

Rory swore. Like Argyll, he was no friend to Lord Murray. "The little minx."

Argyll, who'd been conspicuously quiet and more than content to let Lachlan appease the MacLeod, finally spoke. "Coll's method might have been rather primitive, but you cannot argue with the results. It is a good match, and clearly the lass wants him."

Rory's eyes narrowed at Argyll. He should have kept his mouth shut and let Lachlan handle it. The MacLeod suspected that something else was afoot.

"Only the fact that I am convinced my sister does wish to marry you of her own free will prevents me from questioning you further. But before I leave here, I will have the full story."

Lachlan nodded. By then, it would be too late for it to matter.

Chapter 18

❖

The day of her wedding dawned bright and sunny with nary a cloud on the horizon, but Flora woke feeling chilled. Out of habit, she reached for the solid warmth beside her but felt only empty space and cold bed linens. She experienced a sharp moment of panic before remembering. They'd made love last night, but in deference to the presence of her cousin and brother, Lachlan had returned to his own room. It was the first time they hadn't spent the entire night together since she'd agreed to marry him. It was strange to realize how much she missed him and how alone she felt without him.

He'd been so tender last night, drawing out every moment of pleasure. He'd cradled her against his body as he moved inside her, looking into her eyes with an intensity that made her heart squeeze.

After today, they would be bound together forever. Excitement for the day to come made her eager to begin. She tossed aside her coverlet, she slipped from bed and scampered to the window—immediately regretting her lack of footwear as her bare feet hit the cold wooden planks.

Bright sunlight spilled through the glass, filling the room with a gentle heat that warmed the chill from her skin. From the height of the sun on the horizon, she realized that she'd slept later than she intended. The short

ceremony would take place at midday, followed by a
feast that would last long into the night.

She didn't have much time to get ready. Knowing that
Morag would be up soon to help her dress, she started
toward the stack of half-emptied trunks that still littered
the room, intent on finding the silk stockings she'd misplaced in yesterday's frenzy of sorting through her
clothes for Mary and Gilly.

She smiled, thinking how splendid the girls had
looked last night. Lachlan had been moved by her gift to
his sisters, but she'd never forget the look on Allan's face
when he saw Mary. A year would not come soon enough
for those two.

The evening meal had gone well enough, though
Lachlan seemed distracted. She hoped her brother and
cousin had not questioned him too harshly. He didn't
relish lying to them, she knew, but would do what was
necessary. It was one of the things she admired about
him: He always kept sight of the goal and would do
what he had to do to achieve it.

As she walked toward her trunks, her foot scraped
against something that crinkled. Looking down, she noticed a folded piece of parchment on the floor near the
door.

She wrinkled her brows. Where had that come from?
Curiosity roused, she bent to pick it up and instantly
recognized the seal—the Maclean of Duart. Hector.
What did he want? Knowing there was only one way to
find out, she broke the wax and read.

*I apologize if my rescue attempt frightened you. My
only thought was your safety. I know what Coll is
planning, and you must not marry him. He is deceiving you. My men will be watching the castle gates
should you have need of them.*
    Your brother, Hector

She scanned the letter again, not knowing quite what to make of it. Obviously, the enmity between Lachlan and Hector was strong. It saddened her to think that by marrying Lachlan, she would most likely lose a chance at getting to know one of her brothers. She didn't give credence to his vague warnings, but something did disturb her. How had this letter been slipped under her door? Did Lachlan have a spy in his midst?

Flora glanced outside again to check the time and made a decision. It was growing late, but this couldn't wait. If she left right now, she just might catch him. He and Rory were supposed to be signing the contracts this morning. Quickly, she donned Mary's old dress, as it was the easiest thing to put on, and went in search of her soon-to-be husband.

Lachlan breathed a sigh of relief as Rory MacLeod signed his name on the roll of parchment beside his. It was done. The contracts had been signed, and after what had happened last night, the ceremony was a mere formality. Though Flora might not know it, by Scottish law and tradition, they were already married.

Not only had he assured his brother's freedom, he'd become a very wealthy man in the process. He'd achieved what he'd set out to do, but his pleasure was tempered by the knowledge that Flora would be hurt by her cousin's involvement in their marriage.

The moment of reckoning was drawing near. Tonight after the celebration, he would explain everything—though he knew that making her understand wouldn't be easy . . . or pleasant.

After offering his congratulations, Rory excused himself to attend to some matters before the ceremony and feast got under way, leaving Lachlan alone with Argyll.

It was just the opportunity he'd been waiting for. Without preamble he said, "Where's my brother?"

Argyll's mouth curved slightly. "I imagine the same place he's been for the last two months."

Lachlan's eyes narrowed. "Today is my wedding day."

Argyll took a leisurely sip of claret. "So it is."

Knowing Argyll was toying with him, Lachlan held his anger in check. He would never give Argyll the satisfaction—it would only make him smell blood. But the earl had a well-earned reputation for wiliness. *God's blood, I'll kill him if he tries to wheedle his way out of our bargain.* Lachlan studied the man opposite him. A Highlander, but you would never know it. Argyll dressed and spoke like a Lowlander, with his refined manners and fine silk slops and doublet. But he was no delicate courtier—not like Lord Murray. Argyll hadn't gotten where he was without considerable strength and acumen.

He met Argyll's gaze. "You heard Flora for yourself. She has agreed of her own volition. I've done my part, do not try your games with me."

The other man quirked his brow. "Are you threatening me?"

"Take it how you will. I kept my side of the bargain, and you will keep yours. My brother will be released today, as you promised." This time, there was no mistaking the threat.

Despite Lachlan's much larger size, Argyll didn't appear overly concerned. Though perhaps he'd impressed him, because he stopped his pretense. From inside his doublet he withdrew a roll of parchment. Even from a few feet away, Lachlan recognized the royal seal. He stilled, knowing what it was: Argyll held John's freedom in his hands.

"I have a writ ordering the release of your brother. After the ceremony, it is yours."

Lachlan felt as though an enormous weight had been lifted from him. "And the rest of our bargain?"

"That will take awhile longer. The king must be assured of your cooperation before he decides on the disposition of your castle."

He'd been patient long enough. Nor was he confident in the king's justice. Once he and Flora were wed, he would seek Rory's help—in the form of fighting men—to recover his castle. Argyll could smooth things over with the king . . . later.

Argyll was watching him, a calculated gleam in his eye. "I must say you've impressed me, Coll. I didn't think you could do it."

Flora heard her cousin's voice, and something made her stop outside the door without alerting them of her presence.

"My little cousin has been resistant to any man I've brought before her, but you managed to persuade her. How did you do it?"

"It's none of your damn business," Lachlan replied. "I did it. Without force. That's all you need to know."

"Does she know of our bargain?"

Bargain? Flora froze.

"Of course not. But she will, as soon as my brother is safe."

"Are you sure that is wise? Flora will resent being manipulated; perhaps it would be better if you kept the details of our arrangement to yourself."

Blood drained from her face, and her heart faltered.

"She loves me. She'll understand."

Her cousin laughed. "You have an overabundance of confidence. I hope it serves you well—you'll need it."

Hearing the sound of a chair scooting back and steps moving toward the door, Flora slipped around the corner out of sight just as her cousin left the room.

She couldn't breathe. Her chest constricted, and her breath strangled in her throat. Taking large gulps of air, she forced herself to stay calm. There had to be an explanation for what she'd just heard. *Please let there be an explanation.*

Her hands were shaking as she slipped the folded piece of parchment she'd so summarily dismissed into the folds of her skirt. *There has to be an explanation,* she repeated, though it lacked conviction. Taking a deep breath, she walked through the door and closed it firmly behind her.

"Flora, what—"

He must have seen her face, because he stopped mid-sentence. She drank in the sight of him, wanting to hold on to what she knew. The rugged lines of his handsome face, the hard-muscled body, the dazzling blue eyes, the soft wave of his dark hair—so powerful and unabashedly masculine. He was dressed for the ceremony, she realized with a pang. Wearing a fresh linen shirt and a plaid belted at his waist and secured at his shoulder with his chieftain's brooch. A jewel-encrusted dagger that she'd never seen before hung at his side. Her chest squeezed just looking at him.

"What's wrong?" he asked uneasily.

"What were you talking about with my cousin?" He looked at her blankly. "What bargain did you make with him?"

His eyes shot to hers. "You heard," he said flatly.

"Tell me what I heard was wrong. Tell me our marriage has nothing to do with this bargain. Tell me you did not plan this with Argyll."

He met her gaze unflinchingly.

Say something. Deny it! her heart cried. But he didn't say a word, not one single word.

Emotion balled in her throat. "What have you done?" He took a step toward her, but she jerked away. "I don't need your comfort, I need the truth."

He swore and then dragged his fingers through his hair. "Hell, Flora, it's not what you think. Don't jump to conclusions before you hear me out."

"Then tell me. Explain to me what I heard was wrong."

"You only heard part of it. The least important part. Argyll has nothing to do with how I feel about you." He searched her face, hoping for any sign of yielding, but she looked as hard as ice. "A few months ago, the king ordered me to Edinburgh to appear before the Privy Council. I knew that as soon as I left Breacachadh, Hector would attempt to take the castle, so I sent my brother to court in my stead." His jaw hardened. "But instead of hearing the merits of the case, the king had John tossed in prison to try to force me to accede to the will of the Privy Council."

That stopped her. "But you said that John was—" She stopped herself. *Another lie.* "Why didn't you tell me?"

"I thought you would ask too many questions, questions I wasn't ready to answer. I figured you would realize that because of our bond of manrent I would go to your cousin for help."

"Which you apparently did."

He nodded. "I sought his influence with the king to release my brother. I happened to be there when word of your elopement with Lord Murray arrived. As you can imagine, he was furious. He agreed to help free my brother and use his influence in getting my castle back if I put a stop to the elopement and convinced you to marry me instead."

His words spun in her head. She felt dizzy, trying to sort through the damning words of his betrayal. "So I was a bargaining chip. You and my cousin planned all of this from the start. The kidnapping, the wooing, every-thing." Her chest squeezed. "Why didn't you just force me? It would have been easier than going through this whole charade."

He gave her a stark look as if he couldn't believe she would think that of him.

"Argyll knew Rory would never force you to wed. And your cousin cares for you; he did not want to see you hurt."

"Cares for me? Surely you jest. Neither of you thought of me at all. I was just a means to an end. Argyll wanted to get rid of me, and you wanted his influence. I'm sure a rich wife only sweetened the pot."

He'd never wanted me. It wasn't what she thought . . . it was worse. She'd been bartered and sold like a prized heifer. Flora felt as though her heart had been ripped from her chest and everything that she thought was good and beautiful had been twisted into something black and ugly.

She didn't want to believe it. How could she have been such a fool? How could she have forgotten the one truth that had defined her life since the day she was born—she would always be seen as a prize. Always.

His eyes narrowed, and she could see the muscle in his jaw start to tic. "You've got it all wrong. The bargain with your cousin has nothing to do with the way I feel about you. It might have started out as a means to free my brother and help my clan, but I fell in love with you along the way."

"Isn't that convenient? Of course you'd say that, your plan was to make me fall in love with you." He took a step toward her, but again she flinched away. She didn't want to listen to anything he had to say. Just looking at him hurt. The hard square jaw, the wide mouth, the gorgeous blue eyes that had once held the promise of a future set in the darkly handsome face. "My cousin chose well." Too well. How easily she'd succumbed to his rugged masculinity. Flora felt her heart shatter at her feet like a dropped pane of glass. "God, how could you lie to me like that? How could you be so cruel?"

His face darkened. "I didn't lie."

"You didn't tell me the truth, it's the same thing."

"I told you everything that matters. My feelings for you are the truth; the bargain with your cousin does not change that."

"But the two are inexorably tied together. How could I possibly believe anything you say?"

He gripped her arm, not letting go when she tried to wrench away. "Listen to me," he said in a low voice. "I needed your cousin's help. I did what I had to do for my brother and my clan. But that does not change how I feel about you or how you feel about me."

It changed everything. Lachlan had used her. Manipulated her in the worst way and made her love him. She'd been his pawn and nothing more. Even after he must have realized how much he would hurt her, he hadn't told her the truth. "You could have told me."

"I wasn't sure you would listen." She heard the censure in his voice, but nothing he could say would change the fact that he'd used her. "Would you have agreed to marry me if I had?" he challenged.

"I guess we'll never know, since you never gave me the chance to decide."

"I always intended to tell you the truth."

"When it was too late for me to change my mind?"

"I couldn't take the chance that you would." He gave her a long, penetrating look. "I know how you feel about arranged marriages, and I didn't want to lose you."

She laughed, a sharp sound bereft of humor. "How unfortunate that your plan didn't quite work out."

"But it did," he said quietly.

"You're an even bigger fool than I am if you think I will marry you now."

She didn't like his expression. It made her feel he knew

something she didn't. "What? Why are you looking at me like that?"

"It doesn't have to be like this," he said with a note of warning. "We can go through with the ceremony—"

"No! I won't marry you."

His mouth tightened. "It's too late."

"Don't be ridiculous. The ceremony hasn't even begun."

"The ceremony isn't necessary."

Flora felt a prickle of alarm. "What do you mean?"

He took a deep breath. "The contracts have been signed, and last night we agreed to marry."

She blanched. His strange pronouncement of their intention to marry before her cousin and brother suddenly became clear. "You tricked me," she whispered, though why she was surprised, she didn't know. Hadn't he done so from the start? Her next thought cut her to the quick. Raw emotion tore at her throat, making her voice ragged and tight. "Is that why you came to me last night?" Not to make love, but to consummate their agreement. Consummation following their words of intent to marry would be all he needed to make a valid claim of marriage.

"I would have come to you anyway."

"Yes, but this time there was another purpose." She could feel the pain erupting in her chest. "Wasn't there?"

"I hoped it wouldn't be necessary, but I could take no chances in case Rory tried to put a stop to the wedding. I did it for your protection as much as mine."

Flora made a sharp sound of disbelief. "My protection? You can't really expect me to believe that."

"It's the truth."

"No, the truth is that you've lied to me since the day we met. The truth is that you stood before my cousin and brother and proclaimed our intent to marry, and then you sealed your treachery by using my body." God, the thought that he could hold her so tenderly, make love to her like that, all the while knowing how he was betraying her—it made her ill.

He seemed to be fighting to control his patience. "I have never used your body. You gave yourself to me willingly, Flora. More than once." He pulled her a little closer and lowered his voice dangerously. "Bargain or not, I would never let you go. We belong together, don't you see that?"

Tears burned in her throat as she looked at the man she'd thought she loved. At the man she'd given her heart. She couldn't stand it. It hurt so much. The walls closed in around her. She felt as if she were being backed into a corner. Her darkest fear had come true: She was being forced into marriage.

"Don't do this," she pleaded.

He looked at her stonily. "It's done."

"It doesn't need to be. Not if you don't say anything." They were the only people who knew of this irregular marriage. If neither of them chose to press the claim, no one would ever know. "Please, let me go."

His eyes softened. "Flora, I . . ." He hesitated, but only for an instant. "I can't. I want this marriage, and not just to free my brother. I love you. I know you are hurt, but it will pass—and you will see that this is for the best."

His face was racked with torment, but she was immune. It was all an act. He was every bit as ruthless as she'd first thought. A coldhearted chief who would do anything to win his prize.

She took a step away from him, seeing him clearly for the first time. His betrayal cut like a knife, eviscerating her love for him as cleanly as if it had never been.

She was killing him. Lachlan felt as though he'd taken a whip and lashed it across her back. He'd hurt her, splayed her open, and made her bleed. Even knowing that this was how it had to be did not lessen his feeling of responsibility. The pain that swam in her eyes and trembled in her voice was infinitely worse than he'd imagined. He knew how much she hated being forced into anything, but he'd hoped that she would at least try to understand his predicament.

He'd tried to stay calm in the face of her wild accusations, but it was becoming increasingly difficult since she stubbornly refused to listen. His instincts not to tell her of his bargain with her cousin because of her reaction had proved correct, but knowing that he was right didn't make this conversation any easier.

"Please," she begged. The soft plea tugged at his heart. "If you care for me at all, don't—"

"Care for you?" he exploded, wanting to grab her and shake the truth into her. "Have you been listening to anything I've said? I *love* you. Do you think I want to hurt you? This is tearing me apart. Since the day you slipped the dirk into my side, nothing else has been more important than making you mine."

"That's possession," she said dully. "Not love."

"You're wrong. I've done nothing but try to prove my love to you since the moment I realized what you meant to me."

"You've proved nothing except that you are an accomplished liar."

His mouth tightened as he fought to keep a tight rein on his control when he wanted nothing more than to take her in his arms and force her to listen to him—in the way she could not deny. She was slipping away from him, and he'd never felt so damn helpless. He had to make her understand. He grasped her by the shoulders and stared deep into her eyes, forcing her to listen. "I love you. I've never said those words to another woman in my life. I'm not one of your eloquent courtiers—if that isn't enough for you, I don't know what more I can say. I did what I had to do to save my brother and my clan. I wish that you had not been involved, but you were, and I can't change that."

"You didn't love me enough to give me the truth. I thought I'd found someone who wanted me for myself—not for what I could bring them."

"I do want you, Flora."

"But I can never be sure." She looked at him, her heart breaking in her eyes. "God, I trusted you. I thought you were different."

He was tired of her inability to see past her own blind fears. It wasn't simply her happiness that was at stake here. "Do you think I wanted to lie to you? You don't know how badly I wanted to tell you the truth."

"But you didn't."

"Damn it, Flora. You are so stuck in the past and caught up in your own romantic fantasies that you can't see the real world. You see everything as black and white, but it's not so simple. Sometimes you have to make hard decisions, that's what I do—I'm chief. But you have no concept of duty or what it means to be in charge and responsible. My brother's life is at stake. What would you have me do?" She looked at him blankly, and he continued, "John is in the pit prison now because I was so damn scared of losing you that I tried to make a last-ditch effort to free him—just so I wouldn't need your cousin's help. So you couldn't accuse me of ulterior motives like you are doing right now. But the rescue failed, John was tossed in the pit, and I had no choice but to rely on your cousin. Don't you see that my brother is suffering? Every minute John spends in that hellhole could be his last. Argyll has the writ that will set him free. Would you see him die for your pride?"

She flinched as if he'd struck her. His brother's plight had penetrated her hurt and anger in a way his declarations of love could not. He knew her compassion and her tender heart. She would not jeopardize his brother's life, not even if it tied her to a man she despised.

He knew he'd won, but there was no satisfaction, only despair, in his victory.

She stood stiffly before him, her face a waxen mask. But it was the hollow look in her eyes that sent a trickle of alarm running through his veins.

"You will have your writ," she said dully.

Relief swept over him . . . for only a moment.

"But I'll never forgive you for this."

The cold certainty in her voice chilled him to the bone. She'd cut him off. He reached for her, but she recoiled from his touch. His chest twisted at her rejection, and he dropped his hand to his side. He would make it up to her. She just needed time.

"I'm sorry," he said.

She didn't look at him again, but turned on her heel and left him—alone and emptier than he'd ever felt in his life.

The ceremony and feast passed in a haze. Sitting at the dais that had been set up for the celebration, Flora watched the festivities taking place before her, but they sped by in a blurred whirl of color.

She was detached, an observer. She felt cold and empty, like a marble statue on display.

Not once did she give a hint of the bitterness and heartbreak churning inside. She'd plastered a serene smile on her face and weathered the storm of congratulations from the seemingly endless stream of well-wishers that passed before the table. Only Rory and Mary had sensed there might be something wrong. But she'd dismissed their concerns with a plea of exhaustion—from all the excitement.

Sitting next to him was excruciating. Her unrelenting awareness of him seemed yet another betrayal. That her body could still crave him after what she'd learned was shameful. Every word of their confrontation seemed branded on her consciousness. He'd arranged their marriage with her uncle, tricked her, and then lashed out at her, accusing her of being selfish and not seeing reality. Had he actually thought she would understand that he'd used her?

She'd avoided his gaze all day, not daring to look at him—her husband—because then she might fall apart. Might give way to the agony she'd bottled up inside when she'd realized that she had to go through with this. What should have been the happiest day of her life had turned into a slog through hell. A cruel farce of what might have been.

But it wasn't over. Not yet. She would do her part, but that was all.

So she'd suffered through the agony of her own wedding feast, waiting for the moment when she could leave.

The sounds of revelry seemed smothering: the laughing, the dancing, the lilting sound of the pipes. It was too much. She couldn't bear another moment.

She stood up, legs unsteady. The strain of the day seemed to overwhelm her at once. It had taken every ounce of her strength to make it to this point, and she felt she might crumple to the floor in a sobbing heap at any moment. She'd lost everything.

"I find the excitement of the day has gotten to me," she said to Lachlan on her left and her cousin on her right. "I think I shall retire for the evening."

Argyll frowned. "You look a little pale and have seemed a bit subdued all day. Is something wrong?"

Everything. After what he'd done, her cousin's concern seemed laughable. Argyll had played just as much a part in this as Lachlan. The difference was that from him, she'd expected the manipulation.

"I'm fine," she said a bit too harshly. Then, seeing Lachlan stiffen at her side, she said more evenly, "Nothing that a good night's rest won't cure. I'll send for the healer and see if she has something that might help me rest."

Argyll gave Lachlan a knowing look. "Rest?" She heard the amusement in his voice. "I'm sure your new husband will ensure that you are well rested."

Lachlan ignored Argyll's suggestive remark and gave her a meaningful glance. "I will send for Seonaid and join you soon."

She bit back the angry retort that sprang to her lips. If he thought . . . She stiffened. *Never.*

Aware of their audience, she forced a brittle smile to her face. "No need to rush."

From the angry flicker in his eyes, she knew he understood.

It was a few hours later when Lachlan made his way up the tower stairs to Flora's chamber. It had been one of the most difficult days of his life. The only bright spot was the moment Argyll had handed him the writ. Even now, Allan and a group of guardsmen were preparing to ride to Blackness. If all went as planned, John would be back at Drimnin by sunrise. Only the fact that it was his wedding night prevented him from joining them.

Watching Flora float through the day as if she were a ghost had been hell. Each time she'd forced a shaky smile to her lips was like an arrow darting in his chest. All he wanted to do was enfold her in his arms and soothe the hurt, but he was the last person she wanted comfort from.

She'd looked heartbreakingly beautiful, like a faerie princess in her golden gown and jeweled headpiece. But never had she looked more fragile. As if she were a piece of decorative glass that might break if touched.

And she hadn't worn the shoes. The rejection of his gift stung because he knew it was not the slippers she rejected, but him.

He'd expected anger, but not this haunting cold resolve—cold resolve that was infinitely more worrisome because he didn't know how to break through it. He'd never felt so damn helpless. It was almost as if she'd cut him out of her heart.

He wouldn't believe it.

Once he held her in his arms again, it would all come back. She would never be able to deny what was between them. She was angry, hurt, and stubborn—not a promising combination—but he would make her understand. They'd taken vows, after all.

He stood before her door. For a moment, he hesitated. Perhaps he should give her some time and let her rest tonight?

No. No matter how it had happened, they were man and wife. The sooner she realized there was no changing that fact, the better. He couldn't take the chance that she would slip further from him. This was their wedding night.

He rapped firmly on the door and grabbed the handle to push it open. It didn't budge. Anger surged inside him.

His new wife had barred the damn door.

Chapter 19

❖

The events of the day had taken their toll, and Flora had dozed off in the chair beside the fire as she'd waited. But the rattle of the door had woken her right up.

She stood up and smoothed her skirts, still wearing her wedding gown, a stunning combination of gold silk and velvet embroidered with gold beads and pearls. The shoes he'd given her lay untouched in their box. Instead, she'd worn a pair of simple silk slippers. She wondered if he'd noticed—not that she cared, she told herself.

She fingered the amulet at her neck. The amulet that she'd intended to give him tonight as a symbol of her love for him. Instead, it was an enduring reminder of her mother's fate and of how wrong she'd been about him. The curse, it seemed, would not end with her.

He knocked again, louder this time. She heard the soft rasp of his voice brimming with anger. "Let me in, Flora," he warned. "Now."

Her hands balled into fists at her side. "No."

He swore and jiggled the door harder. "Open it or I'll break the damn thing down."

The low fury in his voice gave her a moment's pause, but she looked at the iron bar across the heavy wooden-planked door, and it bolstered her depleting courage. It would take a small army to knock down that door. "Go away," she said boldly. "I have no wish to see you tonight . . . or any other night, for that matter."

She heard him swear again, and then there was silence. She waited, not daring to move or even breathe. Time ticked slowly by. Finally she exhaled, surprised that it had been that easy.

All of a sudden, she heard a loud bang. She jumped back, startled, as the door came crashing open. Her eyes flew to the wall in stunned disbelief. The force of his kick had torn the latch right off.

Her confidence faltered as she gazed into the eyes of the furious man shadowed in the doorway. His face was a mask of harsh lines, from the taut pull of his mouth to the hard set of his jaw. His eyes blazed like sapphires in the candlelight.

She drew in her breath, and the hair on the back of her neck stood up.

"Don't ever bar me from your room again."

"You have no right—"

"I have every right," he seethed. With three long strides, he stood before her. "You are my wife."

"By coercion and deceit."

The pulse in his neck throbbed ominously. "Don't press me, Flora. I'm trying to be patient with you, but you are not making it easy. We took vows, and you will honor them."

He was acting as though she were in the wrong, when it was he who'd tricked her into a marriage she did not want. She lifted her chin. "Did my cousin give you the writ to free your brother?"

"He did."

"Well then, you have what you want. Now leave me alone."

He grabbed her arm, his eyes boring into hers. "*You* are what I want."

She wrenched her arm from his grasp. "You may have bartered and paid for me, but some things aren't for sale."

He stilled, every muscle in his body flexed. He was

standing so close, she could smell him—the warm masculine scent a drug on her senses.

"What are you saying?"

Her chin jutted up. "You'll have to force me because I'll never come willingly to you again."

His expression turned so dark, she thought he was going to explode. She gasped when he pulled her forcefully to him, her breasts crushed against the granite shield of his chest. He radiated heat. She could feel the force of his blood pounding through his body and the heavy beat of his heart. His breath was on her neck; her skin prickled with awareness. And God help her, she shivered.

"Are you so sure about that?" His voice was like velvet, deep and seductive, seeping into her bones.

She knew what he could do to her. He could make her beg for him, the wretched beast.

Then, as if he would prove it, his mouth was on hers, kissing her with a fierce savageness that stunned her. His kiss was hot and angry, demanding—nay, forcing—her response with the wicked stroke of his tongue. She tried to wrench free, but he only kissed her harder, with a raw hunger that would not be denied.

God, he'd never kissed her like this before. With passion that seemed almost dangerous. He held nothing back. This was the rough, uncivilized side of him that she'd always sensed lurking under the hard reserve. He was raw, primitive, and dominating.

The stubble of his beard scraped her skin. His hands held her tight, cupping her bottom hard against him. She could feel his erection throbbing against her.

The passionate haze blinded her. For a moment, she melted, succumbing to the erotic heat. Responding . . .

No. Tears of humiliation burned in her eyes from her body's betrayal.

She jerked out of his grasp, panting from the loss of breath. All the conflicting emotions he'd aroused broke free. "My mother was right. You are nothing but a barbarian." His face went white, but she was too angry to care. All she wanted to do was lash out and release some of the pain twisting inside her. "How dare you kiss me as if I were your whore! I can't believe I convinced myself that education and refinement would not matter. But you are a brute. I see that now—" Her voice broke. "Keep your vile hands off me."

She knew when he flinched that her arrow had found its mark. She fought the impulse to take back her hateful words. She wanted to hurt him. As he'd hurt her. If the bleak look in his eyes was any indication, she'd succeeded.

"I might be a barbarian," he said roughly, "but you want me." He let the truth of his words fall. "I'm also your husband. The sooner you realize that, the happier we both will be."

"Never."

"Never is a long time, Flora." His piercing blue eyes bore into her. "I'll leave you now, but do not try to deny me again. You are my wife."

She didn't say anything. He thought he'd won, but he was wrong. Very wrong.

He gave her one last long look and left her to her solitude. But Flora knew he'd be back. She hated him for what he'd done to her, but how much longer could she resist him if he pressed her? She wouldn't let that happen. He had what he wanted; his brother's life would be safe. He didn't need her anymore.

The sun had just crested the western horizon when the towering shadow of Drimnin Castle came into view. The light reflected off the sound beyond, creating a magical backdrop of shimmering blue.

Despite the chilly layer of dew that blanketed the moors, Lachlan was hot and sweaty; they'd been riding all night.

He glanced at the man riding beside him—a lad no longer. Their mission had been a success, his brother had been returned to him. But it hadn't taken long to realize that the experience had changed him. John would never be the carefree scamp with charm to spare that he'd been before his imprisonment.

He was thin and dirty, but the changes went far deeper. Behind the scratches and bruises he'd suffered from the failed escape attempt, new lines were etched across his youthful face. Eyes that used to twinkle with teasing now sparked with anger. John had hardened, and the change saddened him. Though he blamed the king, Lachlan knew he was as much to blame himself. He never should have sent John in his stead; he should have anticipated James's treachery. His brother had suffered for his mistake.

And he wasn't the only one. But one look at his brother as he emerged from the hellish pit was enough to convince Lachlan that he'd acted the only way he could. Flora would have to forgive him.

Flora. Hell. His thoughts turned to the bitter confrontation of the night before. He'd bungled things horribly, and the conversation had deteriorated from there. Considering the way he'd broken down the door, perhaps it was understandable. But he'd been furious by her stubborn refusal to listen to reason, that she would bar her door to him, but mostly that she wouldn't understand.

But when she'd told him he would have to rape her, the force of his own reaction had shocked the hell out of him. How he'd ached to prove her wrong. He couldn't believe he'd kissed her like that. Passion, anger, and fear had converged inside him until all he could think about was forcing her to understand. For a moment, he'd been every inch the barbarian she thought him.

He was so furious, he hadn't trusted himself. He knew he had to get out of there, before he did something that he would regret. So he'd joined his men to ride to Blackness Castle to retrieve his brother, giving them both time to cool their fiery tempers.

Her barbs had stung—much more than he would have thought possible. He knew she spoke only in anger, but he also knew there was some truth to what she said. Hadn't he worried about as much himself?

Forcing the confrontation had been a mistake. He could see that now. He should have given her time. And as soon as he returned, he intended to tell her so. He would give her all the time she needed—he owed her that, at least.

But perhaps he owed her more.

He was painfully aware of the roll of parchment he carried in the leather pack attached to his saddle. It was Argyll's letter to the parish minister to record their marriage, along with the fine for the irregular marriage. He'd intended to send one of his men with the missive, but he couldn't bring himself to do it. Technically, he'd fulfilled his promise to Argyll. If she wanted to claim that their marriage had not been consummated, he would not stand in her way.

It would be like cutting himself in half, but if she wanted her freedom, he would give it to her. But he would do everything in his power to convince her otherwise.

John had been quiet most of the ride home, but suddenly Lachlan felt his eyes on him.

"You are truly married?" he asked.

For the time being. He nodded. "Yes."

John shook his head. "I'm sorry that you had to sacrifice your freedom for mine. If only I'd realized what the king intended." His voice teemed with bitterness and anger.

Lachlan fixed his brother with a piercing stare. "You are not to blame for what happened. I should have suspected the king's treachery. If anyone is to blame, it is me."

John looked as if he wanted to argue, but instead he said, "At least we agree on the king."

"And I assure you, marrying Flora was no sacrifice."

John's brow jumped. "Truly?" He smiled for the first time since they'd pulled him from the pit. "Then I can hardly wait to meet the lass who has bewitched my impenetrable brother."

A wry smile turned his mouth. "You won't have too long to wait," he said with a nod to the bustling castle. Even from a distance, the signs of life were easy to make out. "It appears as if the entire keep has woken to greet us."

With a laugh, John urged his mount faster, and they raced the last furlong to the castle, galloping through the gates in a pounding storm of hooves and dust.

But the flash of good humor fled when they entered the courtyard. From the general commotion and the presence of Rory organizing his men, it was clear that this was not a greeting party.

Mary and Gilly rushed forward, crushing John in their relieved embrace.

Lachlan barely had a chance to dismount before Rory stormed toward him—hand wrapped firmly around the hilt of his dirk.

"Give me one good reason why I should not kill you right here. What did you do to her?"

Lachlan looked around at the sea of faces before him. What the hell was happening? Even Argyll appeared in shock.

Before he could question Rory, Mary unwrapped herself from John and ran toward him, throwing herself into his arms. "Oh, Lachlan," she cried. "She's gone."

Gone? Disbelief stopped him cold. And then he knew a bone-crushing blow of utter despair.

Damn her. She'd run from him . . . again.

Chapter 20

❖

As dawn broke, Flora began the last leg of her journey. The *birlinn* had docked at the seaside village of Arinagour on the Isle of Coll, giving her the first look at Lachlan's baronial stronghold that was now in the possession of her brother.

The first thing she noticed was the wind. But as the sun grew in strength, she was able to make out the long stretches of sandy white beach and wide expanses of grassy moorland. Soft rocky crags rose in the distance. She gasped with delight, seeing a white seal scooting around on the beach. Though desolate, it was achingly lovely. Her heart tugged with longing. This place might have been her home.

Instead, it was a place of refuge. She'd run to the only person she could be sure didn't have any interest in her marriage to Lachlan—her brother Hector.

From the moment she'd learned the truth, Flora had only one thought: escape. Just being near Lachlan was torture when every time she looked at him, the pain of what he'd done—and the yearning for what might have been—hit anew.

Their marriage was a mockery. Perhaps she might have forgiven Lachlan's bargain with her cousin, but she would never forgive being forced into marriage. Once his brother was free, she was determined to find a way out of their marriage.

But after the confrontation in her bedchamber, the decision to leave had taken on a decided urgency. Any twinge of uncertainty she might have felt at leaving was banished by the humiliating betrayal of her body. If she stayed, she knew she would succumb eventually. And that she could not abide. All she could think of was getting out of there, no matter how much it hurt to leave or how much she would miss Gilly, Mary, and the others she'd come to care for.

When she saw Lachlan ride out with his men to free his brother, she knew her opportunity had arrived. Although he'd never rescinded his order to his men to allow her to leave at any time, she did not want to take the chance that they would try to stop her. She needed help. So she'd turned to the one person who wanted her gone almost as badly as she wanted to leave—Seonaid.

At first, the healer was reluctant to interfere, but once Flora explained the circumstances and that Lachlan had married her only to free his brother from prison, it hadn't taken much to convince her to help. The prospect of resuming their relationship where they'd left off before Flora's arrival was too sweet a temptation to refuse. It was a prospect that caused Flora more agony than she wanted to acknowledge. The thought of Lachlan with another woman made the dull ache in her chest quicken and throb with something akin to panic.

Thanks to Seonaid, escape from Drimnin had proved much easier the second time around. Hidden in the shadows with a dark cloak covering her from head to toe, she'd waited, trying to calm the frantic beating of her heart. Then, while Seonaid distracted the guards, she made her escape through the landward gate. Once safely outside, she hesitated, experiencing a moment of nearly overwhelming sadness—sadness that crashed over her like a lead blanket with a heaviness that made her knees buckle. She'd never thought she'd be leaving like this again. How could everything have changed so quickly?

She thought of waking up that morning with the sun streaming through her tower chamber and how happy she'd been. It felt as though she'd had everything. She'd *trusted* him. But he'd taken that trust and shattered it into a thousand tiny pieces. Steeling herself from the memories, she retraced her steps to the beach, refusing to look back. But as the castle slipped into the darkness behind her, it felt as if her heart were being ripped in two. Part of her, she knew, she'd left behind.

Hector had not disappointed. She'd barely slipped onto the rocky path before she found herself surrounded by her brother's men, including the friendly face of Aonghus, which somehow made her want to cry.

"We'd nearly given up hope, my lady," he said. "Your brother will be pleased to see you."

Overwhelmed by what she'd just done, she could manage only a nod.

They'd ridden north a short while and then boarded a *birlinn* that had brought them to Coll. She should feel relieved, but instead she felt cold and empty—not to mention exhausted. Now that she'd actually done it, the reality had set in. She'd left her husband, the man she'd given her heart and body. It should have been her wedding night; instead of a night filled with passion and tenderness, she was fleeing in the darkness with men she barely knew. It felt . . . wrong.

She shook off the twinge of doubt. She'd made the right decision. She couldn't live with a man who'd lied to her, betrayed her trust, and tricked her into marrying him. A man who'd broken her heart. And after that scene in her room, her own weaknesses had been blatantly pointed out.

If only it didn't hurt so much. God, she missed him. And it had been only a few hours. The long days stretched out before her like an insurmountable mountain. How was she ever going to make it through?

How could it all have come to this? She'd actually thought she'd found a man who could love her for herself, who didn't want anything from her. She should have known better. But she'd disregarded the lessons of her mother's lifetime for a dream—that was all it was, a foolish girl's dream. She'd been right in the beginning. Not about Lord Murray in particular, but about choosing a husband with cold practicality and not allowing herself to be used as a pawn—making her own decisions.

If Lachlan had used a knife, his betrayal could not have cut more exactingly. If only her memories could be excised so precisely.

And now, in the clear light of day as her eyes roamed the windswept vistas of Coll, Flora felt an acute sense of longing for what might have been.

As she made her way up the beach, she saw a large man sitting atop a fine horse and realized her brother had come to greet her. Her step faltered as she drew nearer. Dear God, though a good ten years older than Lachlan, he reminded her of him. Not in his features, but in his build, stance, and fierce expression. They were both hard, forbidding warriors—men who looked as rough and rugged as the landscape that surrounded them.

Though nowhere near as outrageously handsome as Rory, her Maclean brother was also an attractive man. Unlike Rory, however, he did not bear as obvious a resemblance to her. Nor, strangely, did she feel the instant bond of familial connection.

He dismounted and walked toward her with the same determined stride that Lachlan used. Stopping before her, he crossed his arms and gave her a long, hard look. "You've come. Good. I feared you would disappoint me."

She felt a kernel of disappointment herself, which she

quickly brushed aside. His greeting was nothing like Rory's. Most men weren't demonstrative, she reminded herself, which was why Rory's exuberant hug had surprised her. Perhaps she should have given Rory the benefit of the doubt. *No.* She couldn't have risked it. Even if he wasn't involved in their bargain, his ties to Argyll certainly trumped the feelings of a sister he barely knew.

Still, despite the cool welcome, after her long journey, lack of sleep, and the traumatic events of yesterday, she felt tears of relief swell in her eyes. "It's good to see you, brother."

He must have realized how close she was to falling apart, because his eyes softened. He held out his hand. "Come. You must be exhausted. We will talk when you've had a chance to rest."

Grateful for his kindness, Flora took his hand and allowed her brother to lead her to her husband's castle. Perhaps this wouldn't be so bad.

She was a pretty little thing, his sister. Hector had actually felt sorry for her. When she'd arrived, she'd looked ready to collapse.

In a show of unusual magnanimity, he'd given her a few hours to rest before they talked. Unless he was mistaken, Coll would be hard on her heels. He'd have to raise men first, though, which would give Hector a bit of time to prepare.

He still couldn't decide how to best use her to his advantage.

Flora wasn't the willful, headstrong chit he'd expected. Coll had broken her. Hector supposed he should thank him for that; it would make whatever he planned much easier.

It was a shame. Under other circumstances, he might have warmed to the idea of having a sister around again.

But Coll had to interfere.

And now that Hector held Flora, he finally held the means to put an end to the feud that had been waged between them for too long.

Soon it would be done.

Flora woke to the sound of a knock. For a moment, awash in drowsy confusion, she stretched languidly with a wide smile on her face, thinking she was back at Drimnin. But the swell of happiness evaporated when the unfamiliar maidservant entered with a jug of fresh water. The morose woman made the crotchety old Morag seem like a young girl on May Day. The aura of misery was contagious, and all that had happened came rushing back to her.

"The chief wishes for you to join him for the midday meal," the woman said somberly.

Flora nodded, realizing she'd slept only a few hours. "Thank you . . ."

"Mairi."

"Thank you, Mairi," she said, but the woman seemed disinclined to talk further and assiduously avoided her gaze.

Flora had removed her gown to lie down, and Mairi helped her put it on again. Though wrinkled and splattered with mud from her journey, it would have to do until her clothes could be sent for. She drowned the reflexive wave of sadness with a splash of cold water on her face. The pain would lessen, she told herself—in time. She hoped.

She smoothed her hair in the looking glass beside the bed and left the room feeling if not refreshed, then at least no longer liable to collapse.

As she was led to the great hall to join her brother, Flora couldn't help but notice Mairi's strange behavior. She flinched when Flora spoke to her, almost as if she were frightened by her.

"Have you been here a long time, Mairi?"

She nodded.

"Then you did not come from Duart with my brother?"

"No!"

The vehemence in her voice and the spark of hatred in her dark eyes startled Flora.

Of course it must be difficult, she realized. Hector had taken the castle by force, and the woman was still obviously loyal to Lachlan. Flora was Hector's half-sister, so of course the woman would assume Flora would side with Hector.

She started to assure her otherwise but stopped. What could she say? That she was married to the laird but had left him? She hardly thought that would endear her to the woman. By coming here, she *had* chosen Hector over Lachlan and forsaken her duty to her husband. The realization took her aback. Lachlan's accusation that she had no concept of duty and responsibility that had originally fallen on deaf ears, she now acknowledged might hold some truth. For the first time, she felt a shadow of doubt about leaving her husband.

Mairi had turned her gaze, but there was something in the woman's expression that bothered her. She wore the look of a beaten dog backed into a corner, wounded but ready to bite to defend herself. And what was more, it was clear she perceived Flora as a threat. The animosity she felt toward Hector had obviously spread to his sister.

Instead of trying to make further conversation, Flora studied her surroundings. The place was deathly quiet. Almost like a tomb. A stark contrast to the bustling liveliness and happy countenances of Drimnin. The few servants they did encounter cast their eyes down as soon as they saw her. Almost as if they were scared.

It was unsettling.

As was the state of the keep itself. Much like Drimnin, Breacachadh was a simple tower house construction with a turnpike stair on the southeast corner overlooking the sea. But there the similarities ended. Breacachadh was of much sturdier construction, with thick stone walls, a substantial curtain wall, and a parapet for added defense.

Moreover, she could tell that at one point Breacachadh would have been a very fine home. The rooms were large and richly appointed. Fine carpets were strewn across the wood floors, though mud and muck had turned portions black. The furnishings were much richer as well, carved chairs with velvet cushions, large wooden tables, and cabinets. Tapestries and paintings lined the walls, and fine iron sconces lit the corridors.

It had been easy to make excuses for the signs of destruction along the countryside as they'd ridden to Breacachadh Castle to the south, blaming it on weather, but the woebegone faces of the castle inhabitants—and the condition of the castle itself—were not so easily dismissed.

She knew Lachlan too well to believe he would do this, which left only one person who could be responsible for the pall that seemed to hang over the place.

Hector was already eating when she arrived, having not bothered to wait for her. She turned to thank Mairi, but she'd already disappeared. Flora took the seat beside him and had barely sat down before he started to question her.

"You slept well?"

"Yes, thank you," she said.

She felt his eyes on her face. "You don't look much like her."

"Mother?"

He nodded.

"No." A faint smile played upon her lips as she

thought of her reaction upon seeing Rory. She studied Hector a little closer, noticing for the first time the dark green of his eyes and the shape of his mouth. Though his hair was mostly gray, she could still see the familiar streaks of dark brown. "But you do." And a little of her unease faded with the realization. After her initial impression of the castle and the servants, the connection with her mother seemed somehow reassuring. Hector was her brother.

He seemed surprised by the observation and then shrugged. "Perhaps. Though I hadn't seen her in years."

"What happened to cause the rift between you?"

He eyed her carefully over the rim of his goblet. "She never told you?"

Flora shook her head.

"Not long after my father died, she married a man whom I despised."

Like Lachlan, she realized with a flicker of apprehension. Flora recalled what she knew of her mother's husbands. Only one made sense. "John MacIan of Ardnamurchan?"

Hector's gaze flared. "Yes."

"But he was murdered," she blurted. Something she'd overheard once as a child but hadn't understood at the time came back to her. "Most foully," she finished.

Hector's face grew dark, and he looked at her sharply. "He was an enemy to Duart. An ally of the MacDonalds. Even after the marriage he refused to join us against them. He got what he deserved."

The flash of earlier warmth for her brother vanished, and her unease returned full force. "You killed him?"

His own mother's husband? Surely there had to be an explanation.

"He overstepped his bounds, thinking to marry my mother. And she wanted to soil the Macleans with MacIan blood—I couldn't let that happen. So when the opportunity arose, when I had him in my power, I took advantage of the situation."

He seemed to want her to understand. Hiding the revulsion she was feeling, she asked, "What opportunity?"

"Their wedding. It was at Torlusk, one of my houses on Mull."

This time, she could not hide her reaction. By seizing MacIan at Torlusk, Hector had violated one of the most sacred tenets of Highland life—Highland hospitality.

Her poor mother. Flora's heart went out to her. No wonder she'd so rarely seen Hector. Why hadn't her mother told her?

And more disturbing, what kind of man could do such a thing? Lachlan's warning about her brother came back to her.

She forced her pulse to calm. "But you eventually apologized and reconciled?"

"Apologized?" He laughed. "Why would I do that? It was her fault. No, Mother came to me about the time of Argyll's wedding."

Flora blanched, realizing why. *Because of me*. She'd been bemoaning the fact that she never saw her brothers and sisters and had never met Hector. Her mother had reconciled because of her. How her mother must have loved her to be able to forgive her son's betrayal. She'd put aside her own feelings for her daughter. That was love. Should she have done as much for Lachlan? The thought disturbed her.

She took a deep breath, wishing she hadn't brought up the subject. Surely she was overreacting? This was the Highlands. Blood feuds were a part of their history and not something she pretended to understand. But Hector's actions sounded so treacherous and . . . barbaric. God, she thought, cringing, had she really called Lachlan that?

Hector smiled at her. "But that is all in the past. You are here now, that is all that is important."

He had a nice smile, didn't he? Even though she couldn't help notice it didn't quite reach his eyes.

"Though I do wish you had come sooner," he said. "Why did you refuse to come with my men?"

Flora heard the unmistakable censure in his voice, and it put her on the defensive. "I didn't realize who they were at first. I was shocked. Your man Cormac treated me roughly."

He frowned angrily. "You told Aonghus you wished to stay."

"I did." She paused. "At the time."

His mouth tightened. But when he finally asked his question, he sounded so concerned, Flora wondered whether she'd only imagined it. "Tell me what happened."

Flora recounted the circumstances surrounding her arrival at Drimnin, leaving out her failed elopement. At first he seemed sympathetic, even giving an occasional pat of encouragement on the hand, but when she reached the point of her wedding, his face darkened.

"How could you actually have married him?" he spat, his eyes as cold as onyx.

The mercurial shift of temper was startling. She forced herself to speak calmly. "As I said, I did not have any choice."

He gave her a hard stare, obviously not satisfied with her answer. "But you left before it could be consummated. That is good."

"Yes," she said carefully. "I left not long after the wedding feast. But . . ." Heat rose to her cheeks.

His eyes narrowed. "You gave yourself to him."

"Before I knew the truth." She explained about the declaration that he'd tricked her into before her cousin and Rory.

His face contorted in anger. "You little fool."

The burst of malevolence was truly frightening. He raised his hand as if he intended to strike her, and she recoiled from him, stunned that this cruel stranger could be her brother. *Dear God, what had she done?*

He seemed to realize that he'd scared her, and he lowered his hand, making an obvious effort to control his rage. "It will make it more difficult to claim you were never married, but I will deal with it."

"But—" Flora bit back her denial. This was what she wanted, wasn't it? *Why, then, did every instinct in her body clamor against it?*

Her obvious conflict seemed to amuse him. "You will forget all about him, when you and Lord Murray—"

He stopped. It took her a moment to realize what he'd said. "How do you know about Lord Murray?" She'd omitted that part of the story.

He smiled. "I suppose it doesn't matter now. Lord Murray and I have a little arrangement. He gets you—or rather you *and* your tocher—and I get his influence with the king."

Flora was stunned. The irony was not lost on her. Just like Lachlan, Hector had used her as a bargaining chip. They were both men with steely determination and the single-minded purpose to do whatever was necessary to win—heedless of whom they hurt in the process.

Or were they? Lachlan had seemed so sincere when he'd told her he hadn't wanted to hurt her. He'd claimed to love her. And at one time, she'd believed him. He'd also claimed to have tried to avoid using her by attempting to rescue his brother on his own. Could she believe him? She realized how much she wanted to.

She turned back to Hector. "You orchestrated the elopement?"

He sank back in his chair, stretching his legs out before him, looking well pleased. "Aye. And it was a brilliant plan. It would have worked perfectly had Coll not interfered."

Flora thought of the fate that she'd narrowly avoided. "I won't marry Lord Murray. He is a coward who left me to the mercy of brigands."

Hector gave her a hard stare. "Yes, little sister, you will."

He said it with such confidence, a shiver ran up her spine.

Like Lachlan, Hector was a fierce and ruthless Highland chief. But Hector had a cruel and brutish streak that Lachlan lacked. A lump of dread settled low in her belly. Without a doubt, she knew she'd made a mistake in coming here.

Hector was looking at her strangely. "What's that?" he asked, indicating her amulet. "I've seen it before."

Flora resisted the urge to cover it with her hand protectively. "It belonged to my mother."

He frowned, and before she could stop him he reached for it. Turning it around in his hand, he examined the inscription on the back.

His eyes lit with excitement. "The old curse . . . it's the Campbell amulet from Lady's Rock."

She didn't respond.

"Lady's Rock," he repeated. "That's it."

"What are you talking about?"

But he only started to laugh. Laughter that chilled her blood and made the hair on her neck stand straight up.

A few hours later, she would learn why.

It had taken Lachlan all morning to rally his men . . . and to convince Rory MacLeod not to challenge him to a sword fight.

They were about one hundred strong—including a dozen of Rory's men who'd accompanied him to the wedding. There simply hadn't been time to send for more.

Although Hector's warriors numbered close to four hundred, only half that number were on Coll.

"If you are wrong about this," Rory said as they tied the *birlinn* to the dock at Arinagour, "I will take my men and return to Dunvegan—after we settle our differences."

"I'm not wrong," Lachlan said with more confidence than he felt. "Flora was angry. She acted rashly in running to Hector—which I'm sure she has come to regret. She will be happy to see us."

"Knowing Hector, you are probably right. But as to the validity of your 'marriage,' I am undecided."

Lachlan opened his mouth to argue but snapped it shut just as fast. Rory was right. Though every instinct in his body screamed to hold what was his, it would be Flora's decision whether they stayed married. "I will not press my claim if she does not wish it."

"Damn right you won't." Rory was still furious with Lachlan's deception—as he had every right to be. Only the fact that Lachlan had convinced him of his love for his sister had kept the MacLeod at bay. If it came to it, Lachlan and Rory would be well matched—Rory was bigger, but Lachlan younger—but he didn't relish finding out who was the better swordsman.

It took some time to unload his men from the boats, and Lachlan was surprised when they didn't encounter any resistance. Hector had left the beach and docks at Arinagour largely undefended—something he would never have done.

It was strange.

Rory must have come to the same conclusion. "I wonder where our greeting party is."

Lachlan shook his head. "I don't know. But it makes me wary."

"Aye," Rory agreed.

After they'd marched south the few miles to Brea-cachadh, they had their explanation.

Hector stood outside the gate with only a handful of men behind him. The rest, Lachlan assumed, were stationed in the castle, ready to repel an attack.

The boldness of the man was mind-boggling. Lachlan could easily kill him right now. Though tempted to do just that, he stepped forward. "You have something that belongs to me."

"Your castle? I'm afraid you can't have it. I've rather grown to like it here."

"No, my wife."

Hector pretended not to understand. "If you mean my sister, I'm afraid you can't have her, either." He sneered. "Unless you can swim."

He pointed behind Lachlan out to sea. Lachlan turned, and his blood ran cold. For a moment, he couldn't process what he was seeing. He didn't want to believe it.

Less than a hundred yards from shore, Flora stood marooned on a rock, surrounded by nothing but merciless blue water. But that wasn't all. He'd been wrong about the location of Hector's men. Nearly his entire garrison must be lined up on the beach—a human wall of defense between him and Flora.

Worst of all, Lachlan knew he didn't have much time to reach her. The tide was moving in fast.

Flora had never been so scared in her life. She was cold, wet, and horribly aware of the rising water all around her. She shivered, the thin white sark she wore like some hideous virgin sacrifice a useless barrier to the elements. Except she wasn't a virgin, and she had no intention of going to her death without a fight.

She gazed out to sea, watching and waiting with burgeoning dread. *Oh no, here comes another one.* Holding her breath, she turned her face as another huge wave crashed against the rock, pelting her with a deluge of icy seawater. Her fingers slipped for an instant with the force, causing her a moment of heart-stopping panic before she found her grip again.

God, how much longer could she hold on before he came? *If* he came.

Was this how Elizabeth Campbell felt? Forsaken. Left to die. Praying for someone to come? Never had she felt such compassion for what her kinswoman must have gone through on Lady's Rock. She couldn't imagine what it would be like in the dark . . . alone. At least she could see what was taking place on the shore.

She stood on the side of a jagged rock that protruded from the sea in a sharp peak. There was barely enough room for her to keep her feet flat, and she had to stand with her arms around the slippery rock in almost an embrace to avoid being knocked off. The castle seemed deceptively close—close enough to see the anticipation on her brother's face and hear the orders that he shouted back and forth to his men. So close, but infinitely far away.

The rough waters of the sea were nothing like the placid water of the Faerie Pool, precluding any thought of testing her new water skills. Just the thought of going under . . .

She fought the wave of panic rising in her throat as the memories assailed her. The cold black water covering her mouth, her nose, her head. Struggling to breathe. Flailing wildly, trying to capture one more breath of air.

Not again. This couldn't be happening again.

She'd thought Hector was joking. How could her own blood do something like this? He'd remembered her fear of water from her near drowning in the loch all those years ago and had decided to use her as bait to destroy Lachlan by staging this macabre re-creation of the incident that had befallen Elizabeth Campbell so many years before at Lady's Rock.

She'd stared at him dumbly when he told her of his intentions, believing it only when he'd ordered his men to take her. She'd fought, but it had been useless. There were too many of them. He'd ordered her to remove her gown, and she'd refused—until he'd pointed out that his men could do it for her. Part of her still couldn't believe it . . . until she saw the boat. She'd panicked, and it had taken half a dozen men to drag her down the beach and force her into the waiting *birlinn*. Her terrified pleas had fallen on deaf ears. He'd claimed that she wouldn't be hurt—if Lachlan cooperated.

Lachlan . . .

God, what a fool she'd been. Lachlan was nothing like Hector. She could see that now, when it was too late. Lachlan would do his duty as chief, but his ends were noble: to help his clan and save his brother. Her brother acted for ambition and greed and without compassion. Now, with the benefit of hindsight, she could perhaps see why Lachlan had chosen not to confide in her: Her own fears would have prevented her from understanding had he told her the truth.

She was still furious at him for deceiving her, but she never should have run. She'd reacted rashly, out of fear. Fear that she would end up like her mother. But she'd had one thing her mother had never had, love. And she'd thrown it all away.

She'd left him on their wedding night, shaming him horribly and forsaking her vows. She thought of the things she'd said to him and deeply regretted her harsh words. She'd struck where she knew it would hurt—his pride. Now with his brother freed, she feared he was probably glad to be rid of her.

But Hector had been so certain Lachlan would come after her. And deep in her heart, she knew her brother was right. She was his wife. Lachlan would hold on to what was his no matter how much she'd shamed him. And maybe, just maybe, he did care for her.

God, how she wished they'd been wrong. Her brother's men had watched for his arrival, and as soon as the *birlinns* were spotted, the plan was set in motion. But Lachlan and his men took longer to reach the castle than Hector anticipated, and she was running out of precious time.

Her heart leapt when she first caught sight of him marching up to the castle with her brother at his side. She drank him in, even from a distance making out the hard lines of his ruggedly handsome face. He seemed even larger and more impressive armed for war in his yellow chieftain's cotun, leather trews, and steel knapscall.

Her husband had come for her.

Chapter 21

❖

Across the wide expanse of sea, his penetrating gaze found hers and closed the distance between them. If she'd harbored any doubts of Lachlan's feelings, his reaction told her all she needed to know. His entire body went still, and for an instant beneath the fading amber light of day, she could have sworn she saw him pale. He looked . . . haunted. She'd seen that look before. It was the same expression he'd worn when he'd rescued her from drowning. If only she'd remembered it sooner. Lachlan Maclean was the most fearsome man she knew, but for her, he was scared.

He did love her. Despite her circumstances, for a moment a surge of nearly incomparable pleasure filled her.

There was so much she wanted to say to him: to tell him she was sorry for running, to tell him she loved him, to beg for another chance. And though she knew he could not see all that, she felt that he understood.

He turned back to Hector with his hand on his sword. She tensed, knowing how badly he wanted to attack Hector. She breathed a sigh of relief when he spoke. As the conversation between the two men unfolded, though she could not hear exactly what they said, it became clear what Hector intended—to let her drown if Lachlan did not surrender.

"You bastard!" Lachlan roared.

Flora didn't have to strain to hear that. Lachlan lunged for Hector, but Rory held him back.

"Get my sister off that damn rock right now," Rory said.

"Stay out of this, MacLeod. She's my sister as well," Hector said.

She couldn't hear Rory's reply, but she could tell he took umbrage at Hector's claim of kinship.

"Flora will come to no harm," Hector swore. He gave Lachlan a meaningful look. "Assuming Coll here cooperates."

"What do you want?" Lachlan's voice was deadly calm.

"It's simple. You surrender to me, and MacLeod here will be allowed to rescue Flora." Hector had planned it perfectly. A battle would eat away at valuable time. Lachlan might be able to break through and reach her . . . might. He seemed to have reached the same conclusion, because when he turned back to Hector, she could see the resignation in the set of his wide shoulders.

"No!" Flora didn't realize she'd spoken aloud until the men turned to face her.

Their eyes met, and her heart squeezed. She shook her head. "Don't," she whispered. She didn't want to die, but neither could she bear the thought of Lachlan giving his life for hers. Another wave hit, and she lost her footing but scrambled to hold on by sticking the tips of her slippers into a crevice.

Lachlan swore and then shouted to her, "Hold on just a little longer!" She couldn't hear what he said to Hector, but she knew what he was doing when he dropped his dirk and started to unfasten his baldric. He didn't hesitate, acting without thought. He was surrendering to his enemy, to the man he'd fought his entire life, exchanging his life for hers. Once Hector had him, it would be too late.

God, how could she have doubted his love for her?

A Maclean life is given in love for a Campbell.

The words of Elizabeth Campbell's curse came back to her. She couldn't let it happen. She wouldn't allow the curse to become a reality.

Flora knew what she had to do. Lachlan was right: She was strong. She'd allowed her own fears to be the weapon that had nearly killed her; she would not allow it to kill the man she loved.

"No!" she cried again. "Wait!"

And taking a deep breath, she jumped into the icy blue water.

Lachlan heard her cry and turned just in time to see the splash. His heart lurched. *God, no! Flora!* Panic gripped him. He knew what she was trying to do, but she wasn't a strong enough swimmer for these stiff currents. She'd never make it.

He glanced at Hector, who was even more surprised than he by what Flora had done. Obviously, he'd assumed she still could not swim.

Lachlan realized that she'd given him an opening. Taking advantage of Hector's shock, he pulled his claymore from his discarded baldric and attacked—his only thought to save the woman he loved.

Hector raised his own sword, but it was too late. Lachlan would not be denied. Not this time. Not with Flora's life in the balance. He felt a surge swell through him of almost inhuman strength, and with one mighty swing of his claymore, he knocked the sword from Hector's hold. He spun sideways, rammed his elbow into Hector's nose, heard the satisfying sound of bone crunching, and had his sword at Hector's throat in a single move.

It all happened so fast, Hector's men hadn't had time to react. They did so now, but Rory and his men held them back.

"Call them off," Lachlan warned. "Or I'll stick this blade through your damn throat like you deserve."

Hector's face turned red with rage. He looked as though he wanted to argue, so Lachlan dug the tip of his blade a little deeper, drawing blood. He'd never wanted to kill a man so badly; bloodlust pulsed through him at a frenzied pace. It would be so easy to draw the blade across.

But something held him back.

He was Flora's brother. And despite what he'd done, he knew she would not want him killed. Not like this.

He glanced out to sea, relieved to see her still moving atop the water. Damn, he was proud of her. She was doing it; she was swimming. But even with the tide coming in and carrying her toward shore, she was struggling. The current was taking her east, and she was trying to swim directly toward the beach. "Call them off," he repeated. "Now."

Hector's eyes met his with such hatred, Lachlan thought he might refuse. He hoped he would. Then Lachlan could kill him with impunity.

Much to his regret, Hector lifted his hand and motioned for his men to stand down. It was over. Lachlan's victory was definitive and swift, but strangely anticlimactic. Defeating Hector meant nothing if he lost the woman he loved.

Lachlan twisted Hector's arm behind his back and shoved him toward Rory. Without another glance he raced down the beach, tearing off his cotun and helmet along the way—knowing they would only drag him down. Hector's men parted like the Red Sea, and Lachlan dove headfirst into the waves.

Flora was exhausted, but she refused to give up. Realizing that if she continued to fight the current she would

soon grow too tired, she rolled on her back and floated
as Lachlan had taught her—conserving her strength and
allowing the water to carry her in.

It was growing dark, and she could no longer see what
was happening on the beach, but she wouldn't give in to
her fear, even when a big wave dragged her under for a
moment. She had too much to live for. She wanted Lachlan to hold her in his arms again and tell her that he
loved her. She wanted to call him husband. She wanted
to make a life with him. Her throat squeezed. She
wanted to hold their first child in her arms.

If only it weren't so cold. Her teeth were chattering,
and her limbs had gone stiff. All she wanted to do was
close her eyes. Her lids fluttered. . . .

"Flora!"

The mere sound of his voice jerked her fully awake.
"Here," she cried, tears of relief springing to her eyes.
"I'm here."

"Thank God."

Though it was only a few moments, it seemed to take
an eternity before she caught sight of him. Her emotions, barely contained, shattered when the achingly familiar ruggedly handsome features came into view—the
hard angles of his face made more pronounced by the
shadows of the beckoning night. A pillar of strength in a
sea of danger. He'd found her; the nightmare was over.
With a strangled cry, she swam toward him.

Seconds later, he had her. His steely arms wrapped
around her and pulled her against the solid wall of his
chest. She breathed him in, savoring his strength and vi-
tality. He gripped her tight, his fingers raking through
the tangle of her hair and pressing into her back as if he
would never let her go. She clung to him, taking refuge
in the security of his embrace.

His wet cheek pressed against hers, the scrape of his

day-old beard against her chilled skin achingly familiar. He was breathing hard, and she could feel the heavy beat of his heart against hers. Even soaking wet in the freezing sea, a subtle warmth radiated from him.

Overwhelmed, she started to sob.

"I've got you," he murmured, smoothing her hair. "You're safe." Cupping her chin, he looked into her watery eyes. "You nearly scared the life out of me. I thought—" His voice broke. "I saw you floating like that, and I thought you were dead."

Flora shook her head. "I'm afraid you won't get rid of me that easily."

"Get rid of you?" He pulled her close and pressed a hard kiss on her freezing lips. She tasted of salt and sea, but nothing had ever tasted sweeter. "Never," he said, looking deep into her eyes. And then he kissed her again, longer this time, with an aching tenderness that sent a tingle of warmth to her icy limbs. "Now if we both don't want to freeze to death, I suggest we get back to the castle as soon as possible."

She nodded, and with Lachlan's aid and instruction, they swam for shore—not directly, as she'd attempted before, but diagonally with the current.

Soon she could see Rory and Lachlan's men wading toward them and knew that she'd done it. She'd fought her fear and won. And though she felt ready to collapse, the feeling of accomplishment gave her an unexpected swell of strength that carried her through the last few strokes.

As soon as the water was shallow enough, Lachlan stood and cradled her in his arms, carrying her the rest of the way. She pressed her face against the familiar hard planes of his chest, savoring the simple sensation of being held in his arms again.

Rory rushed toward them. "Is she all right?" he asked Lachlan.

Flora could hear the worry in his voice and immediately moved to reassure him. "I'm fine."

"Thank God." He drew off his plaid, which was blissfully dry, and gave it to Lachlan to wrap her in, covering her near nakedness and providing much needed warmth.

"She's freezing," Lachlan said. "I need to get her to the castle as soon as possible. Have my room prepared."

"Look here, Coll," Rory said, blocking his path to the castle. "I thought we agreed. I'll not have my sister forced into this marriage. It's best if you put her in another room."

Why, he's trying to protect me, Flora realized. Warmed by the show of brotherly affection, especially after what she'd just been through, she gave Rory a grateful smile. One that Lachlan mistook.

His jaw flexed, and she could tell he wanted to argue, but instead he pushed past Rory and said through clenched teeth, "Any damn room, then."

Flora hid a smile and thought about teasing him for a bit longer, but he was right—she was freezing. "I thank you for your concern, Rory," she said to her brother, who'd kept pace with them. "But the laird's bedchamber will be perfect."

Lachlan stopped midstep and gazed down at her, hope glistening in his eyes.

"Are you sure, lass?" Rory asked.

But Flora couldn't look away from Lachlan. The depth of his feeling for her had been splayed open to her gaze, revealing her heart's desire. She would remember this moment forever. Remember how it felt to know without a doubt that she was loved—totally and completely. Despite what he'd done in manipulating their marriage, he'd been willing to give his life for hers.

"Aye," she said softly. "I've never been more sure of anything in my life."

Lachlan squeezed her tight and, not giving Rory the

time to respond, carried her through the crowds of cheering clansmen. The Maclean of Coll had come home.

The door closed behind his serving woman Mairi, but despite her assurances, Lachlan still could not relax. He checked the fire, adjusted her pillow, and tucked another plaid around Flora.

He heard a muffled giggle and whipped around to look at the source. Crossing his arms across his chest, he narrowed his gaze in warning.

A warning the wee harridan promptly ignored. "You would make a horrible nursemaid with that forbidding frown. Stop fussing. You heard what Mairi said, I'm perfectly fine. As soon as I got that wet sark off me, I warmed right up."

His gaze traveled down the length of her, heating at the thought of the naked body underneath. He frowned, realizing that's exactly what she intended—the little minx. "Stop trying to distract me. It won't work, you need your rest."

Her eyes were bright with laughter. She lowered the plaid a bit, revealing a flawless swell of ivory skin. Her brow arched in naughty invitation. "It won't?"

He sat beside her on the bed, pulled the blanket back up to her chin, and swept a stray lock of damp hair from her forehead. His palm lingered to cradle the baby soft skin of her cheek. "God, Flora, when I saw you jump—" His voice broke, and he turned his head slightly, shielding his burning eyes from her view. After a minute, he looked back at her. "I don't ever want to feel like that again. I thought I would lose you."

"But Hector was going to kill you," she protested.

"Aye, but it was a choice I would gladly make."

"But not one I could live with." She hesitated. "What of Hector?"

"Alive, but taken. Argyll will hold him until his punishment is decided by the king."

He could see the relief sweep her face and knew he'd made the right decision in sparing Hector's foul life.

"I know he doesn't deserve my compassion, but I'm glad he was not killed. Defeat and imprisonment is a much better punishment, one for which the pain will endure."

He nodded. "If he'd delayed any longer, I would not have had a choice. I had to reach you." He would never forget the sight of Flora disappearing beneath the waves. That same sense of panic gripped him. "If you ever do anything so foolish again, I will lock you in that tower. My heart stopped when you jumped into the water."

She covered his hand with hers. "Then you know how I felt. I know what Hector intended. I couldn't let you die for me." She pressed a finger against his mouth to stave off his protest. "I was scared, but you made me believe that I could do it. You taught me the skills; I just had to be brave enough to use them."

His gaze softened. "I'm proud of you, lass. But next time, save the swimming lessons for the loch."

"Agreed." Suddenly, the smile fell from her face and all signs of teasing fled. "I cannot believe my own brother could do something like that."

"Hector has the moral compass of a snake. I should have warned you, but I didn't think you would believe me." He shook his head. "I never thought that he would try to harm you."

"His hatred for you was stronger than his feelings for a sister he didn't know. And I ran right into his trap. I never should have left like that."

Lachlan's face turned serious. "No, you shouldn't have. You can't run away every time you are scared or angry."

Flora nodded, chastened. "I know. You accused me of having no concept of what it meant to be in charge and responsible." He started to stop her, but she held him off. "There was more truth in that than I wanted to acknowledge. You were right—I couldn't see past my own hurt to realize the difficulty you faced. You had an obligation to your clan and to your brother. But to me, duty equaled misery. I don't have the family you do. I was raised not to blindly follow my duty. But I never understood that when you loved someone, you owed them . . . something. At the very least, I owed you an attempt to listen."

He cupped her chin with his hand. "I need to trust that you will not run like that again." He gave her a wry grin. "I might not always make decisions that you agree with."

She smiled. "No, you probably won't. I won't promise not to be angry, but I will promise not to look for the first boat."

He stroked the smooth curve of her cheek with his thumb. "You had reason to be angry. I handled it badly. I should have given you time; instead, I forced myself on you." He met her gaze. "I deserved to be called a barbarian."

She squeezed his hand. "I didn't mean it, I wanted to hurt you. Actually, I was more frightened by my reaction." Her cheeks heated. "I wanted to hate you, but my body wasn't listening. I know you would never hurt me."

"But I did," he said quietly, referring not to the kiss, but to his bargain with Argyll. He knew it had struck at her most vulnerable place.

She lifted her gaze to his. But instead of anger, he saw the flicker of understanding beneath the hurt.

She sighed. "When I first realized what you and my

cousin had planned, it seemed that my worst fears had come true. My mother's life flashed before my eyes. All I could see was that I was being used as a pawn. I couldn't separate your duty and your feelings for me. I couldn't accept that you could love me and keep something from me at the same time—not that I don't wish you'd confided in me." She studied his face. "But I understand why you didn't."

"And I'm sorry for that, more sorry than you will ever know. I never meant to hurt you. At first, all I could think about was freeing my brother and getting my castle back, but it didn't take long for me to know that I wanted you for myself. As I grew to know you, and care for you, I realized how badly the truth would hurt you. If there had been another choice, I would have taken it."

"You did what you had to do. Not that I'm planning on thanking my cousin for interfering."

Stubborn lass, he thought with a grin. "I didn't think you would. But marrying you I did for myself as much as for my brother."

"What is important is that I love you and you love me. I can't escape who I am any more than you can. You are chief, and I realize there are times you will have to put duty first. I'll have to accept that I can't have all of you."

"Yes, you can," he said softly. "You have all of my heart and soul."

Her eyes glistened. "For a man who claims not to have a courtier's silvery tongue, you seem to know precisely what to say."

He stroked her chin with his thumb. "Then you forgive me?"

Her mouth twitched, and the naughty glint in her eyes returned. "I might be persuaded. But you will have to work extra hard to prove it to me."

He was more than equal to the task. "I love you,

Flora. If I have to spend the rest of my life proving it to you, I'll be a happy man."

"And I love you."

She leaned over and reached for something on the table beside the bed. It took him a moment to realize what it was. She lifted it up and he bent his head, allowing the amulet to drop over his head.

"It belongs to you now."

A lump lodged in his throat. "Are you sure, lass?"

She nodded, her eyes damp with tears—not of sadness, but of happiness. "You have given your life for mine, and now I willingly give this to you—my husband, my love."

He didn't know what to say, so instead he kissed her gently. Tasting the saltiness of her tears and the warm honey taste of her lips and tongue. Before the hard pull of possession dragged him in, slowly, reluctantly, he released her.

He started to pull away, intending to give her rest, but Flora had different intentions. Her hands slid down his chest, his shirt still damp from his unplanned swim. His blood stirred hot at her touch. She peeked up at him from under her long lashes. "Hmm . . . I was thinking you might care to prove it right now." She feigned a shiver. "I'm feeling chilled. These blankets don't seem to be working. I was hoping you might be able to think of a way to warm me?"

He stilled, wanting nothing more. But he also didn't want to risk overtiring her in her weakened state. Her hand skimmed the waistband of his trews, and he captured her wrist before she could touch him, knowing that once she did, he would be past the point of reason. His need for her was so strong, it would be like trying to harness a lightning bolt.

"Are you sure, lass?" His voice was tight with restraint. "This time there will be no going back. The marriage has not been recorded. If you want out of it, I've promised your brother I would not contest it."

"I'm done looking back. I only want to look to the future. With you."

He let go of her wrist, and when she covered him with her sweet little hand, he groaned into her mouth as he claimed the woman he loved.

Flora tasted his groan of pleasure as she slid her hand over his trews, molding him with her hand. Just touching him again made her flood with heat. He was so big and hard, and she couldn't wait to feel him inside her— filling her as he thrust hard and deep.

Her body pulsed with desire.

She wanted to hold on to every second and make this last forever. But the touch of his mouth on hers was like wildfire, and she knew there would be no containing the passion that burned between them. It was too hot, too intense, too out of control.

After nearly losing him, she needed him too badly.

Her hands skimmed over his back and shoulders, pressing him closer. *God, he was amazing.* So gorgeous and strong. His warrior's body layered with solid, thick muscle that flexed under her fingertips.

He broke the kiss only long enough to pull off his shirt and trews and then slid into the bed beside her, pulling her against him as his mouth fell on hers again. She melted into the heat, wanting to feel every powerful inch of him pressed against her. His warm, smooth skin wreaked havoc on her senses, making her tingle where they touched.

His big hands took command of her body. He touched her everywhere, stroking, caressing, igniting. His fingers plunged through her hair, down her back, and over her bottom. His rough, callused palms were both gentle and possessive as he lifted her against him.

Her body was damp and throbbing—desperate for him. The craving ran from the deepest part of her, taking hold and demanding release.

And he wanted her, though he was struggling to contain it. He kissed her harder, his tongue sliding into her mouth with deep, demanding strokes. But it wasn't enough. She wanted him wild—beyond restraint—the way he'd been in her room last night. The way she felt right now.

"Don't," she murmured against his mouth.

He pulled back, and she could see his confusion. "What's wrong?"

"Don't hold back. I want all of you. You don't need to protect me." She lifted up to kiss him, sliding her tongue along the velvety crease of his mouth. "I won't break."

His eyes searched her face.

"You could never frighten me," she assured him. He was so beautiful, this wild, passionate man. She kissed him again, sliding her tongue in his mouth and circling her tongue with his in a deeply erotic, deeply carnal openmouthed kiss. "Show me," she breathed. "I want to feel your passion . . . unchained." She circled him with her hand. His eyes flared, and the spark of danger urged her on.

Holding his gaze, she challenged him, stroking him, squeezing with long, hard strokes. She wouldn't let him go. He was hers. All of him—even that rough, untamed side of him that he sought to hide.

The flames rose higher and higher in his eyes. . . .

She'd won. His control snapped. She was on her back, and he was kissing her, his mouth moving over her lips, her jaw, her neck. Dominating. Ravaging. Wild and free.

He licked and sucked, making her shudder as his warm breath blew across her damp skin. He cupped her breasts and buried his face between her, the stubble of his beard scraping the tender flesh. She arched against him, needing more. Needing his mouth.

He covered her throbbing nipple and sucked, pulling her between his teeth until she writhed against him. Until her body began to spasm.

He lifted his head and held her gaze as he entered her in one hard thrust. The pleasure made her cry out. So big and thick, he filled her so completely, the pleasure was so acute, she couldn't stand it.

And then he started to move, holding her gaze the entire time. The raw intensity of his expression took her breath away. It wasn't just lust, or even just love, but something far more elemental: a perfect union of two bodies and two souls into one. He was meant for her and she for him.

She could feel the emotion surging in him just under her fingertips, his entire body pulsating with the pressure of everything that had happened between them. How close they'd come to losing each other. He thrust deeper and deeper. Harder and harder. And she met him stroke for stroke.

This was it. He was out of control, utterly consumed. And so was she. Never had she felt so alive and free. She felt the pressure build, knew she was close, but she had to hold on. . . . He sank in her deep, pushing higher, forcing her.

She couldn't breathe. It felt too good. She pulsed with heat, and sensation rippled through her in warm, wet waves.

She felt him stiffen, saw the pleasure transform his face, and heard the deep guttural cry that tore from him as his release gripped his body, and she let go . . . weightless for a long heartbeat before breaking apart with a shattering intensity, her body contracting hard around him, the warm rush of his seed spilling deep inside her.

He was merciless, not even letting her catch her breath. Still warm and tingling, he rocked his hips against her, rubbing her hard against him until she cried out again. Slow and strong, wave after wave of sensation crashed over her. And when the last ebb of her release had faded, he nestled her against him tenderly, as if she might break.

She was moved beyond speech by the magnitude of what had just happened. He'd given her everything: his love, his body, his soul, and his trust.

Lachlan smoothed his hand over her warm, velvety skin, watching as the frantic rise and fall of her chest slowed. He didn't know what to say. Words seemed an imperfect substitute for what he was feeling right now. Happy, content, relieved—all seemed utterly inadequate.

The misery of the past few days had been put behind them. The uncertainty of revealing his bargain with Argyll, the pain of their confrontation, arriving home with his brother to discover her gone, seeing her on that rock, realizing what Hector intended, and then watching her jump into the frigid, churning seas. It had all been expunged, released in a cataclysmic explosion of love and lust.

She'd stripped him to the core, seen behind the veil of civility, and given him only love and acceptance.

He'd made her his wife, bound her to him for eternity, but never had he felt so free—unchained, as she'd called it.

My wife.

She sighed deeply.

"Are you all right?" he asked.

She turned to him and smiled. "More than all right."

He tilted her chin, gazing deep into her eyes. "I love you."

"I know." Her mouth curved in a naughty little grin. "You finally succeeded in proving it to me."

"Thank God," he groaned. "I don't think I could do that again."

But as they found out a few hours later, he was wrong.

Epilogue

✦

August 1608

Flora strolled across the moors with her husband, savoring the last hours of calm before the storm. It was hard to believe a year had passed since they'd returned to Breacachadh. But Mary's wedding to Allan was only a few days away, and soon the guests would be arriving for the week-long celebration, provoking a mix of nervousness and anticipation. For the first time in years, all of her brothers and sisters would be in the same place at the same time—except for Hector, who was still the reluctant guest of Argyll.

She sighed contentedly. That dark day seemed a lifetime ago.

The late summer sun beat down hard and bright, intensifying the vibrant panoply of colorful flowers strewn across the countryside. She inhaled deeply, the sweet, pungent scent a gentle reminder of nature's bounty this year. Everywhere she looked were signs of the largesse that had befallen them since they'd returned to Breacachadh. It seemed almost . . . magical.

"Do you think she's happy for us?" She spoke her thoughts aloud.

Lachlan gazed at her with a quizzical look in his face. "Who?"

"Elizabeth Campbell."

He grinned, and her heart caught. The boyish look on his face was a testament to the transformation wrought by happiness. He was lighter than before, relaxed. The clan thrived, and the constant struggle he'd faced since the death of his father had come to a welcome end. But she knew it was more than that. Their love had been tested by the events of last summer, but as a result it had only grown stronger.

"I thought you weren't superstitious," he said.

"I'm not. But look around. You have your castle back—with the Privy Council's approval, thanks to my cousin. The keep has been returned to its splendor, the crops are flourishing, the cattle are fat and ready for market, the storms that have hit the other islands have passed us by. And then there's . . ." She glanced back and forth between them meaningfully.

His mouth twitched. "Ah yes, there's that."

He turned to her, giving her a view of the tiny bundle he held in his arms. Her heart swelled the way it always did when she saw them together. Nothing could be more moving than the sight of her big, strong husband holding their tiny son in his arms. John, named for the uncle who'd unwittingly brought them together, with his determined little chin and striking blue eyes so like his father's. Lachlan leaned over and gave her a soft kiss on the lips, before dropping another one on the downy head of the matching bundle in her arms—Janet, named in memory of Flora's mother.

Twins. Nature's most magnificent bounty.

He met her gaze in perfect understanding: They had been blessed indeed. "Aye, lass, I think she's found her peace."

As if in answer, the sun caught the silver of the brooch that he wore to secure his plaid, and it flashed like a brilliant heavenly star. The amulet that had once borne a curse had become an enduring symbol of their love.

She smiled, looking deep into his beloved eyes, her heart swelling with love for her incredible husband and precious babes. *Elizabeth found hers, and I've found mine.*

Author's Note

❖

The story of Elizabeth Campbell's trials on Lady's Rock is a familiar one in Scotland even today. On a recent trip to Scotland, our ship's captain decided not to travel up the sound but to take the Sea of Hebrides western route around the Isle of Mull. Thus, I narrowly missed passing by Lady's Rock, which you can still find on maps today. There are many different versions of the tale, but all agree that a Maclean chief abandoned his Campbell bride on the rock to be washed away by the rising tide. She was indeed rescued and returned to her father's home in time to greet her "grieving" spouse. Her brother Sir John Calder of Calder killed her husband many years later. The curse and the amulet, however, are my additions to the story.

The main characters in this book are based on real people. Janet Campbell, Elizabeth's great-niece, was a very wealthy and much sought-after lady who was married at least four times. Her daughter Flora MacLeod did in fact marry Lachlan Maclean, sixth Laird of Coll. Because of the timing of the story and name confusion, "Hector" is really a combination of Lachlan Mor Maclean, the fourteenth Chief of Duart (Flora's half-brother), who died in 1598, and Hector Maclean, the fifteenth Chief of Duart (Flora's nephew). Allan, son of Neil Mor (Coll's great-uncle), was the captain of Drimnin Castle and reputed to be the leading warrior of his day. His wife is unknown. Although an elopement with Flora was pure fiction, Lord Murray was an influential member of King James's court. He succeeded to the title of the second Earl of Tullibardine, and his son John was created the first Earl of Atholl. Lord Murray was one of the commissioners against the Clan Gregor in 1611.

The fight over Breacachadh Castle actually happened a little earlier. Lachlan Mor ("Hector") probably took control of the castle around 1591, and it wasn't returned to Lachlan of Coll until around 1596. The Stream of Heads, *Struthan nan Ceann*, was an actual battle, and bitter feuding between the Duart and Coll branches of the clan occurred for years—including the refusal of Coll to bow to Duart as head of the clan.

Lachlan did execute the men who'd murdered his uncle Neil Mor—though he held Lachlan Mor responsible. One of Coll's first acts as laird was to capture the four murderers who were playing shinty on a beach on Mull.[1] They were hanged at *Cnoc A Chrochaire*, Hangman's Hill, on Coll.[2]

Lachlan Mor ("Hector") did seize John MacIan, the husband of his mother, Janet Campbell, on their wedding night after he refused to switch his allegiance from the MacDonalds to the Macleans. This egregious breach of Highland hospitality has gone down in history as "Maclean's nuptials." When the happy couple retired for their wedding night, Lachlan Mor murdered all of MacIan's men and charged into the room intent on murdering the groom as well. Only his mother's heartfelt pleas stayed his hand. Instead, John MacIan was imprisoned and tortured.

---

[1] Lachlan Maclean-Bristol, *Murder Under Trust*, Tuckwell Press, 1999, p. 212.
[2] Ibid.

Lomond Hills is now better known as part of the Trossachs.

And finally, Scotland is rife with many Neolithic sites: megaliths, stone circles, and cairns. The one I referenced is Strontoiller Stone Circle and Standing Stone.

You can find more information, including pictures and extended author's notes on my website: www.monica mccarty.com.